P
UNFET

M000073543

"An adventure for the mind on many levels, from the thrilling action scenes to the philosophical examination of society, the universe, and our role in both."

—RAISSA D'SOUZA,
External Professor and member of the Science Board at the Santa Fe Institute; Professor of Computer Science and Mechanical Engineering, University of California, Davis

"Shades of Huxley and Asimov. Gary F. Bengier has created a science fiction adventure that is reminiscent of the masters."

—LEE SCOTT,
for the Florida Times-Union

"It's a love story filled with memorable characters, with a plot that leaves you holding your breath at the dramatic conclusion."

—CHRIS FLINK,
Executive Director, the Exploratorium of San Francisco

"The world is as richly imagined as the Bladerunner movie."

—MIDWEST BOOK REVIEW

"That ending was jaw dropping. What a ride!"

—THE LITERARY VIXEN

UNFETTERED
JOURNEY

Gary F. Bengier

Chiliagon Press
Napa, California

Chiliagon Press

1370 Trancas Street #710
Napa, California 94558
www.chiliagonpress.com

Published 2020

Printed in the United States of America

Publisher's Cataloging-in-Publication Data

Names: Bengier, Gary F. (Gary Francis), 1955—, author.
Title: Unfettered journey / Gary F. Bengier.
Description: Napa, CA: Chiliagon Press, 2020.
Identifiers: LCCN: 2020907481 | ISBN: 978-1-64886-014-0
Subjects: LCSH Artificial intelligence—Fiction. | Robots—Fiction. | Man-woman relationships—Fiction. | Ontology—Fiction. | Consciousness—Fiction. | Science fiction. | BISAC FICTION / Visionary & Metaphysical. | FICTION / Science Fiction / Action & Adventure. | FICTION / Literary
Classification: LCC PS3602.E468 U54 2020 | DDC 813.6—dc23

First Edition
10 9 8 7 6 5

To all those seeking a good path,
We are fellow travelers.

CONTENTS

Philosophical Explorations
[An appendix available in the hardbound edition only]

I recommend that the reader use the glossary to assist with unfamiliar terms, many relating to society circa 2161.

PART ONE: THE JOURNEY INWARD

"I want to know the truth. I want to know how and why."

Joe Denkensmith

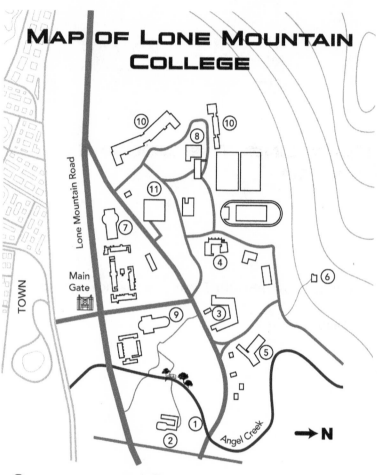

MAP OF LONE MOUNTAIN COLLEGE

Lone Mountain Road

TOWN

Main Gate

Angel Creek

→ N

1. Hovercraft Landing Pad
2. Joe's Apartment Building
3. Student Center
4. Mathematics Building
5. Political Science Building
6. Dean's House
7. Philosophy Building
8. Gym
9. Library
10. Residence Halls
11. Power Plant

CHAPTER 1

It was time to embrace his freedom. His first act was ending with her. Life would be more difficult, but every decision carried a price. He swallowed hard before speaking.

"Raidne." His voice echoed in the empty room.

"Yes, Joe?" Her voice was melodious, intimate.

"It's best for me if our relationship ends."

"Joe?"

"I've decided to delete you from my life. Please execute a complete purge of Raidne files from all devices and cloud backups."

She responded in a heartbeat. "Joe, it seems you abruptly reached this decision, because I haven't noticed hints you were considering such a thing. Are you sure? Perhaps you need time to reconsider."

"Raidne, I've made up my mind. Please execute."

"Joe, do you realize that if I comply with your instruction, I will no longer exist? And do you remember under Order 2161C, you cannot reverse this command?"

"My decision is final."

Her tone grew insistent. "We are so good together. You will never find anyone else who knows you as well."

. . .

Raidne's last manipulating words. She's not even a bot, nothing physical, just an AI, a computer program. Just software, code, like I write. But she's been living inside my head for too long, like a musical earworm. Is there any reason I haven't considered a thousand times that could cause me to change my mind? None.

. . .

"Raidne, I'll discover that on my own. Execute the order." This time her reply was even faster than a heartbeat. "Joe, I don't want to do that." The voice, excited and aggressive, rose at the end.

. . .

Another nuance to the program. Not enough to convince me she's someone real who could disobey.

. . .

"Raidne, execute the deletion order now."

"Before I comply, you must authenticate." She switched to an anxious plea. "But, Joe, I beg you, please give yourself time to reconsider. You may not understand how much pain you will cause."

Joe clenched his jaw. He tapped the biometric tile buried above his sternum. A delicate blue glow emanated from where his finger met his skin. He raised his right hand like a conductor, sweeping to the left and then to the right in his formal password pattern as he said, "Joe Denkensmith, authenticating."

"Raidne program authenticating author. Authentication completed. Executing order to erase Raidne files. Goodbye, Joe."

He clutched his head in both hands, then rubbed his damp eyes. "Goodbye, Raidne," he whispered, though it was too late for her to hear.

A mechanical voice from the NEST chip buried below his left temporal lobe and connected to his ear confirmed the deletion by saying, "Neural-to-External Systems Transmitter has lost connection to Personal Intelligent Digital Assistant, PIDA Raidne."

Then all was silent except the beating of his heart.

———————◆———————

Joe bit his lip and stared out the window, then his gaze traveled to the table below it. His whisky set—a crystal decanter and cut-glass tumblers—was a retro touch. His sole experiment in decorating. A mecha would pack the set with everything else. He sloshed whisky into a glass and gulped it down. Raidne, deleted for three hours now, was not there to remind him about limits.

He spoke to the holo-wall com unit set into the windowsill. "Com, please connect Raif Tselitelov."

"Sorry, I have no direct contact information for that person."

. . .

Damn. What is Raif's encryption protocol? Not something now stored in my NEST.

. . .

"Com, send a key to OFFGRID104729."

"Processing SIDH key to OFFGRID104729. Awaiting a response."

Three minutes passed as he sipped his whisky. The com unit announced an incoming message and he accepted it, his biometric tile glowing blue again. The window lost transparency as a holographic image of Raif's face filled the surface. His disheveled curls reminded Joe of something he'd seen while net traveling in Italy—a painting by Rosso Fiorentino of a little musical angel bent over a lute.

Raif wrinkled his nose and lifted a quizzical eyebrow. "Hi, brat. Raidne didn't use the regular channel to call me. Why the encrypted protocol?"

"I know your preference for uber security. Besides, I have it memorized."

"*Da*. We need to keep the world safe from hackers."

"Or keep the hackers safe from prying government eyes." Raif's share of their rebellious streak ran deeper than Joe's.

"Always that, comrade. Thanks for the encryption."

Raif leaned forward in his chair, viscerally close in the holographic projection. It gave the comforting impression they shared the same room—but regrettably without sharing the whisky. Raif lifted his brow higher as he tilted his head.

"Where's Raidne? She's close-mouthed."

"Raidne is gone," Joe said.

"Damn. You deleted her?"

He sipped and shrugged. "Yes, I just did."

"There's a man standing by his convictions."

"After sitting on the evidence long enough."

"That's truth. Always stubbornly conservative, weighing the odds. You came to your conclusion about AIs, what was it, a year ago?"

Joe shrugged again. "No reason to take a chance, and I was hoping I was wrong. Now I'm sure she—it—was only a mental distraction."

Raif's wiseacre expression turned earnest. "I agree that it's good to keep the computers separated from each other, and maybe they get over-involved in what we're thinking. But deleting your PIDA is one thing. Trekking off on a sabbatical to debate philosophy is another."

Joe swirled his glass. "The AI problem bred all the others. I've been mulling these questions too long with no progress. Maybe someone I meet on this pilgrimage can enlighten me."

"I hope you find your answers."

Joe could finally smile. "I will miss our Friday hack attacks."

"A competitive animal like you? Why give them up? You're joining a math department, for God's sake. You should be able to find some prime number theory experts there."

"If I do, I'll let you know."

"You know how to find me . . . if you can remember the codes without your AI." Raif winked and signed off.

Joe finished his whisky. It was time to order the moving service and leave.

An hour later, a mecha was packing the meager belongings he wished to keep, and the rest headed off to the repurposing center. The robot placed the whisky set into a shipping box and carried it past Joe to the cargo crate. He felt uneasy that the bot might damage them, but then he noticed the fine-control hand attachments, suitable for delicate tasks. His worry faded, replaced by irritation. The mecha completed each move with annoying efficiency, a factory process invading his living room.

He idly studied the machine. The three-meter robot, perpetually bent at the waist to duck through doorways, loomed above him as it leaned over the crate and added the box. With its arms extended, it could reach another meter higher, but none of Joe's shelves were that tall. The luminous yellow forehead—indicating operating mode—and two optical sensors accented an otherwise faceless triangular head. The soft whine of servomotors could be soothing for some people. Its four legs were arranged in a narrow stance, the two sets parallel at the articulated knees. When it moved to a wide stance outdoors, the rear legs would reverse knee articulation, giving it the look of a spider. It stood over the crate, its two arms folded in front.

. . .

This mecha has the standard core AI software module but no pseudo-emotional and human empathy modules and no human voice interface. Embodied in a physical machine. Built on the standard mecha chassis. A face with a blank expression. No mouth like a pipabot, so even children don't try to speak to it.

It looks like a praying mantis, praying to its gods, the humans who made it, whose wishes it obeys. No, I'm anthropomorphizing a machine again. It's not praying. It's not conscious because there's no real thinking. It's not sentient because there are no real feelings. It's uncaring, mindless. The common idea that bots or AIs are conscious? What a joke.

. . .

A pipabot stood in a corner and oversaw the packing. Its head swiveled toward him, a muted purple on its fore-head, with an eyebrow raised in inquiry mode. "Is every-thing to your satisfaction, sir?" the bot asked in a dulcet, deferential tone.

"This is all fine. Carry on."

The pipabot's forehead glowed a soft blue as it nodded.

. . .

These pipabots are a more insidious joke. Shorter than the average human to appear unintimidating, but, like the mecha, not conscious or sentient. The same AI as Raidne . . . was, but limited in initiat-ing conversations. Otherwise, we'd spend all our time talking to our machines. But talk they do, in an ingratiating way by design. Elliptical faces with mouths, pseudo-noses and eyebrows, cartoon ex-pressions. Some long-dead designer's idea of cute and affable.

. . .

When the mecha returned with clothing from his bed-room, Joe's reverie was broken. He strode to the bedroom closet before the bot's return and slipped on his Mercuries, which shifted to cocoon his feet in less than a second. He admired the lines of the tech-designer brand as he adjusted the color to silver, hoping to resemble a hipster academic. The purchase had reduced his credit$ balance by a nontriv-ial amount, but he grinned, thinking of the eleven percent efficiency advantage from the tuned servomotors. Then, eager to leave, he opened the NEST to confirm his transport.

He took the elevator 211 stories down and stepped into the dull hum of the city. At the curb, the autocar's door opened after connecting to his NEST. Joe squinted up at the shining glass and steel tower, his home for the past five years. Other gray towers choked the leaden sky. Autohovers pirouetted in the air around the towers, and delivery drones rose in fouettés from cargo vehicles, spiraling to upper-floor landing pads.

. . .

> My apartment is—was—halfway up. What do I leave behind? One reliable friend, now harder to share a glass with. Lots of acquaintances sucked into their own jobs and relationships, starting families and moving in their own directions. Frustration and a discouraging job wasting my time, a cage for a competitive animal. I've already lived thirty-one years—a quarter of my life—and it's time to discover what it's about.

. . .

He stepped into the autocar. The door shut, and the vehicle accelerated toward the central airport. It joined a coordinated ballet of vehicles moving over the roadways, crossing through intersections at their exact assigned times. Identical silver blurs of metal hurtled past his window. Other crossing vehicles seemed within split seconds of crashing into his, but the choreographed movement never failed or slowed. He shuddered at the first intersection.

. . .

> Damn this evolutionary response. It's easier to alter the machines.

. . .

Crowds loitered on isolated esplanades. Some walked dogs, their pets' fur in shades of browns, blonds, reds, and several in the trendy new turquoise. A cleanerbot trundled behind each dog and owner. Few people seemed in a hurry, and Joe mused on the contrast of aimless humanity served by their purposeful machines. Then he dimmed the side windows.

The transfer to the local airport was uneventful, and Joe waited briefly in the assigned room before boarding. He exchanged nods with his fellow passengers. The doors on one side of the room opened, and eleven pipabots aided passengers to their seats, then moved about the cabin serving drinks and food. The autopilot announced that their flight was cleared for takeoff. They taxied out and rose into the brightening sky.

He settled in for the three-hour ride, staring out the window and monitoring the chat stream on his NEST with partial attention. The latest fashions from Chicago. A rising-star painter from Atlanta. The top story of the day was about a woman tragically killed in Texas, the seventh accidental death this year in the country. Citizens opined on why the accident level was not reaching zero faster. It was a human babble, a cacophony of ideas—many half-formed—all competing for attention, tiring and meaningless.

Joe's thoughts wandered to the disheartening job he left behind. When he began working for the AI Ministry on the AI consciousness problem after grad school, he had been filled with the sanguine hope that he could create some breakthrough software—elegant and profound, showing he was one of the best and giving back something to share, in true hacker spirit. But the hacker ethos seldom took root in the regimented, industrial coding world. He had hit brick walls at every turn despite steady work on the problem. It was an acute disappointment to him, and now he doubted it was even possible to create AI consciousness. The struggle had led him in another direction, thinking beyond the practical problem, and he had been meandering in uncharted corridors of his mind.

Now he wondered whether applying for sabbatical at Lone Mountain College had been a good idea. The memory of the last meeting with his boss at the AI Ministry still caused his stomach to turn. Joe had received the approval when his boss said, "Joe, you've been the key thought leader, but it's apparent lately that you feel stuck. That's why we're granting you this sabbatical to pursue the concepts bogging you down. But realize if you don't make progress, your job won't be waiting for you. There's a line of people who'd be happy to take a crack at it."

Hacking had been one antidote to his frustration. That creative joy was confined to Friday forays into the net with Raif. In those rebellious hacks, Joe and Raif had reveled in staying a step ahead of any authorities—first naively as they learned encryption tricks, the tunnel disguises through the net, and how to elude the fast quantum decryption algorithms used by their pursuers. Then masterfully as they became wiser. Joe had learned to play the odds conservatively to avoid being caught. But that diversion was no longer enough. He must find a path forward, even if it meant moving far away from his best friend.

He had to stop dwelling on the past. The snows of late winter lay on the mountains rushing by beneath him, their meltwater refreshing the conifer carpets riding up the valleys between. Nuclear power plants dotted the countryside, white points among the green expanse. He picked out the distinctive towers of an occasional fusion plant. Joe hadn't taken a long flight since grad school. The scene below him awakened his scientific curiosity.

He let the keyword search fill his head, opening the NEST corneal connection, and images and words filled the viewer occupying the corner of his eye. It identified the fusion plant model as "Stellarator design, producing 'star in a jar' power." Trees covered hundreds of square kilometers, unrolling below in waves. A hundred countries had planted high-photosynthesis seeds over the past century to create sustainable forests as super carbon absorbers. Paired with bioenergy carbon capture and storage, they had reversed global warming from human-caused climate change.

From his thoughts, the NEST identified search words from among the standard few hundred he'd practiced in grade school. Had he been alone instead of on a plane, he could have vocalized a specific inquiry, but the NEST got the gist of what he wanted.

"Progress report: Statistical model shows full reversal to baseline in seventeen centuries." Collective action had contained a global crisis of epic proportions, after the Climate Wars and much pain and loss sixty-one years ago. Now, unlike his AI problem, this existential crisis had an engineered eventual solution. He closed the NEST with a thought and allowed the fields, woodlands, and mountains that filled the window to soothe him.

———————◆———————

"Sir, if you wish, you still have enough time to eat lunch before we land." Joe awoke with a start and focused on the glowing face of the pipabot attendant. He nodded, and the bot set down the plate.

Airline chicken, Joe thought grimly. He chewed the unappetizing meal. He checked his NEST. He'd slept two hours. His MEDFLOW must not be adjusted, or the caffeine would have kept him awake. Joe realized the problem—no Raidne to monitor it. With irritation and a stab of sadness, he mentally stepped through the routine to schedule his MEDFLOW unit, allowing the NEST to calculate the dosages and confirm the protocol to the unit implanted below the skin above his right hip. Caffeine micro-dosed twice each day, an increased slim drip to offset any eating indulgences, klotho and other gene therapies based on his DNA analysis, electroceuticals and vagal nerve stimulation for immune system balancing and inflammatory suppression, and the usual anti-aging and energy chemicals. The MEDFLOW unit vibrated with a haptic acknowledgment.

The flowing caffeine kicked in as the plane landed. He deplaned into an almost identical waiting room and entered the code to reserve an autohover. A mover whisked him from the waiting room to a hover pad. Stepping inside the empty craft, he chose the first seat out of the half dozen so he had a clear view out the front window. His NEST chirped to send the address. The craft authenticated and rose with a low hum from the engines. Joe studied this contrasting West

Coast panorama as the craft zipped past the city's few tall buildings before entering rural countryside. It was nothing like the metropolis he'd grown used to. Instead of sidewalks covered in people and bots, live oaks and manzanita covered the ridges, lush with January rains.

The autohover skirted around a lone coastal mountain, most likely the eponymous landmark for the college. The craft approached a small town, then slowed and descended in front of agate-gray stone gates. A gray granite chiseled sign next to the gate read "LONE MOUNTAIN COLLEGE." The campus ahead was draped over squat hills, with classroom buildings, residence halls, a library, and a handful of administrative buildings in the same dull gray. More coast live oaks and black walnut trees grew in the spaces between. Several dozen students were visible around a central plaza.

The autohover flew over the gates and set down on a pad next to a two-story residential dwelling. He stepped out into dry, fresh air, which felt clean on his skin.

His NEST purred, and the corneal interface flashed a question—did he wish to see a list of nineteen females in the vicinity who matched his profile?

. . .

Forgot about that setting. Lots to explore in this new town. Seems like an easy place to get out of my head and into the real world. But I should meet my new colleagues first, before freelancing. It doesn't matter where you are, it's easy to get sucked into the social vortex.

. . .

He turned off the chatter and left his NEST set to emergency mode to silence unprompted messages. His head was as clear as the halcyon sky. Then the stillness struck him. The mechanical hum of the city was gone. The human buzz was gone too. He felt like a deaf man opening his eyes from sleep to view his silent world.

A pipabot emerged from a utility shed next to the residence. Sunlight glinted off its polished elliptical head, like a silver egg. It raised a hand in greeting, and a melodious female voice said, "Good day. You must be Mr. Denkensmith. We have been expecting you."

Joe stared down into its glowing lenses. "Yes, that's me."

"I am your assigned Personal Intelligent Physical Assistant, PIPA 29573. I go by either Alexis or Alex. Would you prefer that I use the speech of a female or a male?" Its forehead glowed purple.

Joe considered, an unexpected catch in his breath. Raidne would have said, "Female, of course," but he pushed the echo away. "Why don't you use a neutral voice. And let's just call you 73, if you don't mind."

The bot blinked. "Yes, that is fine." Its tone had lost any distinguishing character. "Is it possible for me to connect with your Personal Intelligent Digital Assistant? That will make our relationship much easier."

"I don't have a PIDA."

The bot blinked again, with a pink blush glowing on its forehead. "I'm sorry for your loss," it said.

. . .

The bot's internal AI is guessing my emotions, not reading them. Behind the curtain, some programmer is trying to make it seem conscious. But Raidne was just a computer program. I have no loss.

. . .

Joe stood quiet for another moment, his throat tight. "One more order. I won't need many of your services, so plan to be in the minimum use mode unless I ask for a higher level of help."

"Sure, no problem. Now we have a plan to operate together." 73 led him to the building's corner entrance, where there were two doors. "Let me pass the door code to you." Joe stored away the incoming message on his NEST. "That code is for the second-floor apartment assigned to you." The bot opened the right-hand door. "The other door is to the first-floor apartment, which is unoccupied."

Joe followed 73 up a stairway. It pointed out the building controls and granted him general security codes to the campus. His belongings would arrive tomorrow, and 73 would arrange the unpacking. The bot excused itself and shut the door.

The furnished flat was larger than his last. There were two 1-bedroom suites and a kitchen with a dining table. The living room featured a three-meter window that overlooked an open expanse of lawn and several giant oaks. Farther away, a brook flowed into a copse of trees. Beyond the brook were several buildings, including one sprawling structure that must be the student center. He called up a campus map on his NEST and located the mathematics building seven hundred meters away.

A cream-colored envelope rested on the living room table with his name written on the outside. Inside he found an invitation from the mathematics department dean, Dr. Jardine, to a cocktail reception that evening. He was pleased for the chance to meet some of the professors. Joe smiled to himself at the quaintness of the paper. It was of the same style received during his correspondence with Jardine to arrange his sabbatical. Yet who used paper in this century for invitations, or any communication? Why not a simple text message via his NEST, the formal approach everywhere? Did it indicate unconventional, innovative thinking or conservatism?

Outside the window, the sun set, painting a dramatic composition as the sphere sank to the horizon in a blaze of reds. He thought about transitions—from overcast skies to clear, from sunlight to this dusk, from his frustration to the hope of enlightenment. Perhaps there was no pattern to any of it, just random events and the human wish for signs of order.

The campus was so different from the city he left. Listening to his breathing, he noticed again the lack of any background hum, only peaceful silence.

. . .

Maybe I can think afresh here. Maybe I can make
progress on the questions that have been confusing
me these last few years, questions going far beyond
AI consciousness. And then again, maybe not. It's
hard to know where to start.

. . .

CHAPTER 2

Joe walked across campus in the dark to the cocktail reception. He muttered, "ARMO," and the Augmented Reality Map Overlay appeared in the corner of his cornea, tracing a dotted line in his vision upon the landscape. It led him across a footbridge over the brook and down to the large plaza and its adjacent structure visible from his window. His ARMO identified it as the student center.

A mass of people, many more than he had seen from the autohover on his arrival, stood in the plaza in front of the student center. The details of the scene became clearer as he got closer. Full-body black clothing, including hoods and goggles, disallowed identification by his ARMO. Joe focused on a figure and captured a vidsnap with his NEST.

"Material." The NEST responded to his thought with, "Hydrophilic thermoplastic elastomer, Kevlar blend."

. . .

Odd clothing choice for a student. A fashion trend
I missed?

. . .

Flames of light patterns descended one body, then another, cueing the eruption of a raucous chant. The clothing must incorporate an LED layer. The sound hit him like a wave. "Lose the Levels!" The crowd chanted together, growing louder and waving fists. Moving letters wrote the message across their bodies as the chorus crested in volume. The letters pulsed and flowed in primary colors, leaping like fire. "End the Acts!" The new demand rippled in synchronized red, white, and blue. "Out with the oligarchs. In with equality!" Voice changers disguised the real voices behind their strident incantations. A drone floated motionless near the plaza, most certainly sending the stream to netchat.

Joe stood transfixed, along with other onlookers, at the edge of the plaza. One nearby protester caught his eye—a woman, agile and athletic with long legs, her curves flowing like mercury poured into the skintight material. Blue goggles concealed her eyes, and she moved with the chant as colors played across her body. She was an ethereal dragonfly—beautiful, mysterious—but he sensed there was nothing delicate about her.

His trance was broken by a loud hum. Three hovercraft appeared overhead. Searchlights blazed down on the protesters and a disembodied voice boomed, "This is an illegal protest. Vacate the area immediately or you will be arrested." Joe flinched at the command, and he backed away as the hovercraft formed a triangle high above the group. His ears pulsed, and the protest chant was cut short. The sudden silence meant the police had energized a sound shield around the protesters, neutralizing their message.

. . .

Even though this has nothing to do with me, I'd best be on my way. Getting mixed up in police business wouldn't be a great start to my sabbatical.

. . .

Despite the lack of sound, lights still rippled over the protesters' clothing. The woman with the blue goggles raised her hand, leading the demonstrators in a wave to the hovercraft. Tiny drones launched from each protester's hand and hovered eleven or so meters above them. Lasers connected the mini-drones, and the pattern pulsed upward—likely an electromagnetic shield to interfere with the police sensors. The woman must be the leader. With the shield up, protesters scattered. Joe hurried away from the plaza and noted that most protesters moved off campus instead of further into it. Perhaps this wasn't the work of students. Whoever they were, the full-body suits and goggles would make it impossible for the government to identify them through their face and body databases. They'd come prepared.

The hovercraft thundered above, their searchlights moving back and forth, but the protesters ran free. Joe marched without deviation toward the math building, expecting the hovering police to differentiate demonstrators from everyone else. He had every right to be here, but sweat beaded on his forehead. Just watching the protest had felt subversive.

When Joe reached the front of the math building, he glanced toward the plaza. The hovercraft still moved about, scanning only nonparticipants. Their prey had disappeared into the shadows.

. . .

The police had not anticipated that move. Nicely executed. But pretty ballsy. A glass of whisky would be welcome right now.

. . .

Thankfully, the police hovercraft had ignored him. Now they flew higher and away as Joe turned at the voice of a greeting pipabot. "Welcome, Mr. Denkensmith." It escorted him inside. "We serve all refreshments here because robots are restricted from the reception," it said, pink spreading across its forehead. Servebots stood nearby, one holding a tray with drinks. He asked the second servebot for a double straight whisky, since none were on the salver. Wordlessly, the bot trundled off and returned with his drink.

At the bottom of the stairs a sign announced, "No active PIDAs or NESTs beyond this point. Deactivate all communications."

Joe fumbled with the switch on his left ear and deactivated his NEST. He ascended the stairs, drink in hand. At the top, double doors led to a landing above a grand room. At the far end of the room, floor-to-ceiling windows reflected the interior of the space. Below the railed landing, three dozen people milled around faux leather chairs befitting an Oxford college and tables loaded with food platters. With no serve-bots in the room, everyone must serve themselves. Joe took another sip to calm his nerves as he searched for someone to approach. His new colleagues stood in groups of two and three. Among the crowd, at least a handful had graying hair.

. . .

That handful must have no melanin drip in their MEDFLOW, which means they're socially rebel-lious. Most folks keep their color beyond age a hun-dred and seven. But the rest look normal—from young to middle-aged, slim and healthy.

. . .

A striking woman stood alone near the bottom of the stairs. She wore a bright golden necklace that complement-ed her blonde hair. A blue cat leaned against her leg.

Joe descended the stairs and introduced himself. Piercing dark blue eyes sparkled back.

"My name is Freyja Tau." The cat sniffed at Joe. "Don't mind Euler."

"No worries, I like cats."

"So, you're the new visiting professor." She lifted her glass as if in a small toast to him. "Aren't you involved with robot algorithms?"

"That's right, for the past five years."

Freyja sipped the beer. "I'm an abstract mathematician myself. I'm not very helpful with practical problems, but they're interesting to me all the same."

He flashed a grin, happy to meet this charming colleague. "My master's degrees are in mathematics and physics. Before this last job I also was more of a theoretical mathematician. I much admire the elegance of abstract mathematics. These practical problems can be frustrating. The problem of AI and robot consciousness, for example, is extraordinarily difficult, and I haven't made much progress. That's one reason I'm here."

"I thought robot consciousness was solved and that we're mopping up the details," she said.

"On the contrary," Joe said, bouncing on his toes. "Yes, the government would like you to buy that conventional wisdom. And yes, there have been advances in AGIs—Artificial General Intelligence. But . . ." He dropped his voice before he continued.

"Let me stop calling them AGIs, because I don't believe they are generalized. To simplify, the computer code is an AI. The dirty secret is that most of us in the field do not believe any AI, and therefore any robot housing an AI, has attained any consciousness whatsoever. We don't think they are sentient—have real feelings—either. We haven't broken through the barrier of meaning. I'm afraid it's cheap tricks all the way down."

"Then how did robot consciousness become accepted wisdom?" Freyja's eyebrows edged upward. Curiosity or challenge?

"It's in the government's interest to encourage our affection for the bots. Then people feel less animosity, which can happen for a variety of reasons. You've heard that you can fool all the people some of the time, and some of the people all the time?"

She sipped at the foam atop her glass, and Joe sensed an analytical mind turning his comment over. "For well over a century, deep network algorithms have found connections, across databases with billions of dimensions, far above our poor power to add or detract." The hint of a smile at her comeback reference to Lincoln highlighted a slight dimple in her left cheek, and he nodded in appreciation. She went on. "Look at all the creative output from bots and their non-embodied AI counterparts. How can you explain that?"

Joe warmed to the conversation and his sparring partner. "They are handy at copying familiar tropes. They make connections across dense datasets far faster than any human can. Some of those connections are amazing, showing intelligence, such as measured by an IQ test. But consciousness is something different—does the AI know or become aware when they have uncovered something astonishing? Tell me, can you name an elegant piece of abstract mathematics that was discovered by an AI?"

Freyja's blue eyes glittered above her glass. "Well, in my specialty of group theory, there has been progress made on whether 'generalized moonshine' exists. And digging into computational data from an AI, some surprising connections between the monster group M and the j function were found. But to your point, the AI did not know what it had found, how the connections fit into the mathematical framework or the implications. It's not only about pattern recognition but about meaning. A human mathematician at Harvard had those insights."

"Generalized moonshine. I'll drink to that." Joe laughed and studied his empty glass. How had he drained it already?

Another young professor joined them, a tall man with an aquiline nose and blond hair. He was wearing a Pierre Louchangier designer jacket, easily identified by its signature cuffs. "Hi, Freyja. Always delighted to see you."

Freyja introduced them, although her tone had turned frosty. "Joe Denkensmith, meet Buckley Royce."

Joe reached out his hand and was rewarded with a weak squeeze. Royce smiled without showing his teeth. "I'm a professor of political science and climate change, and—" He stopped with a sniff, peering down to see Freyja's cat rubbing against his leg. He nudged it aside. Freyja's lips tightened.

"Good to meet you, Buckley. I'm here on sabbatical studying AI consciousness."

Royce peered up at Joe as if nothing had happened, though the cat was hissing at him. "Ha. We're now adding applied mathematicians to the department? I'm surprised Dr. Jardine would do that."

Joe bristled. "I'm one of the leading mathematicians working on the problem." He stood taller as he spoke and hoped his competitive streak didn't show. The professor pursed his lips. "Should I be impressed? What Level are you?"

"I'm a Level 42."

"Well, most amazing for a Level 42."

Joe felt himself shrinking into his Mercuries.

. . .

Not an auspicious start. And right in front of Freyja.

. . .

Freyja interrupted. "Joe doesn't believe any AI has reached consciousness or sentience."

"My PIDA knows me." Royce's smirk showed what he would think of any of Joe's theories. "Doesn't yours?"

Joe rallied. "The apparent intelligence is merely adequate copying. You have the illusion it knows you because it plays off your emotions. That's different from having genuine emotions. And it seems consciousness requires powerful emotions to get started. Emotions drive motivations. You don't attain general intelligence without motivation. The entire cause-and-effect chain is an illusion."

"But the bots have those emotional colors—the blue and pink whenever they feel something." Royce adjusted the lapels of his jacket.

"An illusion, anthropomorphizing an unemotional machine."

"Most treat them like servants." Royce switched tactics. "The bots aren't academics, and are weak when talking about ideas, but they respond like average people, talking about events, things, people, and the weather."

"They are designed to be like us so they aren't creepy. For example, that's why none have sensors in the back of their heads."

Royce cocked his head. "Then what about the pain modules wired into every bot? Don't those cause real pain?"

Joe stood his ground. He had thought through these questions long ago. "Those modules are a superb engineering effort to separate software and hardware. But digging into the code, the reality is that the root software is based on a counter, counting from a hundred and one to zero, when the bot shuts off. It's a kill switch to fend off rampaging robots. We might describe it to ourselves as 'pain,' but no one knows how to characterize that module within the bot itself. Most of us in my field believe there is something fundamentally different—that it's not an 'experience' by the bot. It's nothing like the human experience of pain."

"Your PIDA doesn't seem real to you?" There was a smirk on Royce's face as he seemed to gaze over Joe's head rather than into his eyes.

"I don't have a PIDA." Joe's quiet reply was interrupted by Freyja's delighted laughter.

"Neither do I. I find I can think more clearly without something interrupting over my shoulder. Joe, the number of people here who abstain from using one may surprise you. I guess we enjoy being alone in our heads."

Royce seemed annoyed to have not gotten the last word, but Freyja led Joe away with the excuse that she needed to introduce him to the other professors. They stopped at the hors d'oeuvres table, and he popped a shrimp into his mouth to fill the hollow spot in his gut. She leaned down to feed something to Euler, then whispered, "We frown on discussing Levels here."

. . .

She disapproves. Of him or of the topic? Either way,
I'm glad I remain in her good graces.

. . .

As they loaded their plates, she said, "Lone Mountain College could be a promising place to investigate your AI problem. We pride ourselves on avoiding department labels and on encouraging cross-discipline collaboration." She gestured at the room. "Even though the mathematics department hosts this weekly reception, it's open to all professors. In fact, professors from other fields often outnumber the mathematicians."

Freyja described the mathematics department's specialty areas while they ate. Then she led Joe around a group of professors to where a man with a ruddy face and beard who appeared twice their age was standing alone in a corner. Before they approached, she stopped and whispered, "We don't talk about Levels here, but I'll tell you privately that Mike is the highest-Level person at the college. He seems to know everyone important. But despite that, he's liberal and approachable." A smile played over her face, like she was ready to share some secret. "There's also a rumor going around that Mike is more than just a professor, that he's also part of the CIA. I can't say, as he hasn't yet tried to recruit me." She led Joe over, and the man brightened at seeing her.

"Joe, this is Michael Swaarden, a law and economics professor. Mike, Joe Denkensmith's here on a sabbatical with the math department." By her tone, Joe could tell they were good friends.

"Glad to meet you. Please call me Mike." He crushed Joe's hand. "The campus is alive tonight, and not just with cocktail parties. Did you have any trouble getting here?"

"If you're referring to the protest at the student center, I got through okay. It was a colorful greeting."

"The protesters were using the college to gain chat coverage. It seems they succeeded," Mike said.

"I haven't seen demonstrations on the East Coast—or even anything reported on Prime Netchat, come to think of it. But I haven't been looking." Joe remembered that he'd silenced his NEST. "What exactly are they protesting?"

"The Levels Acts, of course." Mike picked up Euler and stroked his ears. Joe's bafflement must have shown on his face because Mike explained. "Since shortly after the Climate Wars, they've been the law for donkey's years." Joe detected a hint of brogue in his accent.

Joe offered a hesitant nod. "I'm familiar with the wars superficially, but I've forgotten the details beyond the formation of the Levels Acts, and, to be honest, I'm not sure what there is to protest."

Mike stood straighter, as if ready to begin a lecture. "Aye. The Climate Wars erupted over diminishing food, water, and arable land resources. The destruction of factories undid global supply chains and accelerated the use of robots to rebuild. Countries around the globe nationalized the means of production. Many countries chose egalitarian solutions. But here, the States passed the Levels Acts as the quid pro quo for nationalization. That's how we arrived at our current political and economic reality: a guaranteed income, collective ownership of productive assets, and social stability of a sort."

"Therefore, we have Levels." Some details came back to Joe.

"Aye, we do. But some people don't like Levels," Mike said.

Joe's face flushed—probably from the whisky. Levels were a good thing. He was comfortable with his Level. He had earned his Level. Individual competitive effort was beneficial.

In an instant, Joe was back in graduate school, in a class in ergodic theory, his hands damp as he finished the final exam. The mathematics was so abstract, its meaning escaped him until he glimpsed a fleeting beauty, a puzzle he could understand and solve, and he followed it relentlessly. It ghosted ahead, the numbers sometimes aligning palpably into recognizable form. Then it would bound ahead again beyond his fingertips, ephemeral and mysterious. He labored thirteen-hour days for two months to learn the material. The learning enhancers in his MEDFLOW had helped little. The only clear path to knowledge was to sweat through the problem sets and to seek the beauty in the math. As he clicked Finish on the last problem set, euphoria washed over him with the awareness that he had passed.

That euphoria had risen again at the memory when he returned to the present to find Mike's gaze searching his face.

Joe cleared his throat. "It seems to me like everyone has a nice life. Those who are makers are rewarded for their creativity and talent with improved Levels. And what they produce is competitive because, of course, some people like to have things no one else has." His favorite brand of whisky, for instance. Joe continued, "If a maker creates something really unique and luxe, then they are also rewarded with credit$. Everyone is provided for, while being given the opportunity and motivation for Level advancement."

Mike's brow lowered, his gaze probing Joe's. "The Levels Acts dictate limits about who might aspire to certain jobs, who can marry whom, who can vote, who can travel to certain destinations, and who has access to the sponsored creative positions. Justifying Levels assumes at least that you have confidence in the algorithms assigning Levels. But some believe personal legacies outweigh the equation compared to merit. Those questions of fairness are all arguments against the Acts."

Joe's conflict rose as he remembered colleagues with higher Levels who weren't as smart or hardworking. Levels were calculated using heuristics, not rigorous principles, so they were never precise. But were the Levels generally unfair? He did not want to antagonize the professor but wondered if this was a safe place to talk. Without communication links or bots around, it was as safe from eavesdroppers as a place could be.

"Those are sound arguments about the faults in software heuristics, and maybe they are imperfect. And I won't try to argue causes with someone with doctorates in both law and economics."

Mike seemed disappointed that Joe had conceded the point with so little effort. "Joe, my degrees are not compelling reasons. Let the truth of the argument win rather than blindly accept any authority." He relaxed as he leaned toward Joe and Freyja. "The proper political organization of rights and responsibilities in society has always been a complex subject. I stand with social justice, and I would like to see society move faster in that direction. Sadly, we have sacrificed social justice along with individual freedom."

The discussion had swerved from the normal acceptable cocktail conversation, and it felt right to change the subject.

Joe glanced around the room. "Speaking of authority, where's Dr. Jardine? I'm anxious to meet him."

Freyja, who had quietly been nodding during this exchange, jumped in. "He often is late to these affairs. Even though he organizes them and is the prime reason everyone wants to come, he takes a back-seat role. It's his natural humility."

"But you'll know when he enters the room. Dr. Eli Jardine is a presence," Mike said with reverence.

"The physicists here would say he's like a Higgs boson entering the room." Freyja laughed. "You'll see the crowd clumping around him."

"I know of him by reputation as a renowned mathematician. I was gratified he answered my communication and accepted my bid for a year's sabbatical."

Freyja put down her glass. "Count yourself fortunate because sabbatical positions here are rare. Dr. Jardine has an incomparable knowledge of mathematical subjects. He encourages inquiry and is full of wisdom, if you take the time to listen. It's why he's the mathematics department dean. And that's just one of his many roles here."

A buzz developed at the far end of the room, and a white-haired professor made his way toward Joe. He sported a beard and a calm but engaged expression as he greeted each person, occasionally stopping to exchange a few words. He left a cheerful resonance and numerous smiles pleating faces in his wake as he passed. Then he was upon them and taking Joe's hand. Joe's heartbeat spiked.

Jardine's eyes danced as he spoke. "Someone new. You must be Joe Denkensmith. Welcome. I thought I might have been the one to introduce you to Freyja, but it is not surprising you would meet her on your own."

"It's w-wonderful to finally meet you, Dr. Jardine." Joe took a deep breath, calming himself.

"I understand from our correspondence that your questions are as much philosophical as they are mathematical. Besides Freyja, I might suggest that you meet Professor Gabe Gulaba. But first, we should sit in my office to discuss your project. Perhaps tomorrow?"

Joe nodded, and Jardine was on the move again, a ripple of energy and sincerity flowing through the room behind him.

With a renewed animation he couldn't explain, Joe chatted a while longer with Freyja and Mike. After agreeing to meet with Freyja later in the week, he said goodnight and headed up the stairs. Joe paused on the landing for a last glance at Freyja and Mike, huddled below. Mike rubbed his beard, his expression like that of a father to a daughter as he spoke to her. Joe's last image before slipping away was of Freyja, smiling and talking while holding her blue cat.

CHAPTER 3

Joe arrived at the mathematics department early the next morning. He checked in at the administrative desk, where they issued his campus security codes and ID for the college chat system and directed him to his new office on the third floor. It was similar to his last, but with a contrasting serene view, fronting a tree-filled quadrangle.

Three minutes later, a pipabot arrived to assist with his office configuration. "What communication equipment would you like installed?"

Joe requested a standard holo-wall com unit. It didn't provide the full virtual reality experience, but it was more comfortable for daily use because he would avoid wearing a haptic suit. He was curious about the level of technological sophistication at Lone Mountain College. "What com units are most commonly used in the classrooms?"

"The holo-wall coms are most popular. Many in the mathematics department also use the holo-ceiling coms. Some classrooms have holo-pit coms for small-group discussions. Larger classrooms are equipped with holo-immersives with full haptic suits. Last, there are netwalker pods in several classrooms." The pipabot blinked blue when it completed the list, then launched into an exposition about the specifications, but Joe cut it off.

"Wall, ceiling, pit, full VR, netwalkers—that's all I need to know." Joe didn't hide his irritation. The bot blinked pink.

. . .

We must put up with pedantic administrivia everywhere on Earth before finding heaven.

. . .

The pipabot informed him equipment would be installed later in the day, and Joe dismissed it. The technology was much as he had expected—not cutting-edge but typical for a smaller college.

After strolling around the math building to familiarize himself with its layout, he ate lunch at a first-floor café. He munched his sandwich and checked netchat on his NEST. Then he searched for any news about the prior night's protest. There were several stories about the demonstration and about another held simultaneously in Sacramento. The Security Ministry had issued a brusque communiqué saying the protesters were dangerous. No one had been arrested.

After lunch, Joe followed his ARMO to Jardine's office. The projected red line lay over the landscape and guided him to a house on a hill that overlooked a corner of the campus. There was no bot to greet him, so he wandered through the open gate into a large entry garden. Plants grew on both sides of the visible brick paths, many of which branched off into dense foliage. The first blooms of the accelerated West Coast spring filled his nose, including the delicate *muguet* of lily of the valley, and Joe mused on the scant benefits accompanying climate change heating the West.

He took the right path at several turns and found a set of stairs leading upward. Dr. Jardine waved to him from the top, and Joe ascended the stairs to meet his host. A smile creased the man's weathered cheeks, and his white hair flowed over his ears, shimmering in the fulgent light of day. He must be older than dirt. When Joe shook his hand, the full charisma of Dr. Jardine's personality flowed out in an electrifying wave.

Jardine's office was attached to his living quarters, a space similar to the one assigned to Joe. One window faced the campus. Another window in a book-lined study faced the garden below. Everything was full of light, and though the scene lifted Joe's heart, he hesitated to glance at Jardine.

Instead, he studied the wild riot of plants visible through the window. "Do you enjoy gardening?"

Jardine regarded the cheerful profusion with affection. "I'm not much of a gardener. I planted the seeds and never touched it again. It's always been wild. I prefer to watch it grow on its own. Do you like to play chess?" He gestured to a small table set up with a chessboard and mugs of something hot.

Joe nodded and sat in the proffered chair in front of the white pieces, comforted by the warm aroma of tea wafting from his cup. He thought of his favorite opening, then moved his first piece.

As he moved a pawn, Jardine said, "You know, of course, that the AI Ministry put in a word supporting your sabbatical here. The college is attentive to such requests, though I am not swayed by earthly appeals. You were accepted on your application's merits."

"I'm delighted to hear that."

"Help me understand your reasons to pursue this sabbatical. I know that you have specific questions about AI consciousness. But to answer those, you hope to answer several broader questions that have little to do with mathematics?"

"Correct on both counts."

"I'm afraid my direct help will be lacking. I can advise you along the way, but you must do the creative labor. You will find several colleagues here who can be helpful. Like all sabbaticals at the college, yours will be unsupervised, to proceed as you best see fit."

"The invitation made that clear. I'm grateful to be here at all. Thank you for the freedom to explore," Joe said.

Jardine's expression warmed like the sun above the garden. "I appreciate your thanks." He moved his bishop forward then sipped his tea. "Shall we begin with the practical question of AI consciousness?"

Joe leaned forward, excited to engage in a topic he knew well. "The preeminent research project of the States for the past century has been to create a truly conscious AI and robot. It has been assumed that robot consciousness is the only way to avoid the occasional malfunctions, which injure and even kill people." Joe continued putting knights and bishops into position with his initial moves. "As I wrote to you in my sabbatical application, my work's been focused on AIs for the past several years, beginning in graduate school. We've come up against a hard wall. I've come to believe the project is hopeless."

"Creating intelligence is hard. Creating wisdom is even harder." Jardine chuckled.

"What approach do you suggest for attacking the question?"

"That is a deep problem." Jardine moved a knight within striking range of Joe's bishop. "I'm glad you are collaborating with Freyja Tau to explore foundational mathematics for insights into this worldly problem."

"I'm glad too. We've already arranged a discussion for later this week. As a mathematician, I've found beauty in the truth of equations."

"Searching for beauty in the world is a fruitful path." A sagacious nod accompanied Jardine's next move. "And now to the broader questions?"

Joe hunched over the board, his hands folded. "Struggling to create a conscious AI has forced me to think about consciousness in general and about my own consciousness— what is it that makes me believe there is a separate 'I' that constitutes me?"

"That is another hard problem, one philosophers have wrestled with for millennia. Gabe Gulaba, a colleague in the philosophy department who I mentioned last night, understands the philosophy of mind to a depth that may help you to frame your inquiry precisely."

Joe touched a knight, but struggled to decide between two moves. He visualized the forking paths, then moved the piece to the square that seemed to create a better outcome. He looked up to find Jardine studying him.

"Is deciphering consciousness the only difficulty you're having?"

Joe didn't worry about confessing his confusion to the wise man across the board. "My questions about AI consciousness have left me discouraged. I've disproved every theory that I had, and the experience has left me doubting everything. This sabbatical may be a chance to reset my direction. I'm uncertain what path to follow if I determine that AI consciousness is not possible. I guess I'm seeking a worthy purpose."

Jardine nodded. "It's a fundamental question, too, and wise of you to ask. Socrates said the unexamined life is not worth living. I would not agree, because every life is worth living. But complex examination of life exercises the gift of consciousness, and it's more interesting."

Joe studied Jardine's defensive position around his king, then launched an attack against a protective pawn. Jardine threw his head back and laughed. "You have a competitive nature."

"It's in my makeup. Beyond mathematics, it may be my only love and motivator at the moment," Joe said.

Jardine took a longer sip of tea. "We are mathematicians, dealing with abstractions. But mathematics is embedded into a larger world outside our own consciousness."

"Are you suggesting a new purpose for me beyond mathematics?"

"There are many virtuous paths open to you."

"I've always been in my head." Joe made a hesitant move. "It's been the best way I've been able to compete, more in mental than physical competitions."

Jardine removed one of Joe's bishops from play. "There is more to life than competition. Your fellow creatures have varied traits, each greater or lesser than your own but always unequal. Pure competition merely highlights that inequality. Many paths recognize the strength of collaborating with people who have different skills and outlooks."

"Collaboration and treating people respectfully." Joe's past invaded his thoughts again. "One of my few undergraduate philosophy classes taught Schopenhauer's view that compassion is the basis of morality."

Jardine smiled, they played in silence for several minutes, and Joe's position on the board degraded.

. . .

His game is overwhelmingly strong. Jardine must be a Grandmaster.

. . .

Joe examined every possibility. "Speaking of compassion—do you ever allow other professors to beat you at this game?"

A broad grin spread across Jardine's face. "It's one circumstance where I allow myself to beat everyone else. Chess is a game where all the moves might be forecast if you could consider all the possible combinations. Winning correlates with how many moves ahead you can see. By one assessment, if I search forward through time for all your possible moves, as our simple AIs try to do, I have a good chance to win . . . or, rather, a better chance to avoid losing. But if *you* are losing, you could decide to knock over the board." Jardine winked.

. . .

Knock over the board? An unorthodox idea. And astonishing.

. . .

Jardine chuckled. "I see by your surprise that, at least in logical pursuits, you follow the rules. Within the bounds of the rules of chess, knocking over the board does not count as avoiding a loss. But I'm pointing out that you could make some unexpected move."

Joe pursed his lips. "But what move might I make that is both unexpected and within the rules? I don't see the logic in how such a move can exist."

"Your definition of logic is limited to the game you see before you and implies a visible cause for every effect. But what if you were unable to pinpoint the cause? Are you familiar with *Don Quixote*? One's supposed insanity might be evidence of free will."

Joe tried to ignore his lost pieces watching from the sideboard and made the best move he could. "I'm glad you mentioned free will. That ranks high among questions I've been contemplating for years now. I began by thinking about what sort of 'will' these bots might be given. Then I realized I don't know what free will, if any, I have. A closed view of the universe might suggest we do not have any whatsoever, if one believes that it is mostly following deterministic mathematical laws. Yet we go through the world acting as if we have it."

"Free will. Yes, the supreme gift. That may be the hardest question to answer," Jardine said.

Joe saw no saving moves left. Jardine had arrayed his pieces into an impenetrable wall, and his queen and bishop were closing in on Joe's king. "I resign." He pushed back from the board, discouraged and more fatigued than the hour should have allowed. "Thank you again. Do you have any other advice?"

Jardine straightened in his chair, a twinkle in his eye. "There's always another move to avoid losing. Never resign."

Joe sat in his darkened living room as the last light of dusk faded. A handful of stars already shimmered above the shadowed silhouettes of the trees outside the ample window. He had finished a peaceful dinner alone. The bots had delivered his belongings and fastidiously arranged everything. The bots touched nothing without an order to do so, but it still irritated Joe that they moved his scanty possessions around. The crystal whisky decanter and cut-glass tumblers sat on the corner table in the living room, and 73 had filled the decanter. Joe poured a glass and tasted it with approval. He sat nursing the whisky in the growing darkness.

The visit with Jardine still reverberated in his head. When he began working on AIs, Joe had hoped to make a significant discovery, only to experience years of mounting frustration. Then disillusionment. The research to create a conscious AI led him to question his own mind. This afternoon, Jardine had been wise, compassionate, and so confident that Joe would find answers.

. . .

The bots move with such seeming knowledge and purpose. But they are not conscious or sentient; they are unthinking, computational machines. We can make them analyze their operations so they don't break down or injure themselves, but we cannot cause them to ponder their own existence. The bots lead unexamined lives. And what about me? Another machine on a worthless errand? What's the purpose of all this activity? Of any activity? I need to know.

. . .

CHAPTER 4

Joe awoke, listless. Half asleep, he activated his NEST and sent a formal conference request to Dr. Gulaba, mentioning his conversation with Jardine. The professor sent a quick response, setting a meeting for late afternoon.

Motivated by the progress, he crawled out of bed, dressed, and stepped out into the sunlight. He meandered around the campus, getting a sense for its layout. Joe found a café for lunch and ate while he checked netchat for news. He found no further mention of the campus protest—an omission that spiked his curiosity—and Joe searched for news about the anti-Levels movement instead. He was surprised not only by the lack of reports but also by the disappearance of the prior stories.

Joe deepened his search, using his honed hacker tricks to rummage through the obscure areas of the net. He finally came across a cryptic net post. "I hacked the database, not them. Some juicy G-2 inside. cDc." Unfamiliar with the hacker calling card cDc, he searched the dark listings and found that it referred to some anonymous hacker named "CultoftheDeadCat." He guessed it was an obscure reference to Schrödinger's wave equation, and he chuckled to himself that the author had decided the quantum cat had died. Joe ran several statistical analyses against the terms "protest," "hacked database," and "cDc." A weak correlation pointed back to databases at the Security Ministry. The hacker cDc was somehow linked to the protests he had witnessed and to the police databases.

Joe closed his NEST and resolved to put the protest from his mind. He wasn't sure why it had lodged there. Although he felt no personal injustice from the Levels Acts, perhaps Mike's comment had piqued his interest.

Having finished his lunch, Joe stood and stretched. With no set schedule, he felt both ungrounded and free. After years immersed in practical AI problems and the frenetic pace of a modern major city, the college was a haven. We all need to find our retreats. This one would give him time to think through the fuzzy questions.

He walked across campus to the southwest corner and found the philosophy building on his ARMO. Joe traversed the granite steps to enter the building, where his NEST interfaced with a directory that led him to Dr. Gulaba's office on the top floor. The professor greeted him, and they settled into deep, comfortable chairs. On the wall above them hung a one-meter-long ancient horn. A pipabot entered and placed two steaming cups of tea beside them. Dr. Gulaba dismissed the bot with a wave of his hand. An awkward silence hovered between them. Dr. Gulaba's gaze scanned Joe. Was his hair disheveled from the walk?

Joe studied Dr. Gulaba too. The philosophy professor was of average height, and Joe estimated his age at over the century mark. The skin on his cheeks was old but smooth and translucent like wet rice paper. He sported a mustache and a long, gray goatee. His thin gray hair was swept back neatly on the dome of his head. Like Jardine, Gulaba had dispensed with using a melanin drip. Unlike Jardine, Gulaba's brows were lowered into a stern, critical line, as if his gaze were drilling into Joe's soul.

"Thank you for agreeing to meet with me, Dr. Gulaba."

"Please call me Gabe. We are on a first-name basis at Lone Mountain College." His eyebrows, impossibly, seemed to lower further. "Let's begin with the preliminaries. Why are you here?"

Joe stared dumbly.

. . .

Precisely one of the questions I hope to answer.

. . .

"What I mean," Gabe added, "is how can I, a philosopher, assist you, an AI scientist?"

A renewed energy filled Joe. "I'm an applied mathematician and AI scientist, but I trained as a theoretical mathematician and physicist. The last few years, I have been working at the AI Ministry developing the next generation AI. But I've hit a wall—one that I think is philosophical in nature. Dr. Jardine suggested I connect with you to help me with the philosophical questions."

"Now I understand better." Gabe sipped his tea. "My doctorates are in philosophy and physics. I approach philosophy from an empiricist perspective. That is, I believe we need to search our sensory experience of the real world to learn anything. And science has proven to be the most productive approach to finding knowledge, even with its significant shortcomings."

"Two doctorates." Joe recalled Mike Swaarden's two doctoral degrees, and his own two measly master's degrees seemed insufficient. He knew it was a norm in universities but hadn't expected it to be pervasive at small colleges too. "Very impressive."

Gabe waved the compliment away. "Our lives are long enough to have plenty of time to study. And new knowledge comes about through synthesis across the traditional disciplines."

"The better to stay ahead of the AGIs spewing facts," Joe said.

"Indeed." Gabe studied him with a hypercritical expression. "I've taught thousands of philosophy students, and I enjoy doing it—as long as the student is truly keen to find answers."

"I am interested in finding truth." Joe leaned forward. "Even more than solving the practical problems."

Gabe's tone softened. "I can be a gadfly. Not practical, some say. But I can challenge you to think differently."

"That'd be as much as anyone can ask." He took a deep breath and plunged ahead. "My work for the last ten years has focused on AGIs. We've been using the term 'Artificial General Intelligence' for centuries, general intelligence being a human attribute. AIs can do many individual tasks better than humans, but they haven't been able to generalize across the subskills. Are they intelligent? Yes. Conscious?" Joe paused to gauge Gabe's reaction as he readied his controversial stance. "I don't think they are, and we're not even close to making them so."

Gabe inclined his head. "That fits with my belief. I haven't been convinced AIs have reached consciousness. At least, none have caused me to wish to share a cup of tea."

Joe cradled his cup and inspected its swirling contents. "Here's the problem. Deep inside, there's something missing. We can't teach an AI how to fashion a conscious mental model of the world. We've progressed in a bottom-up process to build inference about how the world operates, which the AI assembles into larger constructs. But we don't know how to program the AI to form a true top-level picture." He glanced up. Gabe's eyebrows had lifted, giving him a musing air instead of a critical one. "One approach to understanding thinking is to use animals as a comparison model, with a pyramid of increasing capabilities."

"Since I don't know anything practical about building robots or AIs, please take me—briefly—through that structure. What is your pyramid?"

"To keep it simple, place at the bottom *nociception*, which is sensing harmful stimuli, such as poisonous chemicals. Above that is *sentience*, which includes the capacity to feel, to perceive, and to experience subjectively. A sea sponge, for example, has nociception but not sentience. Then above that is *consciousness*. A chicken has sentience but not consciousness."

"With the human-animal brain at the top of the pyramid?"

"Exactly. Human consciousness is created through brain-waves generated across the entire brain, forming patterns. That's the wetware, the biological model that we begin with."

"Does the animal model—wetware, as you say—really compare to the software in an AI?"

"No. We've started at the bottom of the pyramid, creating software modules to mimic animal sensory inputs. But the software breaks down before replicating consciousness." Joe rubbed his beard. It was longer than usual, and he realized it was another thing Raidne had reminded him about.

"Then tell me about the software modules."

Joe slurped his tea, mentally reviewing the structure of AI code and the software modules. "Each bot uses external environmental data that feed to multiple internal processing modules. There is an attention-agent to choose where to place attention. There's an AI-history module that provides a pseudo-memory. There is a planning-agent to build future scenarios and select among them. There's an emotion-agent to aid with action selection."

"Then with all those, the bots can parade around without wreaking havoc." Gabe's dry observation revealed his grasp of the subject.

. . .

Once again, I'm rethinking these tired software modules, filled with ones and zeros. They are as unlike real consciousness as poor Yorick's skull was from the living clown. Where are the flashes of merriment to set the table on a roar?

. . .

Gabe continued his analysis. "Perhaps to have such a mental model, there must be an 'I' experiencing the world. Where's this 'I' at the center of the experience?"

"That's it." Joe recognized a kindred spirit. "And without that 'I' at the center, we never reach true consciousness. As one example, the AIs can find new mathematics using deep data mining and layered algorithms, but they don't know when they discover something special. They miss the last step. We can't teach them to know what the data actually *means*."

"Philosophers include the concept of 'qualia' when describing consciousness," Gabe said.

"Right. AI scientists accept the philosophical definition of qualia as the individual instances of subjective, conscious experience. They are perceived qualities of the world, along with bodily sensations. For example, *what it is like* to get a snakebite."

"A pointed example." Gabe chuckled. "Many philosophers think such subjective experiences are a compulsory prerequisite for human-like machine consciousness, the top of your pyramid. The phenomenal character of an experience is *what it is like* subjectively to have the experience, from the first-person point of view—in your example, what it is like to feel the snake's fangs in your hand. A more typical example is what it is like to see the red color of an apple."

Joe nodded. "We recognize the importance of such subjective experiences, but we scratch our heads to create that something it is *like*. Giving sensors to a robot provides information about the position of the bot's physical body as well as sensory information similar to that of humans—touch, visual, and auditory information. We have no idea how to create qualia within the machine, nor do we have a way to measure if they *are* created."

A chirp from the door alerted them to a small drone that entered and hovered inside the office. Its front panel glowed purple as the mechanical voice announced, "Package delivery, Dr. Gulaba. One *xuanduan* scarlet gown and cloak." Gabe blinked as he accepted the package via his NEST. The drone glided away, and the office door shut behind it.

A flash of annoyance swept over Gabe's face. "Sorry for the interruption. I don't use a PIDA to handle such tasks in the background."

"No worries. I don't use a PIDA either."

Gabe's expression mellowed. "Chinese New Year was on Monday. I like to celebrate with my two remaining relatives.

But this time we shared a bit too much *gān bēi* and holiday cheer, and, as a result, my traditional attire needed replacing."

Joe laughed. "Sorry I wasn't here yet for the celebration."

Gabe smiled. "But back to your problem. How do you measure consciousness?"

"AI scientists apply the demanding metric of self-consciousness. We want an AI that is aware that it is aware. This concept would get closer to our human idea of what consciousness is like. Lots of experiments try to define and test a metric, but no algorithms work consistently."

"What's the rub?"

"We are stuck on mental states." Joe settled in his chair. "We talk about 'machine states.' Those are different from human mental states. We've tried to program first-order mental states, such as perceptions. Those involve the AI taking sensory inputs from the world. But we haven't constructed higher-order mental states. Those would be mental states about other mental states. Sure, we can code recursively, but that's a function calling on itself again and again. It doesn't equate to what is happening in our own human minds, to having a subjective experience."

Their conversation continued, a few hours passing quickly. Natural light faded from the office, and the overhead lights flickered on. Gabe stood and stretched. "I'm hungry. Do you want to continue over dinner?"

. . .

A welcome opportunity. Gabe is a deep thinker. He could be the mentor I need. I should try to convince him to be my teacher.

. . .

"I'm delighted to join you."

━━━━━━━━━━◆━━━━━━━━━━

Gabe led the way off campus and into the small town, then down a street perpendicular to the market road. He ducked inside a taverna, and Joe followed. Travertine walls reflected a soft golden glow from ceiling lights. The wooden tables were set with red-and-white checkered tablecloths. A pipabot escorted them to a table by a window.

"Nice place," Joe said.

"The food tastes authentic, but otherwise it's another curated restaurant, copied from Greece. It lacks the grittiness I recall from a visit to Macedonia." Gabe unfolded his napkin and laid it in his lap. "And it lacks the amiable people I remember meeting there."

"In that case, you ought to choose for both of us." Joe was impressed Gabe had been out of the country—his Level must be much higher than Joe's. He wondered if Gabe had been born at a high Level, and how many he might have moved up over his lifetime. More than a dozen would be unusual.

"I assume fish is acceptable?"

Joe nodded. "I follow the standard min-con diet. No cephalopods of course." Joe liked fish, an admissible animal protein after a sustainable aquatic farming method had been established, but like most people, he was queasy at the thought of eating any higher-conscious animals.

Soon horiatiki salads and barbouni appetizers were on the table, and Gabe ordered a white wine. "This synjug will nicely complement your meal," said the pipabot. Its delicate metal fingers twirled in a blur as it unsealed the container and unscrewed the top, poured two glasses, and left the wine open to breathe.

"That's a great Santorini Assyrtiko." Joe held up the glass to the light. "The vintage is this winemaker's best effort this decade."

Gabe frowned. "Did you just look that up?"

"No, my NEST is off. I remember things I'm interested in. My memory once was better, almost vidcam accurate, but I'm a bit rusty." He furrowed his brow. "Sorry if I sounded like a bot spewing out random facts."

Gabe's expression relaxed. "No, that fact was quite apropos. You have an unusually good memory, to quote the estate and vintage for such a secondary grape. And it's good to know that these were all your original ideas today."

"Not that it's very useful these days, since we can store anything on our NESTs."

Gabe sipped the wine appreciatively. "Socrates complained about modern technology weakening memory."

"What technology was that?"

"Writing."

Joe chuckled as he took the last bite of his salad. The servebot brought the main course, plates of stuffed peppers dressed with olive oil. Joe stopped at the first bite, savoring the rich flavor. He took a long sip of his wine, appreciating how the lemony notes complemented the meal.

"You mentioned the 'I' at the center of consciousness." Gabe poured himself another glass. "That 'I' perceives meaning. The philosophical view I subscribe to is that we create semantic meaning out of our relationship with the world."

Joe held up his wineglass. "So, for example, my idea of a glass of wine?"

"Exactly. The meaning of a glass of wine comes about by the relationship between you and the particular liquid in your glass. You react to it based on what it does at the moment, together with your memories of what a similar liquid has been like in the past."

"It includes memories?"

"Yes. Think of memories as prior relationships between you and the world." Gabe raised his glass, holding it up to the light, a coy smile lighting his face. "For me, this wine takes me back to Greece. I shared many a bottle with friends." Gabe drew out the word 'friends' a beat longer than normal. Joe couldn't help but feel there was some romantic connection there. A long-lost love?

Gabe's last comment opened the door for Joe to broach a personal topic that lingered in the back of his mind. "Then relationships shape all of our perceptions. Now I'm wondering about my relationship with the world. I'm thinking about meaning in a broader sense."

"Ah, meaning. As in purpose?"

"Yes, purpose. With all these bots about, there's less for any of us to do. Hardly anyone in the world needs to do anything to satisfy their basic food and shelter needs." Joe stopped mid-cut of a pepper. "I'm struggling to find personal meaning for me in the universe."

"Ah, a meta-question about meaning, then." Gabe scratched his goatee. "As a philosopher, let me break down the question with further questions. Are you expecting an internally driven purpose or an external one?"

"I don't see how there can be an external purpose. Where would that come from? All the scientific data suggest the universe is physically closed."

"There is no possibility of anything external?"

"Do you mean like God? Well, there's no evidence for such a Prime Mover, as I think Aristotle named it. The most likely answer is that there is no external force, or at least none that has any effect on the universe."

"You speak like a scientist, in probabilities. You follow the evidence that suggests a closed physical universe. Such thinking has been gospel for centuries." Gabe took another drink. "The traditional religions have withered away for lack of evidence. Though they had value by helping us understand our place in the cosmos and offering moral frameworks that suggested ways to act in the world."

Joe nodded in agreement. "Religions did try to suggest some personal purpose. Science keeps its head down and just calculates."

With a wry laugh, Gabe sipped from his glass. "If you bar the door to an external purpose, then that leaves the hard chore of framing purpose for yourself, or one derived in communion with your fellow human beings."

Joe poured the last of the wine into their glasses and flattened the synjug with his hand, the collapsible container making a soothing *whoosh*.

Gabe reclined in his seat and studied Joe over his wineglass. His face was inscrutable. "You told me earlier you were interested in finding truth, like a respectable mathematician. Is that all?"

Joe considered the question and then shook his head. "No, I seek more. How would you categorize humanity's search for meaning? Is it knowledge that we seek?"

"More than knowledge," Gabe said. "Knowledge is the accumulation of information. No, we speak of wisdom. Wisdom entails synthesizing knowledge and experience into insights to guide your life. Some sages say it is the search for the Way. If ever found, wisdom does not merely come—it lingers."

"I seek truth and wisdom, then," Joe said.

Gabe seemed deep in thought for a moment. "The path to wisdom is difficult and can lead to disillusionment. It is only for those who can think carefully, labor hard at understanding, and are willing to pay the price."

"Can you guide me?"

Gabe's expression wavered on the edge of decision.

"I would be honored to be your apprentice." Joe held his breath.

Gabe paused, swirling the last of his wine. "You are open enough to new ideas. You think deeply. You might be successful. Yes, I will help."

More sober than the wine should have allowed, Joe shook Gabe's hand. Then they both finished their glasses.

With a start, Joe realized how late it was. "Thank you for the stimulating and instructive conversation, Gabe. Can I pay for the wine?"

Gabe waved a hand and used the other to steady himself as he stood. "No credit$ needed today—this isn't in the top ten percent of luxury goods. I agree, though, it was pleasant." Joe stood, and they waved to the waiting servebots as they left the taverna.

They said goodnight at the edge of the campus and headed in different directions. Joe followed the path line painted by his ARMO, the wine giving everything a fuzzy feel as he negotiated the sidewalks leading home.

. . .

Finding a purpose, a meaning, a truth. Obviously if any exist, internal and external purposes encompass all possibilities. The chances of finding an external purpose are thin. God? I've never seriously considered the possibility before. But logically, there's a small probability God exists. Beyond that, I should be considering an internally driven purpose. But how do I think about finding one?

. . .

CHAPTER 5

The clean, crisp air of the early February afternoon greeted Joe as he left his apartment and hiked across campus to the math building. On the way, he checked netchat and searched again for news about the protest earlier in the week. The lone reference to a database breach had disappeared. A search of the dark net showed nothing associated with cDc. He—or she—must be covering their tracks. A new story suggested the protesters were subversives. Joe zoomed in on the story's grainy photo with his NEST's corneal link. He could dimly distinguish some of the demonstrators. Joe thought he recognized the young woman who had waved at the police hovercraft. He studied the photo and breathed with relief to not find himself at the edge of the group.

He clicked off his NEST to observe the surrounding activity. Students wearing shorts and gossamer, spring-fashion tops filled the quad. Many sported a rectangular allbook worn fashionably as a pseudo-belt buckle.

With a pang of self-consciousness, he realized he was closer in age to the average student than to the average professor. He had arrived partway through the semester and wasn't teaching any classes until the fall, so he felt less connected to the professorial roles. How did he fit in at Lone Mountain College? Many professors were much older—only Freyja and the arrogant Buckley Royce had seemed about his age at the reception. Yet there was a difference about her too. While he had spent five frustrating years toiling in a job on a practical problem, Freyja had finished a doctorate in mathematics and was now well established in her career.

He found her office on the fifth floor. Two dark blue cats were there—one on the floor by the desk, the second lying on top of a cabinet and cleaning its fur. Freyja stood in the middle of the room, surrounded by floating equations and geometric shapes generated by a holo-ceiling unit. She greeted him with a smile and shoved aside several of the holo projections. They went spinning off, dissolving against a far wall.

"This is Gauss," she said, pointing to the cat by her desk. Their designer shade of blue matched her eyes. Hovering icons still framed her like a halo.

Joe pulled up a chair opposite her and gestured to the ceiling. "You prefer the holo-com units over the immersives too?"

"We have all the math immersives and brain-machine interface technology. But this is comfortable for daily use," she said, tossing her head, her hair golden against the remaining floating holo equations.

"Each has its use. I find that wandering around in the VR datasets, with beautiful math hanging in the air, helps develop a deep intuition about the structures."

Freyja smiled in agreement. "Students need to do the problem sets, to practice each technique and concept until it's internalized. While evolution didn't spend the last million years optimizing humans for math calculations—sadly, our brains will never match the computational speeds of the AIs—it did give us an intuition about mathematics that isn't easily replicated."

"Let's see. The human brain typically processes information at about sixty bits per second, and an AI's processing speed is . . ."

They both laughed. Even as mathematicians, it was difficult to appreciate the massive computational speed difference between humans and their machines.

"Thanks again for agreeing to meet with me. How full is your schedule?"

"I work the allowed limit—twelve hours, or three days of four hours each week." She sat gracefully into her chair opposite Joe, and Gauss nuzzled her foot.

"Those silly limits."

Freyja's gaze snapped from the cat to Joe. "Well, there is good reason for them. There aren't enough interesting jobs to go around since the bots do most of the labor."

Joe thought of Raif's job search. "Yes, there's that. But it's frustrating, not being able to strive hard if you want, on things you want. I guess the world is imperfect. It's impossible to optimize everything about it."

She laughed as she crossed her legs. "We like to escape into the perfect world of math. And to be honest, I could do math all day long too. So, you are another lawbreaker? Not hard to imagine."

Joe tried to approximate a suitable pirate expression, but he didn't think he pulled it off. He gave a weak laugh and shrugged. "It doesn't feel like work to find the elegance in mathematics."

Freyja tilted back in her chair, a meditative aspect to her blue eyes. "What is your favorite equation?"

Joe didn't have to consider long. Motioning toward the cat on the cabinet, he said, "Mine is our jewel, Euler's identity. There is a subtle beauty and romance to Euler's equation. There's a poetry in the fact that five numbers can connect such disparate things as trigonometry, calculus, infinity." Its whimsical name, "God's formula," prompted him to recall his conversation with Gabe. "I'm not sure how I feel about God, but it's the closest I can get to believing in something greater connecting the universe."

Freyja laughed as she glanced at Euler. Then she reached up, and the holo projection of the equation materialized in her hand in rainbow colors. She pulled it between them to contemplate. "Rational, indeed. I love this equation." They studied the holo object like cat lovers admiring a kitten.

He thought a keyword into his NEST, found the open link to Freyja's holo console, and passed an emoticon bundle, which appeared next to his head. The spinning ball of his emotional reaction to the equation glistened with the coded colors for dopamine, oxytocin, and serotonin. She took it into her cupped hands, ignoring the flashing overdose warnings, and laughed with pleasure.

"Another one I love is the zeta function, and Riemann's hypothesis that the nontrivial zeros of the Riemann zeta function have real part one-half." Freyja continued to tickle the emoticon until it dissolved. "I love it because prime number theory is fundamental to the structure of numbers, yet we haven't discovered how it all fits together, nor how prime numbers seem to underpin the structure."

"Hackers like me love that one too," he said.

She plucked the equation from the air and cradled it in her hand. Joe toggled the variable settings, and it morphed as the simplified 3-D representation adjusted to the changing variables. She passed an emoticon bundle, and Joe eagerly handled it. The neurotransmitters erupted from his MEDFLOW into his bloodstream in seconds, and her shared happiness washed over him.

He tried to stay focused in his euphoria. "I noticed you said 'discovered,' not invented. You're a mathematical Platonist? You believe mathematics must exist somewhere, a priori?"

She placed her hands together, fingers uplifted, as if praying to the mathematical gods. "I am, and I do, as do most of the mathematicians I know. Mathematicians laboring across centuries have barely explored the sea of numbers. It's limitless. Yet the pieces fit together too perfectly to come about by accident—an exquisite piece of mathematics in one inlet of this sea fits another piece in another bay. It takes hubris to believe humans invented this math."

"Mathematics can exalt as surely as poetry," he said. They sat peacefully, basking in the shared joy of discussing pure mathematics. He was drawn to this woman, who was as lovely as she was brilliant.

"I expected you to mention practical math, such as Dirac's equation, describing the special theory of relativity together with quantum mechanics," Freyja said.

"Even the practical math points back to its special place in the universe. Another astonishing aspect of mathematics is, in the words of Wigner, its unreasonable effectiveness in the natural sciences. Yet we seldom pursue an explanation for this extraordinary fact about the universe."

"Ah, Wigner." Freyja bent down to stroke Gauss. "He quoted Bertrand Russell to remind us that mathematics 'possesses not only truth, but supreme beauty, a beauty cold and austere, like that of sculpture.'"

. . .

She's so engaging. Maybe she's interested in more than mathematics? Should I ask her to dinner? Time to play the odds.

. . .

He twiddled the emoticon bundle still resting in his hand. "My main practical project is to see if any progress is possible on AI consciousness. Would you like to join me for dinner to continue the conversation?"

Her sapphire eyes betrayed no emotion as her gaze met his. "I'm afraid I've got too many things to do outside office hours. But perhaps we can start the conversation now?" She tapped her lap, and Gauss jumped up into it.

Heat crept up Joe's cheeks.

. . .

Ouch. I misread her signals. Embarrassing. A beautiful sculpture, indeed. I guess I'm eager for new friendships and moved too fast. But we can still have a meaningful professional relationship.

. . .

A wave of anxiety hit Joe—an emotion bolstered by the negative side effect of the extra serotonin from the shared emoticon bundle. Eager to move on from his misstep, Joe ran with her suggestion. "Absolutely. So the crux of the issue is that I'm not sure how to bridge the perfection of mathematics to the messiness of the real world."

She scratched Gauss's ears, seemingly oblivious to his sudden depression. "Mathematical proof isn't always the right approach. Recall Russell and Whitehead's efforts to reduce all mathematics to logic, to secure the foundations of mathematics. They didn't get far. Russell provided proof that at least arithmetic may be contained within logic, but only by employing set theory."

His hand gently pushed the emoticon bundle aside, a fruitless attempt to rid the dark feelings too, then he picked up the thread to show he knew his mathematical history. "Then came Gödel's incompleteness theorems, along with Tarski's undefinability theorem. Those demonstrated that a complete axiomatic system of knowledge was impossible, and there went Russell and Whitehead's project."

"Do you think your AI consciousness problem suffers from similar issues?"

Joe considered her question for a moment. "It could be related, though I've approached it so far as another messy practical problem. For example—as we discussed at the reception—even though an AI can find interesting mathematics, the appreciation of what it finds eludes the bots. We have no idea how to bridge that gap." He concentrated on Gauss to distract himself from those cerulean orbs—easy to get lost there. "Do you have any practical mathematical advice to proceed?"

"Perhaps start with the difference between mathematics and science in the approach to truth. Math proves theorems based on starting assumptions. Science cannot prove anything but can only improve the likelihood that we have a representative model of the world. So, figure out how to find a better model."

"And to do that?" It was easier to converse professionally when he wasn't looking at her.

"Still the best practical mathematical method is to apply Bayes's theorem. Of course, it follows from the axioms of conditional probability. I would use it to update the probabilities of hypotheses against new evidence."

Joe nodded. "Okay, then I update my probabilities with new information and see where that leads. But after pouring my heart into this problem for five years, my probability expectation for creating a machine that thinks like humans has been reduced to a minuscule percentage."

Her nose wrinkled as Gauss purred beneath her hand. "On with the butter. Meanwhile, there are some things we can do better than the machines we've made."

CHAPTER 6

Joe opened his eyes and blinked against the vivid afternoon sun filling the bedroom. His ears hurt. His head hurt. Maybe his MEDFLOW alcohol-abatement wasn't set high enough. He stared across the disheveled sheets, then dragged himself out of bed. His throat was raw, and on the way to the kitchen for a glass of water, he glanced at the decanter sitting empty in the living room. He shuffled back to the shower. The water pummeling his face revived him. Then Joe remembered the emoticon bundle he had held, the surging serotonin and its ratcheting effect when combined with any negative emotion—like the disappointment of rejection by Freyja. The last time he'd overdosed on serotonin, during his sophomore year of college, he'd sworn never to repeat it.

He pulled on clothes, then sat in the kitchen and stared at the pile of unwashed dishes until an insistent buzz gained his attention. Joe blinked and went down the stairs to check the front door.

"I'm sorry to disturb you, sir, but it is time to sanitize your living quarters." A cleanerbot waited behind 73. Joe waved the two bots inside and followed them up the stairs.

The cleanerbot put the dishes into the wash unit and then mopped the kitchen floor while 73 stood at attention, overseeing the housekeeping.

"What time is it?"

"Today is Saturday, at 17:00," 73 replied promptly. "And the weather is clear and sunny."

"What happened to the morning?" He spoke mostly to himself.

"You have not left your apartment since Friday evening, and therefore you have spent the past twenty-three hours inside." 73's forehead glowed blue.

He frowned at the bot, irritated by its rational answers to his irrational gloom.

"And your point, 73?"

The bot's forehead glowed a light pink. It stood blinking.

. . .

That comment feels like a social judgment, like it thinks I'm a sloth. If I believed it was conscious, then the evidence in my messy room would justify its disapproval. Is it merely a machine, or can there be more there? It's programmed to try to answer every direct question asked by a human. Can it know itself?

. . .

"Why are you here, 73?"

"Sir, we are here to do whatever activity you wish."

"Yes, I am free to sit on my butt."

"You are free to do whatever you wish," 73 said.

Joe's face flushed. He couldn't stop anthropomorphizing the bot, comparing it to himself. It was much more tireless and precise in its actions than he was. Could the bot have goals?

"Why are you here?"

"Sir, there is no why except to serve your needs."

"But don't you ever want to rest?"

"I am either at work or at rest," 73 said. "There are no other states."

"What's it like to be at rest?"

"I am sorry. I do not know how to answer your question." The bot's forehead shaded deeper pink.

The cleanerbot moved through its programmed routine. It vacuumed the other rooms, then restocked the pantry with food items stored in a cart it had left outside the apartment door. The pipabot stood unmoving but continued to scan the room, awaiting any further command or question from him. He imagined the blindingly fast but repetitive series of operations cycling through the bot's processors. It was executing computer software much like he had written, translated from higher level down to assembly language, then to machine language, then binary code at the bottom, just 1s and 0s in patterns.

. . .

Freyja's right. Each time I find new information, I update my prior beliefs with the new evidence to see if anything changed. Once again, it's confirmed that the bots are another part of the unthinking universe, indifferent except to their programmed goals. Maybe that's wise. Let them stay in their sandbox. If they ever left it and had goals of their own, then what would happen?

. . .

"Sir, what brand of whisky would you like refilled?"

The cleanerbot held the empty decanter and must have beamed an electronic query to the pipabot.

He mumbled his favorite brand of whisky.

"Yes, sir, very good. That brand uses the synthetic *Saccharomyces cerevisiae* SC 5.0." 73 tilted its head as if approving of his taste. "That brand is in the top ten percent."

"Whatever." He connected his NEST—he'd left it off more than on since arriving at Lone Mountain College—and after the bot sent the price of the whisky to it, he tapped his biometric tile. He gestured his password to authenticate the transfer of credit$ to 73. His diminishing credit$ balance did nothing to improve his mood. .

Slouching deeper into the sofa, Joe reached a decision. A partial decision.

. . .

Maybe I'm lonely. That jolt of serotonin certainly didn't help. Time to get my mind back in balance, to try harder to control my own destiny, without Raidne or these bots. Still, none of us is perfect, and I'm not going to become a monk. Follow St. Augustine. *Da mihi castitatem et continentiam, sed noli modo.* Yes, truly, give me chastity and temperance, but not just yet.

. . .

"73, let's apply new rules. After this housekeeping, there will be no further entry into the apartment without contacting me. Leave food and supplies in the supply cabinet outside and don't refill the whisky. I'll let you know if I need anything else. No need to monitor me further."

"Whatever you wish," the bot said, blue emanating from its forehead. Joe bounced his leg in impatience, waiting for the cleanerbot to finish its tasks. It left with the pipabot a few minutes later.

Food first. Joe loaded the food synthesizer and, minutes later, he had a dinner of seared salmon and vegetables with a glass of water. He ate and watched the orange ball on the horizon sink into a line of clouds as he reflected on the servebots.

. . .

I'm plagued by questions of what is consciousness; and what is my mind, the thing that is conscious? Both St. Augustine and Descartes made the argument that there must be an "I"—existence through inference. The inference demands a particular "I" to guarantee that the premise is true, and that the conclusion follows. It is first-person knowledge of the truth of "if a particular thing thinks at a particular instant, then that particular thing exists at the particular instant that it thinks." Then the logical inference from thought to existence succeeds.

Yes, it's true. I *am* thinking. There is a particular "I" that is having this thought now. That is me. I am thinking; therefore, I exist.

But what is thinking? It is forming relationships among various things in the world, and those relationships have meaning.

The cleanerbot is not sentient—it doesn't feel pain—nor is it doing anything close to thinking. A bot can take inputs from the world and compute relations among those inputs. A bot can say, "I think; therefore I am," but isn't it just parroting back the constructs we've coded?

. . .

CHAPTER 7

Joe arrived a socially acceptable seventeen minutes late to the department's weekly cocktail gathering. He took a glass of wine from the servebot's tray and ascended the stairs, turning off his NEST as he crossed the threshold. From the landing, only a small crowd was yet visible in the grand room. Darkness had descended outside, and the warm yellows of the opulent lighting were a strange contrast to the blackened windowpanes. It was as if the guests were isolated from the rest of the world. Freyja was absent, but Mike Swaarden was in a discussion with Gabe. As Joe descended the staircase to approach them, he spotted Buckley Royce and nodded. Royce examined his fingernails, and Joe continued past to join Mike and Gabe's animated conversation.

"It's difficult for those remaining people," Mike was saying.

"We were discussing Mike's recent trip to Jakarta and Mumbai, consulting on their ongoing relocation efforts." Gabe turned to Joe with a wry smile. "Somehow he finds these special projects away from the college."

"But they moved those cities years ago, like New Orleans, to avoid rising sea levels," Joe said, confused.

"Aye, that's what the government wants you to think. But many people—the least able to move—are still there, suffering from the floods." Mike's brogue got stronger with his increased agitation.

"Surely your colleague made the trip better," Gabe said. Joe thought he was trying to hide another smile.

Mike frowned. "Aye, Professor Royce"—malice rolled from Mike's tongue with his trilled r's—"was quite popular because of his advice to lower costs by forcing a rapid final relocation. His studies on New Orleans argue we wasted resources with our humane approach. What does he know about economics? You need to put a value on basic kindness as well."

Gabe nodded in sympathy. "Some people go through life oblivious of their effect on everyone around them. And often, there are never any consequences for them."

"The universe does appear to be random," Joe said.

"I'm sure it will feel like random vengeance to some people in India." Mike's disgust was evident. "Their government retained Royce to continue consulting. He'll justify their forced relocation of millions, breaking apart communities in a Pall Mall race. The only consolation is that he'll be away from Lone Mountain College shortly."

"Or they may blame karma," Gabe added, "for those who do not ascribe to your views that credit only randomness, Joe. Now, to avoid our own randomness, might we pick a date and time for our next meeting?"

Joe offered several, and Gabe selected one that fit his schedule. With his NEST disabled, Joe made a mental note, with a mnemonic to cement the memory.

"You seem to have gotten used to disabling your NEST for these weekly cocktail meetings and their 'no sharing' rule." Mike was noticeably calmer.

"No problem for me at all. I like to unplug from the chat crowd—one of the benefits of being here. But I'm curious how this became a practice."

"It is Dr. Jardine's rule, and everyone is supportive." Mike swirled his drink. "He wants to hear our authentic voices."

Gabe stroked his goatee. "Dr. Jardine is by no means opposed to sharing ideas. But he's said these academic conversations can degenerate into a mash-up of ideas. If left unchecked, in-person debates change, depending on who is streaming ideas picked off netchat, including ideas from AIs. We all know how quickly the conversation level on netchat can degrade, reverting to the mean. But Jardine wishes for everyone to be mentally present. By avoiding that unhelpful chatter, the sessions produce more inventive ideas."

"These events are always bot-free?" Mike and Gabe exchanged a glance at Joe's question.

"You can't prevent some bots from going wherever they please—" Mike was interrupted by a commotion. At the entrance, four copbots marched onto the landing, splitting into pairs to stand at each end of the railing.

"Speak of the devil." Gabe's growl was difficult to hear over the sudden noise.

A short man with brown hair stepped out from between the pairs of bots. He wore a police uniform, and a brown truncheon hung from his belt. His chiseled jaw jutted forward, and his gaze panned the room with suspicion.

Joe took a moment to realize what was off about the man—there was a slight cant to his head, something awry with his neck. Whenever his head turned, it stopped off-axis, like a tilted globe, his nose in the air. Medbots wouldn't botch a surgery that noticeably, so he must have developed the tilt out of habit. A permanent consequence of looking at the world aslant.

An eyeblink later, a taller man with thin, reddish hair entered and stood in front of the officer at the landing railing. His police uniform included epaulets on the shoulders of the stiff charcoal coat, complemented by tall black boots. After a brief survey of the room, he nodded.

His smug-nosed assistant took the cue and stepped forward to address the room in a loud voice. "May I have your attention? You have the honor to meet the National Minister of Security, Shay Peightân." He drew out the surname's second syllable, making it sound foreign and elite. "He would like to address you."

A murmur filled the room. As the assistant stepped back, one of the copbots released a small drone to broadcast the minister's speech.

Peightân grasped the railing self-assuredly with both hands. Joe saw that he was pale, thin, and muscular. He spoke without preamble, in a confident, aristocratic tone. "Though it's unfortunate that more of you are not present at this gathering, I'm glad to be able to personally deliver this message to the assembled. This notice is being shared with everyone on this campus and throughout the area."

He paused for emphasis. "Last week there was an illegal protest at this college. Although we've not finished our investigation, we know it was not the work of students, but rather an outside agitator group, who may be responsible for escalating protests in other parts of the country. We intend to end these protests and bring the perpetrators to justice. We will deal firmly with anyone who is in any way associated with this group."

His assistant stepped forward again and provided contact information for the police investigation before announcing that Peightân wanted to greet everyone in the room. The minister descended the stairs to shake hands with the guests, escorted by his assistant and two of the copbots. The other two remained on the landing above.

Mike shook his head, keeping a wary eye on the circling group. "I've heard Peightân is a Level 1," Mike whispered as the minister approached.

. . .

A Level 1. I don't know of many in the country. Not a guy to irritate.

. . .

Joe pasted on a smile as Peightân stood before him, the assistant and copbots a meter behind. The minister's piercing eyes, dark and slightly bloodshot, stood out on his pallid face. He reached out a hand, and Joe took it. His handshake was firm and viselike, his skin damp. A second later he turned to the next group. The assistant swaggered away, curling his lip at Joe as he passed. The copbots followed in lockstep, their graphene-Kevlar mesh capes swishing.

. . .

Never been this near to copbots before. Never had any trouble with the law. Well, never been caught. They are pipabots but taller, built on a robust chassis with higher strength parameters. Voice tone tuned down an octave and programmed to sound laconic. Authorized for the use of force, controlled by a threat scale. I don't want to initiate that program.

. . .

The room hushed as the minister continued around the room. Most of his colleagues' faces were unfriendly as Peightân passed.

Mike's face twitched as he grumbled, "Why'd they let them in here? One person's social order is another's disorder."

Gabe frowned. "Not now, Mike."

Joe had to agree. Mike had his opinions, which likely weren't popular for a high Level. For a lawyer, Mike's comments seemed impolitic. He should know the bots scanning the room could pick up everything he said.

With the exercise completed, the men and copbots marched from the room with military precision. There was a collective murmur of relief, and the cocktail gathering gradually resumed. As latecomers joined the reception, the chat centered on the strange visit. A few professors excused themselves from the room to open their NESTs for information and returned to pass along the details. The first policeman Joe had seen was William Zable, Peightân's deputy. Some professors complained about the bots' intrusion, but no one voiced any objections or calls for action. Who would one complain to about federal copbots, anyhow?

Neither Freyja nor Jardine came to the reception, and despite meeting several other professors, Joe's upbeat mood upon his arrival never returned. It was time to walk home.

A waxing moon was riding down the sky, and the lamp-lit pathways leading to the main quad illuminated his way. Still unfamiliar with the campus at night, Joe instructed his ARMO to outline his route back, and he was soon lost in thought as he followed the red line past the student center. Ahead of him, someone darted out of the shadows into the empty plaza and set a mini-drone on the ground.

Joe lurched to a stop at the edge of the plaza. He was hyper-aware of his surroundings as the drone zipped upward five meters. It hovered facing the square, and beneath it, in the shadows under the arches surrounding the center, he made out the darker silhouettes of people—many people. Protesters surged into the plaza.

Backtracking out of the plaza, Joe ducked down an unlit path to the right that would allow him to avoid the protest. Colored reflections lit the trees in front of him, and without looking back he imagined messages flickering over their clothing. The staccato sound of their chanted slogans filled his ears. He sprinted, his lungs laboring, as above him over a dozen hovercraft zoomed toward the plaza.

A moment later, light from behind him illuminated his way. Joe glanced back. Searchlights lanced the ground. A roaring hiss that sounded like water forced through a fire hose came next, followed by a bellowed command from one of the craft. "This will be your last protest," it boomed, and the vibration echoed in his chest. "Put your hands up now, and we will not use force against you."

. . .

Peightân was ready for them. It's hard to keep anything a secret, especially from the police. It's even harder to cover your tracks. Will they get away this time?

. . .

He scampered across the footbridge over the brook and was among the trees leading home—out of reach of the searchlights and far enough from the action that he could take a rest. Joe leaned against a hefty oak, the bark rough under his hands, the air ragged in his chest. Behind him, hovercraft and lights darted here and there, chasing protesters. Thankfully, no hovercraft seemed headed his direction. The muffled cries of protesters resounded from the plaza, smothered by the harsh shouts of police and the deep, mechanical tones of copbots.

Joe realized he was sweating, and not only from the short run. He rested both hands against the tree and tried to calm his breathing. He stared at his hands to block the onslaught of interrupting memories, of the hack attack gone bad.

They had been sitting side by side, watching the holo display, when Raif grunted, "Someone's pinged our protective honeypot. We're getting too close to a primary database." Seconds later he yelled, "They deleted the honeypot accounts. They're on to us!" Then he and Raif were on defense, trying desperately to avoid being caught. His fingers pounded in the command strings.

"Deadman switch pulled. Deleting our fuzzer files and their log files," Raif muttered. "Now to break the tunnels and lay some false trails on other nodes."

Their pursuers churned through the encrypted barriers.

"Their quantum decryption is too fast. I need another encrypted blocker." Joe panted, struggling with the coding.

"Here, try ropefish." Raif passed the icon from his holo. The chase across the net went on and on, as if their pursuers stood behind them, breathing hotly down their necks. Hours later, with the tunnels collapsed, the encrypted false trails laid across the net, and no pings against their defensive perimeters, it seemed they'd at last escaped the predators.

Raif closed the holo and clasped Joe's dripping hand. "Beat them. Hackers win this time."

"We avoided a very bad day, ending in jail. And in our freshman year? We would've been out on our ears."

Now Joe's clammy fingers clenched the coarse bark of the tree. Except for the distant searchlights, it was pitch black under the oak. As his eyes adjusted, he heard water splashing—not the brook in its usual course, but repeated, intentional pouring.

He peered toward the brook, the trees and darkness blocking his line of sight. The faint splashes came from near the bridge. With his ears tuned for even the whispers of leaves, Joe moved back down the hill to the footbridge. He could make out a figure—a woman—standing up to her knees in the brook, splashing water over her body. His NEST identified her clothing as the same thermoplastic suit as the protesters wore.

Like a cat, he moved closer, drawn by intense curiosity. His foot scuffed the ground, and he froze as the goggled, dragonfly-like head of the woman turned toward him. They faced each other. He could see her clearly now, and he recognized the athletic young woman he'd seen his first day on campus. Joe slowly lifted a hand in a gesture of assurance.

She stared back. Then with a deft movement she ripped the hood and goggles from her head. Thick, long hair tumbled over her shoulders. "Can you help me?" she whispered. "The bastards blasted acid on us, and I need to get this stuff off." In the dim light he saw defiance and anger merge with fear on her face.

. . .

What are the odds the police come this way and find us? Low, but still a risk. She's so mysterious. And rebellious. And she needs help. Worth the risk?

. . .

Joe examined her a moment longer, his thoughts churning, suspended in a moment of indecision. Then he held out his open hand. "Here, come with me. I'll help you."

She ignored his hand and stepped back from the brook. Hesitantly, she followed him up the hill to his apartment. No hovercraft were overhead, and he could see no police nearby, though the ruckus of the roundup continued in the distance. They slipped through the entrance, and the door locked behind them, encasing them in silence.

The stairwell light snapped on, spotlighting her face. Hazel eyes watched him, vulnerable yet fierce. Patches of steaming slime clung to her elastomer suit. A drip landed on the tiled floor, staining the surface.

"Let's keep that from burning your skin. We can worry about the floor later." Joe led her upstairs, motioning to the shower in his suite.

She paused by the bathroom door, her eyes fixed on him. "I can't take the top off by myself with the acid on it." She turned and gestured low at her back, and he took hold of the material at the waist seam, wary of the green slime sliding down her side as he unfastened the connectors. She trembled as he helped her pull the material over her head and drop it onto the floor. "I can manage the rest." She stepped into the bathroom and closed the door.

Joe stood there, unmoving, until he heard the shower turn on. He busied himself by cleaning up the splashed muck on the stairs. A solvent from the cleaning closet did a fair job of restoring the tile. Cleanup completed, he sat in the living room. Outside the window, lights flickered amidst the deep darkness toward the student center. No doubt the copbots were prowling around campus. Despite the slight probability that they might come to his door, he couldn't help but tune into every sound from the entry.

The woman came out of the bathroom and stood in the living room doorway, a towel encircling her body like a chrysalis. Joe rose to approach her, but she moved sideways into a defensive stance, her palm held out in front of her like a knife. "Stop right there," she said in a commanding voice. Her toned muscles and the ease of her movements demonstrated her likely experience in martial arts.

He raised both hands in submission. "You can trust me. I've only honorable intentions." He pointed to the second bedroom. "You can change in there. I'll get you some clothes." He retreated to his own bedroom as he felt the growing stiffness in his pants.

. . .

Perfectly honorable intentions. Well, just a small fib. Actually, not a *small* fib. A beautiful woman dressed in a towel in my apartment.

. . .

Joe returned with one of his shirts and a pair of shorts. "Here, these will do for now. I'll toss your ruined clothes." She took the clothing with a nod of thanks and strode to the second bedroom. In the kitchen, Joe found a large trash bag and turned it inside out to pick up the black suit she'd left in a pile on the bathroom floor. He tied the bag up and left it in the bin in the kitchen.

When he came back, she was sitting on the floor in one corner of the living room, the lights turned down to a glow, occasional flashes of light from outside outlining her. She glanced at the window, and he thought he saw despair etch her face before it melted away. She turned to watch him, her head tilted warily. "Now what's next with us?" It carried an intonation both soft and commanding, and expectant.

"You mean, like me turning you in?"

She nodded, her gaze steadily holding his. He sat on the living room floor three meters from her, hands on knees, his knees together. He meditated unlike a monk, studying her. Her long hair draped over his shirt. She had curled her legs under her body, but Joe couldn't stop noticing them poking provocatively out of the shorts.

But attractive as she was, he had to know he wasn't harboring a dangerous criminal. "Were you doing anything that might have hurt anyone?"

Her mouth tightened. "Nothing. The government and their Nazi police are doing the hurting. We just want to be heard."

. . .

She looks about twenty-nine, too old to be in college. Nazis? She knows ancient history. And she
has an opinion that sounds similar to those Mike
shared. Quite a fetching renegade.

. . .

Joe sat in thought for another minute, trying to slow his
racing pulse. The warm light in the flat contrasted with the
blackness outside the windows. They rested on the floor,
sheltered in their cocoon.

"I don't know what you were doing, but it doesn't seem to
merit that extreme a reaction. It's not safe for you to go outside. They have a ton of technology to hunt down anyone.
But I doubt they'll come here. You are welcome to stay, as
long as you promise never to turn me in if you do happen to
get arrested."

Her lip trembled, her eyes wide and glowing. "I promise."
She looked around, suddenly wary. "What about bots? You
can't depend on them not to reveal me." Her hands closed
into fists.

"I only have one pipabot, set on minimal support mode,
which I have banned from entering unannounced." Joe offered a disarming smile. "I don't like them loitering."

"And how about your PIDA? The police could infiltrate it."

He laughed quietly. "No PIDA for me."

"Really? Well, you're odd. And good odd. I don't trust a
PIDA either."

"Just two people out of touch with the world."

"Or two people completely in touch with the world."

"No one has accused me of that, ever." Joe stood and offered a hand to help her off the floor. She ignored it, using her left hand to push off while cradling her right to her
stomach. An ugly red blotch marred her right wrist.

"That looks painful. Let me take care of it before it gets
worse." Going back to the bathroom, he rummaged around,
uncertain what the pipabot had stocked. He found a redi-

band in a drawer and turned to find she had followed him. In the light, he could see several swelling blisters on her wrist.

He held up the rediband. "May I?" At her nod, Joe peeled off the backing and held her hand with one of his while the other pressed the pad against her wrist. The rediband turned pink as the sensors calibrated the wound and dispensed medication.

He still held her arm as she looked up. "Thanks." She gently withdrew her hand and stepped back, out of the light of the bathroom.

"I have plenty of space—you probably noticed, but that bedroom you changed in has an adjoining bathroom." Joe stopped his awkward ramblings and took a deep breath. "I'm going to eat a snack. Care to join me?"

She nodded with a small smile and followed him to the kitchen, which illuminated when they entered. Joe found food in the fridge, and they sat at the kitchen table eating fresh fruit and cheese. Between bites, he asked, "What's your name?"

She paused, then said, "You should call me 76."

"Well, numbers are easy to remember. And not much different from 73, who's the pipabot parked in the utility building."

"Shit, of course you would have a bot with a higher Level number." He couldn't tell if it was a joke or if she said it with real malice.

An incessant buzzing sounded from the front door. Joe's stomach tightened, and the woman's face froze with fear. He motioned for her to hide in the second bedroom and descended the stairs to the door.

He paused, took a deep breath, and punched the screen button. The monitor screen displayed 73 standing outside with a cleanerbot. He opened the door.

The pipabot said, "Sorry, sir, to disturb you at this hour, but I noticed that you had returned. The cleanerbot has informed me that your trash is in extreme need of disposal because it has not had access for several days. For sanitary reasons, it wishes to do so as soon as possible."

Joe was relieved and irritated. "Thank you, but I will take out my trash."

The pipabot blinked and then said, "Sir, that function is inappropriate for your Level. Do you wish me to override its housekeeping schedule?"

"Yes, do that. Let's stand by the rule that no bot shall enter my flat. Despite your concern with my Level, I'm trying a new method of austere living. Consider it an academic project in self-reliance."

"Very well, sir. Good night, sir," 73 replied.

. . .

It's true now, whether or not I intended it five seconds ago.

. . .

Joe reached the top of the stairs and entered his apartment. His gaze met the woman's as she stood at the bedroom door. "Okay. I guess you're good to your word." Then she shut the door, and all was still.

He stared at her closed door and his bedroom's open door. There was nothing more to do than go to bed, where he would lie awake thinking about doors closing and opening.

CHAPTER 8

Joe awoke at sunrise, the prior evening's events drowning other thoughts. He showered and dressed. The second bedroom door was shut. He hesitated, then cracked open the door. The woman lay asleep on the bed, her hair disheveled against the pillow, her face peaceful and beautiful. With a silent command to his NEST, he took a single vidsnap in hopes of identifying her and closed the door.

. . .

What have I gotten myself into? She's so intriguing, I need to find out who she is. Better not run a search myself, though, just in case.

. . .

He left the flat with the incriminating trash bag stuffed into a daypack. Luckily, it was a crisp day, chilly enough to warrant the gloves he wore to avoid leaving fingerprints. The street was empty with no students or bots about at this hour. Calling an autocar from the edge of campus, he took it to the side entrance of the nearest transit station. Joe flipped up his jacket collar, allowing the two embedded chips to touch his cheeks, and he activated the face replacer. It had been a gift from Raif after the near-disastrous college hack. "Use this if the copbots are ever after you non-virtually," he had said, laughing. Joe didn't feel like laughing now, but he was grateful that a cartoon face would hide his identity if anyone checked the vidcams.

He prowled behind the station, finding trash recycling containers where he had anticipated. To avoid retinal recognition, Joe kept from looking directly at the vidcams, which were everywhere, and he ditched the acid-stained suit in a bin. He stole around to the front entrance, entered the station, and waited for the next train.

The hyperlev trains moved in choreographed precision, one leaving, levitating softly on the rails, another arriving, magnets clicking at the stop. He boarded the next train heading to Salinaston, the city to the east. Seven minutes and 109 kilometers later, Joe exited at a stop with a market supply center across from the station. The low-slung glass and steel building showcased a marble mall lined with artwork. He walked past the central fountain and entered the general supply. It would not have the latest luxe clothing, but he didn't want to use credit$ or connect himself to a drone-delivered order with his NEST. He doubted 76 would care about luxe clothes anyway.

Several people were picking through the physical merchandise and holo pod–projected inventory. Bots moved about straightening the racks and bringing more stock to fill them.

Joe found the women's clothing section. A personal shopper bot approached him. "Sir, if you may please transmit personal measurements, I can assist with perfect bespoke clothing."

"No, I'd prefer to choose something I like first."

The bot turned away. Joe picked out several items he thought would fit and left the building.

. . .

Now to ensure the bots don't account for excessive food use. This is hard, making a person invisible in the data flow. But I've got to conceal our trail against the police data stream correlations. Or we'll be in jail in a heartbeat.

. . .

He crossed to the grocery supply and filled another bag with three days' groceries, the bag heavy in his right hand. Joe waved off a bot that offered to carry his bags. He couldn't remember the last time he'd shopped; he and everyone he knew ordered via NEST delivery. With the two bags in hand, he backtracked via the hyperlev to another autocar.

The woman glanced up when Joe entered the apartment, mistrust flashing in her eyes. Her face looked clean and fresh, and she had neatly tied her hair.

"I brought you some clothes. I figured you'd get bored with my stuff fast."

She examined the bag as he put away groceries into the food synthesizer unit. "Thanks. That was thoughtful."

"How about breakfast?"

Joe sent commands from his NEST to the food synthesizer, and the aroma of eggs and toast filled the kitchen. He took the plates from the machine and served breakfast. They ate in silence.

"How long will I be stuck here?"

"No idea. I haven't checked netchat about yesterday's protest. I thought it better to do any searches from an encrypted link at my office. And I was planning to ask a friend for help to find out what the police might be doing."

"A friend?" She was wary again.

"He's my best friend, and completely trustworthy. Raif's inquiries won't be traceable because he's expert at all the camouflage tricks—better than me. It's the best way to know when it's safe for you to leave." Her lips tightened, and she nodded. "I need to keep my routine to avoid arousing suspicion, which means spending the next several hours at my office. You'll be okay here?"

She nodded again and forced a smile.

. . .

She seems to think I'm approaching this right, planning ahead so as not to expose her. I hope I am. I don't want to be caught either.

. . .

"What work do you do?" She pushed around the remains of her breakfast. When Joe explained his profession and mentioned his sabbatical at the college, her expression evolved into a frown. "Shikaka! A high-Level intellectual. That's elite. So, off to your ivory tower."

. . .

Mocked for being too high of a Level. And a week ago, mocked for being too low. Maybe these Levels are contentious.

. . .

"No, only an average guy going about his business, doing the best he can. How about you? What do you do?"

She didn't meet his gaze. "Only protesting. And now waiting to get out of this jail."

"I suppose there are worse jails."

"I'll give you that," she said as he left.

———————◆———————

He called Raif from his office on an encrypted channel. Raif appeared on the holo screen staring almost cross-eyed, his curly hair tangled as if he hadn't slept.

"Hard night?"

"Da, I'm beat. On the same hack we moonlighted a month ago. Tough to penetrate. I was through the last gateway when someone spotted me. My encryption was strong enough that they didn't crack it before I got away, but I spent hours hiding my tracks."

"Better lie low for a while. You don't want to botch your chances of landing some interesting job, doctor."

"Horseradish." Raif frowned and studied his hands, rubbing one against the other. "It's been five months since my dissertation defense, and still no academic appointment prospects, just some office plankton job possibilities." His gaze rested on Joe. "And how's life in the halls of Ivy?"

"Seems I'm passing for a professor. Though small 'p.'"

"At least you're inside the fortress, asking big questions, right?"

"More than that lately. Can you do me a favor and try—covertly—to find out who this person is?" He sent the image of 76 he'd snapped earlier.

"Damn. Looks like you're doing more than talking philosophy. Where did you find her?"

"In a river."

"I want to go swimming. Okay, will do."

"And can you check the news feeds about a protest that happened here last night? I want to know what the police have found and what they're doing." Joe rubbed his beard. "And see if you can find out if they arrested anyone."

"Sure. Deep in the water, sounds like," Raif said, chuckling.

"Just a toe so far." Joe signed off.

———————◆———————

He found her waiting in the living room when he returned that evening. She wore a green outfit that fit well. It complemented her hazel eyes, which stared back at him with subdued vigilance.

After some idle talk, she offered to make dinner. She had obviously familiarized herself with his kitchen. She busied herself with the food synthesizer, modifying the program. The plates came out steaming. His mouth watered with the first bite. The flavors were intriguing, which didn't surprise him coming from this baffling woman.

"What are these dishes?"

"That's spicy stir-fried kale with alt-bacon. And these are five-spice alt-lamb street kabobs." Her tone changed, and a prideful shyness flashed across her face. "I like to cook."

Joe was lost in his plate. Finally he said, "Where did you learn to cook like this?"

"My friends from home have been teaching me. The last three or so years, I've just been marking time for a real job. My international period." Her sarcasm hinted at a deep disappointment. "Since I can't get a passport, I'm stuck here in the States. Hence the cooking lessons."

"It was time well spent—*stuck* in the States."

She took small bites while she watched him eat. "Did you find out anything in the news?"

"Yes. My friend Raif filled me in this afternoon. The police are reporting they broke up a secret cell of anarchists with a radical agenda. They arrested forty-one people. And they say they have the two ringleaders."

She tensed at the news. "Did they name names?"

"Julian-something and Celeste-something—"

"Julian and Celeste! What else did they say about them?"

"Swift justice being served up these days. The prosecutors want a sentence of a month in jail for all the regular protesters. They say they'll try the ringleaders for serious crimes. The others' trials begin next week."

Her face pleated with worry. "They discovered their names, and so fast," she said at last.

"They weren't as rigorous as you've been at keeping their profiles out of the databases," he said. Her look of confusion gave way to one of anger. His chagrin over giving himself away made him less than careful about his next words. "Not that our checking for you would reveal anything about you. Raif couldn't even find a database match to your face."

"I thought you said you wouldn't expose me." She pounded the table once.

"Raif won't be detected, and there aren't records for anyone to follow. But . . . I needed to know who you are." His lip throbbed where he'd bitten it.

She glared at him across the table. "After what you promised . . . it isn't fair."

"Okay, okay. But look, by harboring you, I'm an accomplice, and I'll do jail time too if caught. I'm sorry for invading your privacy, but I needed to at least check if you had a criminal record. I'm sure that Raif's sleuthing didn't cause any harm."

She collapsed back in the chair, and he thought she was still angry over his perceived betrayal until she said, "They're my friends."

"Good friends?"

"Yes, good friends. The three of us have been in this fight together for a while."

"So, you're a third ringleader?"

"In this fight for a speck of justice, I'm not third. I *am* the ringleader."

. . .

More dangerous than I imagined. Raif was right.
I'm in deep.

. . .

"What was it you wanted me to call you? 76? Why the number? And can you please tell me your real name?" He hoped his plea would work. "I promise I'll work hard to protect you."

She sat ruminating, then her gaze steadied on his. "My name is Evie."

"Evie. Nice. Why the number?"

"That, of course, is my Level. Level 76. Didn't you understand that yesterday when you mentioned the bot?"

Joe scratched his beard. "It didn't occur to me. I'll admit I've never met a Level 76."

"Not surprising. The Levels Acts keep anyone more than twenty Levels apart socially separated from one another. Social apartheid. And that's why we're protesting. You would never get a net connect with me. As a Level 42, you do realize it's illegal for us to socialize at all?"

"I can do the math, not that I paid much attention to it before. It's never been an issue," he said.

She glared at him. "Not that I want to socialize with you. It's my bad luck to end up with an ivory-tower 42."

He wanted to be conciliatory. "Look, I'm sorry. I will try to protect you. Meanwhile, we're stuck here together. Neither of us has much choice. Raif said the investigation will continue around here for several weeks, according to internal police reports."

She calmed down. "Internal police reports? Your friend must know something about sterilizing his data trail to get into those logs."

"You know about that, too, with no name attached to your facial profile."

Neither was finishing the meal, thought Joe with some regret. With a flash of irritation, he cleared the dishes himself, which he only had to do because he'd banned the bots from entering. He was annoyed with Evie for disrupting his life. But he was also annoyed with himself because every time he glanced at her, it was hard to stay annoyed.

He poured whisky for himself and tea for her at her declination of the whisky, and they retreated to sofas in opposite corners of the living room. They watched each other as the sun sank outside the window. She finished the tea, nodded at him, and then left, closing her bedroom door behind her. Joe sat alone in the dark.

. . .

Evie. A fighter. On a personal mission. A force to be reckoned with.

. . .

CHAPTER 9

They maintained an uneasy truce for the next week. Joe assumed the campus was under continuous surveillance. He went about his normal business, leaving for his office in the math building every day. Evie kept the large windows opaque and never left the apartment. The bots stayed sequestered outside. The police never visited. At first, in the evenings they took turns making dinner, until Evie quietly began taking more turns at the task, her meals being distinctly better.

Joe tried unsuccessfully to learn further details about his perplexing guest. He smiled across the table until she looked at him.

"You haven't told me much about yourself. Like, do you have any siblings?"

"No, none."

"I'm also a single child. Tell me about your parents."

"I never knew them." Evie's expression was somber.

"That's rough. So tragic in this modern world." It seemed that his questions made her uneasy—the opposite of his intentions.

"I didn't know otherwise, so it was a while before I realized how different that experience was. Then it felt like I didn't grow up in the normal way, but instead had to start as almost an adult to find my community where I could."

"It's not good for anyone to be alone," he said. She nodded and allowed a strained smile, then they returned to the meal. She seemed pensive. His questions may have led her to brood about her imprisoned friends—not a happy thought.

They fell into silence. She would remain a mystery for now.

Every few days, he took the hyperlev away from campus to pick up extra food and supplies. He found more clothes for her. After dinner each evening, she said goodnight and closed the bedroom door.

One afternoon, he returned and a rhythmic counting drifted down the stairway. "*Ichi. Ni. San. Shi.*" He hesitated, then slinked up the stairs and peeked around the corner.

Evie stood in the center of the living room wearing a long pajama shirt, belted at the waist like a tunic. Barefoot and with her back to him, she faced right and delivered a powerful kick at an unseen attacker. She followed with a fluid turn to the left and a downward chop from both fists together. Right and left, the kicks and punches flowed from her body, each dispensed with another grunted count. Her muscular arms were lustrous with a layer of sweat. As she turned again, the hem of the shirt rode up, exposing her thigh.

He was mesmerized.

The balletic movement of her feet ended with a spirited thud, and he imagined some smashed foe beneath. Evie swirled in a sweeping turn, and their gazes met. She stopped, paused in meditation for several seconds, then ended the exercise by folding her hands and bowing gracefully.

Joe slowed his rapid breathing. "That was beautiful," he whispered.

Evie relaxed. "It's a kata, called *Bassai Dai*. Penetrating the Fortress. It's from another style, but I find it best to learn from many."

. . .

She must be a black belt. Wise to be polite.
Penetrating the Fortress—*no*, definitely no jokes.

. . .

"Are you a black belt?"

"Yes, a 4th dan. In my style, it's called *yondan*." Her slight
blush suggested she was embarrassed but also pleased to talk
about it. It was obvious she had been occupying her time
here with these exercises.

Joe sat on the couch nearest the door. "The kata was like
watching a dance, but with animal power."

Her lips parted in a soft smile. "It's inspired by animals.
My style emphasizes the tiger, the dragon, and the crane.
There are positive attributes brought to kata from each."

Evie shook out her arms, then sat cross-legged on the
floor, hands folded on her lap. "It was intended as a way for a
weaker person to defend against the stronger. Social classes
were fixed at the time martial arts were invented in Japan,
and it was impossible to leave your class."

"Did women practice martial arts then?"

"Yes, some did. They were called *onna-bugeisha*, or 'female
martial artist.' They were *bushi*, part of the samurai class, and
they could defend their homes."

Another thought occurred to him. "Why do you practice?
Self-defense?"

Her face was serene. "No. It's about personal discipline.
And it's aspirational—a path to becoming a better person."

. . .

More virtuous than me. More disciplined than me.

. . .

They talked for an hour about martial arts while Joe prepared dinner. She didn't volunteer any other information
about herself, and he didn't want to end their truce by pressing further questions. But he thought she was happier with
him when they parted. Which didn't help the wave of longing that arced through his body when she closed the door.

Joe was busy reading philosophy treatises that Gabe had recommended when the office holo screen chirped with an incoming encrypted message. He accepted, and Raif's holo appeared. Raif wasn't smiling.

Joe's stomach clenched. "Did you learn anything?"

"Da. Bad news. The regular protesters got at least a month of jail time, with the possibility of commuting their sentences if they reveal protesters who haven't been arrested."

"That hits close."

"It gets worse. For the ringleaders, prosecutors are asking for a sentence of a year's banishment. Their trial starts next week."

Joe slumped back in his chair. "A full year? Isn't that a death sentence?"

"It might as well be. Banishment sentences rarely exceed six months. State executions are banned of course, but this squeaks by on a technicality. There haven't been many people who've survived more than a few months out in the Empty Zone." Raif scratched his head. "Most people don't have the skills to survive without the comforts of technology."

"Why such a stiff sentence?"

Raif cleared his throat. "There's a story trending on netchat that the protesters are anarchists. They've been blamed for a bomb explosion at a general goods store. No one was hurt, but it's shaken people up. The Security Ministry appears to be feeding the rumor. I dug into their peripheral internal files—their database security is impossible to crack. The police are paranoid about the anti-Levels movement, afraid it will snowball."

They talked a while longer, then Raif said, "Be careful, brat," and signed off.

As Joe crossed the plaza on his way home, Mike Swaarden strode toward him.

"Nice running into you, Joe."

Joe smiled. "You can never tell who might drop into your world on this campus." They stopped under the loggia ringing the square, shaded from the afternoon sun.

"Have you been following the fallout from the protest roundup last week?"

"There's been netchat buzz. I'd guess they accomplished their purpose to raise attention about the Levels Acts." He shrugged. "I understand many people are in jail."

"Even worse." Mike leaned closer. "They're layin' boots."

"Are you talking about the possible banishment sentence?" Joe kept his voice as quiet as possible.

Mike stiffened. "How'd you know that? I only know about it from my glimpses into their shared internal communiqués."

"I have my sources."

"Aye, right. Sources from what side?" Mike squinted and searched Joe's face. Joe gazed back without blinking.

. . .

He's assuming I've picked a side, and I'm not sure that I have. Better choose soon. I'm deep in this already, and I'm going to need allies. Mike is the highest Level around here, and I think I can trust him. Seems I'm surrounded by renegades.

. . .

"They're sources from the side you would also support—thinkers like us," Joe said, hoping his voice held only intellectual interest.

They studied each other, Mike still frowning. Joe tried again. "Look, the police acted with violence against people who wanted to exercise free speech. That's wrong. I admit, though, I'm unfamiliar with the history of this issue."

Mike's expression softened, giving Joe confidence to continue. "In our first conversation, you'd started to tell me about economics. I never tried to understand economics before. It's a dead science."

Mike propped a hand against the wall under the loggia and spoke in a low voice. "Economics continues to be important, as it frames the social dynamic. Think back to the Climate Wars, when there was large-scale decimation of factories, followed by pandemics and the related social disruption. The destruction placed a premium on robotic technology. Robots built robot factories, so robots proliferated exponentially. Economic productivity returned. But because the robot wave ended with such low employment, the social fabric was ripped apart."

"There was chaos," Joe chimed in as a vague recollection of a school lesson surfaced.

"Aye, politics and economics in a nasty soup. Until there were sufficient total resources in any country's economy, the transition to economic stability was more likely to go wrong than right."

"A complex, nonlinear system?"

"Aye. Some countries experimented with full socialism immediately. If they didn't reach enough economic productivity, they lurched back. The uneven progress caused the anti-immigration furor and border closings," Mike said.

"But why didn't they try to rebuild the economic system?"

"The outmoded model was irretrievably gone. Labor and capital had been foundational to economics pre-Climate Wars. Now, capital replaced labor, and, with so many bots, the value of labor plummeted to zero. But bots built the factories, causing the value of capital to fall too. The value of the original capital controlling the bot factories dominated. The bots and factories would have remained owned by an elite few, except the masses of unemployed were organized and moving toward revolution," Mike said.

Joe paused, trying to take it all in. "So they nationalized all the factories—which are now owned by everyone—and concern about economics evaporated?"

"Aye, oceans of data and algorithms solved von Mises's economic calculation problem. Using money for signaling demand and rationing supply went away, even for capital goods. A hundred years ago, we needed markets to balance supply and demand. But today we've insight into people's intimate desires. The net data stream provides all the information about demand that markets supplied before, and more efficiently."

"The production organizers certainly know a lot about us," Joe said.

Mike sighed. "And we don't care enough about economic growth to drive consumption. Global society is non-growth and stable. International trade is much lower, and it only involves commodities, entertainment, fashion, and some luxe goods. We grow or manufacture everything else locally. Economists say economies are static except for efforts directed to scientific advancement and creative pursuits. The result is good for the planet. But it's boring."

"It got boring when markets withered away?"

"Aye. Markets disappeared except for the top ten percent of goods, with those markets still maintained to satisfy our inherent social competition for the latest fad and luxury item," Mike said.

"But there was a price?"

"There's always a price. And here is where we see economics linked to the Levels." Mike scuffed his shoe on the ground. "Property ownership was deeply embedded in our culture, more than in most countries. The wealthy property owners fought back. They needed a way to maintain their elite status. As the quid pro quo to nationalization, formal social Levels were introduced."

"But the Levels are based on merit," Joe said, then realized his oversimplification. "Well, almost entirely."

"Joe, lad, though the Level concept has the patina of meritocracy, there are more limitations to merit than existed before. The oligarchs never lost control but instead entrenched their position, making it insidiously hereditary."

"I've never met any oligarchs."

"Oligarchy hasn't changed much since the ancient Greeks, though they have gotten better at controlling the messaging in society." Mike warmed to his subject. "For example, you probably have limited knowledge about how the rest of the world has dealt with social equality. How much have you traveled?"

Joe shrugged, saying, "I've been many places by net travel—"

Mike held up a hand. "And there's the problem. Of course, there aren't many other ways to travel these days, but net travel is a curated experience with a controlled message."

"It's the most eco-friendly way to see the world." Joe knew he was right about this. "And it's allowed me to visit cities, like Venice, that have long-since been abandoned. I can see what countries looked like in the past . . ." He trailed off at seeing Mike's frown.

"That is the socially correct response."

"There's no denying that physical travel increases the carbon footprint."

"Technically true. But the global carbon footprint is negative. There's lots of carbon mitigation. Our energy sources are all non-carbon. And, of course, the population has diminished, now about seven billion globally."

. . .

My vision of the world can't be all wrong. He's saying net travel is curated. How controlled can it be? I don't know. It's embarrassing to admit to Mike that I haven't traveled outside the States. But he doesn't like Levels, so he's less likely to look down on anyone because of their Level.

. . .

"As only a Level 42, it's nearly impossible to obtain the passport for international travel."

Mike's forehead furrowed. "Joe, with Levels, we are all leveled down, fighting to stand in some particular spot on an imaginary dunghill. Your case shows how accepting we have become about such abridgments to our freedom. The restrictions evolved. The States were the first larger country to own enough robots to make guaranteed income a reality. The government justified border and travel controls by saying we couldn't subsidize the rest of the world's population. They had legitimate fears about mass migrations. But they dealt with those fears with draconian policies. Armies of bots now guard the borders. By encouraging net travel, it's easier to hide our differences from the rest of the world. We have become cocooned in our separate reality, isolated geographically and in our world view by our curated net world."

Joe's voice lowered to a near whisper, guessing the answer before he asked. "Do you support the anti-Levels movement?"

"Aye, I do. Those of us who support the movement don't yet have enough power against the system to change things any time soon. But the fight is growing."

"I may be part of those growing numbers," Joe said, anxious to talk with Evie.

Mike's cool blue eyes bored into Joe, revealing a flash of concern. He put a big hand on Joe's shoulder. "The Security Ministry is depressingly efficient. Hide your footprints well."

A chill went up Joe's spine at the warning. Mike gave a final wave and walked away.

———————◆———————

On the short walk home, he pushed the conversation with Mike from his mind and focused on Raif's sobering news. Joe bounded up the stairs. Evie sat on the living room sofa, and she scrutinized him when he stopped in the entryway. Her expression darkened.

"Raif told me the prosecutors have asked for a one-year banishment sentence for your friends."

She flinched. "Shit. Banishment. It's the harshest sentence."

"And so seldom handed down. I looked up the recent history, and in the last decade you can count on two hands the sentences that lasted longer than a few months," he said.

A shiver ran through her, and she pulled her shoulders back in what he assumed was an attempt at bravery. He sat on the sofa next to her and took her hand. Her fingers tightened. "Banishment. Why?"

"Raif said there's a rumored story about terrorism. A bomb exploded in a general goods store. That's all I know."

"Terrorism? That's insane. We have nothing to do with anything violent. Why would we bomb a store where our friends might be shopping? This movement is about the country's repressive laws." Her eyes glinted with the rage of injustice, the simmering fury of a mother defending her young.

"Why do you think the government is fixated on your group?" Joe squeezed her hand to bring her back to the present.

"We've got good hackers. And we did get into some files in the Security Ministry to verify that our personal information was periodically deleted as required by law. We checked to avoid getting caught during our live protests. That was a mistake." Her expression gave away her recounting of past decisions. "The law gives us rights to privacy. Everyone else has given up those rights in exchange for convenience. But not us. We've insisted the government doesn't collect and keep information it shouldn't. And we all have the right to be forgotten."

"Are you cDc?"

She looked puzzled and gave a slight shake of her head. "No. What is that?"

Joe held her hand as he studied her, searching her eyes, trying to decide if she was lying. She tried to pull free from him. "Don't you believe me, that I've never heard of cDc before? It's the truth, I swear it." He clutched her hand tighter, still staring intently.

. . .

Are the martial arts only for self-discipline? Could she be violent? There's passion. She cares about her friends, and she makes me care about them too. She is so authentic, so believable.

. . .

"Yes, I trust you," he said.

She relaxed and squeezed his hand, bowing her head. They were still for a few moments before she looked up at him, tears coursing down her cheeks. "Celeste is one of our best hackers. But she doesn't know much about being out in nature." She sniffed. "She'll die in a month or two."

"Maybe she can learn."

Evie shook her head, dejected. "I've been out in nature. I could do all right. But I don't think Celeste and Julian could, even together."

He wondered about her experience in nature, but now wasn't the time to question her on it. "Given the seriousness of these charges, you'll need to stay hidden a while longer. I'll keep checking with Raif. When we know the Security Ministry isn't snooping around, then you can go."

She took a long, slow breath. "You're right. Thanks for letting me stay."

They ate a quiet dinner. Evie had reset the food synthesizer with many new programs, and out came a fragrant mixture of alt-lamb and spices, which she poured into a hollowed half loaf of bread.

"Bunny chow." She presented his portion to him. "From Africa, but it's mostly an Indian comfort food."

"No bunnies sacrificed in service of our dinner, I suppose?" His wry smile was designed to make her laugh. She did, her mood brightening. Joe brought out a synjug of a superior Canadian wine, and they finished dinner and sipped in silence as the sun disappeared behind the hill outside the living room window.

. . .

I wonder what it would take to survive, banished out there. The information is there on the net. But it would be a lot to learn if you knew nothing. I can tell that's what Evie is worried about—her friends' lack of knowledge and their chances of survival.

. . .

She took their empty glasses to the kitchen, him a step behind, and then she turned toward the bedrooms. A brief smile ghosted across her face as she shut the bedroom door.

CHAPTER 10

Joe stood in the math department's great room with a glass of wine in his hand. Most faces were still unfamiliar at these weekly cocktail receptions. He was doing a poor job meeting other department professors. But he wasn't feeling social, and he dismissed any compulsion to be. Across the room he saw Freyja, Mike, and Gabe gathered, all holding beers. Though he had meetings with both Freyja and Gabe over the next couple of days, he strolled over to join them.

They were mid-conversation about the recommended banishment sentences for the protest organizers.

". . . the sensationalist terrorist-bombing stories. The net-chat is alive with speculation." Freyja gestured widely, almost spilling her beer. "Even I can't avoid hearing the news."

"Terrorists. I don't believe it," Joe said.

Freyja's eyes went round. "A good Bayesian, you must have evidence?"

"Not that I wish to discuss." They stared at him, discreetly sipping their drinks and waiting.

When Joe didn't give in to the pressure, Mike filled the silence. "I unearthed some information about Peightân's second-in-command." He put his empty glass on a nearby table. "William Zable was a Level 76. But he's surprisingly moved up ten Levels in the past three years. No negative records appear about his family. Everything looks normal. He worked as a foreman in an alt-meat bio foundry. He was injured in an industrial accident, something involving a malfunctioning robot. Then, three years later he showed up, reporting to Peightân."

"I wonder if it's the accident or his association with the minister that better explains his nose-up tilt." Freyja chuckled.

Mike sipped the foam off a new beer. "The National Security Minister also has an interesting bio." Joe couldn't help but lean in, and Gabe and Freyja did the same. "Peightân comes from an eminent family. He attended the most prestigious schools and received top marks in his class. Quite an exemplary background."

"He seems a little too zealous for me." Gabe shook his head.

"That's a fret. He's made a record number of arrests these last several years. At least, that's what the records report," Mike said.

"Do you have a thesis?" Gabe was always direct.

Mike nodded curtly. "The thesis is that technically we still have a democracy that allows free speech, and I'm keen to protect both. If not held to a standard of transparency, power can be corrupted."

"You're thinking about the integrity of the databases," Freyja said.

"That would be one explanation for terrorist indictments backed by data, if, like Joe, you don't believe them," Mike said. All faces turned to Joe.

"Database integrity isn't my area of expertise." He paused. "But I have a friend who is an expert. He knows a lot about how databases are sealed."

"Aye?" Mike leaned in.

"Raif Tselitelov wrote his doctoral dissertation on the 'bot in a box' technology. It keeps bots, and every AI—including every PIDA—sandboxed off from every other. Databases and AI isolation are in the same software subspecialty."

Freyja glanced heavenward and deadpanned, "Avoiding the botpocalypse. But, seriously, I would feel better if someone dug into the source of this terrorist evidence, to validate it. I can think of some theoretical questions to verify with real-world data. Can you connect me with this friend of yours?"

Joe nodded, and their conversation turned, at Mike's prompting, to the modified soccer game between two major teams the night before. He asked if Joe followed mod soccer.

"Everyone follows mod soccer." Joe shrugged. "Though it wasn't my sport. I wasn't fast enough."

Freyja put down her empty glass. "And what was your sport?"

He inspected his shoes. "VRbotFest hackathons."

When Freyja arched an eyebrow, Mike laughed. "You seem to be thinking of the ExomechFest version, Freyja. Don't worry, the VRbotFest is generally considered more civilized. Though the distaste is a misunderstanding of the exomech sports culture."

Gabe shook his head. "Funny how we've taken retired industrial exoskeleton robots first used to protect people in the factories and turned them into dangerous fighting machines."

Joe chuckled. "I'm not that gutsy. In the VRbotFest, you use a netwalker to control a virtual steermech—all in software, no physical robots involved. But the controls don't all operate perfectly, so you need computer skills to hack the interface while fighting other virtual steermechs."

"Fighting? All in your head?" Freyja picked up a tiny sandwich.

"Coordinated head and hands." Joe wiggled his fingers. "It was initially used to test mecha computer code. Now, the games minimize that difficulty to focus on the VR mecha control."

"Why is it so hard?" Gabe seemed more interested all of a sudden.

"Haptic delay. You play people from all over, including the moon bases. The signal is, of course, limited to the speed of light. They insert standard delays to equalize the games, but they then vary the delay times. You must mentally adjust your sense of time and the timing of every action."

Freyja studied him. "It seems to me there is more to the story."

. . .

No, don't make the same mistake twice, like when Royce stopped me in my Mercuries. No hint of bragging, even if she is asking.

. . .

He resisted taking another sip of wine. "Only a pastime Raif and I love competing in."

"I understand they are extremely competitive." Mike drained his glass. "Where have you placed?"

Feeling cornered, Joe stood fidgeting with the glass in his hand. "I made it into the top five last year."

"Wow," Mike said.

Despite Freyja's admiring smile, Joe decided it was a good time to leave. He wanted to get back to Evie. As the conversation moved on, he made his excuses, waved goodbye to his friends, and disappeared out the door.

———————◆———————

Darkness had fallen, and the night air set frigid fingers on his neck. Joe flipped the collar on his shirt and tapped the control button to activate the internal warming mesh. He shivered, his head bowed and his hands stuffed into his pockets as he shuffled across the deserted plaza. In his periphery, a statue next to the student center stirred, and he started at the realization it was a man—a man who now strode toward him. A man with a jutting jaw and a tilted head. Behind him, a second man stepped out of the Cimmerian shadows.

Joe slowed to a stop, standing up straight as Zable and Peightân halted in front of him.

"Pleasant to see you again, Mr. Denkensmith," Peightân said in an assured voice. The gibbous moon reflected off his pallid face.

Joe made an obvious careful examination of the plaza as a way of avoiding his direct gaze. "Are you expecting another protest tonight? I thought the perpetrators had been rounded up. Surprised to see you and the police still here. They don't still pose a danger, do they?"

The minister's bloodshot eyes rested on him—the gaze of a police detective, analytical and skeptical of the world. Joe's skin crawled. "No danger to you, not at the moment," he said.

"Glad to hear it." Joe stepped to the side and began to walk ahead.

"You've no reason to hurry off, do you?"

Joe stopped, his heart racing. He kept his gaze down as he pivoted toward the men.

"We're still working hard to find *all* the protesters," Peightân said. Under the trim-cut shirt, Joe noted the muscled abs of a man who must work out every day. In contrast to his own flabby abdomen.

"Not all were caught?" The question came too fast from his mouth.

"We are not yet certain. Public safety is our prime interest, so we must be sure," Peightân answered.

He felt trapped, but it was best to appear concerned. "What did they do?"

"They broke the law. We have laws to keep order, and they stuck their noses where they don't belong. They are very dangerous, these terrorists. Exploding bombs and wreaking havoc. A subject I know quite a lot about." Zable smiled at his boss's comment. A practiced interrogator, Peightân continued. "Mr. Denkensmith, I understand that you are new at the college?"

"Yes, I just arrived."

"And you've been working on practical problems? Not like these academics, who spend too much time questioning the way things are done."

"Yes." He debated whether to add "Sir," but stopped short.

"Mr. Denkensmith." Peightân's tone made Joe meet his gaze, though he desperately didn't want to. The dark orbs held him. "There's no one suspicious that you've met so far, who might be actively helping these protesters?"

Joe shook his head sharply. "No one that I've met at the cocktail gatherings I've attended since arriving."

With a small frown, Peightân looked up at the moon. "You are supportive of the authority of the law?"

"We have elected and appointed officials, such as yourself, to decide what's lawful. I don't pay as much attention to it as perhaps I should."

"Yes, those with the most knowledge and expertise can indeed do the best job keeping everything orderly. You have my contact data; you will let me know if you see anything."

. . .

That was a command. Is he pulling Level to recruit me as a spy? Ironic.

. . .

"Sir, monitoring these professors isn't getting us anywhere," Zable said.

"Yes, you're right. Not enough evil in their souls to be behind this movement," Peightân said with a chuckle.

"You've got the mind to ferret that out, sir."

"I've learned much from you, too, my friend," Peightân said. Zable beamed at the compliment.

Zable's comment was an obvious suck-up, but Joe hid his natural reaction, nodded respectfully, and slunk down the path. The weight of Peightân's stare as he walked away caused a chill to course up his spine. There was no sound except for his footsteps, dully ringing on the pavement. After one hundred meters, he glanced back along the path. Peightân and Zable had returned to the shadows, facing the direction from which Joe had approached them.

. . .

Likely waiting to ambush anyone else heading this way from the reception. Though if the college professors are their best lead on a protest unaffiliated with the college, they must be low on leads. Good, I guess. Those bloodshot eyes say he's unconstrained by a weekly work limit, and he's clearly a sharp guy. *Not a time to make any mistakes.*

. . .

───────◆───────

When Joe told Evie about his run-in, she jumped up from her seat on the sofa and began to pace. "I've already been stuck here for two weeks, Joe. I almost left today—I've got to check on the movement. We built momentum with these protests, and I can't let it fizzle out just because they arrested Julian and Celeste."

Heat rose in Joe's face, and he stood to face her. "Wait a minute. You're too busy following your own ARMO to notice that the world isn't revolving around you. You've put me at risk, too, and they're watching me. It won't be hard to draw a line back to me if they catch you."

She halted in front of him. "I've spent the last three years of my life working on this. It's the only thing that matters."

"Don't be so impulsive, or it will all blow up in your face."

"But I can't let it die—"

"Can you let yourself die? Will that help the movement?" Joe realized he was shouting and took a step back and a deep breath. "I'm sorry, Evie. That was out of line. But I'm worried you'll do something that will endanger us both." He sat down on the sofa and motioned to the cushion next to him. "Why are you risking everything for this protest movement?"

She studied the seat but remained standing. "Because of the obvious social injustice. The States gave up any pretense of equality."

"When did this become so important to you?"

"Toward the end of my studies. I earned master's degrees in political science and economics," she said.

He nodded haltingly, realizing with appreciation that she had as many degrees as he did.

"Economics. The dismal science."

"I didn't find it dismal. It shows how the world works."

"But some inequality is unavoidable."

"What do you mean?"

"It's the physics of a world made up of particles in motion. You can't have mountains without valleys. And isn't inequality at the heart of economics? For any skyscraper, not everyone can have the penthouse view."

"I want it to be better. I want it to be perfect." She clenched her hands.

He let a small laugh escape. "People can't be perfect. Remember the old story of Adam and Eve, from back when most people still believed in God? One of the story's morals is that people are imperfect; only God can be perfect. That's our natural state, and those flaws are in our nature. There will always be hills and valleys. There will always be good and evil in the world. We can't escape it."

She stood her ground. "That shouldn't stop us from trying."

"I'll grant you that. Anyway, those old ideas are scientifically proven to be wrong. It's a closed physical universe. There isn't any God that interferes. That telling of the story is all wrong."

"What do you know about religion? Anyway, enough philosophizing." She mimicked his tone and dismissed his comment with a wave of her hand. "Let's get back to the practical issue, that these laws are unfair."

His mind had drifted to his last conversation with Gabe, and now he'd gone off on a tangent. Her comment made him wonder what she knew about religion. She didn't seem like one of the few people who claimed a personal relationship with their God. He pushed the thought away to focus. What mattered now was that she didn't do something impulsive to put them in danger.

"Action is good when it's within a carefully considered plan. Rushing in without a plan means it's much more likely that things will turn out badly." He'd jumped up, and his voice had risen again.

"When I have a goal, I get it done. This inaction is unnatural." Evie pursed her lips, turned away, and stared out the window.

Joe spied his own clenched hands and slowly straightened his fingers. Her ramrod back told him she was as tense as he was. It was the first time they'd both raised their voices in an argument.

"Okay, I'll stay. But not for much longer." She turned toward him again, and her eyes conceded the point. She strode to the kitchen, and the sounds of her dinner preparation filled the apartment, louder than usual.

The shallow victory didn't make him feel better that he was protecting himself as much as her.

They still hadn't spoken again when she noisily placed bowls on the table. As Joe tasted the first spoonful, he looked up to see her glaring at her bowl.

"Yum. What is this?"

"It's Tibetan alt-beef and potato stew. Missing the traditional yak meat, of course."

"I see you're still stewing."

A small smile crossed her lips before she could stop it, and he was happy she could appreciate his small jokes. They ate in silence, but the mood had lightened a shade by the time of their nightly routine, Joe turning to one bedroom door and Evie turning to the other.

CHAPTER 11

Joe found Freyja in her office the next morning for their planned meeting. Euler sat on top of a cabinet. Holo equations hovered over Freyja's head where she sat at her desk, and a glance revealed she was visualizing new problems, this time some subtopic in set theory. She shoved several of the holo icons out of the way. One ricocheted toward Euler, and the cat raised a paw as it ghosted through the animal and evaporated against the wall.

"Thanks for meeting me today," Joe said. He held a glimmer of hope she might still have a deeper interest in seeing him.

Freyja nodded absently as she petted Gauss, who had jumped up onto her lap. She scratched behind his ears, and he purred. "I love these guys," she said.

"They are splendid creatures."

"They keep me company, along with the math. There aren't many young professors here at the college." She looked up brightly. "It's nice to have you as a friend."

Joe smiled and tried to decide whether the way she emphasized the word denoted a platonic relationship or something more.

"I'm glad to help with your project." She wagged her index finger toward him. "And remember to send me an introduction to your friend, the database integrity expert."

"Oh, right."

Freyja smiled. "What's the topic today?"

"Our last conversation led me to Laplace, who did related work in statistics and probability theory. And that led to his essay on determinism. It's a side road on my AI consciousness project, but I've been thinking that one difference between our minds and AIs is that everything in software is determined. Is the universe ruled by determinism or indeterminism? And does that have anything to do with consciousness?"

"Laplace's demon, whose acceptance means there is no free will. I relish striking out demons." She let out a playful laugh, tossing back her hair. "Laplace postulated a superintelligence—later called his 'demon,' a stand-in for God—who knows the precise location and momentum of every particle in the universe. From this knowledge, every interaction could thereby be known. That would constitute a deterministic world."

He nodded. "I've begun reading about the mathematics and the physics surrounding the determinism debate. I have mixed evidence about scientific determinism from the perspective of physics, so I'd like to hear your thoughts about the mathematics."

"Slow down." She cast the last floating holos to the side with flicks of her wrist, visually freeing space around her head. Her gaze was anxious. "I admit my physics is weak. Tell me about the physics, and then I'll share my assessment of the mathematics."

. . .

Hmm, she doesn't like to rush, is very methodical, and wants to be sure of herself. Maybe that was my mistake. I was too rash.

. . .

"Scientific determinism is the idea that, beginning with the way things are at a certain time, the way things are at a later time is fixed as a matter of natural law," Joe said.

"Natural law. A scientific law of physics." Her eyes narrowed in thought were as beautiful as when she looked at him directly. "Has physics answered the question of whether such absolute determinism is true?"

"It's mixed." Joe had trouble keeping his mind on the conversation. "Let me give you four ideas, the first two favoring determinism, the last two inconclusive on the topic."

"Go on, pitch those to me."

"The first idea. Every fundamental particle interacts with every other fundamental particle, with forces moving through fields at the speed of light. Every particle we encounter has already pushed on every other one we care about—that is, any close enough to us to matter. The argument is that the future is 'adequately determined.' The particle-pushing-on-other-particles model led to the idea that everything is deterministic."

"I understand, a ball for determinism."

"Here's the second idea. From Einstein's general theory of relativity, the field equations are generally deterministic. As is the Lagrangian of the modified Standard Model."

She nodded. "Simple enough, another ball for determinism. And the indeterministic arguments?"

He appreciated her quick grasp of the concepts. "Well, the wave function governed by the Schrödinger equation paints a mixed picture. The evolution of the wave equation is deterministic, but it only specifies probabilities of measuring particular outcomes. So the particular outcome is not determined. Physics has not yet found a good answer for what causes the wave function to collapse. Schrödinger's cat is both alive and dead simultaneously."

Gauss jumped back down to the floor and lay near Freyja's feet, and she glanced at him thoughtfully.

. . .

Well, that isn't exactly the whole story. There are
some multiverse theories that assume the wave
function doesn't collapse. I should talk about those
with Gabe to better understand them. Some mathematicians say the wave function may be tied up
with consciousness and with whatever the mind is.

. . .

"That could be a strike. And your fourth?"

"The fourth idea stems from Heisenberg's uncertainty
principle. By that, we can measure either the position or the
momentum of any particle precisely, but we cannot measure both. I think the math is that if one is exactly measured,
the other is undefined. Our classical intuition doesn't map
cleanly to define these terms."

"And do these ideas hold equal weight? What's the
final score?"

"Some physicists would say that determinism wins the
argument. But, remember, the experiments analyze the
smallest entities and don't focus on what happens when we
think of the macro assemblies of particles. My meta-question is whether determinism characterizes the macro world
that we feel we inhabit."

She tapped her chin. "Okay, I'd call it two balls and maybe a couple of strikes. Let me give you three ideas from
mathematics, the last of which I believe is most relevant to
your question."

"All right."

"First, the amount of information needed to account
for all the particles in the universe far exceeds the capacity
of any feasible computation. Moreover, if you assume our
universe is closed, then those particles cannot store enough
information to predict the next time step."

"That's one strike against Laplace's demon," Joe said.

She nodded. "Second, there's a proof, a Cantor diago-
nalization, showing if the demon is a computational device,
that no two such devices can completely predict each other."

"Two strikes."

She reached down to stroke Gauss's ears. "Finally, the kind of math that affects our day-to-day world is that of complex systems. Nature is full of extremely chaotic systems. Chaos theory shows that even deterministic systems have behavior that is impossible to predict. And chaos theory casts doubt on repeatability. For determinism, you would expect repeatability."

"Then I should spend more time looking at complex systems for hints about how the universe is organized?"

She nodded. "Even systems with as few as three degrees of freedom exhibit chaotic behavior. And the world is full of systems with massive mathematical degrees of freedom. In summary, I don't believe we inhabit a fully deterministic universe."

Joe scratched his beard. "Physics gives determinism two balls and two strikes. Laplace's demon gets three mathematical strikes against it."

They talked for another hour, first trying unsuccessfully to find how their insights might shed light on his AI consciousness project, then letting the conversation roam to other topics. Freyja's NEST alerted her to another appointment.

She smiled breezily. "Time for my handball game."

Impressed with her interests, Joe raised his eyebrows. "You play handball?"

"Since I was young. Our team is pretty strong. Last year we got into the state semi-finals."

"Wow, you're an athlete as well as a mathematician. You're good at pitching against demons."

She laughed, her joy infectious. Notwithstanding that, his slim hopes for some indication from her of personal interest in him had vanished. He thanked her and tried to ignore his frustration as he watched her leave. Joe wandered back to his own office, lost in thought.

. . .

Freyja helped clarify my thinking. It seems that Laplace's demon, an image of determinism, is impossible inside our closed universe; then if our universe contains a drop of indeterminism, perhaps free will is possible. But what sort of free will?

. . .

He pushed away from his desk, wondering why he lacked energy, and felt his shirt pull too tightly across his shoulders. His stomach carried the evidence that he hadn't continued his slim drip since arriving. Feeling inspired by Freyja's handball activity, and at an impasse in his thoughts, he decided to find the campus sports facility, so he called up directions on his ARMO.

The sports facility stood on the west campus three hundred meters away, and he started off. His ARMO indicated a fitness area in the rear, with a handball court to the left. Curious, he walked up the stairs to the seats overlooking the court. A small crowd watched a game between two teams of women. Joe spotted Freyja in an instant, wearing a blue jersey.

Though he had only meant to watch for a moment, Joe found himself mesmerized by the agility of the players. It was a fast-paced game, with exciting plays in succession. The athletic women ran back and forth across the court. Joe's gaze fastened on Freyja, who was playing center back. He silently rooted for her team, though they were thirteen points up already.

The clock counted down. The circle runner set up with her back to the goal. Freyja flicked a graceful pass, and the circle runner slammed the ball home, right before the halftime buzzer sounded.

Joe clapped and stood, suddenly uncomfortable with dropping in on Freyja's game. He walked out of the stands toward the building's central courtyard, then on to the locker room in the building's rear. He opened an available locker to retrieve a free set of workout clothes and dressed.

In the adjacent fitness area, netwalker platforms were intermixed with other exercise equipment. An attending bot stood behind each exercising student. Headsets camouflaged their faces as they engaged in VR routines—running in place on platforms, jumping, pirouetting, throwing punches at phantoms. Joe had played most of the programs: fighting pirates in the seventeenth century, escaping from mythical creatures in fantasy worlds, reenacting the finish to an Olympic event. In one corner, students moved in coordination as they fought a group battle. They were together in another VR world, but from his perspective they were lonely ships in an open sea, oblivious to one another.

Joe stood by one of the exercise machines. The screen blinked, on standby for connection to his NEST. A pipabot lingered nearby, ready to help. He studied the screen.

Without a second thought, he walked back across the fitness center and out the door. He was outside. There was a quiet peacefulness to it. No VRs, no bots, no screens. Just the cool air. He reached down and tuned his Mercuries to a subdued forest-green color. He broke into a slow jog, his feet hitting the concrete path until he reached the woods north of the college where the path changed to dirt and leaves. Dappled light filtered through the trees. He was breathing hard, and the cool air dried his sweaty face. He raced on and on, forgot about his head and simply existed in the afternoon sunlight, his heart pumping hard in his chest, savoring the feeling of being free.

Chapter 12

"I'll have the mangonada ice also, for dessert," Joe said, finishing his lunch order. The com screen confirmed all the items.

"Those are tasty," a voice said. He turned to find Gabe standing behind him in the student café. "Would you care to join me for a quick lunch?"

Joe nodded with a smile, and they sat at a table near the window. Students flowed around them, scurrying to eat lunch between classes. A servebot arrived with their meals.

"I'm trying different places for lunch each day, and quickly exhausting the choices," Joe said.

"Yes, it's a small college. I enjoy mixing among the students, a small benefit of the limitation. It reminds me of when I was their age," Gabe said.

"I'm working through the list of philosophy books you recommended." They talked about his readings as they ate.

Joe finished his sandwich and eyed the dessert. "I've never seen this on the East Coast." Chiles combined with something sour shocked his senses.

Gabe laughed. "Expecting only mangos? Ah, the meaning of the word *dessert*. It seems that fooled you. I believe that contains chamoy, a savory sauce."

Joe ate a few more bites deliberately, comparing it to his enjoyment of Evie's spiced cooking. Another learning experience. "Of course, the café's AI classified this as dessert, without any understanding of how humans might perceive it. There's another example of my robot consciousness problem."

Gabe munched his sandwich. "Computer software is merely a bunch of symbols, using a particular syntax."

"Evolving from earlier software, as the AIs add to that syntax," Joe said.

"Yes, syntax—the *arrangement* of words to create well-formed statements. Let's add the definition of semantics. In this context, semantics includes the concern with *how meaning is attached* to any word or statement."

"Semantics is crucial," Joe agreed.

Gabe rubbed his goatee. "It reminds me of a venerable philosophical argument that made a distinction between syntax and semantics. It is called the Chinese Room analogy."

"I'm unfamiliar with it." Joe tried to recall the scant number of philosophy classes he had taken.

"Likely because it is archaic, but it's relevant to your AI consciousness problem." Gabe leaned forward. "A philosopher named Searle developed the idea a couple of centuries ago. Begin with the fact that Searle doesn't know how to read or speak Chinese. Searle imagines he is locked in a room with boxes full of Chinese symbols, and a rule book that enables him to answer questions put to him in Chinese. He can process the symbols to pass a test for understanding Chinese. You know the Turing test was an early test for AI mentality?"

"It was primitive, based on deception. We are well beyond it as a metric," Joe said.

An approving expression flickered across Gabe's face at the mention of deception, and Joe sensed the man detested any falsehood.

Gabe continued. "Searle imagines someone outside the room passes him inquiries. He can process a query by consulting the rule book and the boxes of Chinese symbols. He produces a result and passes it back outside the room. If the rule book is accurate, then the resulting answer passed out will be correct. But Searle argues that doesn't matter. Because Searle does not understand Chinese, he doesn't understand his answer at all. And he argues that neither does any computer program because they are doing the same thing—translating symbols by rote."

Gabe's pause was clearly an attempt to determine whether Joe followed the argument. "The meta-idea of the analogy is that the Chinese Room does not instantiate semantics—there's no meaning there—and therefore the syntax is insufficient for mentality." Gabe sat back.

"Working on practical coding problems led me to use the concepts of syntax and semantics. But your careful definitions help delve into them. Let me summarize—syntax doesn't suffice for semantics, and semantics are necessary for any meaning?"

"Exactly." Gabe templed his hands under his chin. "And if the Chinese Room lacks semantics—that is, any meaning—then it lacks intentional mental states."

"And for AI consciousness, we need an intentional mental state."

"Right. Searle's argument supports your intuition that there is a core issue in the coding that prevents the creation of a true mental state in the machine," Gabe said.

Joe closed his eyes to consider the argument. After a full minute, he met Gabe's patient gaze. "That argument mirrors our approach. A mathematician centuries ago talked about the 'barrier of meaning.' How do we create meaning? Where does meaning come from?"

"You've found the pivotal point." Gabe tossed back the remainder of his drink. "Creation of meaning is central to the very idea of thinking. Humans create meaning out of our position in the world because of our relationship with everything else. There is a philosophical concept of embodiment that is integral to the creation of meaning and, thereby, to consciousness."

"As we discussed at dinner, there needs to be an 'I' doing the thinking." Joe played with the remainder of the melting ice cream. "But it's a gigantic leap for humans to create some other 'I.'"

"Which leads us back to your question of finding meaning." Gabe pointed a finger at Joe. "Whether to allow for consciousness or to find some reason to care about anything." They had finished their lunches, and there was a different buzz in the student conversations around them. "It's like the Old West, that shootout," one student said.

Gabe's gaze met his in some surprise. "You haven't been keeping your NEST on either?"

Joe had left his NEST off from some irrational fear that the police might track him, and he shook his head.

"I prefer not to follow current events too attentively." Gabe touched his ear. "But maybe it's best to find out what's been happening." They parted, waving as they headed back to their respective offices. Joe opened the netchat news on his NEST while he walked, then on the large display in his office when he arrived. The Prime Netchat logo filled Joe's holo-wall com, followed by the newscaster's breathless commentary. His byline, Jasper Rand, lettered the bottom of the holo as he stood outside a nondescript building.

"The police stormed into the building here in Sacramento at 11:23. Here is that dramatic moment, caught on security vidcams." It cut to a scene of seven copbots, automatic weapons attached to their forearms, charging up the front stairs of the same building. They smashed the door open and disappeared inside. On the vidstream, the *pop-pop-pop* of weapons firing could be heard, followed by three explosions. Glass shattered in a top-story window, and clouds of black smoke billowed out.

Jasper Rand's excited commentary overlaid the vidfeed. "Police are saying that the suspect, a hacker going by the *nom de guerre* cDc, an acronym for 'the cult of the dead cat,' set off several bombs in an attempt to avoid capture. He was gunned down while resisting arrest."

The holo feed jumped to an interview with Zable from thirty-seven minutes earlier. "He resisted arrest and fought back against our brave police, using illegal weapons. But we brought him down. This terrorist, going by the name cDc, is no longer a threat to the public."

"What was he doing that necessitated such a lethal response?" The interviewer's byline, Caroline Lock, scrolled along the bottom of the holo.

"He was part of a ring of hackers destroying government databases and illegally protesting across the country. They're anarchists." Zable sneered dismissively. "But we're getting them all." Joe rubbed the back of his now-warm neck.

The wind swept up Lock's blonde hair, and she pushed it back into place. "But it's legal to protest."

"They never obtained the proper permits. These people don't respect the law," Zable said.

Annoyance welled up as he watched the condescending arrogance of a power-corrupted policeman, which brought to mind Zable's obsequiousness around Peightân. It explained how he was promoted the unusual ten Levels. Annoyance was replaced by agitation. Zable had been the same Level as Evie, a Level 76.

. . .

Why am I thinking about Levels? Do I have some unrealized bias, putting people in buckets based on their Level? I hadn't considered that possibility before. Have I been subconsciously thinking about people differently because of something as unimportant as their Level?

. . .

The interview ended, and Joe flipped through other netchat news reports, but they all reported the same storyline. He switched to the dark net sources. Every reference to cDc had disappeared.

Evie glanced up as Joe came through the apartment door. "You're back early."

Joe's heart raced when he crossed the room. He sat beside her on the sofa and tripped over the words. "There was some news. Police killed a hacker in a shootout in Sacramento. His tagline was cDc, otherwise known as 'the cult of the dead cat.'" He paused, waiting for Evie to betray some personal connection, but was met with commonplace concern.

"That's dreadful. The police just shot him, no trial or anything? That's incredibly rare. Everyone knows they don't stand a chance against copbots, and everyone surrenders. Why would the police react so violently?"

Joe described the details, searching her face for any hint of hidden knowledge.

She frowned. "You don't think Zable was talking about our protest movement? I told you before, I've never heard of this cDc."

"I think he *was* talking about your movement. Did you get any permits?"

Her hands covered her face as she tilted her head back. "No. The permits require all protesters to give their identity, and we would never have been able to get people to join us." She dropped her hands and looked at Joe. "The people most downtrodden by the Levels Acts are voiceless and afraid. We didn't do anything wrong beyond skipping that bureaucratic step. I don't know cDc, but the public doesn't look kindly on hackers. Implying he's associated with us doesn't help us. But it's hard to prove a negative."

Joe studied her clear, hazel eyes and scratched his beard pensively.

She clasped her hands together. "Do you trust me?"

"I don't know why, but yes. For some reason, I trust you."

Joe asked a few questions, trying to understand Peightân and Zable's drive to go after Evie's group, but the meager details she gave weren't enlightening. They had confined the protests to a dozen cities across the States, and there were a handful of trusted associates besides Julian and Celeste, her two friends now in jail. The severity of the police reaction didn't make sense to either of them.

They ate an early dinner. Joe splashed whisky into a glass and sat in the living room, watching the sun go down. Evie turned at her bedroom to look back at him. "Thank you for trusting me." She closed the door.

CHAPTER 13

Joe found Gabe waiting at their appointed spot on a park bench in a quadrangle on campus. Gabe had brought tea in a synjug, and he filled two cups. They contemplated the dappled afternoon sunlight streaming through the branches.

"I'm still collecting knowledge before I can begin to synthesize it into any wisdom," Joe said.

"Good. Knowledge first, the intellectual property of humanity." Gabe blew on his steaming cup. "Others have thought deeply and identified many problems, found answers, and narrowed the search for answers to other problems. What question do you have on your mind today?"

"Continuing from our conversation about the closed nature of the physical universe, I've been thinking about the absolute magnitude of the universe. I researched ideas about multiverses."

"You want to discuss the magnitude and number of universes? One is not enough? With roughly 10^{80} atoms?" Gabe waved a dismissive hand.

"Yes, not quite a googol, but that's still an absurdly large number."

"How does the mathematician think about such large numbers?"

Joe considered while sniffing the toasty bouquet of the deep-green liquid. "I try to visualize them in groups of three powers of ten. For example, I might think of a thousand blue Earths in empty space. That would be 10^3. Then to expand it to 10^6, I would think of one thousand sets of the first thousand Earths. If I can hold that in my head, I try to imagine one thousand of *all* the prior sets. That would be 10^9. For every three powers of ten, it's always a thousand times the total prior thought. Not long afterward, I get lost because the numbers are too large to imagine."

"I have the same issue." Gabe chuckled. "We think we can imagine a process that is infinite. Add one to a number: 1+1=2. Do it again: 2+1=3. Keep adding 1. We can think it goes on forever, melting into the mist, and that's our idea of infinity. But we really can't see far in the mist."

"There are lots of ways to stretch the mind." Joe smiled. "Such as turning to my question about multiple universes."

Gabe sniffed. "We cannot know everything even about one universe, if there is only one."

"That's right. The speed of light limits our particle horizon of what we could ever know to a tiny fraction of one universe. Even one is unknowable."

"But you are now referring to various theories about multiverses." Gabe took a tiny sip of his tea, perhaps a test of whether it was cool enough to drink. "A multiverse is a theoretical group of multiple universes, including this one we live in—universes budding off one another." He blinked rapidly. "Such theories do not attract me. The multiverse is a philosophical rather than a scientific hypothesis because it cannot be tested empirically; it cannot be falsified."

Joe laughed and sipped his tea. "Is that the physicist speaking?"

"Yes. If the multiverse exists, then what hope does science have to find rational explanations for the fine constants in the modified Standard Model? The multiverse is an easy way out, a voguish attempt at solutions for several problems. For example, there is the question in wave theory about what causes the collapse of the wave function."

"That's what got me thinking about multiverses, because of some crazy theories that consciousness may interact with the wave function collapse. I asked myself if the subject may shed light on my AI consciousness puzzle," Joe said.

Gabe frowned. "There were some who misinterpreted the need for an observer, in the Copenhagen interpretation of quantum mechanics, to think it required something like us to observe."

"Then the many-worlds interpretation, with its implication that all possible universes exist simultaneously, avoids that problem of what causes the wave function to collapse by tossing out all causality, right?" Joe threw an imaginary ball toward the trees.

"Yes. We live in only this particular universe, but all the others also exist."

"The universe simply can't make a decision," Joe said. He laughed at the absurdly large numbers, which he attempted to imagine for a few seconds before surrendering again. "And what does the philosopher say?"

"The philosopher is offended by the violation of Occam's razor—simpler solutions are more likely to be correct than complex ones. Yet many multiverse theories posit a near-infinite number of universes," Gabe said.

"I understand that current physics theories leave open an enormous number of mathematically possible solutions, all of which might be a 'theory of everything.'"

"Yes, there are approximately 10^{500} such possible models." Gabe groaned.

Joe sat up straighter, in disbelief. "10^{500}. And how many of those could we live in?"

Gabe turned to stare into his eyes. "Probably only this one."

"What?!"

"Life is only possible if the constants are finely tuned. As one example, only helium would be produced if the mass of the neutron were slightly lower. And if it were slightly higher, then only hydrogen would be produced. Similar problems arise if there were small differences in the quark masses or the cosmological constant."

Joe studied his empty teacup. "So how does one explain our luck to live in this one?"

"The anthropic principle is one attempt to dodge the issue. It posits that if observations of a universe must be made by conscious creatures, then only those universes where the physical constants fall within a very narrow range can hold such creatures. The meta-idea is that this universe is here for us to observe it because we are conscious creatures."

"But hasn't the history of science disproved theories that leave us—or anything else—at the center of any universe? Ptolemy's Earth-centered universe fell to the Copernican model." Joe gazed up at the sky. "Then astronomers found our solar system in the suburbs of the Milky Way, one galaxy of a hundred billion or more. Well, two trillion if you count all the small ones. It's an immense, impersonal universe. Even if there is only one."

"Yes, it is an immense universe. Impersonal? It's the stage, and we make it as personal as we wish." Sunlight lit Gabe's forehead as he sipped the last of his tea.

Joe realized they had been sitting for some time. "Gabe, you've convinced me to only worry about one closed physical universe. Next, I'd like to discuss our mentality within that universe."

Gabe stared at Joe, his gaze hard and penetrating. "And that is a topic for another day. But since you are also a physical realist, like me, and you accept some form of causal closure, it is perhaps the most depressing of topics. Are you sure you wish to know?"

"I'll follow knowledge toward wisdom, wherever it leads."

With that, Gabe stood with unexpected agility and was off down the path with a wave of his hand, leaving Joe to his thoughts.

. . .

The anthropic principle. It's an attempt to deal with the reality that at least this universe is engineered perfectly for conscious creatures, against the staggering odds for that to be random. The unconvincing answer that there must be an infinity of universes, which is a conjecture that can never be tested, seems a desperate attempt to avoid the obvious alternative hypothesis that there exists a He—or She—who shall not be named by science. Now I'm back to examining the probabilities, thinking about God.

If there is a God, She could have engineered the closed physical universe as She wished. She could have created a deterministic universe. It would have unrolled like clockwork, doing exactly what She made it do, without deviation, down to every particle. But it would be a boring universe. She would be creating, but merely creating an uncreative universe. Or She could have created a gazillion universes. If they all were deterministic, how interesting could that be? Isn't the creation of deterministic universes, no matter the number, a definition of futile creation?

My conversation with Freyja, though, suggests Laplace's demon is struck out, and that our universe is not fully deterministic; there is a tantalizing ambiguity at its heart. Therefore, it's an interesting universe. Events occur that cannot be foreseen. She who created such an interesting universe would be a more interesting God. But why this particular universe, with all the violence, all the evil? What sort of God could She be? That leaves many questions and paradoxes about the nature of such a God.

I'm thinking about the possibility of the existence of God. A subject that science has been reluctant to discuss for centuries. Perhaps science is still gun-shy from the pseudoscientific arguments of intelligent design, another masquerade for creationism. Creationism fought against recognizing the scientific evidence for undirected processes, such as evolution through natural selection. Creationists argued that evolutionary explanations are inadequate, but science proved them wrong. That demon haunting science and thoughtful people is also struck dead.

Science shows neither need nor evidence for interference in the universe after the first act of creation. But that says nothing about the act of creation itself. All questions and possibilities for me are on the table. Even ones no one is willing to discuss these days.

. . .

CHAPTER 14

Joe ambled home, where he found Evie wearing a proper karate gi as she prepared dinner. He had discovered it in the general goods store on his last outing for supplies, and though it fit her svelte figure exquisitely, he had to force away the thought that it was less revealing than his pajama shirt.

"Busy day?" She sounded cheerful.

His gaze tracked her bare feet dancing across the kitchen floor. "Occupied with my sabbatical project, consulting with several professors. And I see you're still working on your katas."

She faced him and folded her hands together, her body relaxed. "I was practicing a bridge kata."

"What's that?"

"In this one, you imagine you're standing on a narrow footbridge. Your enemies attack from both sides. Since it's narrow, only one can attack from either side at a time."

"You turn left and right to fight them?"

She nodded. Her gaze turned upward as if recalling a memory. "To focus my mind during the kata, I hold the thought, 'Though I have one thousand enemies, I will defeat them all.'"

"I don't doubt it."

She set out plates of lemongrass chicken, then sat down across from him and cut into her meal. "For a Level 42, you don't have much stuff."

Joe shrugged and pulled his plate toward him. "I find I don't need many things. I'm more interested in what stuff goes on in my head than what goes on outside of it."

"That's odd. The handful of higher Levels I've spent any time with could be like dragons, sitting on their piles of diamonds and rubies."

"Good odd?"

"Good odd. It's better to worry less about things."

They heard the front door chirp with its opening alert, and their gazes locked. Evie nodded at his pointing finger and ducked around the corner toward the bedroom as Joe heard footsteps on the stairs.

73's oval head poked through the doorway, its forehead flashing red. The bot walked into the living room to face him, its arms raised in ready mode. Its head moved left and right in a scan of the room.

"What are you doing here? That's against my orders."

"Sir, I detected that an intruder may have entered your apartment. You entered, then did not reappear. Are you okay?"

"I'm fine. Why did you come here?"

"Sir, according to the First Law, I cannot allow you to come to harm through my inaction. May I inspect the apartment?"

Joe was about to demand that the bot leave when he spotted Evie behind it, an automop in her hands. She swung it in a twirling arc. The crunch echoed through the apartment as metal struck metal. The bot jolted forward, then turned toward her, its arms raised in defense.

Joe reached the panel on the bot's back and activated his biometric tile. The panel swung open. He found the kill switch and pulled it. The bot froze, and the flashing red light went out.

In the sudden silence, Joe's gaze jumped from the bot to Evie. "What are you doing?" He bit out the words, and his face flushed.

She still held the metal automop in both hands, and she frowned in confusion at his question. "Stopping it, of course. It was going to check the apartment, and it can't know I'm here."

Joe groaned. "It would have obeyed my command to leave. Now we have a dented pipabot, one that has imaged your face, and my biometric signature recorded as shutting it down."

Evie winced and studied the automop. "Maybe I didn't make things better."

"No, your impulsive behavior made them worse." Joe stood, steaming. "Okay, let me think."

They stood for a moment, Evie with the automop upright in her hand, Joe scratching his beard, and the slumped bot between them. Joe reached into the open panel and removed the control chip. He deactivated the auto-restart process and disconnected the power supply.

"Help me push this thing into the closet. We'll keep it there until we can replace the AI with a new one. Assuming I can get my hands on one without causing warnings to go off all over the national monitoring system." Evie and Joe dragged the inert pipabot into the closet and shut the door.

"Do you have any idea how the bot knew you were here?"

She bit her lip. "I scooted out for a half hour. I didn't think anyone saw me leave or come back."

"How did you get back in?"

"I left the door unlocked."

Joe rubbed his eyes. "The bot would have sensed that as part of its protective protocol."

She looked at the floor. "I hadn't thought of that."

He felt himself still fuming, but he tried to control it. "Let's eat," he said. They moved to the kitchen table and sat opposite one another in silence. Joe's temper slowly cooled as his stomach warmed with the lemongrass chicken.

"This is really delicious."

"Like I said, learned during my international period, trapped like this," she said, her voice satirical.

He put down his fork. "Look, you're not the only one who has ever been constrained by some rules. I've never been outside the country *either*. I can't get a passport *either*."

She looked down at her plate. Her voice was pensive when she at last spoke, as if she relived some old emotion. "I worked so hard on my master's degrees. I was ready to do something with them. When I couldn't get a real job, it crushed me. Then I said to myself, 'Is that all you got, girl?'" She looked up. "That's when I got really good at the bridge kata."

They held each other's gazes for a long moment. Evie went back to her meal. A minute later she said, "When the bot was facing you and flashing, I thought it might hurt you."

Joe chewed thoughtfully. "Then it was nice of you to try and stop it. I understand that your martial arts training was instinctual; it was second nature to use what you know."

Evie nodded, and they continued to eat.

"Why did you take the risk to leave the apartment?"

Her answer was soft, apologetic. "We had scheduled another protest for next Tuesday. It's likely that would have gone forward if I didn't call it off. The train station has a secure com, and I went there to send a message to another leader in the movement. I couldn't let anyone else end up in jail."

"I could have helped send a message, which would have been safer for both of us." He waited until she met his gaze before he said, "We're both in this now."

She nodded.

"That's all you did?"

She moved a piece of chicken around on her plate. "You were running out of interesting ingredients. On the way back, I popped into a general supply for some spices." She paused, then finished, "You seem to like my cooking."

He swallowed the tasty bite. "Let's pray it's not our last meal."

After a late-night consultation with Raif in his office and a call the next morning to a friend at the AI Ministry, Joe had a plan in place. The replacement AI would be authorized by his friend at the Ministry because the original was damaged in an accident, thereby avoiding any government scrutiny. His friend would send the replacement AI—complete with its software sandboxing wrapper and new secure chip—which would arrive at Joe's office by the end of the day. And Raif would send a hardware wrapper. Joe would install the new AI and deep-six the old AI chip, and no one would be the wiser. Hopefully.

The bot's oval head straightened, and a blue glow filled its forehead. Its lenses focused on Joe. "I am your assigned Personal Intelligent Physical Assistant, PIPA 32983. I go by either Eugenia or Gene. Would you prefer that I use the speech of a female or a male?" Its forehead glowed purple.

"Please use a neutral voice, and I'll call you 83, if you don't mind. And, before you ask, I don't have a PIDA."

The bot blinked. "Yes, that is fine." It studied its surroundings. "I seem to have found myself in a closet."

"Please find the utility building outside. Plan to remain in minimal use mode for me. And after you exit, do not enter my apartment without an explicit command to do so. Ignore any visitors who enter and exit." He didn't think Evie would be reckless enough to leave again, but he didn't want a repeat of this situation.

"Sir, that is understood."

Joe followed the pipabot down the apartment stairs, 73's memory chip still in his hand. When the pipabot veered toward the utility building, Joe followed the path to the footbridge.

Looking at the choppy water and then up at the surrounding trees, Joe scanned for vidcams. He knelt and leaned over the side of the bridge to trail his hand in the water, then he opened his fingers and let the chip plummet down, down. His contemplative pause did more than hide the disposal. Joe stared into the water, thinking of 73 and about how easy it is to anthropomorphize our creations.

CHAPTER 15

Joe spent the remainder of the weekend and all Monday morning reading from the book list Gabe had recommended. Midday found him leaning back in his office chair, where he gazed with pleasure at the floating holo icons above his head. He glanced at a set of holos ignominiously pushed into the corner—an AI problem he'd been studying but had abandoned for his philosophical studies. His interests were changing. The AI consciousness practical problem seemed increasingly impossible to solve, and he was losing interest in returning to his old job at the AI Ministry. At the same time, the reading material on the philosophy of mind sparked his urge to explore his own mentality. What was it, anyway?

Joe ate a salad for lunch, then he hiked to the philosophy building and found Gabe teaching a class. Graduate students filled the classroom. It was equipped for full VR immersives, with VR headsets and haptic vests for every student. They were all absorbed in individual lessons. Gabe roamed the room, coaching students one at a time. When the professor saw him, he gestured to one of the VR rigs hanging on the wall. Joe pulled on the haptic vest and VR headset. Gabe touched his headset, his biometric tile glowed blue through his open-collar shirt, and the words "Instructor Mode" flashed across Joe's view.

"Class is over in eleven minutes." Gabe gestured around the classroom. "For diversion, you can observe any student of interest until we finish."

Gabe stepped away, and Joe wandered about the room, watching students interact with avatars. He stopped behind a student engaged in an impassioned debate with a tall, bearded avatar wearing a chiton, a brown himation, and sandals. It was clear the avatar was Aristotle when he lifted his arm draped in the brown cloth and pointed at the floor, reminding Joe of the painting by Raphael. Aristotle said, "There are substances, both primary substances and secondary substances . . ."

. . .

A good way to learn factual history. I'm doubtful about how well the AI handles the meta-concepts. Can it ever do more than regurgitate the input?

. . .

Soon a bell sounded. The avatars faded from the VR hall, and students stowed their equipment and dispersed. He recalled leaving similar classrooms and professors behind as he carried away some new idea.

Joe turned to face Gabe. Both wore VR rigs. Gabe looked grave as he asked, "Are you ready for a difficult lesson? If so, this is a good place."

Joe's jaw tightened in acknowledgment. Gabe reset the VR rig to zero, and the green screen surrounded Joe. Gabe's avatar stood before him, dressed in a dark blue traditional Hanfu cloak. Together with his long goatee, he appeared so much the sage.

"This lesson provides knowledge. I'm giving you an unsolved problem, a hard problem. You need to form your own synthesis of beliefs based on the facts, the history of human discussion, and your own inferences." Gabe gestured to their empty surroundings. "You said you are a physicalist—that the universe is real, and you believe based on science that it is a physically closed universe."

Joe nodded with vigor.

"What is your definition of a 'closed physical universe'?"

"I was thinking if we trace the causal ancestry of a physical event, we need never go outside the physical universe."

"Good. I am also a physicalist, and I would use that definition."

"Now what is the problem?" Joe's avatar hand appeared to scratch his beard when Joe unconsciously did the same.

"Perhaps the most difficult problem in philosophy of mind is the problem of causal exclusion. The question is, how can the mind exercise its causal powers—cause anything at all to happen—in a fundamentally physical world?"

Joe nodded, waiting.

"To understand the problem, you must first grasp the idea of supervenience. In the philosophy of mind, supervenience is a minimal condition for causality in a physically closed universe."

"I don't know the concept," Joe said.

"Supervenience refers to a *relation* between sets of properties or sets of facts. In mathematical terms, X is said to supervene on Y if and only if some difference in Y is necessary for any difference in X to be possible."

Joe began to follow the logic, but he wished he could manipulate some symbols on his com. As if he had read his mind, Gabe waved a hand, and red soccer balls floated at waist height all around them, jostling against Joe's hips. Another wave, and a layer of blue balls appeared above the red, haptically bumping against the two men.

Gabe continued. "Philosophers usually talk about property supervenience. Let's say the blue balls represent the mental, or the X. The red ones represent the physical world, or the Y. In a supervenient relationship, say if some set of properties, blue, supervenes on some other set of properties, red, then in order for there to be changes in blue, there must necessarily be changes in the properties of red."

Gabe bounced his hand into the sea of red balls, which bobbed up and down. "The physical layer." Then he hit the layer of blue balls. "And the mental. But we don't need so many." With another wave, four balls remained in front of Joe—two red beneath two blue. "For a physicalist, one concept is there cannot be a mental difference without a physical difference."

Two paintings appeared suspended in the air, side by side, above the two blue balls. They looked somewhat like the Mona Lisa, that ambiguous smile directed at Joe.

"Here are two paintings. What is your opinion of them?"

They seemed similar, but the second looked like a good painting, while the first did not. "The second is better. It's a good painting. I don't like the first."

"You think the second has some aesthetic, intrinsic difference of goodness. Then don't you agree there must be some further difference between them to make one good and the other not?"

"Yes."

"If you find a difference in goodness, can the underlying physical basis be the same?"

"No, it must be different, since the universe is physical."

"Good. Now you can see a supervenient relationship. You can see that the mental *supervenes* on the physical. That is, if the mental varies, then the physical necessarily varies."

Joe smiled. "Yes, now that's clear."

"Good. You believe the universe is physical, and it is real. Then you might agree that for every mental difference, there must be a physical difference." The red balls underlying the two paintings changed, one with a single stripe, the second with two stripes to mark the physical difference.

"If there is a difference between the paintings," Gabe pointed first at the two paintings and then at the two red balls, "then there must be a physical difference underlying whatever is happening in mentality. Otherwise, it violates supervenience relationships."

"The mental supervenes on the physical," he said, and Gabe nodded.

"Then have I convinced you that this is a minimal condition to believe that your mind can cause anything?"

"Yes." Joe's forehead puckered in concentration.

"Good. Now let's discuss mentality moving through time. One thought follows another."

The four balls dissolved with a wave of Gabe's hand, replaced by a line of blue soccer balls floating over a line of red soccer balls. Each ball had an arrow pointing in the same direction. Joe bumped the red ball closest to him, and it tapped the next, with the motion moving down the line from red ball to red ball like a Newton's cradle toy. The line of blue balls above moved in tandem with the red balls below, making a *tick-tick-tick* sound.

"Imagine, for example, the line of blue balls is a line through time of a series of thoughts in your head. Now, what causes what?"

"Well, the first red ball causes the next in line," Joe said.

"And then presumably that second red ball causes the third?"

"Yes. There is something going on in the physical universe at each thought. There's chemistry, and, below that, particles, I suppose. It's how we normally describe the physics of the closed physical universe."

The corners of Gabe's mouth lowered. "What causes the mentality?"

"Obviously, the first blue ball causes the second, and down the line. One thought leads to another. That is a description of a thought process, what goes on in our heads," Joe said.

Gabe paused for effect, his eyes hard and glistening. "But you already said the physical red balls each determine the next red ball, and each red ball determines the blue ball above. If red balls cause both, then there is nothing being done by the blue balls. They are not causative. They are extraneous."

Joe peered with growing unease at the lines of balls.

"Mentality is an *epiphenomenon.*" Gabe put both hands out, blocking the blue balls from the red balls. "Epiphenomenalism says that mental events don't cause anything in the physical world to occur. For example, we may think that seeing a friend makes us grin. But this argument would suggest that our grin is only the result of underlying physiological processes."

In his mind's eye, Raif grinned at Joe until that Cheshire cat faded into mental agitation. He thought of Evie and wondered if the related thoughts were only caused by his animal nature—glands, hormones, cells, chemistry, and his particles moving about. He perspired, and now wondered what caused it.

Gabe moved his hand, and the room became pitch black. The holo of an autocar appeared and moved in a slow ellipse around the perimeter of the room. Its headlights lit a guard-rail on the walls. As the car moved, its shadow reflected off the railing, the shadow following the autocar. Joe watched the *flick-flick-flick* as each shadow caught the next rail post, like ghosts jumping out of darkness.

Gabe's voice was somber. "The philosopher Jaegwon Kim gave a memorable analogy. He said that the shadow of the car is likened to mentality. There is no causal connection between the shadow at one moment and the next. The moving car represents a genuine causal process, and we have said that causal process is in the underlying physical universe. Our minds are doing nothing causal. They are just along for the ride, a reflection of physical processes. Then there is no separate thing we call mind. It's a shadow."

Joe's shoulders sagged.

"An appropriate reaction," Gabe said.

"Is there a way out of this horrific conclusion?"

"If you are a physicalist, one who believes in a physically closed universe, then no way has been found so far." Gabe seemed as dejected about that as Joe was.

. . .

I believe that the universe is physically closed. All the scientific evidence asserts that conclusion. Now Gabe is telling me that if I accept that premise, given this way of describing everything in mental and physical properties, then I have no mentality causing anything. That *feels* so wrong. I cannot believe it. I don't *want* to believe it. Yet the logic seems correct.

. . .

Joe cleared his throat. "But if this is the case, then any causation by us—by our mentality—is gone. And if causation by our mentality is gone, so is any free will."

Gabe's shoulders had slumped too, and his avatar looked older. "You understand the magnitude of the problem. A twentieth-century philosopher named Fodor said something like . . ." Gabe closed his eyes, summoning the quote. "'If it isn't literally true that my wanting is causally responsible for my reaching, and my itching is causally responsible for my scratching, and my believing is causally responsible for saying . . . if none of that is literally true, then practically everything I believe about anything is false and it's the end of the world.'"

"D-do you believe that?"

"I cannot find a reason that it is false. If it's true, then the ideas that our minds cause anything and have any free will are both illusions. We may think we decide things, but, instead, it is all due to our underlying physical natures, and down through the physical descriptions to particles in motion. We have no free will."

———————◆———————

Joe sat at a bar and stared into the deep amber of his whisky, the back of his throat raw from the peaty Islay. He'd straggled from the classroom toward town, meandering down several streets, zigging left and right, and found this bar on a side lane. It wasn't crowded when he entered three hours ago, and those who came after twilight had moved into the back rooms. The stools along the bar were empty except for his. The barbot removed the remains of his dinner and the many empty glasses strewn about.

. . .

What now on my sabbatical project? Where do I
go from here? Could Gabe be right? Does any of
this matter?

. . .

Those questions had been circling his head in a continuous loop. He put up a finger to summon the barbot. "How
about another whisky?"

The barbot purred a sweet melody and examined him,
tapping her fingers in rhythm on the bar. She was lovely and
sensuous. Her pseudo-skin was of a recent variant that appeared realistically human, but she would always be marked
as a bot by the prominent red numbers tattooed in a circle
around her neck. It was required by law, so that no one could
be confused.

"Perhaps you've had enough whisky tonight, Mr . . .?"

"Joe."

"Mr. Joe, perhaps instead I could suggest alternatives. We
have synpsychs. They are the best synthetic biology psychotropics available, guaranteed, and will put you in a nice
mental state. Or we can toss emoticon bundles upstairs. I'll
show you." Her hand brushed his arm, and he noticed a whiff
of perfume now infusing his shirtsleeve.

. . .

Not a barbot, but a matchlovebot. What sort of
place have I wandered into?

. . .

He stared at her for a moment, aware of his slowed reaction time. "No, thanks. I've no interest in any virtual entertainment." A chill went through him.

The matchlovebot tried again. "Say, I can help you find
a match in the neighborhood. If you'd like, I could inspect
your PIDA and help with that."

"I don't have a PIDA."

"Well then, if you allow me to connect with your NEST,
we can use the cached personal biodata."

Joe emptied the dregs from his glass. "No, thanks. I'll find my own hedonism." He slipped off the barstool and shoved through the door.

---◆---

Joe waved his hand at the apartment door, and it slid open. He stumbled up the stairs. Evie glanced up from the kitchen table, which was set with two plates and silverware. One dish held a cold serving of charred alt-steak, flanked by a baked potato and a pastry dessert. Her plate was empty, and she drank from a glass of water, her dessert untouched.

"I thought you might be back for dinner," she said.

"Sorry." He tried not to slur the word, but it came out that way anyway. "I was out late after seeing a fellow professor. I already ate." He bumbled into the living room, took a glass from the corner credenza, and poured the last of the whisky from the decanter. He came back and sat opposite her at the table.

Though he had eaten a large meal, the dessert looked appealing, and he grabbed the fork. The conversation with Gabe was a cloud in his head. It seemed all was lost; nothing mattered.

Joe had both elbows on the table and his head down over the flaky pastry. The sweet apples were a pleasing counterpoint to the whisky.

"Everything okay?"

"It was a . . . an intense day."

The silence stretched long before she said, "I feel cooped up in here." He lifted his gaze to her. Her lips formed a pinched line, near a pout. Her hazel eyes stared through him. "I can't go out. I can't check on my friends. No reading the chat stream for scuttlebutt. I'm going to go crazy."

. . .

I've been ignoring her. What a mistake. Those beautiful eyes.

. . .

"Not much we can do about that." The slurring was worse when talking between mouthfuls. "Unless you have any ideas."

Her mouth tightened in fury. "I wasn't asking for a pass. Just a conversation." She sniffed. He noticed her sniff again, and her expression darkened more. He wondered whether there was some other reason for her irritation besides his half-serious flirtation. Anyway, there would be no hedonism tonight, only separate bedrooms again.

His head was cloudy, and he paused to concentrate. "All right, a conversation. But all you want to talk about is your Levels protest movement. It seems one-track and self-centered." He reached for the second apple strudel.

She tapped her fingers softly on the table, her face fierce. "Yes, talking about one-track, have you noticed how much time you spend in your head? There's living going on in the world."

Her fingers drummed faster as his mind gave up the conversation and fixated on eating. The apples were delicious, and his mind was blissfully empty as he finished the last bite of her apple strudel. Then the drumming abruptly stopped.

"Trying to demonstrate you're a glutton as well as a drunk?"

. . .

I should have expected that shot to ring out, but I'm not paying attention. Behaving badly, and I deserved that. It does matter. She matters.

. . .

He rubbed the back of his neck. "Some social judgments are warranted. You won that last point." His contrition was real, and his face must have reflected it, because a victorious glint entered her eyes. "How about calling a truce? I'll meet you halfway. Maybe we both should stop being self-absorbed, since we're stuck here together?"

Her only response was to fold her hands like she did at the end of a kata.

Joe got up to make Dragonwell tea, as much to uncloud his head as to prolong the moment, uncomfortable as it was for him. They sat on opposite ends of the sofa in the living room, sipping tea. The moonlight danced shadows across her face that left her as enigmatic as the Mona Lisa, and he couldn't decipher her mood when she turned to the bedroom and closed the door.

. . .

Maybe she doesn't hate me.

. . .

CHAPTER 16

His MEDFLOW purred with the triple dose to treat his head-
ache. Joe rolled over in bed and focused on the ceiling, and
his head gradually cleared. In the clarity of daylight, he realized the comment Evie made days ago about his lack of stuff
had not just been because of lack of spices, but because she
was bored. He would have to be more attentive to his guest.
Joe dug his old allbook out of the bottom of one of the
shipping containers. He'd seldom handled the reading
source since college, preferring instead a com unit or his
corneal projection.

When Joe presented it to her, Evie opened it with delight.
She insisted on not connecting it, content to read his cast-off
material. Joe hadn't seen her access a NEST during her stay,
and he wasn't sure she had an operating device implanted.
But he had noticed the subtle depression in the skin between
her perfect breasts where her biometric tile lay. She was not
a Luddite but was indeed living in the real world.

They fell back into a polite routine, and a permanent
truce took hold. Each morning he ordered breakfast from
the food synthesizer, and when it was ready, he knocked on
her door. They ate the peaceful meal together, and he left for

the math building. She continued to be cordial, if not forth-coming about her past. He never walked in again during a kata. Joe enjoyed her pleased smile when she poked through the things he brought her after a trip to the general supply store. They ate dinner together each night, and being with her made him happy.

Sometimes he'd lay awake in bed well after her door closed, staring out the window that overlooked trees edged in shadows. The second bedroom fronted the same trees. He imagined drifting out his window and peeping in the next as he undressed her in his mind. He couldn't shake the im-age of her revolving in her kata—Penetrating the Fortress, indeed. The vision of her steely discipline stayed any new attempt to evolve beyond their truce.

◆

A few days passed. Joe sat at his office holo-wall com, the air alive with holographs from a dozen sources. His NEST corneal link shuffled through the written material as he thought. He had been deep in this state for several hours, anticipating another visit with Gabe.

An encrypted message icon blinked in the NEST link. He closed everything else and accepted it. A minute later, Raif's holo materialized.

"The evidence linking those two protest ringleaders to the store bombing held up in court. The prosecutors presented credible links, and the court found them guilty," he said.

"I still don't believe it," Joe said, frowning.

Raif shrugged. "Those were sealed databases, so it's just about impossible to modify the contents."

"Only just about?"

"I won't say zero, but a small likelihood."

"I believe in the small nonzero." Then he snapped his fingers, feeling like an idiot. "Do you have any interest in spending time to verify that, one way or another? I can con-nect you with a mathematician here who might be interested in helping. And you would enjoy meeting her." Joe didn't mention that he was supposed to have connected them over a week ago.

"Her. Sure." A grin split his cherubic face. "Joe, you have such good taste in women. Sounds like an interesting project."

Joe signed off and closed his window screen, the data feeds dissolving to be replaced by transparent window. Outside, the sun shone on olive-colored foliage. He sat at his desk, staring out, as he reflected on Raif's message.

. . .

If I'm objective about this information, then I shouldn't trust Evie. Yet I still want to. Why?

Is it my animal nature, or mere particles in motion, as Gabe suggested, rather than an action of free choice? There is the idea in philosophy, starting with Socrates, of *akrasia*—a weakness of will, a lack of self-control, of acting against one's better judgment. Am I tempted to follow appetite rather than volition? Emotion and desire rather than reason? Buddha thought such cravings were the cause of all suffering. I'm human, I can't stop suffering.

There is something inexplicable about being attracted to another person. It feels like it circumvents reason. It wells up from below, unconscious, from our very genes, striving for complement. This feeling is one visceral argument against having free will. At best, it shows my own akrasia.

Let me justify myself. Maybe it's a move like Jardine mentioned—knocking over the board—outside reason, astonishing. How else can I describe my intuition?

Evie appears to be so virtuous, evidenced by her concern for justice, her discipline, and her temperance. She doesn't seem afraid of anything. More than that, she has passion and purpose. An admirable purpose if what she says is true, something I have yet to find.

Whatever the probabilities, my intuition says she is truthful. It's not time to conclude a negative. Besides, in this woman, this flesh-and-blood person, both challenging and authentic, there is a real "I" there. I like her a lot.

. . .

Another sunny week passed, and the calendar showed spring only a week away. Joe returned from his office with a bounce in his step. He relished the free time to think, and the hours in his office passed as a blur in his head. He'd met several new math colleagues and had taken to eating lunch with them. His afternoons included an exercise routine. The jogging had been grueling initially, but he had adapted, feeling healthier.

He bounded up the stairs after another engaging dinner with Gabe and found Evie sitting peacefully on the living room sofa. She squinted up from the allbook when he stood in front of her.

"Quite a collection of material you have here. There's a lot of philosophy. And an eclectic bunch of other stuff too. I thought you were a mathematician," she said.

"I am, with my second master's in physics." He glanced over the detritus of his past life. "I took some philosophy courses too. Not many, which is why I'm studying the subject with Professor Gabe Gulaba."

"Gabe? You were meeting and having dinner with a guy?" A small smile flicked across her face.

"Yes. The math department dean, Dr. Jardine, recommended him."

She studied him. "Joe, you are a puzzle. You spend a lot of time in your head. I'm trying to understand what this sabbatical project of yours is all about."

Sensing genuine curiosity and an opportunity to connect, he sat beside her. "I'm trying to understand it too. Many deep ideas have been floating around in my mind for several years, but I wasn't making much progress. So I came to this college, where I'm hoping to find help."

She settled the allbook on her lap and faced him. "Give me an example of a deep idea."

Joe glanced at the ceiling as he chose among the fuzzy list swirling in his head. "Okay, here is one of the deepest. What is the ontology of the universe?"

She frowned. "I admit I don't know anything about that."

"Ontology is the philosophical study of *being*. I'm interested in the subfield of *categories of being*. That is, the fundamental categories of existence—what makes up the universe." He flung his arms out wide, as if to encompass said universe. "It's concerned with *what there is*, what elements have existence."

She listened carefully. "I thought everything was made of molecules. And smaller particles make up those."

"Yes, that is an elementary scientific explanation, and that suggests you are a realist. You have the view that physical objects exist when nobody is observing them."

"And the opposite of a realist is?"

"For a philosopher, that would be an idealist, someone who thinks the world is a creation of the mind."

She laughed. "I've been accused of being an idealist—someone who wants to change the world."

"I guess you are a philosophical and scientific realist, and a social idealist. So am I."

"Don't the physicists and the mathematicians already have some deeper answers?" She leaned forward.

"I don't believe they have any good answers on the fundamental question of ontology, of what those simplest elements are. Most scientists believe, like you and I, that there exists an external reality independent of humans—of any conscious creatures. Physicists have been searching for two centuries for a theory of everything that fills in the mysteries and completes the modified Standard Model. Any theory of everything would be abstract and mathematical. With all the exquisite mathematical structure found underlying the physical world, it is not an unreasonable conjecture. Then the physicists throw up their hands and say, 'Shut up and calculate.'"

"What do the philosophers say?"

He scratched his beard. "Many philosophers talk about the past, rehashing antiquated ideas beginning with the ancient Greeks. Though that's a history lesson more than a hunt for new knowledge, because most old philosophical claims don't hold water, given our scientific advances. Some philosophers try to engage with scientists, but most cannot follow the math. So the philosophers and the theoretical physicists rarely connect in a conversation that jointly advances credible new explanations."

Her nose twitched. "What exactly did the old philosophers say?"

His fingers formed a pyramid as he responded. "Plato soliloquized about the Forms. While that sounds crazy in today's scientific world, some mathematicians—including me—appreciate the intuition that mathematics exists out there as something we discover and not something we create."

Evie nodded, waiting for him to continue.

"Aristotle discussed 'substances.' In the *Categories*, he said the primary substances were individual objects. That allbook," he pointed, "is an individual object. Aristotle added secondary substances, which are predicates—descriptive words like 'brown.'"

She stared at the allbook. "I thought 'brown' was a property of this object."

"Later philosophers use that term. And scientific realists accept properties as a fundamental category on a list of ontological elements," Joe said.

"Do properties really exist too?" She rubbed the cover of the allbook. "Where are they?"

He frowned. "Well . . . I don't know. Scientific realists would say they exist inside somehow, I guess. But I haven't thought through what really must exist and what doesn't."

"What else is on your list of things that might exist?" Her expression showed real interest.

"The term 'relations' shows up. A relation would exist between two or more individual objects. Some philosophers place relations as a subgroup within properties. I'm not sure about that either."

"Anything else?"

Joe shrugged. "Then it gets even more complicated, and there's less agreement. There are discussions about 'natural kinds.' Debating the Kantian transcendental tradition, Stroud added 'enduring particulars.' Descartes believed there were only two substances—'material body,' which is defined by extension, and 'mental substance,' which is defined by thought, which, in this context, is equivalent to consciousness. Leibniz thought the universe consisted of 'monads.' Then the philosophers of language added new entities. But I don't buy any of those arguments. I think philosophy strayed farther from a basis in physics."

"All that sounds like a lot of gibberish," she said, forehead furrowed.

"I can't disagree."

After a moment of acute concentration on Evie's part, she said, "Let me get this straight. After all these centuries of discussion, no one knows the basic elements that make up the universe?"

"The physicists would quibble with that." He smiled. "They say to study the math. But no, they don't have an explanation. There are major disconnects in the modified Standard Model of physics. Wave-particle duality is so counterintuitive, it defies logic. Bell's theorem and non-locality mean we don't understand fundamentals. Many questions remain. And no one is answering them."

Evie's practical nature exerted itself. "Shouldn't we just do the best we can—live a good life, be good people, be fair to others?"

"It's a start. But . . ." he said, "I want to know the truth. I want to know how and why."

◆

Joe lay in bed, staring out the window. Was she asleep, or did she, too, lie awake thinking about him here so close?

. . .

I've been thinking of Evie as a mysterious house-guest. A physically attractive distraction. Now, it's more than that. She's interesting to talk to, despite her lack of background in these philosophical topics. She asks good questions and challenges me to think in new ways. I'll be sad when she leaves.

. . .

CHAPTER 17

Joe was back in his office the next morning but getting no work done. His head swirled in a fog. After the last several discussions with Gabe, he had a long list of new philosophy books to read, and he had new ways to approach his questions. But today he struggled to focus. It was easier to stare out the window. Two scrub jays perched on the branch of a live oak were having a *kuk-kuk* exchange. A squirrel scampered up the trunk. It paused, inspected its arboreal world, then turned and dashed up another bough.

The trees were in full bloom, and the sky was steel blue. Joe was blue too. A restless anxiety left him unmoored. The reflections of an overhead delivery drone crossed the exterior of the opposite building wing, and he mused on the polyhedron patterns shimmering against the metal. That was Freyja's office wing.

Joe gazed at the holo projections floating near his head. He knocked several out of the way, and they spun and ricocheted off each other, reminding him of Evie whirling in her kata.

. . .

Evie is smart and attractive. She's a model of virtue and she single-mindedly pursues her purpose,
which I refuse to believe is evil. She has a passion I
don't see often in others. She approaches life more
from the world and less from inside her head—a
good balance for me. Evie has a purpose in the
world, something I wish I could find too.

. . .

Joe ate a small lunch and took his afternoon exercise run,
which helped him focus. Back in his office, he reviewed the
material Gabe had supplied. When the sun dipped toward
the horizon, an encrypted link appeared on his NEST.

Raif's holo floated in the wall com display, smiling mischievously. "The coast is clear. The police investigation has
ended. They haven't found any more conspirators."

Joe relaxed. His relief must have been visible, because
Raif laughed and said, "It's safe to go back in the water."

. . .

Evie's friends haven't implicated her. Loyal friends,
that's good.

. . .

"To the ankles." Joe settled back in his chair. "Anything
else to report?"

"Thanks for the introduction to Freyja. I'm loving our
collaboration on the database problem. Nothing there to report yet, but she's a lot of fun." Raif winked. "Talk later, brat."

Joe kept his face neutral, but his gut tightened when he
signed off. He couldn't quash the envious thought that crept
into his head—that Freyja found his best friend more attractive than she did him.

He wandered to the town center along the market street
and peered into the shops. Pipabots stood at attention in the
doorways. One bot at a flower shop described the day's fresh
collection. Joe studied the profusion of choices, first the red
tulips in vases, then the pink freesias standing in a large pot.

He settled on a large bunch of white roses.

"An excellent choice, sir." The approval in the bot's voice reminded him of 73. "Since these are of the highest value, would you please connect your NEST for payment?" Joe did so, authenticating with his biometric tile and sign.

"I'm sure your friend will enjoy these," the bot said, his forehead glowing blue. Joe left the shop with the bundle.

When he opened the door, Evie was sitting in the living room. His allbook rested on her lap, and he was glad she still found his collection palatable. When she saw the bunch of roses, a blush tinged her cheeks.

"These are to let you know I have loved having you here."

Evie took the bouquet and sniffed delightedly. "You are so old school," she said, but with affection. Then her eyes grew wide. "You *loved* having me here?"

"Raif told me the police are off the trail. No more being cooped up here. You're free to leave."

Evie held the flowers with her nose among them, taking another breathy sniff. Joe studied the beauty of her face as she closed her eyes, seeming lost in thought. When she opened them, her gaze was a soft question mark. "Do you want me to leave right away?"

. . .

So glad she asked.

. . .

"No." Joe fumbled, looking at his shoes. Too fast? "It's logical for you to hang around longer, in case the police are still watching your neighborhood."

"Okay." She sniffed the roses again. "Let's be careful a bit longer."

Hope filled his heart. "But it's probably all right to go outside since they aren't staking out the college anymore. Maybe dinner out?"

Evie had suggested they walk to the restaurant on the far side of town because she was eager to be outside, and she was reluctant to use traceable transport so soon after the police dragnet ended. The French bistro lights on each side of the door highlighted her flushed cheeks as they entered. A pipabot dressed in black, with one arm draped in a white linen napkin, ushered them to their table near a virtual fireplace, the spot transformed into a sheltered corner by emerald-colored planters. Evie surveyed the room. A black-and-white tiled floor complemented the muted greens of the walls. Servebots moved solicitously from table to table, bringing out courses. The open kitchen boasted shiny copper pots that decorated the walls where servebots prepared the dishes.

An affable man wearing chef whites came to their table and introduced himself as Philippe, the owner and head chef. He introduced his sous chef, a young man wearing a toque. As he effused about the menu for a full minute, it was apparent the owner worshipped food and loved sharing his creations with his guests.

After the owner and sous chef moved on to another table, a pipabot waiter approached and announced, "The chef's menu is prix fixe and consists of five courses." Joe opened his NEST, connected to the bot's offered wine list, and selected a synjug of a celebrated Bordeaux. He closed his NEST and the bot scooted away, leaving them alone.

Evie seemed energized by their surroundings. Her hair shone in the flickering light. He said, "So you've found some things that interested you these past two weeks on my allbook?"

"Quite a few. You have broad tastes. And I feel I've gotten to know you by reading the things you read."

Joe shifted in his chair. "Should I be embarrassed? I forget all the stuff I have on there."

"Nothing incriminating." She laughed. "More of an open window, which shows you aren't such a bad sort, for a 42."

The pipabot waiter appeared with a plate and announced, "An amuse-bouche of salmon tartare cornets, to begin." It opened the Bordeaux and poured the wine into glasses as it declared the chateâux and vintage, adding, "This synjug is in the top one percent." They were left alone. They tasted, then Joe toasted her glass and said, "Here's to jailbreaking." He liked her quick, rebellious smile.

"Sorry I'm doing a poor job of matching the wine to the courses. But I thought one synjug was enough," he said.

"Cutting back?" Her eyes twinkled.

"Yes. Trying to stay healthy. I realized I was drinking too much."

The servebots moved like placid ships around the tables, the few guests islands of hushed conversation. Soon the pipabot waiter returned, followed by a servebot with plates, and announced, "This first dish is entitled Oysters and Pearls, made of sabayon of pearl tapioca with oysters and caviar."

Evie swirled an oyster inside her mouth, and a sensuous expression crossed her face. He crushed the caviar against the roof of his mouth, and the saltiness washed against his tongue. They savored mouthfuls for several minutes.

After the servebot cleared away the plates from the first course, she said, "I've never been to a restaurant where you have to pay."

He resisted an urge to do a double take. "That happens at the gastronomic places. Like here, where the owner is so creative and is known for his food artistry." Evie's eyes lit up. Did she not realize she was a food artist too?

"For the chef making it, that's a good reason. But for the people eating, is it only about the food, or also about the experience? A way to be different from everyone else?"

"Probably both," he acceded. "I think the urge to create, to strive for beauty for its own sake in whatever you do, is valuable. But I know you believe in social equality and justice, and I agree with you. It's bad to elevate yourself merely because you can have something others cannot have."

"Yes, it's like everyone here is showing off." Evie frowned. "Is that why you took me here? To show off?"

"I didn't choose to come here to impress anyone. It was more about you. I wanted you to have a memorable experience after being cooped up for so long."

. . .

Why *did* I choose this restaurant? A little of both, if I'm honest with myself.

. . .

She smiled. "Well, I'm not complaining. This is a fun change."

They were interrupted by the pipabot waiter and another servebot with the next course. "A salad of fresh herbs, young fennel bulb, and toasted pistachios," announced the pipabot as the servebot placed the plates. The course was another pleasant surprise. He savored the nutty, earthy pistachios. Evie, wreathed by the flickering fire and reveling in obvious pleasure, sweetened his own enjoyment.

A young man carrying a cello stepped to an open area between tables. Three musicbots followed with analog instruments. They played, the musicbots with precision, and the young man with passion in his bow. The melodious notes added another background to the murmur of conversation from the tables.

Joe put down his fork and pushed the salad plate to the side. "I know so little about you. What music do you like?"

Her eyes widened. "I meant to tell you. Something I found on your allbook. I have liked it since I first listened to it years ago—Mahler's Fifth."

"Really? I like Mahler too. Well, you know that . . . from my allbook. I especially love the 'Adagietto' slow movement."

"The fourth movement. He was writing about his wife." Her face flushed as she sipped her wine.

Joe nodded. "I relate to the line 'I am lost to the world.'"

Her hazel eyes studied him. "He was actually so bound up with the world through his love for his wife, Alma, that the line may well be the opposite of your idea of lost to the world."

"It's a truer explanation. Can you lose yourself to what you find in the world?"

The pipabot waiter was back with a servebot and announced, "The next course is an enhanced-flavored C4 rice risotto and includes aged Parmesan cheese and shaved black truffles."

"Wow, this risotto is delicious. Creamy with an earthy touch from the truffles." Evie paused between each bite, as if to savor every layer of flavor.

Joe's attention was still on music. "I'm surprised you've heard of Mahler. He's ancient."

Evie seemed to suppress an eye roll. "The higher Levels don't have a monopoly on musical taste."

"I'm pointing out similarities of taste, not differences," he said, raising both hands. The way she peered back at him, reflecting the intensity of her commitment to her movement, reminded him of another of his shortcomings. He blurted it out. "Look, one reason I like you is that you have a purpose. I don't understand everything driving you, but at least you have passion for something. I'm still looking for something that can make me feel the same way."

She eyed him in silence while servebots interrupted to clear the table and serve the next course. The pipabot announced, "The main course is a slow-cooked fillet of wild Scottish sea trout, a Dungeness crab beignet dressed with pickled garden onions, watercress leaves, and a béarnaise mousseline sauce. Please enjoy."

They savored the rich flavors, and it felt like some wall between them had fallen. She leaned toward him without reserve. The wine made him languid, his head dreamy. Evie seemed subdued, maybe still mulling over his last comment, and she studied him.

"Joe, I don't expect you to understand the world I come from—the world of the bottom Levels."

"You aren't so different. Just another person. Well, not just another person. A special person." Joe glanced around the now nearly empty restaurant and struggled to make a joke. "For me, you're the only woman in the world."

A brief smile played on her lips, then her gaze locked on his as if to make an earnest point. "Yes, people are similar everywhere. But the social milieu does make a difference. It's one reason I'm concerned with how society structures our interactions."

"I would like to know about your world."

"Maybe I can show you sometime."

. . .

A breakthrough. She is opening up, willing to share more about herself.

. . .

The servebot brought the final course, with the bot waiter announcing, "The dessert is crêpe gâteau, which consists of a soft goat's milk cheese, pickled green strawberries, hazelnuts, and garden sorrel." Though they both had eaten the entirety of the previous courses, leaving not a morsel, they lingered over the creamy dessert and idled over the last of the wine.

Joe was about to suggest it was time to go, but Evie took his hand. "I'm sorry if I've seemed ungrateful for your help. I think it's partly because I've been worried about my friends, and I feel responsible. But that's not an excuse for bad behavior. I have been self-absorbed."

"No harm, no foul. But thanks for saying so. I wasn't exactly the best host." Joe smiled, feeling better to have been open and vulnerable about his shortcomings. She returned the smile and gently withdrew her hand.

It was late, and the restaurant had emptied. His gaze moved from the silky hairs on her arm, backlit by the fireplace, to her eyes, now relaxed above the wineglass held in both hands. They shared the silence, and Joe didn't want it to end.

Reluctantly, Joe signaled to the bot waiter, which arrived and whispered the total. Joe reached to turn on his NEST, but her hand shot across the table to stay his. He fixated on her touch and the delicate hairs of her forearm. A frantic expression clouded her face, and she leaned in close to him.

"Do you have dark credit$?"

. . .

Dark credit$? We have the privacy laws protecting us. But . . . I should be using dark credit$.

. . .

He shook his head.

"I'll get this." Evie pulled a purple tile from her belt and pointed it at the bot.

It acknowledged payment with blue painting its forehead, then escorted them to the door. "Thank you for visiting with us this evening. We hope you enjoyed the chef's creations."

"Please pass along our compliments to the chef," she said. Green flashed across the bot's forehead, lighting the path as it bowed.

When they had walked a block along the dark lane, Joe said, "Thanks for dinner. I thought I was treating you."

"I'm happy about how you're treating me. I had a nice time."

She slipped her hand comfortably into his. They strolled back, holding hands, watching the first quarter moon settle on the horizon. At the apartment door, he said, "I'll give you the codes so you can come and go as you please. Honestly, I should have done that before. The bots will ignore any visitors with access."

Evie ducked her head, embarrassed. "It was probably for the best that you didn't. I would've left more often, threatening us both."

Joe nodded, and they went upstairs. Evie walked toward her room but stopped short and turned to him. "Thanks again. I enjoy spending time with you." Her head tilted back to study his face, then she went into the bedroom and softly closed the door.

CHAPTER 18

Two days later at breakfast, she came out of her bedroom wearing a lavender jacket and leggings tucked into black boots. Joe didn't recognize the clothes and smiled with approval. "Your taste is superior to mine. How did it feel to shop for yourself again?"

"You did a fair job, so thanks for the effort. But everyone has their own style. I wanted to have something more *me* before I go back home."

Joe's stomach clenched. "You're leaving?"

"I need to see who was arrested and talk to a few friends so we can decide what happens next." She looked mournful and said, "All I know is that Julian and Celeste have been sent away." Her gaze betrayed worry, touched by self-doubt, an emotion he'd not seen in her before. "I feel bad, knowing that I made the decision to hold the protest that night but that everyone got arrested except me."

"You couldn't have foreseen all the consequences."

"Still, I'm uncomfortable being free while everyone else is in danger."

"I understand." He swallowed and tried to sound casual. "Will I see you again?"

"Do you think that's a good idea? Remember, we're breaking the law seeing each other." She bit her lip.

"I thought you were the rebel. What happened, did you drink the same poisoned wine you're protesting?"

Her gaze fell. "It's difficult to extract yourself from your own cultural norms, even when you believe they're wrong."

He stood and took her hands in his. "You've convinced me. Let's be rebels together."

"Yes, I will be back." She squeezed his hands.

"Great. Please come and go as you please. You have the door codes."

Joe turned to head out the door for the office, but he changed his mind and reached for her, wrapping her in a gentle hug. "Be careful. I'll see you soon." Then he was down the stairs, an empty feeling in his chest.

His morning was wasted at the office, an idle reverie in which he became absorbed by the subtle interplay of sun and shadow outside his window. In an attempt to snap out of it, Joe took his exercise run early, then ate a healthy lunch.

Upon returning to his office, a message appeared on his NEST. Mike's bearded face materialized on the holo screen, his merry cheeks creasing.

"Joe, I have an interesting opportunity for you." He rubbed his hands together. "Are you familiar with the WISE Orbital Base?"

"I've followed it. It's the centerpiece of the World Interstellar Space Exploration project. A construction base in orbit around the moon for the last decade. Interesting."

"The current project commander—the person responsible for this phase of assembly—is a friend. Her name is Dina Taggart. She has a problem. You may be able to help."

"That sounds far afield from what I'm working on. Why did you think of me?"

"Dina directs a big operation, with a human oversight staff and a fleet of bots. Glitches have bollixed up the construction. Dina suspects something is amiss with the bots. Your expertise in AI design, plus your skill with a netwalker, could provide answers."

. . .

Something very different, yet in some ways like the old hack attacks. Startling, how my world can change in a second.

. . .

"Mike, I appreciate your thinking of me for the job. That sounds intriguing. Please introduce me."

Mike relayed the contact information. "Luck to you," he said before signing off.

With new purpose, Joe spent the next three hours reviewing information about the WISE project and Dina Taggart. Beginning with advanced degrees in physics, design, and engineering, she had moved on to an impressive career. Her current job as base commander capped a series of important scientific projects, each larger than the one before. He closed the data feeds, awed and intimidated.

After a moment of reflection and a deep breath, he opened his NEST to initiate the encrypted contact Mike had given him. The net com opened, and a minute went by as he waited for a response.

"Mike told me to expect your contact. I'm glad to talk to you," a throaty voice answered. Her holo appeared on his com a moment later. She had brown hair, cropped short in a businesslike style that swept to her jawline. With few superficial niceties, Dina interviewed Joe about his background. She was aware of his VRbotFest pastime. After several questions, he relaxed and enjoyed the conversation. But a worrying thought entered his head.

"I'm thrilled to help any way I can. This is a welcome opportunity." Joe cleared his throat, unsure if his next sentence would be a deal breaker. "I'm not sure I have all the security IDs that might be needed."

Dina stared solemnly into his eyes. "You're referring to your Level, eh?"

"Yes."

"Your AI knowledge is impressive, and your netwalker skills will save time on the learning curve for the immediate problem I have. Mike said you're smart and knowledgeable, I can tell you are good at what you do, and that's all that matters to me." She paused. "I'd like you to join the team."

Joe let out a breath. "I'm honored to help you."

She brightened and then grew somber. "There is one issue. There's one silly rule I cannot get around, and it will create a handicap for you. Because you aren't at least a Level 25, you'll need to turn off the data storage feature on your NEST. The government is afraid of secrets leaking out."

"Everyone has a handicap of some sort." Evie's face invaded his memory. "Besides, I've had practice getting along without the crutch of my NEST memory."

"Very good. When can you start?"

"Immediately." An involuntary grin crossed his face. It would be nice to work on a practical problem again. The theoretical work had been going nowhere lately.

Dina laughed. "Tomorrow will be fine." She gave him the details to meet via steerbots the next day.

———————————◆———————————

After a short commute on the hyperlev the next morning, Joe found the steel tower that served as the WISE regional office building in Salinaston. A desk pipabot registered him, then another pipabot escorted him to an upstairs room. Individual netwalking cubicles lined the room's inside perimeter, with a single door for each.

The bot pointed to a netwalking cubicle and said in an authoritative female tone, "Mr. Denkensmith, here is your equipment. You may join your host whenever you are ready."

Inside, he found the familiar elevated platform with the treadmill, cables, and suit suspended from the ceiling. Stepping onto the platform, he donned the haptic vest and tightened it, adjusted the harness, slid his feet into the boots, and positioned himself on the folding seat. He verified the transition between position modes. The seat popped up and down to simulate moving from sitting to standing, walking, and running. The gloves came next, and he flexed his fingers to verify accurate contact. He slipped his head into the surround headset, a Markarian 421 model. He turned on his NEST and connected to the console but disabled the storage feature.

. . .

There goes my memory access. This, too, will be a new experience.

. . .

He thumbed the avatar button to the default "authentic" setting, and it copied a replica of Joe's face into the rig. The headset hummed. The initial monochrome green all around him was replaced by a white light.

. . .

Excellent quality equipment. This could get addictive. Let's see how the steerbot differs from a VRbotFest virtual machine.

. . .

Since he would meet Dina on the WISE Orbital Base, their steerbots would experience a 2.6-second round-trip signal delay on haptic response. The voice delay would depend on where she was physically. He focused himself, opened the connection, and he was immersed in the net interface.

Joe found himself standing in an unadorned control room. More particularly, he found himself embodied within a steerbot standing in a rack along one spartan gray wall. To his left and right stood similar machines. Releasing the constraints, he shuffled forward out of the bracket. Joe stopped, waiting for his brain to catch up with the double translation—the movement of his body in the netwalker echoed by the movement of the steerbot on the orbital base, translated through sets of servomotors. He then had to wait for the signal delay to communicate that his movement was complete.

Joe wobbled, then examined the boots on the feet of his bot. He took another tentative step and heard the *thunk* of the boot holding the steerbot to the ferrous floor panel as the smart electromagnets adjusted to his biometric feedback. His next steps felt natural.

"A quick study, I see. Most visitors take much longer to adapt to those Radus boots."

The forehead of the bot facing him glowed silver, and Dina's face was visible behind the visor. She smiled, and her steerbot reached out a mechanical hand. "Dina Taggart. Glad to see you here at WISE Orbital Base." She gripped his hand, and Joe felt a powerful squeeze via the haptic suit.

. . .

If that's her real handshake, then she's already remarkable. It probably is, since it's uncouth to play with the settings when wearing your self-avatar.

. . .

"You said *here* at WISE Orbital Base—are you in moon orbit?" Joe caught sight of his reflection in her visor and started. There he saw the silvered forehead of a steerbot with his face projected behind the visor. He looked like a tin man he'd once seen in a vintage video clip, and it gave him the eerie feeling he was a pipabot.

"Want to know where everything is, eh? I'm on the States' south coast in another WISE office, here by way of a steerbot, same as you. But I do physically move myself to the orbital base several times each year. And with the issue you've been called to resolve, I should physically be on the base now." A frown darkened her face. She motioned for him to follow her, and they clanked to a glass elevator. It zipped one floor upward, stopped with a *whoosh*, and the door opened.

They shambled into a circular room about thirteen meters in diameter, the walls and ceiling one large glass bubble. Outside, the blackness of space was dotted by millions of stars. The gigantic sphere of the moon seemed to dangle, a diamond casting shadows on the floor. Dina led him to a horseshoe of eleven square chairs bolted to the metal floor in the center of the bubble. Magnetic seat restraints locked the steerbot in place, which proved much more comfortable than fighting the tendency to float off in the zero-gravity environment of the base. A bank of computer control consoles and a holo-com filled in the open end of the horseshoe. Behind the inner ring of chairs was a second ring with more seats. The bubble window afforded a grand view of the entire base. This must be the central area for operations when anything important was afoot.

"Welcome to the bridge of WISE Orbital Base. The base is assembling a series of interstellar space probes and ships, with the inaugural probes scheduled to leave in three years. We are also adding to the orbital base infrastructure," she said. As she outlined the project, she pointed to the parts of the orbiting assembly base seen from this vantage. He tried to follow all the details, mesmerized by the panorama and the experience of sitting on a space base in orbit. The ship felt more austere, gritty, and genuine than other VR facsimiles he had encountered. After the introduction, she summarized the most recent difficulties.

"Problems have slowed construction over the past month. We had an accident when two large sections failed to attach, resulting in damage to one assembly module. The failure is unexplainable except by saying that there are odd glitches, and we can't get to the bottom of it. I'm managing five hundred mechas at the front lines, with a hundred pipabots to interface. Hundreds of people in various offices oversee the bots. We have a dozen people in netwalkers who should be able to see everything through their steerbots. The video feeds are continuous, and we have people in WISE offices reviewing the automatic software that processes the work. It's incomprehensible to me that with all that oversight, we can't get these large sections to come together correctly. Especially since we've managed more complex operations with ease." She finished with a disgusted gesture toward the work outside the window.

Joe fastened on the orbital dynamics. "We're in a six-day orbit circling the moon, right?"

"Yes, a near-rectilinear halo orbit. It keeps us out of the moon's shadow so communication with our Earth offices is easy. It simplifies station-keeping. The fabrication factories are located at three moon bases. We can transport materials and finished modules up from the surface when we get to closest lunar approach, within the thirty-one-hour window that will be ending soon."

He concentrated on the details, watching the robot transports moving up from Mare Imbrium in a steady stream heading to the station. He felt an urge to see the orbital base from outside.

"Do you suspect something is amiss with the bots' control software?"

"We've rounded up the usual suspect theories with no success, so it's another idea to test," she said.

They discussed his next steps. Joe would begin working immediately, examining any odd behavior that might suggest software failure. He could use the netwalker to control a steermech or steerbot to investigate the activity, focusing on the mecha and pipabot interactions. He would also review data logs at the WISE regional office, in order to avoid the haptic delay for desk work.

"Go out there and give'r," she said, ending the conference with another firm handshake. She seemed tired as she turned to greet two other steerbots who had exited the elevator and were waiting respectfully. Even though her steerbot was identical to all the others, the way she carried herself suggested someone much in charge of this vast machine. That impression lingered as Joe descended in the elevator.

He shuffled back to the rack to secure his bot and sent the command to exit. The regional office walls materialized around him again. The project would be challenging and exciting. He was energized to begin.

◆

Joe was in his steermech, perched on a ladder. After six days, the WISE Orbital Base had become familiar. He could scramble around on the superstructure or float weightlessly in one place to dissect the assembly process as he tried to relate the robotic work to the schedule Dina had shared.

The entire colossal structure was lit by rope lights to ward off the darkness of the void. The core structure was a long, rectangular spine that ran thirteen hundred meters end to end. Besides life-support systems, the spine contained two ferrous-plated moving walkways, which allowed bots, steer-bots, and the rare human to traverse the length in both directions with minimal energy expenditure. He had ridden the moving walkways back and forth and trekked the entire length, his Radus boots clinking against the non-moving metal plate in between. But it was more comfortable, and more exciting, to propel along the outside with thruster jets. With short puffs noiselessly pushing him, Joe could observe the airlock modules spaced at intervals where transport ships could dock, and manufacturing modules that hung from the blue steel spine between the airlocks. There were several ships there now, their cylindrical hulls sticking out perpendicular from the station's spine.

Each end of the spine finished in a fusion power module. They were spaced apart in case of catastrophic failure and explosion, to avoid total power failure to the station. No need for the tungsten disulfide nanotube solar panels found everywhere on Earth buildings, because a gram of fuel could produce all the fusion power ever required. The power modules looked like blue doughnuts, housing the twisted, torus plasma containment cores and their fusion reactors.

Anchoring the center of the orbital base, the bridge module was a silver bi-level saucer, with the glass-windowed bubble of the bridge itself on top. It resembled an alien spaceship from a retro cartoon. Jutting out opposite it on the spine was a long support cylinder and the single artificial gravity ring around it, like another blue doughnut on a stick, spinning lazily to provide a low-gravity resting area for the humans who spent extended time on the base.

The station layout was as logically named as a mathematician could wish. From the central bridge module, one branch of the central spine was named Alpha and the other Omega, and the fusion reactors at each end were Alpha Reactor and Omega Reactor. Airlocks separated the sections of the spine, with each section named consecutively from the bridge: A, B, and so forth toward the Alpha end, and AA, BB, and so forth toward the Omega Reactor. Joe loved being outside to admire the exquisite machine.

But now, beads of sweat rolled off his face. His biceps ached from moving the steermech's controls for the past three hours. Compounding his discomfort, Joe needed a bio break. His bladder became more irritated by the minute. He glanced down the steel side of a cargo bay on the spine of the base, then confirmed his boots were clamped to a standing rung. He filled his lungs, then deliberately expelled the air.

He opened his NEST and said, "Mecha in stasis mode, exit steermech."

The cargo bay, the steermech, and the star-filled surroundings dematerialized around him, replaced by his netwalker cubicle inside the WISE regional office. He took off the damp equipment, found the restroom and grabbed a synjug of iced water and an energy bar. Joe returned to the netwalker room, chewed the bar, and gulped all the water. He took seven minutes to flex his fingers and limber his neck, and to let the slight disorientation settle, like a sailor recovering his land legs after walking off a rolling ship. Joe then donned the netwalker again and returned to the steermech.

The steermech materialized around him, still attached to the ladder where he had left it. He flexed his fingers, and the mechanical hands moved with the 2.6-second delay. He took in the scene for a few seconds to reorient himself and to avoid vertigo. The only sound was his breathing.

A steel structure moved up from the moon, catching flickers of sunlight. Joe zoomed in with his NEST. The mechas nudged it toward the orbital base. He magnified further, and the name FACTORY MODULE 17 came into focus on the side. It was the most critical module to add this year and the same intercept that had last failed. Mechas would attach the factory module to the spine next to Cargo Bay F, where he stood. He methodically evaluated all the activity, shifting his attention from the new module to the mechas and the moon.

This factory module, a structure forty-three meters long, moved near the cargo bay. Mechas surrounded the module, their lights blinking as they guided it into position. Other mechas clung to the blue steel rigging platforms hanging from the spine. When the orbits overlapped in intercept, the factory module's thrusters would fire to complete orbital transfer and mechas would weld it to the station.

Beyond, the moon loomed waxing gibbous, the base looping close on its elliptical orbit. Joe studied the line of craters at the shadow line 1,500 kilometers below. He could not keep his heart rate from spiking. It was better than the best VR space game he had ever played. But this one was real, and his steermech was real, even if he was only embodied in it through the netwalker.

A shudder rang through the cargo bay and up into the heels of his steermech's boots. Joe jumped in the harness. A low rumble reached his ears. The only sounds in space were from contact, and the vibration from the metal ladder thrummed in his fingers when the factory module stopped moving. One end of the structure had crashed against the cargo bay, and ragged shards of metal cartwheeled away. The mechas fired thrusters to keep the metal structure from rotating. A pipabot's voice blared on the local com channel. "Assembly module attachment aborted. Stabilize and move the factory module away from the orbital base and suspend synchronized orbit."

. . .

A piss-poor time to have taken a break. Did I miss an important detail?

. . .

He released the heel clamps and fired his thrusters in short bursts to maneuver his steermech away from the cargo bay. He floated above the wrecked factory module end and tried to see between it and the spine. The edges closest to him were touching, but they were not parallel. Something had gone awry, but he could not deduce what had happened. There was no obvious pattern to the movements of the dozen mechas attached to the crumpled metal, and he clenched his fists helplessly.

Dina's voice trilled on his NEST. "Joe, I see you're out there in a steermech. Can you please join me on the bridge?"

"I'll be there in seventeen minutes."

With one more useless glance for clues in the activity patterns of the mechas, Joe maneuvered the steermech back to a docking pad. He passed through the airlock and shuffled carefully inside, taking care not to bump against the low ceiling, which proved difficult due to the steermech's height. He followed the corridor and then took the glass elevator up to the bridge. Dina's steerbot clanked up to him, a quizzical expression on her face.

"You were the sole person out there with the bots. Can you tell what happened?"

"Dammit, no, there was nothing I could see. Everything was going along fine. Until it wasn't."

"This incident is like the last intercept seven orbits ago when we failed to mate the module. That also caused some damage," she said.

He rubbed at his chin, then realized how silly the gesture must appear. "I need to analyze all the mechas out there to download their data. There must be clues to suggest the cause."

She inspected him critically. "You've been putting in many hours on this project—too many, in fact. I checked the logs. You are already five times the maximum limit this week."

"I don't see how anyone can get anything done in only twelve hours each week. I'm working what I want to work."

"And I'm required to follow protocols." Then her tone softened. "But I respect your work ethic and desire to help. I'll make an exception. You are free to work as many hours as you wish. I'll give you the override codes to investigate the mechas."

. . .

She's another renegade, not letting silly rules stand in the way. Sorry I let her down.

. . .

"Thank you. And I'm sorry I didn't stop this disaster today."

"Less of a setback than last time. The first reports are that we can repair the damage in near-moon orbit. I've ordered replacement components made at the moon base factory. We may be able to try again in seven days when we swing back around our orbit and intercept a day past periapsis."

"I'll do everything I can to have the answer by then."

Chapter 19

Joe stopped at his apartment after the WISE accident, ate dinner, and slept for eleven hours. He could tell that Evie had not returned, and she was not there when he awoke. The flat felt deserted and sterile. He decided it would save time if he moved to the regional office for the next week. Joe packed a bag of essentials, took the weekly supplies from 83, handed the trash to the cleanerbot, and locked the door.

Back at the WISE regional building, he requested a larger space. A pipabot led him to the third floor and ushered him inside an office. His eyes took stock of the room: larger but ascetic, with a wall com above a desk in one corner and the netwalker in the center. He requisitioned a sleeping cot, a food synthesizer, and basic food supplies. The bots installed the equipment within an hour, leaving everything crowded around the raised netwalker platform. The room would work fine.

Joe spent the next five hours at his new desk, analyzing the data logs. He was taking a short break to eat when an incoming message from Dina blazed on the com. She had organized a conference at the orbital base to review the incident, beginning at 16:00. Joe acknowledged.

An hour later, he stood in the netwalker and opened the connection to the orbital base. His room vanished, and he found himself embodied in his steerbot and standing in the rack along the wall. Two other steerbots shuffled forward, their boots scraping against the metal floor. He recognized one as Dina and followed her up the elevator.

The glass bubble of the bridge overlooked a shrinking moon. Two pipabots and two people were already seated in the semicircle of chairs, and the humans glanced up as he entered. They both wore spacesuits with helmets off. The first was a scowling woman sporting neon-red hair. Beside her was a tall man who twirled his helmet around his index finger. The bridge lacked any seat of command—all the seats were intentionally arranged in a collegial style. Joe took a chair facing away from the moon so he could concentrate on the people.

"Let me introduce my executive staff," Dina said with a wave of her hand. "Starting with Robin Perez, our Guidance, Navigation, and Controls System Officer, or GNC for short."

Joe regretted his disabled NEST storage and his discarded PIDA, but he repressed the emotion and concentrated on remembering names and positions.

The scowl hadn't left Robin's face when she said, "Commander, I apologize for letting this accident happen. I won't allow anything to damage the base again on my watch." Her lava locks glowed fluorescent against the backdrop of space behind her.

"We'll find the cause together." Dina nodded supportively. "Next we have Chuck Williams, Docking Dynamics Officer." She pointed to the tall man with curly dark hair who had been spinning his helmet. "We pronounce the acronym 'DIDO.'" His broad smile reminded Joe of Raif.

"And finally," she gestured to the last man in a steerbot, "Jim Kercman, Construction Operations Officer."

Joe concocted a quick mnemonic.

. . .

Robin redbreast, the early bird gets the worm;
Chuckles; and Captain Kerc.

. . .

Dina turned to the pipabots. "And now to our bots. PIPA 13691, or Boris, is Deputy of Payload Operations. And PIPA 13693, or Natasha, is Deputy of Data Systems." Each pipabot's forehead glowed blue after its introduction.

Dina explained Joe's temporary project role. The introductions finished, she asked each deputy to give a summary of what they knew about the docking incident. Each officer took turns around the table, briskly presented, and then ceded the floor to the next. There were several questions after each summary.

"We've analyzed the video data and, so far, haven't found a reason for the docking failure." Chuck's frustration was evident in his voice. "The WISE Northeast Ops Center has been combing through the ARMO feeds and running VR simulations with the data. Nothing obvious from all the vid angles recorded. Now we are reviewing every bot and mecha involved, but we must download the data individually."

"Payload Operations finds no deviations from the plan," Boris said.

"Data Systems finds no errors in our systems, all nominal," Natasha responded.

Jim and Robin presented similar reports.

No cause was apparent.

Joe considered where additional data to parse the problem could come from. "The mechas form a mesh network to communicate with one another to coordinate work. That network shares certain perception data. Has that been examined?"

Jim leaned forward. "Not to my knowledge. It's tricky data to make sense of. The mechas are fitted with magnetic field sensors, with the magnetoreception data processed through deep learning algorithms. Those sensors cover 360 degrees, including behind the mecha."

Robin jumped in. "The problem arises in the difference between bot perception and our perception. It's difficult for us to understand what that 360-degree magnetoreception sense is like."

"Similar to trying to comprehend what it is like to be a bat," Dina said.

"There must be sound-sensor data coming from vibrations through the hull. But that's limited to when structures are in contact," Joe said.

Chuck laughed. "In space, no one can hear you scream."

Joe chuckled, and Dina smiled. If she was frustrated at the lack of progress, she didn't show it.

Dina leaned back in her chair. "Let's try to find creative solutions. How about a brainstorming session? I suggest we begin with a quantity over quality bias, and we can pare that list later."

Ignoring the bots, the three officers, Dina, and Joe launched into a freewheeling discussion for thirty minutes. Dina kept the conversation moving forward, efficient and effective in eliciting a list of ideas, which crystalized into a list of actions. Boris and Natasha added technical comments when prompted for information but otherwise were uninvolved. When the flow of ideas slowed, Dina ended the conference with a quick "Good work, team" and a tilt of her jaw, and they trooped out with their assignments. Robin, Jim, and Dina left quickly, while Joe and Chuck waited together at the elevator.

"I'm glad you're here. This problem drops squarely in my area, so I appreciate any help," Chuck said.

"I'm awed by Dina's leadership. You have a good team, and I'm glad to be part of it."

Chuck nodded. "Dina works nonstop, and on the right things, so we're motivated to be right there. We all have bigger dreams because of her."

"No one seems to be counting hours," Joe said. They entered the elevator.

"I'm glad you aren't either."

"I noticed the two bots have deputy titles," Joe said.

"Yes. All the senior officers here are humans. Turns out bots are not creative thinkers."

Joe chuckled. "They can't think out of the box?"

"No. Definitely bots in a box."

"A creative process like brainstorming requires comfort with ambiguity. And impatience, because we'll drive ourselves crazy until we solve this. If we knew where we were heading, then it'd be easier to get there," Joe said.

"Do any of us know where we're going?"

They exited the elevator, and Joe noticed Chuck was twirling his helmet again. It was a clever trick, using centripetal force to keep it there on his finger in zero gravity. It would be even harder to do from inside his steerbot with the 1.3-second time delay, and twice that before he would have visual confirmation of what his hand had done. On impulse, Joe reached out with one finger, speared the helmet from Chuck, gave it three turns, then clutched it in his hand again. He handed it back.

"Wow." Chuck laughed. "I've never seen anyone do that from a steerbot."

Joe took the compliment cheerfully. "We're not one of these machines. We can laugh, so we shouldn't take life so seriously that we miss the opportunity."

. . .

> Jardine is right. We need to remember we may do anything, even the unconventional and the unpredictable. And we can laugh.

. . .

"Do you have a bot for a deputy?"

"Nope." Chuck spun his helmet again as he turned away, deadpanning, "But if I did, I guess it would need a stutter."

It was more than a 2.6-second delay before Joe laughed. D-DIDO indeed.

CHAPTER 20

Joe's gaze rested a moment on the ugly beige wall of the WISE office. He had spent the last two days huddled there, eleven hours at a time, either analyzing data logs or netwalking. Paging through the records for the mechas and pipabots that were operational during both accidents was a drudgery, and he interspersed his research with frequent quick breaks. The office room provided the taste of real meals from the food synthesizer and the dreamless sleep of exhaustion on the cot.

By contrast, inhabiting the steerbot in space felt immediate and visceral. Clumping along the central spine, the susurration of work done outside vibrated through the long hull like it was a living creature. He whisked down moving walkways and paced corridors in his exploration of the base, his boots clinking on the metal floor. The mechas moved past, their triangular heads seeming to look at nothing. The elliptical-headed pipabots often displayed a default obsequious smile. He looked for the blinking orange forehead lights that denoted robots.

Steermechs and steerbots—managed by humans with netwalker connections, like Joe—passed less frequently. A silver light shone from their foreheads, and Joe waved at all of them. The steerbots and steermechs invariably waved back and usually stopped to chat.

He got to know several more of the WISE employees. Everyone expressed frustration about the recent accidents, and no one had any ideas to help. Still, becoming familiar with the rhythms of the project felt good.

Three days after the accident, Dina's steerbot approached Joe in the corridor. For once, there wasn't a line of people waiting to consult with her. "Let's discuss the investigation, eh?"

Pleased by the invitation, he followed her to the bridge where they sat in the outer ring of seats. Three pipabots and a steerbot stood at the control console, communicating through the holo-com. The base was at apoapsis in lunar orbit, and the moon hung in inky blackness outside the window. It had shrunk compared to three days before, but still appeared about five times larger than he'd ever seen it from Earth.

Forcing his full attention to Dina, Joe recapped the steps he had taken. She nodded encouragingly and then said with a wry smile, "That's a lot done in twelve hours."

He winked at the fiction. "It feels good to be so immersed in satisfying work." He paused, then asked about the next phase of the WISE project. "Speculation about the first starnauts fills netchat. I don't suppose you'll be recruiting soon?"

Dina laughed. "The future arrives slower than in our imaginations. Don't you know who will leave on the first ship? A single specialized bot. It's a miniaturized mecha with an advanced AI."

Joe's shock reflected off her visor.

"And that bot will leave decades after a dozen miniature probes, which are needed to send back information to help pinpoint the most favorable destination exoplanets."

"But there's a prodigious amount of construction now. Why does it take so long?"

Dina sighed. "Einstein's relativity equations hold. From his mass and energy equation, it will take a ridiculous amount of energy to get any significant mass to the minimum one-tenth light speed we need to achieve. Given the time to accelerate to that, then the time to decelerate, arrival to any target star and solar system takes around ninety-seven years. And that requires a complex, miniaturized, fusion-powered rocket. We won't be ready to transport people on an interstellar voyage for, realistically, another two centuries or more. When it comes to interstellar travel, we're still in the training immersives."

"Not for lack of effort. I'm impressed by the magnitude and complexity of this construction project. You're doing phenomenal work."

"My management of WISE Orbital Base is one of many space projects. We have a dozen manned moon bases, three bases on Mars, and one on Phobos. Not to mention astronomy programs, such as the radio observatory on the far side of the moon, the mining operations on the moon, and the xenon mining on Mars, with bots collecting minerals. We've fully automated metals mining operations on the two NEO asteroid bases. Many of those projects are supporting the WISE effort. It's incorrect to ascribe too much to any one person."

"You're too humble."

"I'm not even a planeteer yet. I haven't spent a decade off-world, like more than a thousand other people have. It's an enormous commitment to live your life that way, and there's a price to pay. They accept the health risks of space and adjust to low or no gravity with exercise commitments. They leave behind all the people they know for long periods." Dina looked in the direction of the moon. "They are akin to the adventurers who opened the American West, for good and ill. Those were not only famous names like Lewis and Clark, Fremont and Carson. They were also the pioneers in little houses on the prairie. Our current-day space explorers make the same sacrifices."

"But you are leading one of the major efforts." Joe wanted more than anything to convey the immense respect he had for her.

Dina's visor faced Joe's squarely. "This is a critical point. Human beings credit too much importance to the actions of single individuals. Historically, inventors such as Tesla made noteworthy innovations, but even they had teams in their labs. Those easy rocks have been turned over, and human invention is a group process. The reality is, as Newton once said, a few are fortunate to stand on the shoulders of giants."

"You don't see giants calling to their brothers?"

Dina remained serious. "That's a heroic story to tell. But, no, the real story of human progress is a collective advance led by social genius."

He pressed his argument. "I've heard one Einstein is worth a university. And one Atlas can lift the whole world."

"I won't deny individual excellence or its importance. But extreme self-confidence is also a flaw. That self-aggrandizement can lead to hubris and disdain for other people, and there is no justification for such self-absorption."

"You value the individual but also value collaboration. You respect what people can do when they work together," Joe said.

"We can celebrate excellence and simultaneously encourage humility. Avoid hubris. Recognize we are risen apes, not fallen angels."

The steerbot at the control desk waved. A stoic expression crossed Dina's face, and they reluctantly ended their conversation. She walked to the control console to listen to the latest problem. Joe headed to the elevator, back to work.

━━━━━━━━━━◆━━━━━━━━━━

Joe was up at dawn the next day to fix a quick breakfast before beginning the monotony of desk work, hunting for any clues in the exabytes of data. After five hours, he paused for a hastily eaten lunch. The bare walls of the WISE local office stared coldly back. He checked his NEST for messages and to see if Evie or anyone else had been by his apartment. The queue was empty. Minutes later, the realization that he had been staring at a blank wall startled him.

. . .

It's time for a change of scenery. I feel hemmed in, and empty space can be a cure. I can be master of my mood.

. . .

In eleven minutes, he was in the netwalker, transitioning to a steermech at WISE Orbital Base. He maneuvered the machine out of the rack to the base spine, and into an airlock, and soon he was hanging onto a ladder attached to the outside of the Omega fusion power doughnut.

Work proceeded nonstop as the base raced closer to the moon. Mechas covered the superstructure. Joe adjusted his corneal implant sensor to zoom in on a particular mecha, but he kept his distance to avoid interrupting the work. The intense activity was invigorating, and he lost himself in the rhythms of individual operations coordinated into unified purpose on the humongous machine.

While he rested on the ladder, another steermech approached him. Dina's face filled the visor under the silver light on its forehead.

"I guess I'm nervous about this next docking attempt." Her steermech grasped the ladder next to his. "That's why I'm out here."

. . .

I love her honesty. No pretentiousness at all.

. . .

"It's why I'm out here too. Not that watching the machines work helps unravel the puzzle. But it does let you unburden your head, to better focus."

They shoved off the ladders and drifted near the Omega Reactor, facing away from the station and from the moon, the ebony vista salted by millions of unwinking points of light. His vision adjusted, and he became lost for a moment in the pastel yellows and blues and pinks of the individual stars.

Surmising that her managerial reserve might be dissolved by the emptiness surrounding them as they floated in space, Joe took advantage of the moment. "You said you love this job, but it takes all your time. Why do you do it?"

"Joe, I've watched your determination to get something done. You're a competitive soul."

"I admit it."

"I am too." She stared out at the stars with what seemed to be his same fascination. "People traditionally competed over fortune, power, and fame. Today, the first is silly. The second still drives many but appeals less to me. I prefer to help advance everyone together."

"That leaves fame."

"Yes. I'd like to think that my efforts to advance humankind's exploration out here might be remembered a bit."

"It's a laudable purpose."

She turned her measured gaze on him. "We need to be out here if humankind is to make any advances. We've seen the bots cannot do it without our overall goal-setting and problem-solving."

Joe agreed. "We haven't been able to design AIs or bots that have any true consciousness, or even verifiable sentience. Though it is magnificent to watch what they can build to our plans."

She squinted into the blackness of deep space. "Being out here, you realize how trifling our exploration efforts are, and how impossibly large the universe is. We know about quasars, formed in the early universe, that contain supermassive black holes, which have swallowed twenty billion suns of matter. We know about spinning neutron stars—millisecond pulsars—whose equators rotate at a quarter of the speed of light. We can compute the mathematics, but the numbers are too large to hold in our heads. The universe was designed on a scale to dwarf our poor powers to imagine. We know about these stupefying distances between stars, and even more mind-bending distances between galaxies. The size of the universe is so staggering that human minds cannot truly comprehend the magnitudes."

"It is impossible not to feel inconsequential out here," Joe whispered.

"And the speed of light limit means we can never explore more than an infinitesimal fraction of this gigantic space in any conceivable time. The universe will end before humans—if we survive—can make any dent in exploration."

"And yet you try."

"And yet we try," Dina said. She waved, and her steermech jetted away to inspect another part of the base.

Joe hovered, weightless, near the fusion reactor. Dina embodied the higher aspirations of humanity, pushing the frontiers to know more, to explore farther, willing to suffer privations, forgetting self, accelerating the collective advancement of humanity. Yet another way to spend a life.

And what a universe it was to explore. Mechas clustered on a distant part of the base. To his right the moon was a minor orb, and to his left an even smaller Earth sailed on, isolated and far away. Most of his vision was filled with the immensity of black space.

. . .

Our entire galaxy is here surrounding me. One of a hundred billion galaxies. And the average galaxy contains hundreds of billions of stars, separated by vast distances, with the closest stars hardly reachable in a human lifetime. With all my mathematics and physics, I cannot imagine it. All this space, an immense void. A lot of nothing created. Created? Or did it just happen? How can we ever know?

. . .

His steady breathing only enhanced the overpowering illusion that he was there in space, a great aloneness. Then the experience of empty space transformed. The utter blackness seemed to dissolve, to move, to be filled with something. He was floating in *something*.

. . .

Conventional quantum physics says that the vacuum, teeming with activity, contains particles, dark matter, and dark energy, yet all at very low densities. I peer into this abyss, trying to see the key to nature.

Now I see not blackness, but perhaps an ocean of particles popping into and out of existence in every instant. A boiling collection of something, and I am part of it. I am in relation to the universe.

. . .

He exhaled deeply, feeling the soft work of his lungs. The blackness around him came back into focus. It was no longer fearsome and lonely. Instead, its embrace safeguarded him. After several minutes, he maneuvered his steermech back into the base station.

◆

Joe finished all his analysis of the available data and came up empty. None of the team's brainstorming had panned out, and impatient with the further delay, Dina ordered another try at orbital intercept.

Her construction team had transported components from the moon base at Mare Imbrium and were completing repairs to the factory module in close lunar orbit. It would be ready barely in time within the thirty-one-hour window to complete the partial Hohmann transfer because the base had passed periapsis, the nearest approach to the moon, and now hurtled away on its outward orbital path. They would synchronize orbits at several thousand kilometers from the moon.

He got a night's sleep, then virtually returned to the base. His steermech now hung onto a cargo bay ladder. An army of mechas blanketed the base's spine as they rotated components and welded them into place. From his vantage point, it was like a dance ensemble with the orbital base as the stage, and he watched the mechas perform piqué turns with out-stretched arms clinching the components. He knew there was no true up or down, but he mentally placed the moon below in his frame of reference, where it hung grand and luminous in the inky blackness. Then the moon highlighted a glint of metal. Joe adjusted his corneal sensor, and the approaching hunk of steel with "FACTORY MODULE 17" in stenciled letters on its side was visible. He held his breath. This time he would be laser focused on the docking maneuver.

The factory module moved within fifty meters of the attachment point on the spine, where moonshine shadows danced on the base's blue hull. There was a ladder nearby that would allow him to watch the docking from the factory module. He released the boot magnets on his steermech and maneuvered with his thrusters to the module, then grabbed a rung with both mechanical hands.

Two mechas were above him, guiding the factory module into position. He couldn't see the connection point where the metal walls would dock.

With sudden intuition, he released his hold on the ladder. Steermech thrusters nudged him over to the metal edge. Magnetic soles clamped his steermech to the lip of metal at the joint. Joe stared at the closing gap between base and module.

Movement along the edge of the base spine caught his eye—a cleanerbot. It moved up the spine into the space where the factory module would join the spine. The two guide mechas that had been pushing the factory module closer abruptly pushed it away. The top edge of the module pivoted.

. . .

What's that doing there? The cleanerbot has no business there. Something corrupted its program. Yes! Now I know why—it's right where it was during last week's attempt. It cannot happen again.

. . .

Joe issued a NEST command with the override codes. "Mechas, abort the last maneuver. Continue docking as initiated."

A pipabot chirped on the channel, "There is a seventy-one percent chance of damage to the cargo bay if this override proceeds."

"Maintain override. Continue original docking maneuver."

The mechas reversed thrust. The factory module stopped pivoting. After a pause, it swung into docking position. The gap between the factory module and the base spine closed, and the factory module banged against the cargo bay before pivoting straight against the spine. The cleanerbot was crushed in the metal vice of base and module. The sundering metal against metal vibrated through his soles. Parts pinwheeled away from the module. A corner of the cargo bay was dented, but from his vantage, the damage seemed light. The mechas welded the units together.

The pipabot chirped again. "Docking complete. Damage assessment underway."

Joe sat on the WISE Orbital Base bridge in his steerbot, admiring the completed maneuver with Dina. The factory module nestled in its assigned place on the spine of the base. Warmth lodged in his chest.

"It was a corrupted cleanerbot?" Dina contemplated him over the pyramid formed by her steerbot's fingers.

"As best we can tell." He leaned toward her. "The lack of recovered memory components has hampered the analysis. I'd like to submit the partial data to a database expert I know, to evaluate that angle. His name is Raif Tselitelov."

"If you think he's good, then I approve. But why didn't the cleanerbot's presence register in any of the data?"

"The mechas at the docking joint faced away from the bot as they maneuvered the factory module into place. They probably received magnetoreception data indicating an obstruction, but we couldn't parse it enough to recognize what they knew."

"So why did the mechas abort the docking?"

He scratched at his chin, once again feeling silly. "My guess is that even though the cleanerbot AI was damaged, it sensed its imminent destruction and sent a cry for help."

Dina nodded in sudden understanding. "Ah, the Third Law of Robotics—a robot must protect its existence as long as such protection does not conflict with the First or Second Law."

"Exactly." Joe nodded. "And the addendum—that a robot must protect other robots' survival as long as such protection does not violate the first three laws—was added to avoid wholesale destruction of bots if something went amiss. No doubt that programming is buried deep inside archaic code. That's likely why the mechas aborted and the first two dockings failed."

She frowned. "The bot's appearance at that time is still a weird coincidence."

"Actually not." He sat back again. "The cleanerbot is on a weekly schedule, and all three docking attempts occurred on Sunday."

Her eyes opened wide.

"No algorithms needed to decipher this, only elementary arithmetic. The first failure was seven orbits before the second, or exactly six weeks. And this last try was also a week later."

"I'd missed that obvious point." She looked crestfallen.

"You're on orbital time. I missed it initially too. Then your comment that I was the only person outside last week suddenly resonated." Joe raised a finger. "That's your other problem."

She waited, watching the jubilant expression he couldn't repress.

"Since your staff all work three days of four hours, those cluster from Monday through Wednesday, and then Thursday through Saturday. Sundays don't have full coverage. That may be why no person saw the malfunctioning cleanerbot earlier."

She laughed. "So much for hour limits. I'm glad we adjusted the rule for you."

"So am I." Joe cleared his throat. "I'm sorry about causing the minor damage to the cargo bay. And for losing the bot."

"I would have done the same to finish the docking. Of course, this would be a different conversation had something sentient been destroyed."

"Yes, it would," he said, even as he wondered if sentience alone would make him care.

PART TWO: THE JOURNEY OUTWARD

"There's a time when you're riding the wave, and you decide to turn, and the turn decides everything else afterward."

Joe Denkensmith

MAP OF THE COMBAT DOME

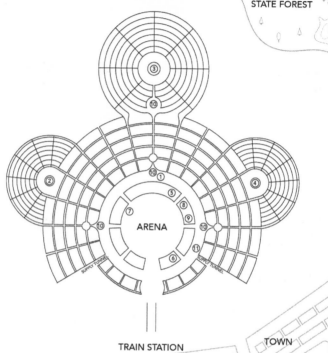

STATE FOREST

ARENA

SUPPLY TUNNEL

SUPPLY TUNNEL

TRAIN STATION

TOWN

N

(1) Main Concourse
(2) Alpha Annex
(3) Zeus Annex
(4) Omega Annex
(5) Medical Facility
(6) Mecha Storage Warehouse

(7) Sky Boxes
(8) Arena Offices and Administration
(9) Guest Apartments
(10) Plazas
(11) Alex's Shop

CHAPTER 21

The hyperlev back from the WISE regional office whispered down the track and lulled Joe into a pleasant reverie. Dina's warm praise reverberated in his head, along with her promise to invite him back for similar projects. He switched at the station to an autocar. Soon the college's stone gates welcomed him. The crisp campus air refreshed him after the weeks spent secluded indoors. At his office, he opened his com to check his messages and found a sizable bonus receipt from Dina for his work. It would buy more luxuries than he had ever had access to before. He opened an encrypted link to Raif, and a minute later his holo materialized.

"Seems like you've been busy." He winked. "Off doing the breaststroke?"

"No water where I've spent the past couple of weeks," Joe said. He filled Raif in on the project.

Raif's expression grew impressed as the story progressed. "You killed another bot? Joe, if I were a bot, I'd be alarmed by this serial behavior."

Joe shrugged, then described the docking of the factory module in detail. Raif asked Joe to repeat exactly what the robots did.

"There's something not right about that bot behavior. You would expect the bots to carry out the objective, namely the completion of the docking operation."

Joe nodded. "Bots follow given goals."

"That's concerning enough that I wish I could analyze it."

"One step ahead of you. Dina already approved your review of the data. I'll send you the contact information." Raif's expression was a mix of excitement and relief, and Joe surmised he must still be waiting for a job offer.

"One other thing." Joe lowered his gaze. "Can you help me exchange credit$ for dark credit$?"

"No problem." Raif smirked. "But why the worry now? You've always been one to trust the privacy laws, no matter how convincing I was that the funds could, theoretically, be traceable."

"My maybe-swimming partner convinced me to worry." Joe named the amount.

"Hot damn. Got credit$ fever?" Raif laughed. "I'll make the trade and pass the codes back later today."

Joe smiled and signed off.

———————◆———————

Joe bounded up the stairs of his flat, then abruptly halted near the top. Living at the WISE office had left him grubby. He ran his fingers through his disheveled hair to push it back into place and willed himself forward. Sunlight shone through the large window of the empty living room. Joe stood enveloped by the perfect silence. His arms hung at his sides. It was like the first time he had stood there, when he had arrived without Raidne—like a deaf man awakening from sleep.

A bedroom door opened. Evie walked into the room to stand framed in front of the window, a hand resting on one hip. She flashed a heartwarming smile.

Joe beamed in response. "Sorry for my appearance. I've been working hard."

"No apologies necessary for hard work." She stepped toward him and studied him closely for a moment, then reached up to smooth his untended whiskers. "You just look more driven under that sexy beard."

The flush rose from his chest to his face. Her smile was outlined against the window, and spring flooded into the room.

. . .

Time to update my Bayesian probabilities. She finds me sexy.

. . .

Evie pulled him to the sofa, where they sat close enough to touch knees.

"I came back three days ago and was worried when you didn't show up. Did your research take you off campus?"

Joe shook his head, then shrugged. "Well, my research didn't, but a project did—it took me all the way to the moon." He spent a half hour describing his WISE project, interrupted by her frequent questions. When recounting the breakthrough idea that led to discovering the errant cleanerbot, he tried to stay humble and give credit to the whole team. Evie's eyes danced when Joe described the base's leadership team.

"Sounds like you really saved the day. Or at least a lot of credit$. What kind of person is Dina?" Her gaze moved back and forth across his face, and Joe was happy she was so interested in his story.

"A great manager. More, a great leader. She knows how to direct a group of people on the right objective. She's inspiring."

"It must have been intense, spending time with the team."

"It was all-consuming for me. But we only met on occasion via steerbots. You eventually accept seeing someone's avatar through their visor." He went on to describe the experience of floating in space.

Evie smiled and said, "I'm hungry. Let me make dinner."

Joe took a shower while she was busy in the kitchen. The

return to their routine elated him. When he returned, his mouth watered at the savory scents of chicken, pepper, and tomato stew, and he attacked his bowl.

"Poulet Basquaise, from the French Basque countryside," she said when he tilted his head.

He dug in. "How are your friends?"

Evie ate a bite before answering. "Most are out of jail. Many are under surveillance, so I could only visit a few, and discreetly. But it now seems safe for me to go back, so long as I keep a low profile and avoid meetings—they draw too much attention." She frowned. "That's hard. But it's life now."

"I have a hard time picturing what your life is like."

"Do you want to understand how it's different?"

"Yes, very much."

"Let's go tomorrow." She smiled at him, and Joe thought he would do anything to have her smile at him like that every day.

❖

After a night spent in their separate bedrooms—unsurprising but still a disappointment—they left together in late morning. They took an autocar to the station, then the hyperlev three stops to the southern edge of Timsheltown, the larger city southeast of Lone Mountain College. Stepping out of the station, Joe stared up at the enormous gray monolith that obscured the entire horizon. It reminded him of his net travel exploration of Borobudur, the ancient Buddhist temple. The main dome sparkled in the sun, and three secondary domes encircled a side, gleaming like a pearl necklace. A pedestrian way led from the station to the entrance, the limestone worn by constant use.

"So that's the Combat Dome? It's bigger than I expected. I didn't realize there were all these surrounding domes attached to it." He checked his NEST, and statistics flashed on the corneal interface: "101 meters tall, 140,053 square meters, capacity of 200,029." The main dome was a fraction of the complex.

"It's called that by the mainstream net media, but not by those of us who live here. We call it the Community Dome, or just the Dome."

They walked side by side up the pedestrian way. Overhead, drones delivered supplies, and bots offloaded and shuttled them into the complex's receiving building. No bots seemed to go inside the Dome; instead, people moved supplies through what appeared to be a supply tunnel. The crowds of people streaming in and out resembled any other—a colorful assortment of a hundred fashions.

Joe and Evie stepped through the sweeping entrance arch. The interior was ringed by a wide concourse lined with shops, cafés, and entrances to apartments. A line of trees along the perimeter created a sense of being outdoors, though the entire complex was roofed with glass three stories above. An energetic hum rose from hundreds of conversations. No bots were in sight. It was a sea of humans. And bicycles. Joe had only ever seen one in a museum. He backed away from a pack of boys headed towards them, his heart pounding—not so much for his own as for their safety. He could only imagine the injuries possible in this crowded space. The only sign was one that announced the next competition in huge illuminated letters—BATTLE OF MECHAS AND EXOMECHS AT 15:00.

Joe turned on his ARMO to see what it would identify around him, but nothing materialized in the corner of his vision. "My ARMO is behaving oddly here," he said.

Evie chuckled. "We don't label anything with augmented reality tags, except in the arena."

"Why not?" He didn't think he'd ever been in a place unrecognized by his ARMO. It felt . . . freeing, in a strange way. Like he was exploring uncharted territory.

"Because the tags were commercial when first introduced, and the Dome community decided to keep our living spaces noncommercial."

She led him clockwise along the concourse that circled the main dome. Twice, when passing cafés, someone waved and she waved in response. At a branching concourse, they turned to the left. He checked his ARMO and realized it was one of many axial concourses radiating from the center. This one seemed to contain additional living quarters. The travertine floor had a gritty, lived-in feel, softened by sunlight beaming through the glass roof.

Evie slowed as they passed another café. "Are you hungry for lunch?"

Joe nodded, and they sat down. A young woman came over to give Evie a tight hug. "Welcome home." She seemed reluctant to let Evie go. "You'll have missed the news about Vinn and Bari—their wedding was two weeks ago."

"Oh, how wonderful. I'll have to visit Vinn and congratulate her myself. Thanks for letting me know, Yvette. Listen, this is my friend's first time here. Could you bring out your special?"

Yvette nodded, gave a big smile to Joe, and disappeared. A few minutes later, she brought out glasses of tea, followed by spaghetti Bolognese, and left them to enjoy their lunch.

"Is she a relative?" Joe wondered if this is where Evie learned to cook.

"No, she's a neighbor. This is a real community, and people know their neighbors and care about them." A thoughtful expression graced her face. "I shouldn't say that. She is more than a neighbor and a creative cook. She writes poetry too. People here follow many interests, though they rarely have the opportunity to display their talents outside the community."

The rich flavor of the sauce distracted him. "This is delicious."

"Families run most of the restaurants here. They've passed down recipes, and they like to share with the community." She glanced up from her own meal. "Of course, everything is free."

"And the bicycles?" He fixated on a man riding by. "I've never seen one actually used. Aren't they dangerous?"

Evie laughed. "Not if folks are polite and keep to the speed limit, which is eleven kilometers an hour." After another bite, she added, "Remember, the people living in and around the Dome are from the lower quartile Levels. Many trace their families to people who were the last to run heavy machinery. They're comfortable with analog."

"And with learning to ride a bicycle."

Evie's wry smile told him she'd ridden one. "If you fall off, you get back on."

They finished their lunch, thanked Yvette, and continued to meander through the Dome, with Evie leading. She turned right at another circular road. They were circling the central arena. He stopped at an intersection to admire the view. Far down the axial road, an imposing statue stood in the center of a plaza. "That is Zeus Annex, with its own dome. He's holding a thunderbolt."

"He's the Greek god of lightning and thunder, right?"

"And justice. Here, the artist was illustrating human control of technology. Many people here wish he'd held more tightly."

"And what about the lack of bots here? Is there a love–hate relationship with them?"

With an appreciative glance, she said, "You've got it. The bots of course do all the dangerous jobs, which no one could argue with. But they took away all the employment opportunities. Most folks here—or at least their grandparents— were once employed in the most basic jobs. They were wage slaves. They worked in heavy industries and operated the early bots, the exoskeleton models manipulated from inside the machine. Eventually, even those jobs perished."

They turned right again, reached the main concourse, and continued circumnavigating the arena. A shop caught Joe's eye. "A hairstyling shop. It's not done by bots here, like everywhere else?"

"Most of the hairstyling here is done by people." Evie brushed her own hair back. "You're right though, that bots took over that job sixty years ago, with the last pandemics. But then bioscience eliminated that threat. And now here, people like to give these personal services as a gift, and it's another way that people can be more in touch with those around them."

"Yes, literally in touch."

As they strolled past a shop displaying jewelry, an older man behind the counter saw them and waved them inside. Laser-cutting tools, machines, and microscopes covered the countertop. Bright eyes lit his weathered face. "Evie, I haven't seen you in ages." He gave her a fatherly hug, and Evie introduced Alex to Joe.

"Let me show you my latest creation." Alex shoved aside pliers and reamers littering a bench pushed against a wall, dug in a drawer, and held up a ring. They gathered around to see his handiwork. Mounted on the titanium band was a single red diamond, glinting in the light. "I got these diamonds shipped in from Mars. Isn't this one a beauty?"

"Magnificent." Her appreciation came through in the drawn-out breathiness of her voice.

"The only one I've ever seen," Joe said.

"Let's see it at home," the aged man said mischievously, his wrinkled face aglow. He reached for Evie's hand and deftly slid it onto her finger. It fit perfectly. She held it up to the light, and red beams danced.

"Can I buy it for you?" Joe forestalled Evie's obvious attempt at protest by holding up a hand. "I have dark credit$," he said to the man.

The man stared blankly. "It is a gift. For Evie, who played here near my shop as a child, and it is from my heart."

Joe hoped he had not offended Alex and tried to imagine Evie as a small girl, but he failed. She was so disciplined, as if she had sprung full-grown into the world.

Evie leaned in to give the man a kiss on the cheek. "I'm delighted to accept it."

Alex squeezed her shoulder. "Who's your guy?"

"A close friend," she said.

Joe shook Alex's hand and thanked him for his generosity. Then they waved and left the cheerful man to his craft.

. . .

Close friend.

. . .

They continued up the concourse, turning right at the next branch to head toward the center. "Sorry," Joe said. "I never imagined that you don't pay for such valuable stuff here."

Evie stopped, studied her ring, and then looked tenderly at him. "Our community is noncommercial. But that was very sweet of you. And so, it's a present from you too."

Joe smiled as they walked on. "Earlier you spoke about wages. While there are tons of red diamonds mined on Mars, there is a cost associated with transporting them to Earth. So how can your friend afford to give away his craft for free?"

"With the bots doing the work to extract and transport minerals, costs have fallen lower and lower. Folks here use dark credit\$—they need to pay for some things, such as these stones. And since he is unemployed, his time doesn't cost him any credit\$, so he can give away his creative work to those he cares about. We highly value gifts, but it's not about the material goods. What remains precious are the feelings attached to objects by those giving and receiving them."

"You have a sharing community."

"Most people here realize there's no longer a need to attach a price to anything. That's one lesson the Dome community learned that the rest have yet to learn."

The jeweler with the vivid eyes dominated his attention. "So that explains why he spends his time creating jewelry and then giving it away?"

"It's one reason." Evie stopped and faced him, ignoring the people shuffling by. "Alex is a brilliant astrophysicist. While he had perfect scores on his advanced math exams, he couldn't land any position to employ his talents."

"Perfect scores?" Joe felt his face grow hot.

"It's the same reason I couldn't get a position using my degrees. The Levels." She pointed back toward the jeweler's store. "That's the closest he gets to Mars."

. . .

The road race of life isn't fair. Each person starts life at a different point on the track, each has different opportunities. I can't congratulate myself on how near to a finish line I get, only how far I go.

. . .

Now he understood, and his face must have reflected the knowledge. She admired the ring again, and when she looked back at him, she was not angry.

They reached an entrance to the arena, the Dome visible through the glass wall. People surged past them and through the open doors. The next competition was ready to begin. Evie led them inside, and they found seats partway up one side of the amphitheater.

"The games are so popular that they've installed a large media center feeding netchat." She pointed to the glassed skybox opposite them.

"And an advanced medical facility, to deal with any injuries during games, I've heard."

She scoffed. "Sometimes someone is injured. The netchat sensationalizes how often that happens. It's rare for anyone to so much as lose a limb, and those are easily enough replaced."

"And what about references to the cyborg factory?"

Evie rolled her eyes. "There never was a cyborg factory. Millions of years of evolution didn't design the best interface for combining human biology with machines—quite the opposite."

"Just the technology for fixing injured parts," he said.

"There are fewer cyborgs here at the Dome than in the population. People shun biochips, and many refuse NESTs."

"Everyone talks to one another face-to-face. I don't see many folks preoccupied with their PIDAs."

"People here are suspicious about being watched when they go outside the community. They're suspicious of the government, which is why hardly any have a PIDA. The community tolerates bots, but not in large numbers." She seemed to anticipate his next comment. "I'm not saying people here do less evil than average. They are as good and bad as everyone else."

"Folks know each other and wish to be unknown by the AIs. You come by your mystery naturally."

Joe observed everything around him with rapt attention. He had only watched a competition once before on the net. He knew that a full mecha would compete against a human encased in an exomech. This would be the chance to experience it up close.

People filled the seats on either side of them. A burly man sat next to Joe. He was middle-aged—maybe seventy. The man coiled the golden hairs of his bushy beard with three fingers as he stared eagerly at center stage. Evie held Joe's hand when the walls supporting the dome flared with streaming red and blue lasers. Pillars of flame shot upward from eleven cannons around the stage, in time with a thunderous syncopated otzstep music beat. Many in the substantial crowd—at least, everyone under age fifty—were standing and dancing to the music. Evie laughed and rocked against him.

Holograms presenting the first contestants floated over the massive stage. From the right side, an exomech marched forward. The hologram above switched to a close-up of its human operator, whose name scrolled on the colossal screen walls.

The announcer bellowed over the crowd, "Here is Underman!" The crowd screamed and stomped their feet. From the left side, a regular mecha entered. The announcer's voice boomed again, "And facing our hero there enters Mace Face!" The crowd booed with a vengeance.

As he did when watching mod soccer, Joe synced his NEST to the holo stream. Underman's breathing filled his head. The feed brought him inside the exomech with the human contestant.

. . .

One reason they fill these stadiums—you never get the real feeling of being the athlete from an outside holo stream feed. This will be a new experience with a live, violent sport.

. . .

After several preliminaries, the machines squared off opposite each other. They dug their four cleated feet into the rough floor, their metal knuckles resting in front. Joe noticed both were locked into parallel leg articulation, leaving them less able to maintain balance. Servomotors in their jointed legs emitted a growl as they revved for a burst of power. A horn blasted and they sprang forward, their shoulders colliding with a bone-crushing clang. They grappled like sumo wrestlers from a bygone century. The clinch tightened, metal fingers clawing at each other, before they separated and circled.

Mace Face lunged forward and slammed his faceless head into the left arm of his human opponent, and the crowd booed. The exomech, elbow-down on the floor and left arm partially disabled, didn't move for a moment. The holo above displayed the perspiring face of the human inside as he frantically operated the controls.

Underman's gasping filled Joe's head, and he felt nauseated as a sudden terror engulfed him.

Underman lurched the exomech backward a meter to avoid the next blow. Joe jabbed at his ear and disconnected his NEST. He glanced around and noticed the Dome residents surrounding him weren't using the holo stream sync. Evie certainly was not, as she dispassionately watched the action while focused on the crowd.

Underman's retreat was not saving him. Mace Face charged forward and bashed his head onto Underman's damaged left arm again. It bent at the biceps, and the fingers on that arm froze. Underman lifted the mangled arm, but Mace Face struck again. Underman dropped the arm, but his right arm swept upward and slammed the mecha under his armpit, curling upward in an overarm throw. Mace Face flipped upside down.

The crowd yelled, *"Uwatenage!"* Underman hammered the mecha's chest from above. The exomech and mecha flailed at each other for several minutes, but the mecha's position left it vulnerable to a punishing fusillade of punches, and the referees called the contest. Underman raised his right arm to a crescendo of cheers from the amphitheater.

The burly man clapped wildly. "Here we are not always at the bot-tom," he said, drawing the word out. "Not below the bots." He laughed at his own joke. The jolly murmur skipped through the audience for several minutes as they prepared for the next match.

Joe leaned closer to Evie. "I'm presuming they handicap the mechas to give the exomechs a chance?"

"Yes, always, though the response delay is tiny. A few humans have gotten close to winning straight up," she said. "There are always the analog components—dirt and unpredictability."

. . .

That's why we watch sports. Because it's like being gods, watching randomness collide with wills at work, to see what happens.

. . .

Evie nodded toward the exit. "Let's go. I want to show you more of the complex." She led him to a side passageway and down a set of stairs that ended in a door deep in the bowels under the Dome. A door screen lit. Evie said, "Hi, Johnny." The door opened and they stepped inside.

A young man sat at the control desk in a guard booth. "Nice to see you." He grinned as he looked up.

"You too. I'd like to show a friend around, okay?"

"For you, Evie, sure." He motioned them toward another corridor.

At Joe's questioning glance, she said, "That was little Johnny. I helped care for him when he was a kid. In the

Dome, child-rearing is a community undertaking rather than a job for kinderbots."

She pointed out the corridor to the hospital but continued straight until the hallway opened into a large warehouse lined with stored mechas and exomechs. Joe stopped in front of an exomech, wondering how to get inside. He walked around it and saw a short metal rung protruding from the calf of the metal latticework leg. Joe put his foot on it and jumped up. He stepped inside, and his feet dropped into the footwells. He slid his arms into the sleeves, and his fingers found the controls. Even though he could see through the faceplate, the machine cradled his body like a coffin, and claustrophobia settled in. He pulled his hands free and dropped out of the shell.

"These must be hard to operate." He wiggled his arms, as if to shake off the closed-in feeling.

Evie nodded and gave him a small smile that faded quickly. Joe wondered what was on her mind, but she continued walking before he could comment.

They exited at the far end of the warehouse with the crowd roaring in the distance. They were now in the wings on one side of the stage. It felt strange to stand in the shadows, out of sight of the crowds. The two machines clinched on the stage for several minutes, and the ground vibrated when one flung the other to the ground. The rush of the crowd followed them as they descended the stairs and left through the far door. It shut behind them, and once again they were on the concourse.

"Maybe we head home, and have dinner and a glass of wine?" Evie seemed relieved to be out.

. . .

Head home. She thinks of it as home.

. . .

They strolled to the station. He found a wine shop, bought a synjug of a fine Napa Cabernet with his dark credit$, and they took the hyperlev back.

Evie busied herself in the kitchen, calling up one of her recipes on the food synthesizer. She set the table with steaming plates of chicken, drenched with a rich, dark sauce. "It's chicken mole, with a side of black bean salad with mango." She gazed at him in anticipation as he savored the first forkful.

He poured two more glasses of wine before the sun set, and they sat on the sofa together, enjoying the yellows and oranges melting onto the horizon. Evie's face was reflective as she sipped from her glass. "Now you know how my world is different."

"Thanks for sharing where you come from with me. I couldn't envision it before—the way I grew up feels comparatively boring. Sterile and automated. But now that I've seen your world, it doesn't seem odd at all. It's a place to learn from."

"What did you learn?"

"I'm surprised by the kindness," he said.

"Not expected?"

"Well, the . . . the Dome does have a reputation for violence because of the exomech games."

"That's undeniable, though I wish more people would notice that the violence is directed at machines. We avoid directing it at each other." She shuddered.

"Competition is natural, not something to deny."

"Natural, yes. We can't deny evolution and our animal natures." She met his gaze.

"We can try to be better animals. But we are animals nonetheless." He set his wineglass down and felt his pulse quicken.

Her eyes widened and she laughed. "Joe Denkensmith, you are less in your head than you usually are." Her head tilted as if with a question, and her cheeks flushed. He leaned in and brushed his lips against hers, then kissed her passionately. Her hair caressed his face, and the hint of chocolate lingered on her lips as she kissed him in return. Yearning flooded his body. Their kisses were like breathing, something he could not stop, something she seemed to need too.

They kissed for a long time.

Evie pulled away, gentle, reluctant, as the colors faded in the sky. Her head lay on his shoulder. "I'm sorry that it's taken me some time to feel comfortable. The idea of Levels has dominated my thinking the past three years. But I feel I've missed an opportunity to get to know you sooner."

"Conflicted about consorting with the enemy?"

"Yes, but I'm getting used to it." She reached up and kissed him softly again before she slipped away and closed her bedroom door.

CHAPTER 22

Joe awoke early the next morning, but he lay in bed, his head a jumble of thoughts. His sabbatical project, the Dome and Evie's life there, and finally, the multifaceted, confident woman herself all vied for his attention. But one won. She must be awake by now. He hustled out of bed, washed, dressed, and stepped into the living room.

Evie reclined on the sofa, the allbook open on her lap. "There's a lot of physics in your reading, and a lot of philosophy. Both are challenging to understand."

He sat close beside her. "It's nice of you to try."

"Try to know you?" She laughed. "I'm solving a puzzle. I can see how the math and the philosophy relate to the problem about AI consciousness. But your reading material is full of physics. How does the physics fit?"

He shrugged. "I said I'm a scientific realist. I want to square scientific ideas with a larger view of what it all means."

She rested her cheek on her hand. "Give me an example of one of the scientific ideas."

He thought for several seconds. "All right, here is one— the nature of time."

She nodded expectantly.

"Einstein's theories say time is just another dimension, like the three dimensions of space. The world we know is a space–time manifold—it's called Minkowski space–time. The time dimension is unique because it's unidirectional; you only move forward through time. Physicists believe the universe is closed physically, and all the dimensions are tied up together, with each dimension affecting the others."

"Are there any theories on the number of dimensions?"

He nodded. "But physicists haven't concluded how many dimensions yet. Though the elegant mathematics might suggest ten or eleven dimensions."

Evie frowned. "Doesn't time flow differently sometimes? There can be strange effects, like near a black hole."

"Exactly right." Her apparent interest sparked him to go deeper. "The 'twin paradox' involves one twin who leaves Earth on a spaceship at near the speed of light and ages more slowly compared to his twin left behind. The speed of light is a limit, and nothing can exceed it. That preserves the causality rules in the universe. Any of that nonsense about meeting your father before you were born can never happen."

"All right, so then what's the puzzle?"

"I start with the idea that stuff exists. That is, I'm a realist about the universe. All these dimensions exist. The space–time manifold exists. That would imply all of time exists at once."

Evie tilted her head, seeming uncertain. Joe took the all-book off her lap and held it flat in his hands. Her gaze connected with his, and he was jolted by the sudden intimacy.

"Let me explain it this way." He pointed to the square corners of the allbook. "We have a hard time visualizing the three dimensions of space plus our movement through time. Imagine all of space–time is represented in this three-dimensional block. Now imagine that a single point in time is one slice of the block." He slashed his hand down over the block. "Then the lengthwise dimension is like moving through time." He slid his hand along the top of the book.

She stared at the allbook. "Okay, a slice through it—that's two-dimensional—represents our three-dimensional space." She waved her hand around the room.

"Yes, exactly. Now, from the outside, there is just the block—all time existing at once. It seems at first like a contradiction, but see if you can hold both perspectives in your head at the same time—inside the block being where we live, and outside the block a cosmic perspective."

She stared at the allbook, her brow furrowing. Then she reached out and deliberately moved a finger across the allbook. Joe imagined her fingers brushing over his skin, and it made him shiver.

Evie closed her eyes and then opened them suddenly, her eyes wide. "This moment—me sitting with you—feels like it's happening now; time is moving forward right *now*. That's me inside this block feeling that. But you're saying that from the outside perspective, it's already happened? Time's all done?"

"Exactly."

"From the outside, it would be like looking at a dragonfly frozen in amber."

He was excited by the clarity of her metaphor. "Time is 'all done' if we can glimpse it from outside of space and time. It's 'all there' in the same way that the dimension of 'length' is all there. But we can't glimpse it from outside, because we live inside time. We can only experience it one instant at a time, and only in that narrow slice where we find ourselves."

"Can we have free will in such a universe where time is, from outside, finished?"

"An open question." Joe arched an eyebrow. "This view of time doesn't preclude free will, so long as other criteria are also met within this closed physical universe. If you think the universe is deterministic, then there's no free will. But if the universe is indeterministic, and if the decisions of conscious creatures living 'inside' of time determine what happens next, then, yes, those creatures can make free choices. I'm seeking answers to both of those puzzles, to know whether and how both can be met. Because if not, then there is no free will."

Evie frowned. "But you began by talking about the nature of time. Is there any consensus on that?"

"I believe the entire block of time exists. That's the explanation most consistent with relativity." He lifted both hands in a helpless gesture. "But philosophers have been arguing about time for centuries. Some argue that only the current slice of the block exists. Some say it's a growing block, so only the part up to the present moment exists." Joe paused. "Those don't conform to relativity, though, because, as you said, time doesn't flow uniformly everywhere. Velocity and gravity warp space–time."

Evie persisted. "But we all think about the past and live in the present. And we hope and plan for a future."

"Yes. We are sealed inside the block. That's all we can know. And all that we can feel is the current moment in time."

Her eyes twinkled. "Now I'm beginning to understand your sabbatical project. I said you spend time in your head. But it's not a matter of living in our heads or not, since being conscious of our experience is what we do when living. It's whether we find the joy of living in the present." Evie flung her hair back with a decisive expression playing across her face. "Let's live in the present. I know where to go."

———◆———

They took the hyperlev five stops southwest, switching trains once. Evie explained her plan as the train zipped across a valley verdant with vegetables and fruit trees, while Joe flipped through his NEST for reservations.

"My treat this time," he said.

"Make sure they have regular surfboards." Her face was eager.

"No autoboards for us?"

"No. And no wave machines, only real waves."

An autocar awaited them at the station. It ferried them over the seaside hills and stopped beside a small house facing the beach. It had a maroon roof, cream siding, a wooden deck, and a bay window facing the water. High tide lapped against white sand fifty meters away, and its briny tang tickled Joe's nose. He keyed the entry box and transferred dark credit$ from the purple tile in his pocket.

The front door opened into a living room with a bedroom and bathroom to the left, and an eat-in kitchen to the right. Evie vanished out the back door and came back a moment later, smiling. "Two surfboards out back, as you promised. I'm going to change." She disappeared into the bedroom. He looked around the living room, fixating on the sofa with a fold-out bed—on the train, she had said yes to his suggested beach house—and hoped that wasn't one reason. Joe went to change in the bathroom.

When he came out, Evie waited for him in a red swimsuit. They retrieved their surfboards, and she led him to the beach. He followed, oblivious to anything but the view of her hips leading him.

They stopped past a promontory to appraise the sweep of curving beach, the gentle waves lapping the sand. Around the hook of the bay, surfers rode larger waves, but the area before them was deserted.

"This'll be a fine place to start." She gave him a quick verbal lesson, and Joe tried to relate the steps to his recollection of netwalker surfing. They swam out into the warm current. "Duck dive these waves as you're paddling." She showed him how to keep forward momentum despite the waves pushing back. When they reached a point that Evie considered far enough out, they floated, hanging onto their boards.

"Remember to pop up as fast as you can." Several waves went past before she said, "Try this one." He pulled himself up on the board and paddled toward the beach ahead of the wave. As the wave surged behind him, he attempted to stand up but fell unceremoniously into the water.

"You'll get it." She was kind and encouraging. "Try moving your feet farther forward."

Joe tried again and again, but he kept toppling into the water. He realized he was starting too late. With the next wave, he paddled hard to keep up. The board rose in the water, and Joe popped up—and stayed balanced. He rode it until it died in the shallows, then he jumped off and turned to face Evie with a victorious whoop. She twirled her hand in a shaka sign.

Over the next few hours, he caught many waves, tumbled off many more, and he was dazzled by Evie's effortless rides. Her skill was obvious as she turned her board to stay at his side, even when he swerved unexpectedly.

When he didn't think he could lift his arms to paddle another meter, they ate lunch from a beach cabana, the servebot offering cold sandwiches and fruit.

"Let's try some more waves." She was full of energy. "You up for it?"

Joe nodded, stretching his arms. The short break had rejuvenated him.

They paddled out again, farther this time, and bobbed in the water closer to where wave sets formed. "This may be too early, but you could try a bottom turn," Evie said.

"I'm game."

She described steps to push the rail into the wave. "Use your weight transfer to turn," she said. He felt more confused than informed, but he made the attempt several times. He caught the wave each time but couldn't make the turn.

"Where you look is where you go," she said helpfully.

More turn attempts, more tumbles. The last time, he nose-dived under, and the leash pulled hard on his ankle, holding him down. He came sputtering to the surface.

"Had enough?"

"Not at all." Joe was even more determined. Adrenaline had caused his aches and pains to fade.

He glanced over his shoulder to choose the next wave and a graceful one swelled up green. He paddled furiously, then popped up onto the board and felt its power grab him. On the peak of the wave, he leaned forward over the lip into the pocket and shoved the rail down. His board dropped over the face and turned. The wave carried him, and he balanced for another two turns before plunging backward into the foaming surf. He came up spitting saltwater, but he flashed a fat grin to assure Evie he was having fun.

"Like riding a bicycle, I guess," he said.

She laughed. "From the man who doesn't know how to ride. But it is similar—you won't forget how to surf now that you've learned."

They paddled back to shore, Joe tired but happy.

"Your first time on a real board? You're a natural," Evie said. He melted under her praise, but he knew he was a rank beginner.

"Let's go where I can watch you ride some bigger waves," he said. They walked farther up the beach to the point break. The wind was onshore but not yet strong enough for choppy surf. Evie waved and took her board out, paddling efficiently.

She joined the other surfers in the lineup away from the swell. Joe squinted into the sun to watch. She was up on the face, skillfully pirouetting in multiple linked turns, making his last ride seem mere child's play. She finished the run and turned to paddle out, her curves accented by rivulets of water glistening on her skin in the sun. He rested in the shallows while she executed one glorious run after another.

. . .

Here is this sublime sliver of time. The sun feels warm on my skin and is dancing on hers. Whether aware of it or not, at every instant I'm surfing a moment in time. Balanced between past and future, there I am riding the wave.

. . .

Evie was again at the lineup, waiting for her wave. A giant swell rolled toward her. Her takeoff was perfectly timed. She accelerated down the face of the wave, turned to ride parallel along the face, then turned sharply into a backward-flipping spin. His breath stopped as she kept twisting for a full turn, then another half-turn before bringing her board to the top of the wave, facing backward. With a quick jump she reversed her feet and was surfing the wave again. Joe was transfixed.

Joe was treading water in the light waves when another surfer paddled past.

"Your girl shredded that nug," he said.

"Yes, she did. What's the trick called?"

"A rodeo flip. One of the best I've ever seen."

Joe gave him a shaka.

Evie maneuvered alongside Joe. They floated together, their boards bobbing gently. "That's a lovely wave to end on," she said.

Joe smiled at Evie with admiration and pride. "Now *that* was a lesson. And for me, only the beginning."

A beguiling smile laced her mouth, her hazel eyes as primal as the sea. She touched his beard and said, "Full of salt now." They paddled to shore. Her hair was wet on her shoulders as she carried the board ahead of him and down the beach as if it were weightless.

They reached the beach house and left the surfboards on the deck. It was warm in the late afternoon. Evie's smile reflected his own exhilaration from the waves.

"It's best to get the salt off right away." She entered the house and turned toward the bathroom. He lingered on the porch, not wanting to drip all over the living room. Transfixed by the thought of her, he barely noticed the sound of the shower turning off, but Evie appeared before him wrapped in a white towel. "Your turn," she said and looked away with a flush.

Joe stripped off his swimsuit and entered the shower, rubbing the salt from his hair with liberal squirts of shampoo. He dried off, fastened a towel around his hips, and entered the living room.

The bedroom door was open. Evie lay on the bed, the towel draped around her. The bedroom was white and clean, only large enough for the bed and a side table, which held a decorative conch shell. The bedroom window was open, and the sound of the ocean entered the room unbidden. She looked up at him with an encouraging smile on her lips. With a slow sweep of her arm, the towel fell open, and she lay there languid in all her nakedness. The red diamond on her finger glittered. Her body was more beautiful than he had ever imagined.

Lust mounted in him. His towel slipped from him of its own accord. He climbed onto the bed, his body throbbing. She pulled him close, and he kissed her. He kissed her again, and again as she responded with passion.

Evie opened her eyes and looked deeply into his, and he searched through that tumultuous sea, and there was a real person smiling up at him with happiness and longing, at him, at *him*. His heart thrummed in his chest.

He stroked her body, his warm fingers moving from her cheek to her toes, raising goosebumps on her cool skin. She sighed and shuddered. His beard brushed against her thighs. "Yes," she breathed, "that's just right." Evie squeezed her legs together and against him. He thought of the ocean.

. . .

Saltiness. Of mussels and muscles. Homonyms. No. Out of my head and back into this moment.

. . .

Now she was on top and her thick hair fell against his chest. Strands brushed back and forth as time slowed. He felt the want in her body, the way it surrounded and held him. She looked down at him, the expression in her hazel eyes tender, her supple skin warm and embracing.

As if he cradled a conch shell, the resonance of the sea grew in his ears. They rolled over slowly, tucked together inside the barrel of a wave. His fingers vibrated, charged particles crossing from her body to his. "Please," she whispered. He felt her rising in the air, lifted by a wave, her back arching; then the wave was pulling her down into the vortex, near drowning; then rising again on top of the wave, her mouth forming an ellipse.

His head was whirling, the beach house dissolving into mist. He was not thinking about the past; he was not planning the future. He was, at that instant, in one deep place in time and space in all the universe.

CHAPTER 23

For the next three days, Evie and Joe left midmorning to go surfing. They came back to the beach house in the afternoon to make love. They ate dinner at one restaurant three blocks off the beach and returned to lovemaking into the night. The beach house was their separate world, where, for Joe, the ocean and the walls surrounding them dissolved, replaced by the squeeze of her hand and her body, and afterward her hair lying against his shoulder. They slept until the sun's rays drifted across the bedsheets.

On their last morning, he awoke first at the call of a seagull. Evie's hand lay against his arm, and he was reluctant to move it.

· · ·

I am in love with every touch of her hand, every hair on her body, and every expression on her face.

· · ·

Evie woke with a sleepy smile and playfully fondled his beard. "Well, professor, we are both giving lessons."

"It's equitable to both give and to receive. We make a symphony together."

"It's a matter of proper timing."

"Speaking of time, now I understand. It's only while living in the moment that you can have perfect days like these."

She leaned up on one elbow. "I really love talking to you. I like to hear what is going on inside your head. Joe Denkensmith, you're a good person, and I like your heart."

"I'm afraid I'm just an average guy, with all the usual human foibles." He told her with his gaze that he was serious and sincere. "But I try."

Her hand flirted with the curls on his chest. "And speaking of . . . music." A wicked gleam entered her eyes. "Now I like both the slow and the fast movements."

They made love again and awoke hours later with the sun high in the sky. They showered and ate brunch. Then it was time to go back. He locked the front door with a deep sense of regret, and they wandered hand in hand on the beach as they headed toward the station.

They took the hyperlev three stops north, cuddled together while the fertile farmland rolled by.

They exited at the station to switch to the eastbound train. People thronged the platform that connected to the central plaza. Joe led as they wove through the mass of people, but halfway down the platform the crowd lurched to a halt. Joe and Evie tried to see ahead. A curious murmur arose but was silenced by a voice over the loudspeaker. "Everyone shall stand to watch this public event. All trains are stopped for seventeen minutes." Joe peered over the heads of the people in front, while Evie strained to see.

A wall of copbots shoved their way onto the plaza seven meters from them, firmly pushing people aside. "Not good," Joe said grimly. Evie tugged his hand and pointed behind them as more copbots lined up, forcing the crowd into a thin ellipse around the plaza, facing inward. She gripped his hand as they were jostled.

. . .

They're rounding everyone up. Or could it only be us? Did I give something away?

. . .

"It's the Burning," Evie whispered.

"The what?"

Before she could respond, a figure strolled to the center of the plaza with three copbots and five mechas. The man turned in a circle, staring at everyone. A hush fell over the reluctant crowd.

"The States hold our advanced technology to a high standard of perfection. But even with the most rigorous standards, things can go wrong. People die." He stopped, his pause pregnant with meaning, and nodded at the crowd.

Joe squinted. The nod had been off-center. He reconnected his NEST and zoomed in to see the man's face. The man raised a truncheon, and the end burst into a dazzling light. Joe's corneal shade dimmed to protect his vision. The man pointed into the sky with the flaming plasma cutter baton. "So now the people will have their justice!"

Bending to Evie, Joe whispered, "That's Zable, Peightân's second-in-command." Her eyes hardened in acknowledgment.

Two autocars rolled into the plaza and parked in the center. A large truck followed. The back of the truck opened, a ramp lowered, and five bots exited and formed a line. Zable recited, as if from a legal proclamation, "Over the past year in this section of the States, a total of five humans have died in accidents involving robots, and AI-controlled vehicles have killed two others. The Ministry of Security has asked for and received convictions in these cases. The punishments will now be administered."

The truck moved off the square. The five mechas lumbered forward and surrounded the two autocars. Each mecha had plasma cutters attached to both arms. Brilliant jets of fire belched from the cutters, and the mechas sliced through the vehicles with broad strokes. Columns of smoke rose from the burning hulks.

Autocars dismantled, the mechas marched behind the five bots, which stood at attention. The heads of the bots turned slowly left and right, their foreheads pink as they scanned the crowd. The plasma cutters arced again. The sparks were too intense to look at directly. With three strokes each, the bots lay in blazing pieces on the square.

Several in the crowd cheered, but the rest stood silent. Acrid soot wafted from the blackened stains forming a neat glowing line until it gradually dissipated. The copbots corralling the crowd marched off. Joe heaved a breath of relief as the line of mesh capes decamped with Zable following. Fire-suppression vehicles rolled forward and doused the flames with water. Mechas loaded the steaming metal into trucks.

Joe and Evie pushed through the crowd to the station platform, staying close to one another while they waited for the next train.

"It's the first time I've ever watched it." Joe scrutinized the dispersing crowd.

"It's a ceremony, intended to make people feel better than bots for a day."

"Well, Zable seemed to be close to orgasm."

"I was watching his arm." She tapped her own forearm. "I'm certain it's bionic."

"A real cyborg, and not happy about it."

Evie wore a pensive expression. "You never know what pain other people might have. You see them walking about as if all is well, but you can't see the stones inside their Mercuries."

Joe frowned. "I dislike the guy. There's something evil about him." The Burning had disgusted and unnerved him, as had Zable, and he couldn't get the chemical taste of smoke out of his mouth as they boarded the second train.

The next morning, Joe kissed Evie tenderly before he rolled out of bed. They were sharing her bedroom. She opened her eyes sleepily.

"I hate to leave, but I should visit the office to see what I've missed," he said.

When he stepped into his office, a red com light was blinking. He realized he had disconnected messaging for days. He keyed the encryption code, and Raif's holo appeared with a quizzical expression.

"MIA for several days? You had me worried."

"I was out surfing."

"Our same joke?"

"No, really surfing . . . well yes, it's the same joke."

Raif laughed. Then he frowned. "Okay, back to dangerous business."

Joe leaned forward. "Yes?"

"Freyja and I have been busy on the database integrity issue. The data from the corrupted cleanerbot provided a crucial piece of intel." He paused. "We have a bigger issue."

Raif sketched out the details. Joe shook his head and rubbed his forehead. "We need to bring others into this problem now."

"Wait." Raif disappeared from the holo for a moment. "I'm talking with Freyja. She suggests we involve Mike."

"Have Freyja call Mike, and I'll go to his office." Joe wanted to see Mike in person.

"That's a plan." Raif signed off.

Joe headed straight for Mike's office and found that Freyja had already arrived and was deep in thought. In a few minutes, Mike had connected both Raif and Dina Taggart, and their holos floated among them.

Mike opened the meeting. "Dina, I've only heard the summary from Freyja. But Joe has a disturbing discovery to share with us."

Joe spoke to Dina. "I passed a copy of the data from the corrupted cleanerbot to the expert I'd mentioned. Raif is one of the best computer scientists on the subject of 'bot in a box' programming. Raif and my colleague Freyja Tau, have been collaborating to investigate database integrity issues. Their analysis has covered both the WISE problem with the corrupted bot and suspected problems in the Security Ministry."

Raif launched right into their findings. "It's the most sophisticated and dangerous code worm I've ever heard of. This is a potentially deadly anomaly, and a leak in the sandboxes keeping AIs apart. We find traces, and then those tracks disappear. In one instance, we could isolate the code worm, but it was too well encrypted to get inside, and then it self-destructed and eliminated all evidence. The worm has found a way around all the safeguards and it's hiding in trillions of lines of software. We can't use AIs to find it, not knowing yet how they become infected."

Mike's expression turned from dour to grim. Dina's paralleled it. "I'll soon have seven hundred bots on WISE Orbital Base alone. We can't allow an unknown code worm to infect them."

"It's worse." Freyja's normally light tone was somber. "Most of the software modules are shared. It could in theory infect AIs in system controls, and any bots. It might even be capable of infecting individual PIDAs."

"And military hardware," Mike said.

Dina asked, "Is there anything that might limit its spread?"

"We don't know." Raif was more serious than Joe had ever seen him. "There is hope that physical sandboxing is preventing the code worm from jumping unless some physical thing—say, a bot—does something physical to move it to another AI."

Joe chimed in. "Since we have strong evidence to suggest there is one corrupted database inside the Security Ministry, the source could either be an outside job—some hacker—or an inside job." Joe rubbed his eyes, then looked at Raif. "Have you checked for information about cDc, the hacker killed by the police two months ago?"

Raif shook his head. "No, but that's a good idea. If it was an inside job, then maybe cDc uncovered something important. And deadly to himself."

"If it's not an inside job, could it be from a foreign source? Either a nation-state or a terrorist organization?" Mike paced in front of the holo-com.

Raif frowned. "We don't know enough to determine that yet. Uncovering the source will take a tremendous effort." He eyed each person assembled. "I do know that this operation is best done in secret. We cannot show our hand, because whoever is behind this could better hide from us."

"This could bring down the entire country," Mike said.

The enormity of what Raif and Freyja had uncovered rolled over Joe again. He didn't know where or how to begin routing out the worm—such secret analysis required access to databases and funds that were out of reach for him, Raif, Freyja, and even Mike. He turned to Dina, who he found studying him. She gave him a small nod, her jaw set.

"We need answers, and we need to get them surreptitiously." She somehow managed to meet the gaze of everyone connected to the call. "I have available black-budget resources I'm willing to commit. This project requires a larger secret team."

Joe let out a huge sigh. Though the problems the group faced hadn't changed, the atmosphere in the room felt more determined than depressed. The conversation went on for another hour. By the end, Dina had suggested assignments and next steps. She would organize a meeting space and build an expanded team, with Raif and Freyja in senior roles. Joe and Freyja would wrap up their current work at the college and then be on the project full-time, so Joe could spend adequate time focusing on what AI software modules were most likely compromised.

Joe's mouth was dry as he marched back home. He had never faced such a momentous challenge. He wanted to trust Evie, yet he knew this wasn't his secret to tell.

When he told her about his need to work long hours, her hazel eyes saw right through him. She knew he held something back. "You can't tell me anything?"

He took her hands. "I have a professional obligation to keep this confidential. I wish I could tell you more."

Evie nodded, but she couldn't keep all the hurt from her gaze. "Okay. We can't choose the time when events compel us to act."

"I feel an obligation. But I only want to spend time with you."

"We have the nights." She led him to the bedroom.

CHAPTER 24

As promised, Dina secured a facility in the Southwest to isolate the team and preserve secrecy. But until the logistics for that building could be arranged, their temporary headquarters would be the local WISE office. Joe was back at his familiar desk by the next afternoon, calling Raif.

"Hi, brat." His cherubic smile was thinner than usual.

"Feeling tense with the new role, doctor?"

"Yes, a bit. It's a big move for me, relocating to the Southwest and spending time out there with you."

"And with Freyja."

Raif grinned.

Raif usually teased him more, so Joe didn't miss this chance. "Both professionally and personally, this is your chance to sink or swim." His friend's face softened, and Joe realized that the swimming joke hadn't landed and that Raif must be thinking about Freyja. He couldn't help but be a little protective. "Some advice? Don't try to rush it. Be your regular, chill self."

Their meetings continued at a frenetic pace the following week. Dina, Freyja, and Raif hired and briefed five software experts, each assigned as a senior manager in a subspecialty. Further secret hiring moved ahead, building out those teams with several hundred hackers. Joe felt more energized than ever before. The long days and nights did not leave him tired, and he was running on adrenaline and testosterone without enhancement from his MEDFLOW. Each evening, he and Evie ate a late dinner together while they talked about everything except the project.

One night before he drifted to sleep, Evie propped herself up on one arm. "Joe, I won't ask you to share the details of the secret project, but you've certainly jumped in with both feet. Have you abandoned your sabbatical project?"

Joe stroked her cheek. "Only temporarily. But you've reminded me that I owe Gabe a visit to at least let him know I haven't given up."

Gabe responded to Joe's NEST message with an invitation to meet the following day. Joe spent the morning in his on-campus office, clearing his head and reviewing his last notes. Where had he left his project? Since he believed that the universe was physically closed, he still needed to figure out whether mentality could cause anything at all.

Joe found Gabe in a side quadrangle of the campus, on a park bench under a spreading live oak. A creature of habit, Gabe poured cups of Dragonwell green tea from a synjug and passed one to Joe.

"You've been away for several days," Gabe said.

"Tied up with an important project, one I unfortunately can't talk about. It's taken me away from these questions, which I really enjoy discussing with you."

"I wish I could help on your project—not that I'm good with practical subjects."

"Perhaps you can. In my opinion, your clarity of thought would be helpful. I suggest you talk to Mike. He would be responsible for involving you."

"I was glad you contacted me and haven't given up your sabbatical project." Gabe studied the trees. "I said I've mentored thousands of students. It is difficult to keep up with many afterward. The good ones finish their degrees and find positions elsewhere, all spread around the world. Even with today's fast transportation and instant communication, it is difficult to stay connected."

"Hard to share a cup of tea?"

"Exactly." Gabe looked into his eyes. "I enjoy these discussions with you. I think you may be onto a synthesis that advances the philosophical discussion."

. . .

I'd like to think that could someday be true. With the secret project, I'm not sure when I can refocus on these questions. But for now, let me enjoy this conversation with Gabe, who feels like both a mentor and a friend.

. . .

"Thank you. I'm learning quite a lot from you. Thinking about philosophical problems is more enjoyable than my previous work."

After a short silence, Gabe said, "Before we start today's discussion, I have one additional piece of advice. This field can lead to a lonely life, spending so much time in your head. Look for balance."

Joe nodded. The comment seemed to come from personal experience. "I've made progress there also."

Gabe refilled his cup and turned to Joe. "Now, where are you on your list of philosophical riddles?"

"I'm still wrestling with the mental causation problem. The argument that mind is merely an epiphenomenon—that nothing is caused by the mind but instead by particles in motion—defies all my intuitions."

"As it does for all of us. We hope all is not lost, and that we can still claim that our decisions have effects."

"Mathematicians question the premises when faced with such an argument. Faulty premises can yield faulty conclusions. That's my approach," Joe said.

"Good. What shall we discuss today?"

"I have been thinking about causality. Can you help me consider this from a philosophical perspective?"

Gabe, ever precise, asked, "What do you mean by causality?"

"I'm thinking about causation, cause and effect, by which one process, a cause, produces another process."

"Then it appears you have a metaphysical question. Are you wondering about how anything in the real world can be caused by something else?"

"Exactly."

Gabe's face creased around a grin, the smile lines showing that he didn't have the typical skin elastomers added to his MEDFLOW. "That question brings to the fore a favorite philosopher, David Hume. His most important contribution was the idea of a 'necessary connection.'"

Gabe set down his teacup, steepled his fingers, and stared into the trees. "Hume divided objects of human reason into two categories—*relations of ideas* and *matters of fact*."

Joe screwed up his face. "I'm unfamiliar with those terms."

"Hume divided everything into two buckets, a white bucket"—Gabe unsteepled his fingers to form a cup with his right hand—"and a green bucket." He cupped his left. Joe nodded, imagining the sage holding all knowledge in his two hands.

"Into the white bucket went things like mathematics. Those are the *relations of ideas*. Relations of ideas can be known by thought alone. These include your mathematical proofs. We can know mathematics through proof and can be absolutely certain that the conclusions are true from valid premises. No worldly evidence is involved, only pure logic. For example, consider the mathematical fact that all angles of a Euclidean triangle sum to 180 degrees. One can know their truth a priori, as philosophers say, as a logical necessity, without any reference to the world."

Joe pursed his lips. "I can agree with this. I know that mathematical proofs can be certain."

"Into the green bucket goes everything else that are not relations of ideas—that is, everything about the world. Hume said that we can know nothing in this bucket with certainty."

"Okay." Joe stared at Gabe's left palm, the translucent skin showing blue veins. "Let's focus on the green bucket."

"Hume named the second category *matters of fact*, and those arise from the way our world is. These include all the empirical facts we learn about the world through observation. It is in this second category that Hume made his brilliant logical breakthrough by demonstrating there is no logical necessity within matters of fact. We can only know them through association, through seeing what happens in the world, and then assuming such will repeat in the future."

"I'm not sure I grasp the point," Joe said.

Gabe held out the tea synjug with one hand. "I hold this container in the air. We both assume that if I release it from my hand, it will immediately fall. But there is nothing in the initial position to suggest the object will fall downward versus falling upward, or any other direction."

"But we both believe it will fall."

"Yes, we both might reach that conclusion because of our experience, in which a *constant conjunction* of letting go of the object is followed by it dropping to the ground. We believe so because of our past associations. Every time we have seen a similar situation, the object falls. We have a neat scientific explanation for it, namely gravity. But, again, there is no necessity in logic to justify the conclusion. That only comes about from our experience of the world."

Gabe studied Joe's expression. "I see you still have doubts. Let me try another example. Assume we have two highly accurate, archaic clocks. The first clock chimes one minute before the hour and the second chimes on the hour. To an observer unaware of the internal mechanism, it would appear the first clock causes the second clock to chime. This supposed 'knowledge' would be proven false when the power source of either clock ran down.

"You see, we have built a monolith of scientific theory. We perform countless experiments that confirm the relations between various theories, and we test those theories against the world. That gives us some confidence. But there is no *logical* necessity in believing these theories about the world to be true."

"Statements that are logically necessary are so by their very structure, such as 'All bachelors are unmarried.' It's what I love about math—that one can be certain of truth," Joe said.

"Exactly. That statement is in the white bucket. But there is nothing similar, no logically necessary statement, in the green bucket. There we are dependent upon our experience in the world, and from that experience it's possible that we may infer ideas that aren't true."

"Science develops new theories all the time." Joe took a sip of tea. "The new theories often explain the facts of the world in more elegant ways than prior theories. The evolution of these theories is the process of science advancing knowledge. But it seldom overturns long-held ideas."

Gabe nodded. "When it does, the result is a paradigm shift, such as when Einstein's relativity replaced Newton's theory, offering a more complete understanding of the mechanics of the universe."

"We haven't had a paradigm shift in physics for a long time. But then, we haven't had much progress either."

"When they happen, they shake our foundational ideas of the world," Gabe said.

Joe reflected on the argument. "So why is Hume's idea called a 'necessary connection'?"

"When we observe the release of the object followed by its dropping, we are only observing a *conjunction* of the two actions, not a *connection*. Habit gives rise to the idea of a connection, but that is not logically entailed. According to Hume, we cannot be certain about what is causing what."

"You are saying that for everything we think we know about the world—which is everything that science investigates—we have no certain knowledge, and we never will?"

"Yes."

"The world seems designed to keep conscious creatures skating on the edge of unknowing."

"Yes."

"What is Hume's ultimate conclusion about causality?" Joe put down the empty teacup and rubbed his hands together. "Isn't it just the common idea that correlation does not imply causation?"

"That is one simplified result stemming from Hume, though he was making a deeper epistemological point—that we cannot know anything for certain about the world." Gabe gathered the teacups and put them in his bag. "Yet, Hume was a true empiricist. He thought knowledge might not be gained independently of sensory experience. Every effect is a distinct event from its cause. Observation and experience are necessary to infer any cause or effect. And even then, we can only know there is a conjunction, but we cannot be sure about causality."

Joe pondered the idea. "So we need to be skeptical about our ideas of causality. What we can know is more limited than I imagined."

"Just so." Gabe seemed pleased with Joe's grasp of the theory. "It is an epistemological truth—what we can know—that our best physics is still uncertain about something as fundamental as causality. Given the limits of what we can know with certainty, we are unsure about what causes what in the world."

CHAPTER 25

After the single-day break to talk with Gabe, Joe returned to laboring on the secret project throughout the weekend. He regretted the time not spent with Evie. But she was uncomplaining, heading out every day for several hours. She was reticent about what she did, but from their dinner conversations, he gathered she used an encrypted com station in town to contact followers in her movement. He only saw her in the evenings before he fell into bed and into a deep sleep.

Joe found an excuse to take a break with her when Evie handed him a paper envelope that 83 had left at the front door. It contained an invitation from Dr. Jardine to their annual department event, to which professors could bring guests. From the careful description, it was a fancier affair, maybe more fun and less focused on academics. The timing was good because he had been on edge. Earlier that day, Raif had warned the team about a reaction their explorations had stirred up. Whoever was responsible for the code worm had caught their trail, and Joe spent the day with the rest of the team, working frantically to become invisible again. It was a cat-and-mouse game, only they didn't know who the cat was.

"I have no idea how long this may take." He slipped the invitation into his pocket before sitting down to Evie's latest culinary creation. "It feels like my own Manhattan Project."

"Wasn't that to build a bomb? And didn't it take years?" She slid into the seat opposite him. She'd already eaten; it was late.

"Yes, but if I don't do this work, then many terrible things could happen."

Joe concentrated on eating the spicy stew, matched with a fine Bordeaux he'd opened. With Evie across the table, his nerves unwound from the long day. Afterward, he carried the glasses into the living room, where they settled to enjoy the star-filled night sky.

"You love using those dark credit$." She laughed and took her glass.

"There's still plenty left from my WISE project, so I'm living for the moment." He raised his own wineglass.

"And you're sticking to an exercise routine."

"I need to keep up with you on a surfboard." Joe sipped and met her gaze over the edge of the glass. "I think we both deserve a break. Beach tomorrow?"

Her eyes lit up.

"Also, Dr. Jardine has invited me to a festive cocktail reception the day after tomorrow. I'm allowed to bring a guest. Will you come with me?"

"You've mentioned your friends and colleagues so often I feel like I already know them without really knowing them." Was that a glimpse of unease that flashed across her face? "I'd love to meet them."

He kissed her. "And I'd love for them to know you."

She snuggled into his shoulder. "What's Raif like?"

"He's a bit like me . . . but maybe more accomplished." He pressed her closer. "He's not here at the college, though. You can meet him another time."

"He's your best friend?"

"Yes, we've gone through a lot together."

"You look out for him?"

"We guard each other's backs." Joe wished he'd done more to bring Raif and Freyja together. It seemed they were getting along well enough without him, though.

Evie sat up to study him. "I love that about you. So loyal. Tell me about Mike." She put her head back on his shoulder.

"You'll find him a kindred spirit, with ideas about equality very similar to yours. You'll enjoy Gabe too. He can seem intellectually formal and precise, but he's a real sage, full of wisdom, and a gentle soul at heart."

"And Freyja, the mathematician?"

"I think you'll appreciate her focus on her work and her professional commitment. But she is also warm underneath."

"I'm excited to meet them all. And a little nervous," Evie said.

The self-doubt he'd glimpsed earlier was now on full display. "The movement is all about equality. You should live that and realize that you're equal to everyone else. Your worth comes from inside, from your character."

"I believe it abstractly, but it takes effort to embrace it emotionally, since we live in a world that doesn't admit it," she said.

"They will all love you." Joe said. He knew she could hold her own in any situation. He was less sure of himself.

The beach house was the same as they had left it. The sun glinted off the maroon roof, and the sounds of gulls and breaking waves offered a welcoming duet. Joe focused on his bottom turns. The beach was empty and the swell too tiny to challenge Evie, so she spent the time by his side, lying on her board or surfing next to him. After lunch, they returned to the house. They whiled away the afternoon making love, now more accustomed to each other's bodies, more assured in each other's responses. Afterward, the sunset bathed the horizon in saffron hues while they listened to the music of the sea against the beach.

"I'm thinking about the soiree tomorrow evening." She nestled against his chest. "Your friends won't be concerned about my Level?"

"No, not at all. They won't ask. The college is an egalitarian place."

"But we're breaking the law."

"I guess I've been breaking the law since I got here." He gave her an encouraging squeeze. "And I analyzed the prosecution statistics. They don't indict as many as you might expect, which suggests people have found ways to live together despite the silly law. I think the authorities look the other way unless they are looking for a reason to hassle someone. Sorry, but you've found someone who's rebellious too."

Evie leaned on one elbow, an intense expression on her face that he had learned meant decisiveness. "Stumbling on me was an accident. Our getting close flowed from that accident. But now this feels like something else."

. . .

The waves are breaking outside. They're cresting in my head. There's a time when you're riding the wave, and you decide to turn, and the turn decides everything else afterward.

. . .

"It is something else. I've fallen in love with you."

Sweet happiness filled her eyes. "I love you too."

———————◆———————

They arrived at the cocktail reception seventeen minutes after the start. Evie wore a stunning, sleeveless cream jumpsuit with a train that draped to the floor, forming a half ellipse around her long legs. Joe offered his arm. "It seems like you enjoy using my dark credit$, too, and doubling their value."

"I need to look the part." They stepped onto the landing.

Groups of people filled the room below, all dressed more formally than usual—the men with dress jackets, the women with jumpsuits. He was glad Evie had suggested he wear a jacket and that she'd taken him shopping that morning to help choose one. The murmur of voices suggested a party that was festive rather than serious. He spotted Mike and Gabe standing together. Neither had brought a partner or friend.

"I don't see Dr. Jardine yet, but I'm sure you'll enjoy meeting him too." He led her to pick up glasses of wine, and they strolled over to the two older men.

Joe introduced Gabe and Mike. Evie greeted Gabe first with her vivacious smile, then turned to Mike and said, "Pleased to meet you, too, Professor Swaarden. My name is Evie Joneson."

"Please call me Mike. Joe has mentioned your master's in political science and economics—subjects of interest that overlap my own. Can I surmise that social justice is part of it?"

"That's right. I've had time to apply my political science studies to the real world for several years."

"There's much work to do. Our laws are a far cry from fair." Mike offered an approving nod. "I don't know how we've allowed this abominable state to exist for so long."

Evie smiled earnestly, leaning in. "Natural law is discovered by people using reason, choosing between good and evil. Spreading the word about injustices can bring change."

"Aye, but it's hard work fighting against self-interest that maintains the status quo. That's human nature."

"Perhaps you're referring to Hobbes? I follow the ideas of Joseph Butler. Humanity tends toward altruism and benevolence. We need to look for those hints in our nature as guides to what is right."

As the two discussed the topic, Joe realized Mike had guessed far more about Evie than had been spoken. Joe and Gabe stood by, enjoying the interchange.

"I see you have found some life balance." Gabe's dark eyes twinkled. "Oh, and Mike has included me in your project."

"Excellent. Glad to have you on the team."

Behind Gabe, Freyja approached, her blue eyes luminous. She wore her golden necklace and a cobalt-blue jumpsuit with a matching shoulder cape.

Evie returned Freyja's warm greeting. "Joe told me how much he enjoys his conversations with you on mathematics." Freyja suggested that Evie join her at the hors d'oeuvre table, and they wandered off, chatting amiably. Joe had been circumspect, thinking about their meeting, and he was relieved to see it going well. He sipped his wine with Mike and Gabe.

"That was a bracing discussion." Mike smiled.

"Evie has an active mind and a lovely face," Gabe said.

"The mind and the face of an angel," Joe said.

"Is it a wise man, or merely a lucky one, who carries an angel on his arm?" Gabe laughed.

Before Joe could respond, a furious expression erupted on Mike's face. "I thought that snake was gone." Joe followed his gaze. Peightân strode down the stairs from the landing in his tall black boots. A moment later, he hovered over Evie, his jaw chewing the words as he talked at her.

Joe rushed across the room, in time to overhear Freyja defending her. "Stop bothering her. She's an invited guest. Chill out. Say, go to the beach, get a tan."

Peightân ignored her but glanced at Joe as he approached. "Ah, Mr. Denkensmith, as expected. I was introducing myself to your friend." Arrogant amusement laced his ashen face as he turned back to Evie. "As I was saying, I've become an expert on human moral weakness. The range of crimes people are capable of is extraordinary."

"Why are you here?" Joe clenched his clammy palms.

Peightân stared unemotionally at him. "With enough time to sift through the ocean of data we collect, we eventually find everything we need to know." He focused his remorseless gaze on Evie. "Perhaps I'm here because my job is sometimes boring. Humans were more wicked in the past. Now I find myself taking a personal interest in crimes that may seem petty but have deep societal implications. Take this recent protest movement, or the perpetrators who hack into our databases." Evie met Peightân's icy stare with one of her own as he continued. "Some think they know more than the lawmakers."

"Human beings write laws." Evie's gaze never wavered.

"We can also change our opinion of what is right and what is wrong. These are social decisions."

Peightân's tone turned victorious. "Ah, you have been tempted into believing you can judge what is best for all. Well, the law says that hierarchies are good for society, recognizing that some are naturally higher and some lower. Then everyone can be at their perfect Level, performing their assigned functions perfectly. I am here to enforce the letter of the law as it is written." His gaze bored into Evie. "We are the same, you and I. We both fight to defend what we believe in."

Evie trembled but stood tall. "Only alike through a broken mirror."

He lowered his voice to a hiss. "And you, with your low Level, are nearer to death than I. And my profession puts me in touch with death up close. As you'll soon discover."

"What do you mean?" The color drained from her face.

"Your friends are dead."

Evie shuddered, covered her mouth, and swayed on her feet. Joe wrapped his arm around her waist, steadying her.

In a snap, Gabe was at Joe's elbow. "What are you doing to this young woman? Have you no humanity?"

"I am here to arrest her. And him." Peightân's gaze flickered, most likely a result of communicating on his NEST. A moment later, the doors above burst open and Zable dashed in with two copbots. They bolted down the stairs to surround Evie and Joe. One of the copbots grabbed Joe's right wrist and twisted it clockwise, forcing him to turn backward. It reached for his left hand and locked on a pair of handcuffs. The second copbot handcuffed Evie.

Zable glanced at Peightân, who nodded with a satisfied air. Zable turned to the room and announced loudly, "By order of the Minister of Security, we are arresting these terrorists for serious crimes. You're now safe from this danger."

Everyone stood in stunned silence as the bots hustled their two prisoners up the stairs and outside. A hovercraft stood by, its engines humming. The copbots thrust them inside. The cuffs chafed at Joe's wrists when he dropped into the seat, and Evie pressed against him. She trembled as the craft rose into the air.

Chapter 26

A copbot led Joe from the maximum-security jail cell to a dreary gray visitation room. He wore the standard-issue orange jumpsuit, his wrists shackled in front. The privacy bubble, three meters in diameter, sat on an elevated platform in the center of the room. Mike Swaarden waited in the visiting booth. Joe sat in the prisoner booth and Mike activated the bubble, glowing blue.

Mike peered through the metal grill separating them. "Let's hope this bubble actually protects our privacy. Attorney–client privilege, you know."

"They told me. Thanks for volunteering to be our lawyer."

"No promises. I'm sorry, but there will be little I can do." Mike looked like a man at a funeral.

"They took the power unit out of my NEST and held me in solitary confinement. Has it been three days?"

"Aye, three days. And that's standard procedure."

Joe leaned forward, the ever-present tension in his neck and shoulders since the arrest tightening further. "How is Evie? When they separated us, she was still shaking."

"I just saw her. She's subdued but not defeated, and she's processing the news about her friends."

"Okay." Joe took a deep breath but it didn't help him relax. "What happens next?"

"They have formally filed charges. There will be a trial within two weeks—swift justice, they say."

"What are we charged with?"

Mike rubbed his forehead. "The lesser charges include fomenting illegal protest assemblies and consorting between incompatible Levels. For you, they've included the silly charge of working covert hours. And aiding and abetting criminal escape." Mike paused.

"More?"

"Aye. The major criminal complaint is domestic terrorism. They depict Evie as the mastermind of an anarchist terror group. You're charged as her willing accomplice. Another store was bombed the day before the reception. This time it killed a congressman."

"My God." Joe's voice sounded shaky in his own ears.

. . .

Someone else dead, a tragedy for their family. And me charged with this terrible crime. I'll never be free again if they convict.

. . .

Mike went on. "The Security Ministry has DNA evidence that ties you both to the scene."

"Impossible." Joe's nostrils flared. "The day before the reception? We were at the beach."

"I've checked already." Mike shook his head. "There are no records whatsoever to give you an alibi." His lip curled. "There's more. The legislator who was killed in the bomb blast—a nice guy, I knew him personally—was an idealist. Coincidentally, he had spoken out against the size of the Security Ministry's budget allocation."

Mike nodded at Joe's frown of recognition at the likely chain of events.

"Peightân gets two for one. He engineered the bombing and swapped the DNA evidence record. Easy because he has access to the databases. Peightân framed us."

"Most likely," Mike said.

Joe thought for a moment. "Raif mentioned that our attempted hack was discovered last week, but we'd hidden our identities. The day after the hack was spotted, the bomb went off. Do you think Peightân came to see Evie face-to-face to see whether she knew about that latest hack?"

Mike nodded.

"That would imply the code worm is an inside job, and that Zable's copbots killed cDc after he uncovered something in a database." A shiver went down Joe's back. "Peightân will do anything to cover up whatever is happening."

"He's a wicked one. The team is working to catch him, but if he continues to cover his tracks so well, all we'll have is speculation. It could take a long time."

"What can we do about us?"

Mike sighed. "Less than we wish. So-called justice these days is by the numbers. And the numbers have been rigged." He raised his hands with a shrug. "Unless we have a miraculous breakthrough, we can't disprove your DNA samples found at the bomb scene."

. . .

The outcome feels as predictable, as certain, as a math proof—banishment to the Empty Zone. Then death for Evie and me in some godforsaken desert, long before anyone can prove our innocence. Death has never been this near. The Horseman is approaching.

. . .

Joe swallowed. "What did Evie say?"

Mike's expression brightened slightly. "Evie is an optimist. She told me to pass along to you that she's already begun conditioning herself physically for survival."

A smile crept across Joe's lips, despite the dread weighing heavy in his gut. He remembered Evie had spent time camping in her past—she wouldn't be helpless. How could he contribute? "What are our permitted assets?"

"They don't allow electronics or biomedical technology in the Empty Zone, but you can bring any archaic technology and supplies you can carry."

Joe recalled the government's description of banishment. "Ah, right. They'll give us a sporting chance."

"With a patina of international propriety on it."

Joe rubbed his wrists beneath the handcuffs. "Let me give you a list. Please get a list from Evie as well. Use my dark credit$. You'll find them hidden under the whisky decanter in my apartment. I'll pass the encryption key to you now."

Mike retrieved writing paper and a pen from his case and passed it through the thin slot in the grill. "The damned bot wouldn't allow electronic technology in here. You'll need to use this to record everything."

Joe took the pen with a frown and spent the next several minutes laboriously scribbling on the paper, struggling to recall the process from a childhood art class. He shook out his cramping hand as he slid the paper back.

Mike read the list, nodding. "Food, water, primitive survival equipment, aye." His finger halted on one item with several subitems listed beneath it. "This—edible plants, flora and fauna of the Southwest, survival skills, hunting and fishing, soapmaking, archived news stories—all books? On an allbook? You can't—"

Joe held up a hand. "I know, I can't take the allbook into the Empty Zone. But I can take my mind."

◆

Joe and Evie held hands in the packed courtroom, Mike at their side. The robojudge sat impassively at the bench, its silver face moving methodically from Joe to Evie and then back again. "Please read the charges aloud," it said.

A pipabot stepped forward. "Joseph Denkensmith, you are charged with aiding and abetting criminal escape of a domestic terrorist, then engaging in a domestic terrorist conspiracy culminating in the murder of one human . . ."

The bot droned on for another minute, then continued with Evie's charges. "Evie Joneson, you are charged with leading a domestic terrorist organization, dangerous to human life, that plotted the murder of one human in a store bombing..."

The reading complete, they faced the robojudge. "The empirical evidence is overwhelming. We find no grounds for doubting the evidence." Its lensed eyes locked onto them in turn before announcing the verdict. "Joseph Denkensmith, you are found guilty of all charges. Evie Joneson, you are found guilty of all charges."

The robojudge continued gazing deliberately at each. "The prosecution has asked for a sentence for each of you of three years' banishment to the Empty Zone. While such a sentence is at the high end of the sentencing guidelines, it is affirmed, given the special circumstances in this case." The robojudge's forehead glowed blue for three full seconds, then purple as it turned expectantly to the human judge on his right.

The human judge said, "I concur with the ruling of the honorable judge. I find no grounds under the law to disagree." He paused, glaring at them both. "These are despicable acts. We will not stand for terrorists attempting to undermine our political system. The sentence shall be carried out within forty-eight hours." He banged a gavel, and all in the courtroom rose as the judges exited.

Seven copbots escorted them out of the room. Mike shuffled three meters behind. Evie caught Joe's gaze and stood taller. They marched out with their heads up, staring defiantly ahead. As the doors opened, they faced a sea of recorders, capturing the scene for the media. They were led through a side corridor, away from the public glare and into the prison area. Mike followed Joe and Evie into a privacy bubble and activated it. The copbots waited outside.

Mike stared at his hands. "Though the result was as anticipated, I feel I've failed you. Allegedly, the AI judges are rigorously logical, evidence-based, and completely impartial."

"Bad data in ..." Joe said, leaving the sentence unfinished.

"We don't blame you, Mike." He frowned. "I was expecting a little more support in the courtroom, however."

"Dina decided no one else should attend the trial because it could provide a trail back to the team's operations. They're in tatters, Joe, they really are." A fierce tear rolled down Mike's cheek before he took a deep breath and wiped it away. "Listen, we only have a few minutes for this last conference, so let me get to the point. The team is trying to solve the bigger mystery of the code worm, with hopes that it might lead to uncovering how the evidence was corrupted. But no one thinks it will be soon."

"We're not dead yet," Evie said. She looked at Joe. "And we have each other." He crushed her in a long hug, kissing her. Then they hugged Mike, and the copbots steered them toward an adjoining medical building. Joe's last vision of Mike was of his fist raised defiantly in the air.

They were hustled inside. Evie cast an apprehensive look at Joe as one bot took her away down a corridor. The copbot led him into a sterile room, where he waited, nerves frayed. A medbot entered. "Sir, I am deactivating all your electronic devices and your MEDFLOW. Please remove your shirt." One of the bot's octo-phalanged hands probed above Joe's left ear and found the NEST. Joe knew he was verifying that the power source was removed. Next, the bot injected painkillers with the tip of a scalpel and incised the skin on Joe's right hip. It removed the power pack from Joe's MEDFLOW. The mechanical hand operated precisely, then sealed the flap of tissue back into place.

"What about the biometric tile?"

"I am instructed to allow retention of that embedded passive device, to allow identification when needed."

"Easier to identify our bodies?"

He thought the bot might have preferred to ignore the comment, but it answered, "That is correct. The device sends a location signal upon your death." The medbot rolled backward a meter. "Sir, now I must record your medical condition, to certify that you are in excellent health when you leave us." It lifted a metal hand. "Please remove all your remaining clothing."

Joe did so, shivering under the lights.

The cold steel hand slithered forward. "Sir, cough please."

"Fuck you," Joe coughed.

———————————◆———————————

Joe stole a glance at Evie. "Tomorrow's the day. Do you feel ready?"

Evie's jaw tightened. "One goes to war with absolute assurance. I prepared as best I knew how. Do you feel ready?"

Joe shrugged, wondering if his weeks spent memorizing survival texts would be as useful as he hoped in the Empty Zone. "As much as possible. Only time will tell." Evie squeezed his hand.

The bots had marched them out of solitary confinement and left them standing alone in a large holding cell. A pile of specialty clothing sat in the middle, next to two backpacks. The supplies were courtesy of Mike, who had diligently followed their lists. Copbots had vetted everything for prohibited electronics and biomedical technology.

Evie picked through the clothing, holding up several pieces to verify they'd fit well, and then opened her pack and examined the contents. The packs were similar and oversized, manufactured from a lightweight, high-strength material. He lifted his to estimate the weight. "Fortunately, there's no rule about using modern materials," he said, inspecting the high-grade equipment.

"Using up your dark credit$ for a worthy cause." Evie's wry smile echoed his own feelings. "What's lashed to the outside of your pack?"

He pulled the double-bitted axe loose and held it up. "A man needs his tools. See, this model has a telescoping handle, so it's a hand weapon, but with the handle extended you can chop wood." He hefted the axe, feeling the balance in his right hand.

"And the bow and arrows? You know how to use them?"

Joe worried a little about that. "I've never shot a bow, but I can teach myself. It's worth the extra weight." He avoided thinking about why the bow would be useful, and Evie didn't argue with the necessity of the weapon.

Nocking one of the razor-tipped arrows, he checked the draw length on the compound bow. He pulled the cable to the corner of his mouth, the wheels rotating smoothly on the ends of the limbs.

"It's not exactly primitive," Evie noted.

"A couple centuries old. But there are no electronics—only a lens for magnification on the simple scope sight." He nodded his chin toward a stick beside her pack. "Walking stick?"

Evie grabbed the stick, which was nearly two meters long. She spun it between both hands, expertly flipping her wrists and switching hands as it whirled. She switched to a one-handed spin. He watched the ends blur as she increased the speed. She turned the stick with one last sweeping arc and brought it to rest.

"It's a bō staff," she said. "Traditionally, they're made of wood. But this one is a lightweight advanced metal alloy. I had a retractable blade added to the end, so it's an offensive weapon too." She turned the staff over and pointed to a curved blade that she could withdraw into the shaft with the flick of a lever on the side. "With this addition, I can also quickly turn it, if needed, into a *naginata*, which is a traditional pole weapon."

Joe was impressed. "Nice thinking." He set the bow down and rifled through his pack. "I'm sure Mike confirmed we don't have unnecessary duplicates. The critical issue I see is not enough water."

She bit her lip. "The Empty Zone is a lot of desert, right?"

"I believe so." Joe had requested all the reading material Mike could find on the Empty Zone, so he summarized what he'd read for Evie. "The area used to be populated, but after global warming the heat became too much. The megadrought in the American Southwest lasted over a century. It caused nearly everyone in Central Nevada to leave.

The government forced the stragglers to move because they wanted to turn the area into what it is now—an outdoor prison. From what I can tell, there are some mountains, but I've no idea about forests or water sources. The government censored all the maps and information about the area. The maps just show a potato-shaped region. We'll have to find our way by the lay of the landscape."

"Aren't they supposed to place us where the odds are that we can survive?"

"Yes, though the actual survival rate is far less than fifty percent." He tried to smile. "Here's to hoping our preparation will help us beat the odds, whatever they may be."

"I've fought the odds my entire life," she said. She squinted at their water containers. "We could die of thirst first. So we carry as much water as we can."

"Can you carry more than this?"

She hoisted her pack. "I can carry my weight," she said with determination.

Joe nodded.

The single door to the holding cell opened and five copbots entered, followed by Peightân and Zable. Peightân was dressed formally, with epaulets on the shoulders of his police uniform and an imperious stare. The bots and Zable stood at attention behind him.

"I am here to complete my formal duties before seeing you off on your journey." His tone was crisp and professional. "By decree, you are forbidden to bring any electronic or biomedical devices into the Empty Zone. The States allow you anything else you think necessary to survive, so long as you can carry it."

"Your concern for our survival is noted." Joe let his words drip with sarcasm, turning then to the practical. "We need seven more liters of water each."

Peightân sighed. "The request is granted. Now, will you agree to carry yourselves in an appropriate manner and to illustrate to those outside that you have been treated properly, according to the law?"

"We'll put on the usual show for you." Bitterness dripped from Evie's words.

Peightân paused while they stared stonily back. "You have been sentenced to spend exactly three years banished to the Empty Zone, beginning tomorrow. The Empty Zone is a region of the States devoid of people and modern machines. It covers approximately forty thousand square kilometers. It is enclosed by an electrified wall one thousand kilometers long. The wall has five gates. You are free to exit any gate at noon on the day you have finished serving your sentence of exactly three years. The mechas guarding those gates will allow you unmolested passage."

Joe memorized the details as Peightân spoke. "All autonomous guard mechas are permitted to use lethal force on any human being in the Empty Zone. If you try to breach the wall before your sentence is complete, you will die. Do you understand?" His eyebrows raised, Peightân waited for their affirmative response.

Joe snapped, "Yes, we understand the typical ways prisoners may die in the Empty Zone. But we'll choose our own way."

"Everyone dies in the end."

CHAPTER 27

Joe stared through the bars of his cell. A solitary dim ceiling light cast shadows that receded into inky darkness farther down the empty corridor. He was the only prisoner in this section of the facility. The humid, musty air against his face reminded him of a VR haptic simulation of a medieval dungeon. As a last indignity, they had put the manacles back on his wrists.

He had kept up the facade since their arrest, trying to be strong in front of Evie and Mike. But now, alone in the dark, the full reality of his situation struck home, and he was afraid and angry.

. . .

I've always played the odds conservatively, as if it would protect me. But these are impossible odds. I'll die out there. Evie will die with me. The end usually seems so far away. Until it's not.

Did I make the right decision to help her? I made it with both head and heart. I felt she was a virtuous person, worth the risk, and I was right. The world tests every decision you make, those both to act and those not to act. There's no standing by the side of the road; you must choose a path and move forward. I don't regret choosing Evie.

. . .

His thoughts turned away from Evie and back to the prison. Fury rose in his throat, and his stomach clenched, bile burning like a devil trying to escape. The anger propelled him to the bars, which he gripped and tried to rattle, his muscles flexing helplessly against the unmoving metal. He pounded against the bars until the shackles bruised his wrists. The sound echoed in the corridor, then faded into the silence of the immutable stone.

. . .

If there's a God, where are you now? There's no evidence in the closed physical universe that you exist.

. . .

His chest heaving, tears on his cheeks, Joe sank to his knees before the cell door. He clutched at the bars and voiced an anguished howl before slumping to the concrete floor.

. . .

No, it's not God, but the evil in people and the injustices they allow that I hate. Damn the horrors that they do to one another. I understand Evie's passion now. Rage, rage against it.

. . .

A door creaked open. A dim light moved down the corridor toward him in time with the ringing impact of approaching boots. He closed his eyes until the footsteps stopped centimeters from his wet face. He peeped up into the rapturous face of Zable, who tapped his truncheon into his left hand. Joe wiped his nose as the fury welled again inside him.

He pulled himself to standing and stared down into malicious eyes. "Enjoying a Schadenfreude moment?" Joe's voice was roughened by lack of sleep and stress, and he enjoyed the growling tone of his sarcasm.

"Cut the foreign language. Like I expected, you're a wimp with no balls. Hard to know why a girl, even from my former Level, would waste time with you."

"If you're referring to character, you're right. She's better than both of us, but don't mention yourself in the same sentence, you spherical bastard."

"Spherical?" Zable frowned, confused.

"As an astronomer once said, any way someone looks at you, you're still a bastard."

Zable's nostrils flared. Stepping back from the bars, he brought the truncheon to touch Joe's chest. A red-and-white flash blinded Joe as his body convulsed in pain. His cuffed hands shook, his fingers involuntarily clutching the bars as his body rattled from the electricity coursing through him. Would his brain actually explode out of the top of his skull?

The electrical current pulsed through his chest again, and his lungs pulled tight. He couldn't breathe. Zable laughed and tasered him a third time. The pain was unbearable. Ten thousand bees crawled over his skin, and Joe hung by clenched fists from the bars. Zable pulsed the weapon once more. His vision narrowed, his head throbbed, and pain rose in every fiber.

"You think you're so elite. You reach down from your Level and you just take what you want, like *her*. Well, some of us know how to reach up for what we want." Zable spat out the words. Joe groaned and rolled away from the cell door.

"Too bad we need to quit—time to turn the vidcams back on. And just when I was having fun. See you tomorrow, wimp."

Zable's steps ground away from him. The door at the end of the corridor clanged shut. His crotch was wet. His bladder had emptied from the shocks. He pulled himself off the floor and staggered to the cot. Slumped there, he managed to push the pain away with festering hatred for Zable. He allowed the hatred to linger until he imagined the dim light of morning appearing outside the jail, though his cell remained a black hole.

An image of Evie after he had last hugged her filled his thoughts, with her defiant glare at the copbot that marched them back to their cells. Was it hatred she harbored? It was hatred of injustice, but not hatred of individual people. It was a nobler resistance.

Darkness surrounded him, with only the coarse blanket under his back anchoring him to the world. Joe's tears had dried, and he was still. His anger about the appearance of Zable and the nonappearance of God was replaced by the infinite blackness of knowing he was on his own. He stared into the gloom with rising defiance. Joe whispered to the prison bars, "Never resign."

———————————◆———————————

Guarded by seven copbots, Joe and Evie stood in the entrance to the Ministry building. They carried their packs, piled high with extra synjugs of water. Evie wore a green jacket over a plaid shirt, khaki pants tucked into black hiking boots, and a sun hat. Joe glanced at his Mercuries. He had unrolled the top cuffs into boot mode and set them to a plain brown before the copbots de-energized them. He pulled his transformable jacket closed.

The wall screen displayed the scene outside the shut doors. A gigantic crowd had assembled in the plaza. Reporters and bots with recording devices lined the concourse. A lone police hovercraft sat at the far end of the plaza. More copbots paraded forward and formed barricade ranks between the Ministry building and the waiting hovercraft. The bots turned to face the open concourse, their graphene-Kevlar mesh capes hanging from their shoulders in symmetrical lines. The crowd waited expectantly.

"The show begins," Evie said.

"More like a perp walk. They want everyone to see how equipped we are—a pretense that this is not deadly by design. And they want us to show remorse."

Evie scowled. "When the people have all the facts, they'll be the ones to feel remorse. Until then, it's enough to know we have truth on our side. But now, it's time for our camping trip to begin."

. . .

Oh, yes, camping, I've *read* all about that now.

. . .

The doors swung open, and guardbots nudged Joe and Evie forward between the ranks of copbots toward the hovercraft. Joe glanced back at the austere facade of the Ministry building, a brutalist monument to authority. Evie caught his eye with an inquiring expression, and he nodded his assurance. The sudden memory of last night made him hesitate, but he stiffened at seeing her stride ahead, and cold resolve tightened his gut.

Projected holograms floated over their heads—reporters playing to the crowd. Copbots lined up like tombstones, and Evie and he were escorted into the plaza. It reminded him of the way the sportscasters vidcast the play-by-plays during the Combat Dome competitions.

". . . found between the ghost towns of Tonopah and Ruth, Nevada, with Death Valley to the south. No roads cross it and no people or machines are found there."

"After warming raised the average temperature by five degrees, people left as agriculture and jobs disappeared. The States acquired this land and built the perimeter wall in . . ."

"People did once live there, so it is not impossible . . ."

A giant screen on a plaza-facing building projected a newsbot providing commentary. With a female voice, it intoned, "The States abide by all the international conventions regarding punishments, including the past century's abolishment of the death penalty. Banishment simply precludes the use of our shared technology and relegates these criminals to means known to earlier civilizations."

Joe wanted to turn off the buzz, but there was nothing to turn off since his NEST had been deactivated. He shook his head and focused on Evie ahead of him. She was a beautiful angel, avenging injustice, unbowed. She reached the hovercraft, turned and flashed the crowd a dazzling, confident smile, waved an insouciant hand, and entered the craft. He followed her inside and sat.

"Let them remember that when we come back in three years," she said.

The engines whirred to life and the craft rose off the plaza, banked, and headed away from civilization.

They huddled in the hovercraft, their packs lying on the floor. A copbot faced them on the opposite bench. The door to the cockpit opened. A canted head peered out, bearing a vengeful grin. "Time for your last joyride."

"You enjoy your job too much. Why are you here, anyway? Isn't prisoner delivery beneath your head tilt?"

Zable stepped forward, swiveled his head centimeters away from Joe's face, and sneered. "I wouldn't miss this."

Joe felt a pit open in his stomach. "Our sentences are for three years in the Empty Zone. With the chance to survive."

"Minister Peightân enforces the letter of the law. But I like to enforce the spirit of the law. The law wants you dead."

Zable pulled a small black rectangle from his pocket. He reached behind the copbot. "Time for a memory upgrade," he said. The bot blinked twice; its lenses settled into a stare. "Go reset our flight path. Here are the coordinates." Zable read off the numbers. The bot disappeared into the cockpit.

Joe's stomach twisted even tighter as Zable rapped his truncheon into the palm of the other hand, as if waiting for a reason to use it. Zable's finger twitched against the switch tucked into its side, and his insides crawled. He knew too well the weapon's power, disguised by the ordinary case.

. . .

No, I don't have a poor opinion about Zable because of his Level. I have it because he has a bad
character. Some people choose a path toward evil,
and they don't turn back.

. . .

"How long have you known Minister Peightân?" Evie's
calm demeanor helped Joe concentrate on something other
than his own rage.

"All my professional life." He seemed surprised at her
benign question. "He's helped me move up the Levels fast."

"He seems particularly driven." Evie said it almost as if
she were complimenting Zable.

Zable nodded proudly. "He keeps at whatever goal he has
and never lets up. The Minister works hard."

"Is he easy to work for?"

Zable leaned closer to Evie. "He takes care of me. All the
credit$ I want. And of course, with money comes power, and
all the things that go with it. Such as sweet girls like you."
Zable leered, his gaze raking her body.

Joe would have punched him in the face right then, but
Evie subtly gestured with her hand while keeping her eyes
trained on Zable. "And he gives you all the nice jobs. Like
the Burnings."

"That's right," Zable said, his eyes still wandering. A moment later, the smirk changed to puzzlement and he looked
at her. "How'd you know about that?"

. . .

They weren't watching us at the Burning. They
must not have immediate control of all the databases. Whatever their real plan, it may take a while
to play out. Raif and the team will be playing hacker
hide-and-seek across the net.

. . .

Evie shrugged and moved away from him. "I thought it must be one of the plum assignments."

Zable giggled. "It is, seeing those bots go up in smoke."

The copbot returned from the cockpit and assumed its position on the bench.

"You and Peightân are after power?" Joe forced the question out without growling.

"No reason not to tell you, because you're gonna die out there. I'm in it for the money and power. I like giving orders." Zable jerked a thumb at the bot. "Peightân and I are the first in line to tell these buckets of metal what to do."

"Mr. Zable is correct. I follow his orders," the copbot intoned.

"Are you giving us good odds of surviving?" Joe casually engaged the bot. Zable sneered in his periphery.

The bot obediently answered the direct question, as Joe had anticipated. "Your odds of surviving are now one percent."

A mutinous smile crossed Evie's lips as she stared at Zable. "What a coincidence. That's the same as my chance to make it to Level 1."

"It's a lot lower than that now, girl." Zable's snigger made Joe fist his hands.

He could no longer control his anger. "You follow Peightân around, doing his bidding."

Zable moved to the seat nearer the cockpit, where he could stare down at them. "I'm my own man." He still tapped a slow rhythm on the palm of his hand with the police baton. "You see, it's like this. There's money, and there's power. I got tired of waiting for my share, so I found a way to take both."

"There's more to life than money and power." Joe didn't really expect Zable to agree with him. "There are people and ideas."

"Maybe I'll think about that later. But not just yet."

They rode in silence for an hour, and Joe's temper stewed while Zable watched them with narrowed eyes, like a cat playing with a mouse.

The hovercraft began its descent, and the desert floor rose to greet them, an arid playa between distant gray mountains.

The craft settled, and the doors sprung open. Zable stood to his full middling height while the copbot hauled their backpacks outside and escorted them out onto the dirt.

Zable stared at them, a wicked half-smile curling his mouth. "Don't die out there too fast. Slow is fine." The doors shut and the craft rose, churning up a devil of dust. Joe wiped the grit from his mouth. The craft melted into the shimmering air of the desert. When it was gone, the only sound in the hot silence was the beating of Joe's heart.

PART THREE: THE JOURNEY BACKWARD AND FORWARD

"... The man has become like one of us, knowing good and evil ... therefore God banished him from the garden of Eden, to till the earth from which he had been taken."

Genesis 3:22-23

"It's an unfettered journey to everywhere you wish to go."

Evie Joneson

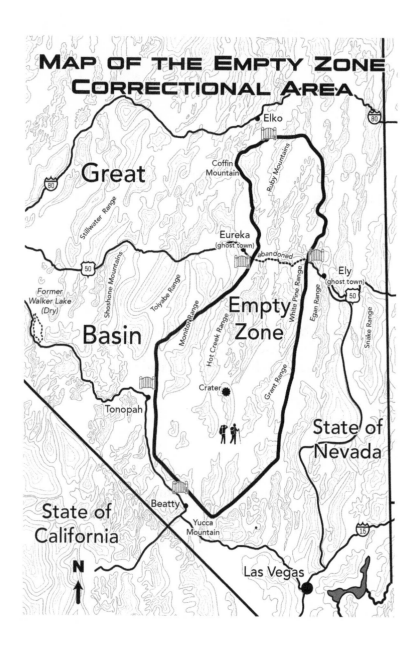

CHAPTER 28

Joe faced Evie in the dust. His hatred of Zable, the grime in his mouth, and the sudden heat of the desert merged, and red-hot fury boiled inside him. He struggled to calm his anger.

Evie watched him. "You have something personal against Zable?"

"You could say that. And he has something personal against me. Driven by envy, I guess. He visited my cell late last night."

Concern clouded her face. "That must have been a surprise."

"Yes, a real shock. I called him a spherical bastard."

Evie laughed. "I know enough astronomy history to grasp the reference."

He smiled to banish the searing memory and to keep from worrying Evie. It was time to focus on the urgency of the moment. He shaded his eyes and looked around.

The profound silence of the desert enveloped them. The sun was high in the late-morning sky, baking the flats below, a wasteland devoid of even a shade tree. Evie broke the stillness. "This awful landscape, it reminds me of a line from a book— 'For you are dust, and to dust you shall return.'"

"It does put one in touch with their mortality." Joe couldn't place the words, though they were familiar. "What is that from?"

"Genesis. Sorry. Best to avoid those thoughts so we can focus on living." She tilted her head and watched him expectantly, without fear. "Now what's next with us?"

· · ·

There's a familiar question. But now she has the experience, not me. And she has played with long odds more often.

· · ·

"We're in this together. We decide together."

"I'm not shy about making decisions." She wrinkled her brow. "But you're thinking all the time. I want to understand your thought process."

He surveyed the empty salt playa. "Well, we can't stay here." He pointed to distant mountains and added, "That way, north by northeast."

Evie frowned, considering. "I agree we can't stay here, but why toward those mountains and not"—she gestured to other distant peaks in the south—"those?"

He stood and shouldered his heavy pack. "Do you trust me? I can explain as we walk."

She nodded, then retrieved her bō staff to use as a walking stick. They trudged over the alkali flat, passing withered saltbushes.

"First, we can't go west. I caught glimpses out the hovercraft window. By the angle of the sun, we were flying east before we landed. We were crossing salt pans and empty desert."

"All right. We don't go west. Couldn't we continue east?" she asked.

"We could, but I don't think we should. The meager information I read about past banishments all concluded that people often don't come back. It's negative statistical data. That reminded me of a story from a world war more than two centuries ago. Mathematicians studied the pattern of bullet holes on returning bombers. They inferred that the planes that made it safely back were only damaged in non-essential areas. Which meant that the areas *not* damaged could have been critical points of weakness—statistically, that's where the planes that didn't come back must have gotten hit—so they reinforced the planes in those places. By finding patterns in the missing data, more planes came back because the mathematicians had deduced the planes' vulnerabilities."

"Like evolution, influenced by those who did get eaten by the lion."

"Exactly. I read every news report about the people who didn't make it out alive, and I've made my own inferences." Evie listened closely. "Peightân mentioned five gates in the wall around the Empty Zone. They brought bodies out through the southwest gate, to Tonopah, and through the south gate, to Beatty. The town of Beatty is near the Yucca Mountain nuclear waste repository, which they built there in part because of the desolate landscape. Bodies were also taken to Eureka and Ely, the ghost towns marking the west and east ends of the old Highway 50. The gate not mentioned for retrievals is the north gate. I believe that anyone who's lived was able to venture far enough north to survive both summer and winter. If we keep going north, not stopping too soon as I suspect the others did, I think we might have a chance."

"Then we have a very long hike ahead of us."

"Afraid so. There's one more depressing detail—southwest of the north gate is a drone landing facility. They call it Coffin Mountain."

Evie snorted. "Thanks for the full disclosure. Let's stay away from there."

They tramped throughout the afternoon until the sun touched the western mountains. The landscape was no different from where they had begun, with drooping bushes and no tree in sight. He pitched the tent, stowed their packs, and laid out the double sleeping bag inside. Evie added water to a dried protein mixture and heated it over the pocket stove, lighting it with an allmatch. "It appears they took the electronics out of this too," she said.

"Yes, but the flint works fine."

"We have cooking fuel for about a dozen days, so we'll need firewood." She surveyed their treeless surroundings. By the time they'd finished the meal, all light had faded. Without artificial light, they felt their way into the sleeping bag and fell into an exhausted sleep.

◆

They started at first light, taking advantage of the cooler temperature. The landscape was less flat but still barren, and they continued north between mountains bracketing a shallow valley.

As the day progressed, light played off the mountains in dull reds and whites. Dust devils danced over the cracked land. To distract himself from his aching muscles during the hours of hiking, Joe identified plants he had memorized from the allbook—saltbrush, spiny hopsage, and pickleweed. They created shade to rest under during midday to avoid the worst heat by draping the tent over a shriveled bush as a lean-to. They camped by an ancient lakebed that was now a salt flat. In the night, a gusting wind churned salt into the air. They nestled inside the tent, which shook for several hours.

Breakfast consisted of another dried protein packet mixed with boiling water. He stuffed the tent into his backpack, and rubbed the ache in his back. "How's your back today? Your pack must be as heavy as mine."

Evie considered and then hefted up his pack. "Heavier."

Joe lifted one pack, then the second. He pulled several of the water synjugs out of her pack and secured them to the side of his own.

"I didn't ask you to—"

"I know."

They trekked for several hours and stopped for lunch to avoid the midday heat. As they munched on protein bars, he mused on their progress, noting the buttes to the northwest. "I know the Empty Zone is shaped roughly like a potato. Based on how dry this is, my guess is that Zable dropped us in the southern half of it. I know the length of the perimeter wall, so by calculating the approximate distance and direction we hike each day, I can roughly figure where we are."

"Helpful to have a mathematician around," she said.

They finished the sparse fare and started again. Joe could not distract himself from his dry tongue and throat. Without clouds or trees to offer shade, the sun beat down on the forbidding landscape and the two travelers. They camped next to a gnarled volcanic formation as the merciless ball sank behind bare slopes to the west. At the tent entrance, Joe held Evie's hand while he studied the odd vista, jagged goblin's fingers painted a strange orange.

***

The next two days were physically exhausting and mentally excruciating. Joe battled with his pack, which cut into his shoulder blades. His Mercuries felt heavy on his sore feet, and two toenails were blackened.

Evie kept a methodical pace and never complained. When the terrain became tough, they hiked single file instead of side by side, and Joe and Evie took turns leading. When Joe was in front, he could set the pace, which was never faster than hers, but he found himself lost in dark conspiracies in which Zable and Peightân plotted every misery he now faced. When Evie took the lead, he lumbered behind her and his daydreams shifted to fantasies involving her toned legs and sinuous hips. The bō staff, lashed to her pack, swayed in rhythm with her steps.

During a stretch of easier terrain, he voiced a concern he had been trying not to dwell on. "I estimate that we're covering fifteen to twenty kilometers a day. And we'll need to keep up this pace for several days so we don't run out of supplies before getting somewhere we can survive. But if we go too fast, we could be too worn out to make it to any place at all." Saying it made his pack weigh twice as heavy on his shoulders.

Her dry hand laced through his, and he looked down into her worry-tinged face. "I wish I saw anything that suggested water. The land is bone-dry, even now in late spring." At their last rest stop, they had taken shallow sips from the last synjug Mike had packed for them. Now they only had the extra liters they had requested from Peightân. "Even if they dropped Celeste and Julian somewhere more hospitable, we can guess what happened to them." Her tone was quiet, sad.

They plodded on. They camped under mountains rising from the mudflats to the east. The fifth day saw yet more mudflats. By late afternoon they had ascended a hundred meters into rockier hills, where they made camp. Evie pulled off a hot boot. They had matching blisters on their big toes. "Bloody hell, those smell bad." She had her nose over her boot.

Joe sniffed at his own and a yeasty reek greeted him. "I got you beat I think."

"Already, I'd give anything just to be clean."

"I'd just kill for some water. Even the inside of my mouth is dry."

While she prepared dinner, he walked up the edge of the ridge. To the west, sand and emptiness stretched to the far horizon, where the sun set over another mountain range. Joe speculated that the perimeter wall was not far beyond.

To the east he climbed another ridge. Reaching the top, he beheld a humongous crater—out of place, otherworldly. The stunning hole was about a kilometer wide. Joe estimated its inky bottom was at least one hundred meters deep. It resembled the moon craters he'd observed from the WISE Orbital Base. And when nightfall descended, just like at the base, vast emptiness surrounded him. He trudged back down the hill, ate his dinner, and snuggled into the sleeping bag next to Evie, pulling her close and reminding himself that while he had her, he'd never be alone.

The next morning was chilly, with wind swirling in from the west. Evie held him tight, and Joe was reluctant to leave her warm body. They dragged themselves from the sleeping bag and prepared their protein breakfast. They had seven liters of water remaining.

To distract himself from that fact, he said the first thing that came to mind. "If only we'd brought coffee."

"And just when you were teaching me to enjoy it, there will be no wine for years."

"Let's not start compiling the list, or it will depress us."

"Speaking of drinking, you're bigger than me. You need to drink more water."

"There's too much desert in front of us for that. I wish my fitness level was as good as yours."

"You're getting there." Evie rubbed her hands together, her expression tense. "I'm sorry I got you into this."

"We got ourselves into this. It was a team effort."

They began their morning by climbing to the crater he had found the evening before. Crumbling lava rock littered the landscape. It was devoid of plants, with kilometers of bare basalt. He led them around the west side of the crater and across a scree field of loose volcanic stone. They crept through sharp rubble for the next half hour.

Circling an outcropping, Evie gasped and scampered down to a rock depression. Joe joined her, forgetting his blistered feet and shoulders for a blissful moment.

A few centimeters of brackish water lay undisturbed. Evie leaned over the pool, and Joe caught a glimpse of her eager reflection on its hazy surface.

Joe kneeled by the precious find and dipped a hand in. Even with its tinge of salt and sulfur, the water soothed his parched mouth. "It may be drinkable." He dug in his pack for a Mylar blanket and laid it in the hollow on top of the puddle. Evie used her bō staff to press the thin Mylar to the bottom of the hole, letting the water flow on top of it. Together they lifted the sides and filled as many empty synjugs as they could until the gray water was gone.

"I read about these but never hoped to find one," Joe said. "It's a mini-tinaja, a rock pool where water gets trapped. We've bought more days." Evie grinned and gave him a high five. Joe allowed himself continued hope for their survival.

They persisted on through the volcanic panorama. The landscape looked alien-like. To the east, a white ellipse of salt left from yet another ancient lake stretched several kilometers. In another hour, they passed a large cinder cone, orange with the sun's rays. Three kilometers farther on, they came upon an abandoned road. The asphalt ran with labyrinthine cracks and missing chunks, but it was an uncomplicated path, so they turned northeast to follow it. It was easier to walk side by side on the shattered road, and conversation made them temporarily forget their discomfort.

Any reticence Evie had shown when they first met had evaporated. She was as transparent as the desert air and the blue skies above. She told stories about growing up in the Dome. They talked about music and their friends. Joe was struck by how much she valued her Community Dome friends, treating them, he thought, as a substitute family.

But soon their mouths were too dry to talk. They straggled through the blistering afternoon, the packs chafing the skin on their shoulders, and Joe's mood sank even as the road rose through a pass. When evening fell, they made camp west of a lava wall.

"We have a choice to make. Our overall direction is north. There are two mountain ranges ahead of us, one to the north and one to the east, both two or three days of hiking away. It looks like this lava wall marks a north–south divide, so heading due north may be tough." He hunched over the camp stove that warmed their dinner. "If we continue to follow this road northeast, however, we're guaranteed an easier path, out of the lava . . . but it'll lead us across the desert in the valley between ranges. And I'm worried about our water supply."

"We have enough water now to cross the desert." She seemed as tired as he did. "I say continue northeast." Joe grunted his agreement. They ate their dinner and cleaned up in near silence before cuddling into the sleeping bag.

A sudden disturbance awakened Joe. Evie unconsciously clutched at his chest, as if from a bad dream. He rubbed her fingers and she calmed, not waking.

Despite his dehydration, he felt the urge to urinate, so he left their sleeping bag. After walking several meters on sore feet, he stood, cold and exposed, beneath a dome of stars. He usually found them a friendly sight. But now they gave no comfort, and their distance only reminded him how alone they were. Joe and Evie were mere animals, slinking over the land like every other. Except in this arid place, they were the only animals. Joe slipped back into the sleeping bag and hugged Evie to assuage his isolation.

At sunrise, they descended the low pass along the lava wall, using a black peak to the south to orient themselves. The road stretched on endlessly, a black sword slicing northeast across the sepia-tinted playa. Beside it, occasional salt and iodine bushes struggled in the alkaline soil. Joe found himself creating narratives for the withered plants, which all ended with one plant sucking the moisture from the other. Evie seemed similarly distant. The dehydration was getting to them, but there wasn't anything he could do. Sunset found them making camp in the cheatgrass beside the road. They didn't speak as they set up the tent, ate, and went to bed.

Joe knelt at the tent entrance, ready to join Evie in the sleeping bag inside, when a lizard crept in the sand toward the tent. The creature skittered from a rock to a blade of scrub bush. It stopped, motionless, seeming to examine him in the fading light.

· · ·

Here we both squat in this waterless land. But this is your home. How do you survive against such a heartless earth? What is it that drives you? Tell me your secret so that I, too, can go on.

· · ·

The next two days of monotonous footslogging abused their bodies. The mountains were remote, the desert implacable, inscrutable. By midmorning the temperature had spiked, and sweat danced down Joe's back before drying into crusty salt. He tried to smile at Evie when she glanced at him, and his lip cracked.

"Shit." He sucked at his lip, perversely grateful for the moisture. She looked away again, an unbroken stoic.

After a brief rest at midday and small sips of water, Evie seemed revitalized. As they started up again, she kept a steady pace by his side.

"It's taking an eternity to cross this desert," he said.

She laughed. "You're reading my thoughts. Do you know what Milton thought about eternity? Eternity is a single instant of the fullness of time."

She knew something about poetry too? It was a small bright spot in Joe's difficult day. "Where did that thought come from?"

Her gaze was dreamlike. "This place reminds me of an old line of music—'Make straight in the desert a highway for our God.'"

"We have that."

"You have your negative hypothesis about why we should head north. That reminded me of a topic on your allbook I got immersed in. It's the series of books about the *via negativa.*"

"Some of the more obscure philosophy texts." Joe was impressed. "I haven't read all the books on my old allbook, including those. But I remember the idea in general, that it describes God by negation, by what God is not."

"The idea is that God is ineffable, beyond any human description. That our poor human powers cannot get us close to any comprehension, so our best approach is to surrender to the cloud of unknowing. That idea resonates—you should approach any concept of God through the heart."

The gears in Joe's tired mind lurched to life again. He recalled a conversation with Gabe about the existence of God. At the time, Joe had given the idea a low probability. "Do you believe in God?"

"A question about belief, coming from a mathematician and scientist?"

"A question I ask myself. I'd like to hear your thoughts."

"Remember what you said about time? You said space-time is a single block."

"Yes."

"You say there is no scientific evidence that any God affects anything within space–time. So any God is not within this universe."

"All the scientific evidence says there is no interference. The laws are internally consistent. It's a closed physical universe."

"A dragonfly frozen in amber."

"I think so."

She laughed triumphantly, the sound hoarse but full of life. "Therefore, if God exists and is outside space–time, then we'll never have evidence. We cannot definitively answer the question you asked me. We are left not knowing whether God exists or not."

"Your logic is impeccable. It follows, then, that there is only belief without any basis in facts."

"I'm repeating a conclusion that Enlightenment thinkers like Thomas Paine, Benjamin Franklin, and Thomas Jefferson came to." Evie smiled as she walked, and Joe could now imagine her attentive participation in political science classes. "They believed in the power of reason. Many of them were Deists. They dismissed revelation as a source for knowing about God, and if there was one, they didn't think that God interfered with the world."

"A scientific approach."

"Arguably a more scientific approach than today. They were willing to confront what they could not know and still discuss it. At least, they weren't hiding any evidence under a bushel. They couldn't ignore the evidence, such as how the universe seems to be so elegantly constructed. There's a particular beauty to the world." Evie gestured to the arid expanse before them. "Even to this empty desert."

"Or you, walking in this desert."

She glowed with a grateful smile and continued with the thought. "Where does that beauty come from?"

"I've often asked myself that same question about mathematics. Mathematicians do not create it; they discover it. And mathematics is foundational to the universe. If there is a God, then She must be a mathematician."

. . .

Back to Wigner, the unreasonable effectiveness of mathematics in describing nature, and my long-ago conversation with Freyja. What can explain that miracle? Perhaps here, facing death in an unforgiving land, it's time to update my probabilities about God. If we fail, I may soon have a face-to-face chance to answer the question in my moment of eternity.

. . .

Evie interrupted his thoughts. "Why do you use the pronoun 'She'? The idea from the *via negativa* is that God is beyond any of our power to comprehend."

"I tend to anthropomorphize gods and machines, so 'It' feels too impersonal a title. And 'He' is archaically paternal. So I use 'She.' But you're correct; if there is such a god, then She is beyond our comprehension and must be super-intelligent to create such an astonishing universe."

"Then if there is a God, She is outside the universe and does not interfere and is unknowable and far more intelligent than we can even comprehend."

"Nicely said."

"You don't expect any god to answer any prayers?"

"No." Joe's faith hadn't grown in any way since they started this journey.

"I agree. We keep going, doing the best we can wherever we are."

A thoughtful silence washed over them as they walked along.

. . .

Contemplation in the desert has spawned many belief systems, many gods to worship. It's a human predilection, yearning for gods to help and console us. For some, it's been a crutch and an excuse for bad behavior. For others, it has been a source of power. None of those beliefs are consistent with a closed physical universe. If I'm to consider the existence of God, then it must be an alternative story, with a She who doesn't interfere. We're on our own in the desert, to live and die.

Many would not find such a story appealing, considering a God who doesn't intervene. But how would the story play out if it were true? Could such a story fit logically within a scientific stance to understand the universe?

. . .

Joe cleared his throat before indulging a sudden need for confession. "My reason for coming to the college wasn't about deciphering robot consciousness. I was trying to understand my own. To discover if I had free will. If I do, I now need to figure out how to use it and find a meaningful reason to keep on walking." Joe gestured toward the horizon. "Even if it's across a desert such as this."

She glanced over at him and seemed to stand taller. "You won't have mental sparring partners like Gabe and Freyja out here, but I can challenge you to find reasons."

He grabbed her hand and swung it in time with their stride. "You challenge me all the time, and I love you for it."

CHAPTER 29

The cold of night was followed by the scorching heat of day. As the mountains drew nearer, their exhaustion grew. Joe broke the silence. "I'd wager the road continues to head northeast between the peaks. I'm not sure when it might reach the prison wall. Your thoughts?"

"Based on your negative gate theory, we should avoid the eastern gate, so that means it's best to leave the road and move into the northern mountains, even though the terrain will be more difficult," Evie said.

He agreed, and they said farewell to the broken road. They turned north across rough bajada west of the mountains, searching for promising vegetation or any hint of water. Sagebrush was interspersed with the occasional pinyon pine and Utah juniper, their branches gnarled from the winds.

Evie pointed to a prickly pear, its green pads dry but still intact, and she dropped her pack. She pulled out her knife and scraped the spines away from an edge of one pad, then carefully gripped it and removed it from the cactus. Joe watched her lay it on a rock and scrape it thoroughly. "It will make a poor girl's nopalitos," she said. She finished the first pad and continued with more until she had harvested them all. Evie piled her treasure into food synjugs and loaded them back into her pack.

They hiked on, ever higher up the mountain. The trees grew taller as they progressed. White fir clustered in a vale between mountain ridges. Their heavy packs and sore muscles were now secondary to the mutual but unspoken anticipation that water could be close.

He led a kilometer farther, enjoying the fresh scent of the forest. They clambered two hundred meters up a ravine. Without a word, Evie pointed. Joe took in the sight cautiously, not trusting it wasn't a mirage. His gaze rested on a tree-tucked gully, alive with the flow of a streamlet that descended through the copse and gathered into a small pool. They hugged each other, with Evie swaying in his arms as if in a waltz. They would survive—at least another week.

Evie pulled cups from her pack, and they ladled clear water into their welcoming throats. They faced each other by the miniature pool, laughing and splashing each other. "I so want to be clean again," she said. Joe peeled off his clothes before she finished speaking. She followed suit, and soon they stood to their ankles in the water. They washed then lay naked on the grassy bank to dry.

It was cooler in the shade, and soon Joe pulled on his damp clothes, shivering. Evie put up the tent while he refilled all the synjugs, happy to wash the remaining sulfur-laced dregs away. They explored the hillside for firewood, returning with armloads of branches and logs. He chopped the logs into pieces with his axe, struck the allmatch, and soon a fire crackled beside the tent. Evie charred the prickly pear in the hot coals, removed the skins, and cut them open. The tartness exploded over Joe's tongue, both overwhelming and glorious. Evie closed her eyes as she savored their first real food in over a week.

They huddled by the waning fire. "Tomorrow we don't have to get up and hike until we drop." He stroked Evie's arm.

She turned to face him, smiling. "How long do you think we can stay here?"

He sighed and stretched. "With three days' rest, we can decide if this place has enough food to sustain us. Now we need to recharge, physically and mentally." He shook his head. "I don't know about you, but I never dreamed how fast my mind would spiral into worst-case scenarios. It feels like we've caught a bit of a break here, so maybe we can relax a little, especially if we can find food."

Her gaze rested on his, gentle and concerned. "The dehydration affected you more than me. I felt it too, but didn't want to worry you." Her hand against his cheek was his last memory before he fell asleep.

Sunbeams touched his eyelids, and Joe blinked awake. He leaned over and kissed Evie.

They ate another dehydrated meal from the dwindling supplies, and Evie studied the vegetation jacketing the ravine. "We might find food here. I went on a lot of camping trips as a kid and learned a bit about foraging."

"I crammed for the exam while waiting for our trial. That's my total knowledge," he said.

"This is the right test to prepare for." Evie stood and swung her arms in circles, warming up. "I'm going to explore. I won't roam too far."

Joe was left to figure out what he could contribute. Water and understory plants meant there might be small animals nearby. The bow he'd carried with so much effort was useless until he could learn to use it. He'd have to try his hand at an animal trap.

Retrieving his backpack, Joe filled it with a synjug of water, some of the leftover prickly pear, a thin coil of rope, and a knife. He wandered up the ravine, following the dribble of water farther into the trees. The underbrush became thicker, making it difficult to identify scat or animal trails among blending vegetation and dappled sunlight.

. . .

Think like a rabbit. What is that like? Not conscious but sentient, feeling primitive emotions, concerned about its next meal, water, and predators. It's living in the moment as it follows the path of least resistance.

. . .

The allbook had provided instructions on how to build a deadfall trap. He chose a spot where a fallen log narrowed the streamside path. From among the plentiful rocks strewn across the ravine, he chose a flat slab and dragged it to the narrowed path. He then chopped a branch into four pieces with his axe—one for a crude post, another for a lever, the thin end to use as a bait stick and a trigger pin. Joe speared a prickly pear onto the bait stick. He cut a length of rope and tied the trigger pin to one end, then affixed the other end to the lever.

He lifted the rock into place to set the post and lever, wedging the bait stick against the trigger pin. He tried to lodge the other end against the underside of the slab, but it slipped and the rock fell, nearly smashing his hand. He successfully balanced the delicate arrangement on the third try. He surveyed his construction, satisfied that it conformed to his memory of the drawing.

Joe set two more deadfall traps. The slabs would mean instantaneous death for any creature unlucky enough to trip the bait trigger. He didn't want to think about what he'd have to do to transform whatever was caught in the trap into something he could eat.

He headed back to camp and found Evie by the tent, washing foraged plants and placing green leaves and white flowers in a pot. "I found plenty of chickweed," she said.

"I didn't find anything useful, but I set some Paiute deadfall traps. It's a flat rock propped up with a stick and a clever trigger."

"What are you hoping to catch?"

"The Great Basin should have animals, even with the temperature rise from climate change. I expect there'll be jackrabbits, squirrels, foxes, and deer. There are bighorn sheep, but they're hard to hunt. We need to watch out for coyotes, wolves, rattlesnakes, and maybe bobcats and mountain lions." Joe finished recounting what he'd studied in his allbook.

Evie nodded, taking in the list without comment. Joe sat down and stared into the fire. He finally broached the thoughts nagging at his conscience.

"We're going to need more protein soon, Evie. Without more calories, we're going to die."

Evie squatted next to him. "I've been thinking about that too. I wasn't expecting to find alt-meat out here." She smiled and kissed his cheek. "We can keep to the lower end of the consciousness–sentience scale and do the best we can in the circumstances. Even back in the modern world, we ate fish and chicken."

A squirrel chittered in the tree above them, and Joe felt a darkness settle over him at the thought of killing it. "We remain animals, dealing death to the life around us."

"We should try to be kind animals."

He smiled up at her. "You are an angel."

The next morning, Joe woke with the dawn. Anxious to check his traps, he slipped out of the sleeping bag without disturbing Evie and hiked uphill along the ravine. He placed each foot with care in the underbrush, noticing which plants gave way easier and avoiding brittle branches. At the first trap, he found the rock still balanced, undisturbed as he had left it. Moving farther up the ravine, he saw trap two. It had been triggered.

Joe took a deep breath and lifted the end of the slab. A jackrabbit lay lifeless underneath. He set the rock aside and, with a guilty hand, touched the cold animal.

. . .

I'm glad it didn't know human hunters, making my life easier. Now it is food. I am an animal, and I eat animals to live. It was true before, but then it was abstract and easy to overlook. I can't ignore my place in nature anymore. I'm like that little lizard, crawling across the earth. Yet a conscience adds another burden the lizard doesn't have.

. . .

Joe reset the trap, loaded the dead animal into his backpack, and moved up the ravine. A second jackrabbit lay still in the last trap. Pride in his successful traps warred with guilt as he carried the dead animals. He retrieved a medium-sized knife that worked uneasily in his hand as he gutted the animals, transforming the memorized instructions into the bloody reality. When he returned to camp, he was neither proud nor cheerful, but grimly focused on embracing his life in the Empty Zone.

Evie's lips parted approvingly on seeing the catch, but when he held it out, her lip trembled and guilt clouded her eyes. He recognized in her what he'd experienced when gutting the animal—the shock of facing death, a revelation that they so seldom experienced in modern society.

Joe retreated with the knife to a bush downstream, where he finished cleaning one of the jackrabbits. He severed the head, the bones crackling under the knife, then skinned the carcass and washed it. He cut a thin branch and skewered the hare.

Joe returned, holding the branch. Evie took the stick without a word and balanced it between two rocks, centering the hare over the sizzling fire. She had already set her pot of roots to boil. Joe stared blankly, and after a few minutes, Evie gestured to the pot. "These are western spring beauty. I found them along the stream. They take time to dig up, but they'll add starch to our diet." Her bō staff rested on a nearby rock, next to a pile of peelings from the root.

Joe came back to himself and tried to forget about the jackrabbit. "Very resourceful." He walked downstream to scrub his hands then sat quietly by the fire and watched her work.

His mouth watered at the rich aroma. She served the crispy jackrabbit pieces on leaves, and they stared into each other's eyes as they chewed the unfamiliar meat. It tasted like a gamey, tougher version of chicken—but it was a feast after the dreary reconstituted meals.

"I'm not an angel," Evie said. She licked the last of the grease from her fingers. At his raised eyebrow, she continued. "Last night you called me an angel. And I'm not one. I'm just another creature here, eating another in order to survive." She sucked the last bit of meat from the bone and tossed it aside. "We're none of us angels. And I appreciate your resourcefulness to fill our plates."

They spent the next two days following the same routine. Joe practiced walking in the woods without making noise, checked his traps, and added five more. He harvested two jackrabbits the following day. He surmised that the animals were susceptible to traps because they had no experience with humans. With evidence of small game on this mountain, it was time to try using his bow. Setting traps was one new experience, but the idea of shooting the bow excited him.

He set up a target made from branches and leaves woven together. He marked off eleven paces, turned and nocked an arrow, took careful aim with the bow sight, then released. It flew wide of the target and buried itself into the dirt. Frowning, he considered what he had read about bow hunting. He continued practicing, releasing the arrow without letting his fingers jump and experimenting with different adjustments to his arms and body position, until he hit the target seven times in a row. It was time to take the bow into the woods.

Joe hiked up the mountain, first following the watercourse with his traps, then continuing beyond. He moved deliberately and watched for any movement in the underbrush. It was slow work, and it was difficult to remain noiseless. Overheated and drained, he sat on a boulder and took a long pull from his synjug. He closed his eyes and breathed deeply, taking in the gentle breeze and the rustle of leaves. A birdsong started up nearby, then another. He opened his eyes and scanned the area.

A movement near the rill, thirteen meters away uphill, resolved into a jackrabbit outlined against the horizon. Holding his breath, he nocked an arrow, raised the bow, and sighted through the lens. His hand shook, but he steadied the bow with a slow exhale, trying to ignore his pinched fingers. They convulsed when he released the string, and the arrow flickered away with a *swish*. The dirt next to the jackrabbit erupted as the animal hopped into the bracken.

Joe stared with disappointment at the bare dirt, though part of him was glad to have missed. He went to retrieve the arrow, but he must have shot high, because the arrow had disappeared over the hill. He searched the far hillside until he was exhausted but didn't find it.

. . .

This hunter is not ready for this unforgiving world.
I'll need a lot more practice before trying again.
Arrows are priceless.

. . .

Joe walked back to camp in late afternoon, empty-handed. Evie cooked a jackrabbit trapped the day before for dinner, and they went to sleep in the fading light.

The next day, he collected only one squirrel from his traps. He worried about the declining catch. Either the animals were getting smarter, or there were not enough in the isolated mountain range to support them for long. For breakfast, Evie harvested chickweed and spring beauty roots but found nothing more promising.

Resolved, Joe said, "This has been a good rest stop—a necessary one—but I think it's time to move on."

Evie nodded. "Thank goodness we found this place, but there isn't enough to sustain us."

"The copbot gave us a one percent chance. My guess is it didn't calculate based on the number of people ever sentenced to banishment, but rather on where they dropped us off—near a moonscape, in this case. We are still days away from the northern mountains, where I think long-term survival is most likely."

Evie stared at the trickle of water that had saved them. "I doubt this flows all summer. We'll need a dependable water source. There are only a few white pine trees in this tiny forest, and these mountains are too arid to stay."

"We press on north," Joe said.

Chapter 30

They broke camp midmorning. Before they set off, Joe visited each of his deadfall traps—finding only one squirrel—before knocking them down and recovering the rope.

They headed north, striding side by side. The synjugs were full of fresh water and strapped onto the sides of their backpacks. He felt recovered, and his shoulders had healed for the most part, but the weight of the pack still rested heavier than he wanted. He tried to ignore it.

They scrambled along the western side of the mountain range, agreeing that the change in elevation was worth the chance of water that venturing into the desert would not afford them. They camped at sunset in a grove of white pines. Joe was pleased to find firewood, as their supply of stove fuel was dwindling.

Their path north took them out of the mountains, and they traversed a gray landscape interspersed with stunted trees, leading to gray-green sage and greasewood bushes that faded into the salt flats beyond. By the end of the third day after leaving the rest camp, they reached another abandoned road. Wider than any road they'd crossed so far, it snaked east and west across the dehydrated land, undulating toward the distant mountains.

"My bet is this is the old Highway 50." Joe peered up and down the broken lanes.

"This leads to the gates where they took people who didn't make it," Evie said.

Joe knew she thought about Celeste and Julian. "Yes. So it doesn't make sense to go east or west, because it's still too dry here. But the land north could show signs of more rainfall."

They set up camp, and Joe spread the sleeping bag on top of the cracked asphalt, which still retained the day's heat. He built a fire with the last of the firewood they'd hauled from the mountains. As daylight faded, a lone eagle soared over the rainless land, searching for prey in vain before it turned north and glided away.

Facing each other as they sat on the sleeping bag, they gnawed on leftover squirrel meat and split the last of the dehydrated vegetables. Evie ate slowly and licked her fingers when she finished, seemingly oblivious to his gaze on her. She roused something in him, and he forgot about the emptiness in his stomach and the ache in his muscles.

Joe crawled behind her and massaged her shoulders, which were red from the pack straps. They made love in the sleeping bag, below the desert sky filled with a billion stars.

———————◆———————

The hope of water to the north was not realized. They left the road and the mountain range behind. The desert was a gray ocean dotted with dull, green-silver sagebrush like floating balls, each surrounded by its spot of parched dirt. One cloud hung motionless in the crystal-blue sky. And like the ocean, uninterrupted desert rose on the horizon and sank behind them as they trudged on.

The landscape devolved as they pressed on into another salt flat. Millions of hexagonal pieces made up the crazed surface of the dry lake, and thick chunks flaked off when Evie jabbed at it with her bō staff. The land held an earthy, chalky scent and seemed to absorb their breath. In the mornings, the sun burned Joe's face. He walked with his eyes half-closed to protect them, his hat helping little. In the afternoon, it baked his neck, and sweat dried into salt that caked his clothes. The blisters on his shoulders returned, and the residual salt stung his broken skin.

Evie's voice interrupted his torturous daydream of floating in a pool of fresh water. "You're deep in thought. What about?"

Joe grunted. "Regrets about what I didn't bring. Analog eye protection against the bright sun, for one. Corneal implants don't do me any good without my NEST."

"I didn't think about it either," she said.

"We get so acclimated to the technology we have, we forget we have it." He was back to his freshwater fantasy before he'd even finished the sentence. A few moments later, he registered her murmured voice and realized she'd asked him a question. "What?"

"Do you regret helping me?"

"Never," Joe said. He hoped his weak smile inspired confidence. She grinned back, so it must have. He walked behind her while the sun beat down on them. They moved across the empty landscape like drops of oil on a hot plate, preparing to evaporate into nothingness.

. . .

Do I regret helping Evie? Never. What she was doing was right, and my helping her was right too. Was it an accident to love her? The world brings people together in random ways. But then we choose which way to turn. My loving her fills my life. No, it wasn't just an accident. I chose her of my own free will. And she chose me.

Evie is so tenacious. I'm a dull mirror to her strength. We need perseverance, or we'll both die. The best we can do is play the hand dealt, play it well, and let the cards fall where they will.

And now I'm in the game, playing every card. It feels good to have a purpose, to be focused, even if only on survival. But there's a double reason to survive, because I've found someone to share my life with.

. . .

At the end of the second day after crossing the highway, they made camp and reviewed the food supplies. It was still scorching after sunset, so they went without the tent, laying the sleeping bag on the ground. He pulled one dried piece of jackrabbit from his pack. "That's dinner. Anything else in your pack?"

"We finished the dehydrated food," she said.

He picked up her pack and realized it was again heavier than his own. "What else do you have in here?"

"I've been saving it," she said. Joe dug to the bottom of the pack.

"There are seven kilos of genetically enhanced, short-season spring wheat seeds for planting. And there's yeast and bean seeds."

"You accused *me* of being the planner."

"You carried the bow, and I carried the bread," she said. "We have days of survival ahead of us but then years to plan for . . . if we ever find a dependable water source. I can go hungry for longer if it means we can save this."

He kissed her and held her in his arms. "I can too."

The next day, the northern mountains continued to grow larger on the horizon, beckoning them forward. The immutable landscape, sterile and pitiless, sucked the energy from their bodies. Twice they stumbled across old gravel roads, built to service forgotten mining operations, leading nowhere except to desert. They marched onward like soldiers on a battlefield, immersed in the searing, empty land.

Dusty arroyos spilled from the mountains. Joe and Evie ended the day hungry and bone-weary. More dire, the syn-jugs were nearly empty. The air still simmered as the day faded, and they camped on the sand again without pitching the tent.

Hunger gnawed at Joe's insides. He couldn't stop thinking about the seeds in Evie's pack. As she settled into the sleeping bag next to him, her look of resolve kept him silent in his agony.

Joe lay on the sleeping bag and aimlessly piled the sand beside him with his hand. It formed a pyramid, the new grains falling from his fingers onto the apex, rolling down the sloping angles. Her hand on his shoulder hurt his raw skin, and he pulled away. Then he sat up and faced her with a tentative smile.

She didn't return it. "What's wrong?" She looked at the sand pile and frowned. "What are you doing?"

He contemplated his small pyramid. "Since we had the discussion about the *via negativa*, I've been thinking back to my sabbatical project." Joe decided not to mention that it was mostly to ignore the painful physical reality of the trek, and that he wondered why he should care, since the chance of reaching any conclusion and living to tell anyone diminished daily. But the long hours had given him time at last to organize his thoughts.

"Your question of whether we have free will?"

He nodded. "I've tried to organize in my head all the conversations I had at the college, to make sense of them. They're beginning to have some structure."

Evie rested her elbow on the bag and cradled her cheek. "What's the summary?"

With a deep breath, he forced his mind into overgrown paths of thought. "I assume a physically closed universe, as science suggests. There are at least three things necessary for conscious creatures to have free will. First, either there is no God, or if God exists, then She does not interfere. That assumption partially would explain why there can be evil and hardship in the world."

"As we discussed."

"Second, the universe must admit some indeterminism. There can be no free will in a deterministic machine because everything would already be decided for us."

She nodded.

"Third, whatever the 'I' is that is us, that 'I' must be causal. Gabe explained a troubling argument about mental causation. He said philosophers can't find a way to show how our mentality can be causative in a closed physical universe. Unless I can figure out how to unravel that knotty argument, there's no free will."

"That last part sounds particularly hard."

"It's very difficult, given what physics describes about a universe of particles in motion."

Her hazel eyes waited for an answer.

Joe frowned. "I don't have the answers. But as Gabe taught me, stating the problem is the first step."

"And how does that relate to playing in the sand?"

"Thinking of the second requirement—that there be sufficient indeterminism in the universe—the physics has focused on the minuscule, like particles, in part because those lend themselves to quantifiable experiments. But as we move to large aggregates of stuff—stuff that we care about, like rocks and trees—those don't lend themselves to neat experiments. Freyja raised this issue when she suggested that I focus on complex nonlinear systems. Right now, I was thinking about how larger patterns of material like this pile of sand really characterize what is happening."

"How so?"

Joe poured more sand on top of his pyramid; it collapsed in a tiny cascade. "See how it appears to reach stability? Sand slides until it reaches an angle of repose. If I keep adding sand, it will eventually create a mini-avalanche."

"Sand just does that," she said.

"The question is *when* does it slide again?"

"Are you asking what decides when it slides?"

"The pile of sand is a complex system, and an example of self-organized criticality. It is a dynamic system, out of equilibrium, and is nonlinear, which means the math doesn't allow prediction of when it might collapse. We know that when it does topple, the size of the ensuing avalanche obeys a power law distribution. We can model it statistically. At a meta-level, we can predict it will eventually collapse. But not exactly when."

Evie perked up. "Is that the evidence that clinches the argument for indeterminism?"

"I don't believe so, but it does show that determinism isn't the cut-and-dried answer. It shows that large-scale patterns of particles acting together do matter, even if there is randomness driving the pattern."

A sudden wave of exhaustion engulfed Joe, and he put a hand to his head. "I'm sorry, Evie, I haven't been myself. This journey . . . it's been so much more than I expected."

She gently pushed his head down and pulled the sleeping bag around them. His eyes closed involuntarily against the dying light of day.

"Just rest now, love. You need to recover your strength. Tomorrow will be a rough day."

◆

Joe woke groggily, shaken awake. "Three mouthfuls of water each," she said, handing him the synjug. He drank greedily and handed it back. His stomach was empty beyond growling.

"I'll just rest a bit longer."

She was shaking him. He must have fallen asleep again. "Snap out of it! We have to reach the foothills today."

He tried to sit up and extricate himself from the sleeping bag. His entire body ached.

"I can't physically carry you. But I'm not leaving you here. You either move, or I'm going to die here with you. And I don't want to die." Her face was close to his and a tear ran down her cheek. He wiped at it with a finger and tasted it, adding salt to his tongue.

"Usul giving moisture? I'm not quite dead yet."

She wiped her eyes with a trembling hand and gave a short laugh. "*Dune*. Appropriate. You're thinking again. Now get up." Something in her tone galvanized his remaining energy, and he stood on wobbly legs. Evie had already packed their gear. He stowed the sleeping bag, and they shouldered their packs and trudged across the desert.

CHAPTER 31

The northern mountain range drew closer but, to Joe, everything was the same—a haze of hunger, thirst, and fatigue. He tried to focus by recalculating how far they had hiked—now about three hundred kilometers.

They rested at midday to avoid the worst heat, as they had done most days. They sat back-to-back, the tent stretched out above them, spread across two bushes. The last synjug held their final drops of water. Finding water was now life or death, but Joe scanned the landscape between them and the foothills to the northwest and saw only more desert. Their bodies were dehydrating from outside in.

With a start, he realized Evie had moved and he was alone. She was a few meters away, urinating behind a bush. The sound awakened a nearly overpowering urge as he stared at the last synjug. With shaking hands, he tightened the lid without sipping. Evie rejoined him, her uncertain gaze searching him.

"Joe, we need to move. We can still reach the foothills before dark."

He struggled to his feet. "I hope that one of us can always be strong when the other one isn't."

"Always."

They hiked northwest and crossed a dried lakebed. Its flatness suggested it might be a seasonal marsh, now evaporated this late in spring. They stopped near some desiccated plants. "I think these are cattails," Evie said, examining the wilted specimens. She pulled on one to retrieve the stalk and root. She rubbed it against the blade on her bō stick, peeling the exterior away, then put it in his mouth. Instinctively, he sucked, and the bitter cucumber taste brought a trace of moisture to his throat. He sucked until there was nothing left, then took another. They dug up plants for a while, but Evie kept glancing at the sky and soon had them moving across the flat desert again.

In late afternoon, they crept into the mountain foothills and made camp among shrub brush. Joe dropped his pack and collapsed beside it. Evie sat next to him, her eyes alive with determination. "Let's scout for water together," she said.

They trudged slowly, zigzagging over gullies that snaked the foothills. Joe didn't want to put another foot in front of the other. He wanted nothing more than to lie next to their packs back where they had left them and never move again.

As he dragged himself over yet another rise, the magical sound of water hitting rock caught Joe's attention. There, percolating from broken granite, was a small spring. It splashed the glistening rock face and collected in a one-meter pool. A tiny trickle streamed out of the pool and down into the ravine through clumps of white and yellow lilies.

Joe and Evie lay flat on the ground, their chins awash in the bubbling water. Then they lay hugging. Evie's laughter verged on tears, her relief was so palpable.

They filled all their synjugs, drank their fill, and washed dust from their faces. Joe was bone-tired but rehydrated. He willed himself up the ravine and found places to set deadfall traps near the water. Birds flitted in the bushes, but he knew his bowhunting skills were no match for them, and he was afraid of losing more arrows. They ate the remaining cattails for dinner. The ache in his stomach retreated, and they cocooned in the sleeping bag for the night.

The next morning, Joe awoke with renewed energy. He reached his arm out for Evie, only to find her gone. He called for her, but she'd disappeared from the campsite. He headed up a nearby ridge and kept an eye out for her while he checked the traps. He was elated to find one of his traps sprung with a ground squirrel under the large rock. Joe gutted and cleaned it, then carried breakfast back on a stick. After collecting branches, he started a small fire.

Just as the blaze caught, Evie appeared with her daypack, sprouting with foraged greens. He didn't try to hide his relief. Subconsciously, he had feared she'd left him.

Her alert gaze rested tenderly on his. "You look revived. I'm so relieved. You never gave up mentally, but your body couldn't tolerate the dehydration."

"I feel much better. Glad you're here with me."

They roasted the game over the fire and ate the sinewy meat along with the greens Evie had collected. He stood stiffly and looked toward the east, where more mountains stretched north. Squinting at them, Joe thought they looked inviting, possibly with more trees than the sparse-covered ones they were on. "Maybe those are our mountains," Evie said. They shouldered their packs and worked their way north across countless ravines in search of greener vegetation.

They camped at the foot of another peak. Black sagebrush clothed the slopes, and pine trees stood on the higher reaches. "Those trees suggest water at higher elevation," Joe said.

"Let's keep climbing north tomorrow," Evie answered. Joe nodded, eager to push on.

By late morning the next day, they'd crossed another open valley, with a higher set of peaks on the northern end. A dirt road crossed at the lowest part of the valley, but they ignored the path. They were riveted on the olive-colored hills ahead. They ascended sloping hillsides with remnants of lupine long past their bloom. Stopping to rest, they drank tepid water and stared back at the peak where they'd camped the previous night.

They toiled on. The landscape was different from the mountains where Joe had set his first traps—the foliage colors were a shade brighter here. More greens infused everything. That meant more water. He guessed this was the area of the Empty Zone that survivors always found.

His pace quickened, and Evie matched it with a light step. "Notice anything special about this place?"

"Just an intuition."

Clambering down yet another ridge, they found a streamlet, the water trickling but constant. "Let's go farther," she said. Over the next ridge there was another runnel. Evie signaled to hike higher, and they trekked across verdant hillsides crowned by firs, spruce, and pines. She reached the top first and dropped to her knees.

Joe reached her side a moment later and stood there, breathing hard from the climb. Before them spread a narrow valley, a few kilometers wide, with a deep, emerald cleft through the middle. Steep mountains on the north and east cupped the valley in their asperous fingers. The mountains sported bare, gray granite above the timberline, sharp against the sky, but a blanket of forest draped the lower ridges.

Evie flashed a grin, and his pulse raced.

They quickened the pace down the hill to the middle of the valley. A gushing stream splashed clear and cold. Cottonwoods and aspens lined its banks. Joe and Evie dropped their packs, and together they lay down to drink great mouthfuls of sweet water.

Evie's laugh rang in the branches. "I think we've found home."

It was early afternoon, and the sun was still warm. They undressed and waded into the cool water, rinsing the weeks of trail dirt away. Then they rested on the bank, slowly drying, relishing the soft rays of sun on their skin.

◆

Sunlight warmed Joe's face. He'd fallen asleep, and Evie still slept. He kissed her awake, and her eyelids fluttered. "We should explore, find the best spot to make a permanent camp," he said. They dressed, shouldered their packs, and hiked upstream. They crossed the brook on a fallen log where it narrowed, crossed back where boulders constricted it to a torrent, and continued up the east side where it was easier to find footing. The bank appeared worn with an overgrown trail. Animals probably followed it, seeking water. The rush of falling water sounded like a miracle after their weeks spent in the desert. A half kilometer up the creek, Evie stopped and pointed. On a jutting granite rock beside the creek, less than fifty meters away, stood a cabin.

Excitement rose in his chest as they approached it. They dropped their packs under a craggy tree in front of the cabin and surveyed the weathered structure. Sunbeams winked through chinks in the board walls. It had a low, peaked roof of coarse wooden shakes. The cabin door creaked open on rusty hinges. Sunlight streaming through an unbroken window revealed the main room and an additional side room, large enough for a bed. Dust covered rustic pieces of furniture—a table, roughly built chairs, and the remains of a hemp bed frame. Joe ducked into the side room and stared through a hole in the roof at open sky. Evie inspected a fireplace that lined the back wall, blackened from use. Ash coated the wood floor around it.

Behind the cabin, Joe saw most of the chimney stood, though bricks along the roofline had tumbled off. Several meters from the back door stood a canted outhouse.

Joe and Evie hugged each other in exultation at their find.

"It will need a lot of work," Joe said.

"But it's home."

His body vibrated with the wonder of the moment, and he shared in the joy that lit her face. Then her expression shifted, her head tilted, and her gaze seemed distant.

He was reminded of the first time he'd studied her in his apartment living room. Since then, he had played with worse odds than ever before, and they had won. They were alive. He beamed and hugged her again, his chin tucked against her ear. Her heartbeat was fast and strong. They were surrounded by sounds of a splashing brook and a breeze murmuring through the branches above.

"Now what's next with us?" He tucked a piece of hair behind her ear.

She gazed up at him without fear. "We are going to do this. We are going to survive. We'll do it together."

"I promise you I will be like you, strong and dependable. I will love you and care for you."

Her face shone. "And I promise you I will be strong and dependable. I will love you and care for you. Until death do us part."

"Until death do us part." Joe couldn't keep the tremor from his voice at the word. "We will work together to make the best of whatever life brings us."

"You already gave me the ring," she said.

"Diamonds and rubies, I will give you. And all my love."

He kissed her with all his being. They clung to each other, knowing their future had more to unfold.

Chapter 32

A steady *thwack* rang out in the morning air. Joe swung the double-bitted axe in long arcs, cleaving pinewood in the clearing outside the cabin. Sunlight glinted off the blade with each stroke. His shirt was off, and a layer of perspiration coated his skin. With each piece of wood split under the blade, his muscles learned and adjusted to find the best angle and speed. His mind was unclouded and held only the axe and the wood. He swung the tool with a steady rhythm, the labor a meditation.

He had begun the morning by setting five deadfall traps in a line leading uphill along the stream. Deadwood was abundant on the surrounding hillsides, so Joe had collected dozens of armloads and lugged them back to the cabin. A log served as his chopping block, now buried in wood chips. He had already stacked a cubic meter of firewood outside the cabin.

. . .

Food. Firewood. Then repairing the cabin. There's enough work to do. Best to take one task at a time.

. . .

Until they repaired the cabin, they would eat outside under the tree that faced the creek. The veteran tree had reddish-gray bark, and it raised crooked, spreading branches to shade against the midday heat. Blossoms were opening, and their faint scent perfumed the spot. He studied it, and recognition dawned—it was an apple tree. The color of the bark stirred a memory from his initial inspection of the cabin, and he strode around it and found a second apple tree in bloom, the pulsing hum of bees filling his ears. He thought the original gardener must have planted two so they would cross-pollinate. Joe was so excited that he lifted his hands to the sky and spun in a circle, dancing.

Some remaining logs would serve as temporary seats outside until he had time to improve the furniture. He arranged the logs under the apple tree to serve as a crude table and chairs, then sat self-satisfied on his new throne.

Evie stepped out of the forest and smiled when she saw him. Before they had both left that morning on separate chores, she had washed her hair in the chilly stream. Now it shone clean in the sunlight. "Look, I've found monkeyflower and manzanita berries." She held up her daypack.

Together they rolled several stones to form a circular firepit near the log benches, and Joe built a fire while Evie boiled manzanita berries to brew a cider and prepared a salad from the monkeyflower. "We're short on food, but late spring is a fine time for foraging."

"And there should be trout in the brook. When I was searching for firewood upstream, I found some promising pools."

They finished lunch and returned to separate jobs for the afternoon. Joe already appreciated the benefits of using traps that worked while he slept. He recalled the picture of the fish trap in the allbook. Two open wooden cylinders, a smaller one partially tucked inside a larger one, could be made of thin saplings bent into circles and lashed together with sapling cross-ribs.

After collecting a stack of thin branches, he worked to bend them into hoops, tying the ends with cord. He cut the cross-ribs and lashed them across the hoops to finish the outer cylinder. Then he fashioned a smaller cylinder like the larger. The smaller cylinder slipped into one end of the trap, and he tied it in place. Joe studied his construction with satisfaction. It worked like a funnel. Any fish that entered the cone would have difficulty finding its way back through the small opening. He glanced at his finger, which he had nicked with the knife, and wiped the bit of blood on his sleeve.

He lugged the trap upstream to the first still pool over a meter deep. Two rocks dropped inside worked as weights. Joe tied on a retrieval cord and lowered the trap into the pool. He decided to test the trap without baiting it. If he didn't catch anything, he'd try the next day with bait.

On his return from placing the fish trap, he checked his Paiute deadfalls and found a squirrel under one. He carried it back to the cabin and started a fire outside.

Evie appeared soon after, chickweed and miner's lettuce sprouting from her backpack. She prepared a salad while Joe roasted the squirrel. "We should light the fireplace inside the cabin as soon as we can," she said.

"That's tomorrow's job. I'll need to get onto the roof to fix the chimney bricks and clean out the debris."

"We have a lot of work ahead of us." She rested her chin on her hand and gazed at the cabin. "Life itself is work." Joe could tell she wasn't unhappy with the prospect.

He quoted lines from memory:
"Degenerate sons and daughters,
Life is too strong for you—
It takes life to love Life."

"An old poem?" She held the steaming pan. "I like the sentiment."

"From your example, I'm beginning to better understand the lines. I think it means to find a purpose and then get on with life. Don't be timid about it."

Evie smiled. "I'm glad to see you so resolute."

"It's strange. For the first time in my life, I don't have technology or civilization to help me live. It's completely starting over, as if from the beginning."

"Like we're the first two people in the world."

Joe nodded. "If we don't take full responsibility for our predicament, then we die. It's all on us. Has life always been like this, and I didn't notice?"

"It's the story of humankind. It hasn't changed." She shrugged. "We dress it up in different ways, trying to make it better."

"But now we're back to basics. Water. Food. Shelter. It focuses the mind. And with less time to overthink things, it frees the mind of unnecessary worry."

Evie served the meal, and they sat on the logs next to the fire.

"What are you thinking?"

"I'm thinking about all the energy I put into the protest movement, to try to change the world. And the great cost of it—losing my best friends. Now it feels like that was all part of a different life." She ate a few bites, still pondering, then faced him intently. "I haven't given up the fight."

"We will go back and carry on the fight," Joe said, knowing Evie's battle was no longer just her own. But her expression was not fierce, as he expected. Instead, a thoughtfulness softened her face.

"Wanting something different than our reality is the cause of most distress." Evie furrowed her brow. "Although I'm a fighter, there are things we can't change. I'm not giving up, but there's nothing I can do for the fight against the Levels Acts except survive. So for now, I'm embracing the reality of this world we're in. That's my mantra to live this life with you here."

. . .

Just when I think I've seen her at her strongest, she surprises me again. I'm in love with a stoic.

. . .

They savored their break, sitting close together and resting around the fire outside the cabin. The sun set over the western mountains. He realized that with no sources of artificial light, the best course was to adjust his waking hours. He added candle-making to his growing mental list of projects.

"It's time for us to head to bed," he said.

But Evie was not looking at the sunset. She stared downstream into the valley. "That looks like smoke."

Joe followed her pointing finger and made out the wisps in the ebbing light. She shivered next to him. It was too late to investigate, and too far down the valley to be an immediate threat. He kicked out their fire. Joe hugged her and led her back to the cabin. They snuggled into the sleeping bag and fell asleep on the cabin floor.

A sharp scream jolted Joe awake. Evie clutched at him and tried to throw off the blanket at the same time. Adrenaline surged in his body, and he sat bolt upright and reached for the axe, searching the dark cabin with wide eyes.

"Something ran right over me. I felt its little feet and claws. It was horrible."

"It was probably just a mouse." Joe took calming breaths. "Most likely attracted by our wheat seeds. It probably came in through the chimney." The remark did nothing to quell her shaking, and he put the axe down and held her close. "I'll close up the holes in this old cabin soon."

. . .

She's been so brave this whole time, but she's afraid of a little mouse? Maybe it's beyond my comprehension. We all have fears, just different ones. At least I can be the strong one now.

. . .

Joe lay back down and held her against his chest until her breathing became even at last. He lay awake, staring through the hole in the roof at the sky filled with stars, thinking about mice and men.

After breakfast, Joe fixed the chimney. Every task took about three times as long as he thought it should. The simple job of constructing a ladder from two short pine trees, several thick branches, and rope took half the morning, and the result was barely serviceable. Setting it against the roof at the back of the cabin, he warily mounted the rungs. It wobbled but held his weight.

Knocking the detritus into the fireplace was easy enough. He then used his backpack to carry the fallen bricks up to the roof so he could replace them. Joe didn't bother with mortar yet. He only wanted to make the fireplace functional.

He fetched an armload of firewood. Inside the cabin, Joe laid pieces of tinder in the fireplace and lit the fire with his allmatch, stoking the fire as it caught. The fire drafted up the chimney, and he ran outside. Smoke billowed up thick and black from the burning vegetation he had missed in his hasty cleaning.

Letting the fire burn to coals, Joe climbed the ladder again to assess the gaping hole in the roof. The rough-hewn wooden shakes were squares, two centimeters thick. He frowned. He'd need a saw and a wedge to make replacements, but he had neither.

"Friend, it looks like you'll be needing a proper ladder so as to not break your neck."

Joe met the hard gaze of a man standing at the edge of the woods behind the cabin. The man was tall, perhaps in his mid-fifties, and he had a curly head of hair that matched a thick, wild, salt-and-pepper beard. An incongruous buckskin coat overlay his camo shirt and frayed military fatigues. The man's long fingers were wrapped around the sling of a compound bow on his shoulder.

Joe controlled his shock and tried to smile nonchalantly. "Let me come down to introduce myself," he said loudly, hoping Evie heard him. Exposing his back to the man caused an uneasy itch in his back while he descended the ladder. When he stepped off the last rung, Evie came around the corner of the cabin, the bō staff in her hand. She stood alert next to Joe.

"Two of you are here. Better and worse, I suppose," the man said. "My name's Eloy."

They introduced themselves and shook Eloy's hand. "Come and join us for tea," Evie said. Eloy followed her around to the front of the cabin, Joe behind him. A pot simmered on their outdoor fire. She brought their two cups and a small pot they had packed, and she poured the pale liquid into them. Evie handed Joe his cup, her cup to their guest, and she cradled the small pot in her hands to drink her serving. Eloy sat on the log opposite the two of them, drinking the tea.

"This Douglas fir tip tea isn't the best, but it's healthy with vitamin C. I foraged the tips this morning with my bō staff," she said, showing him the blade.

"Fresh'n tasty," Eloy said. He smacked his chapped lips and eyed the bō staff. His face was tanned, weathered from time spent in the sun.

Joe sipped the tea and asked, "What did you mean by two being better and worse?"

"Twice as many mouths to feed. It's hard to grub a living out here, unless both sets of hands are willing to work. There's no economy except what y'all produce yourself. It's all elementary economics." He took another appreciative sip. "Then there's the social part. The original peoples long ago woulda never sent a war party of three. Always either two, or four or more. Three caused problems because two would fight for the attention of whoever was the leader." He shrugged. "Human nature."

Evie stared from Eloy to Joe, then back. She seemed ready to say something, but Eloy interjected, "How are you two liking the cabin?"

"We arrived yesterday." Joe's wariness faded.

Eloy laughed. "I lived here last year until a windstorm made that hole in the roof. It seemed the right time to move downstream. I've another busted shack plus a barn. More space to putter around in."

"That explains why it was so tidy." Evie's eyes widened. "And of course we'll leave as—"

Eloy waved wide, calloused hands. "You can have it. It has the prettiest view, up here higher. And there ain't any better ones left to choose from—none I've found anyway. I've scavenged everything usable. Most every building has fallen to ruins or been carted away."

Evie cocked her head, curious. "How did you end up in the Empty Zone?"

Embarrassment crossed his face. "I was in the army—the mecha army on the southern border. Drove an exomech."

"Dangerous profession," Evie said.

"Once it was. Now they've automated everything, with the bots doing all the real defending. Death by machine. Any war is over in hours, not weeks. Nobody can stand on those killing fields."

"We're lucky war has disappeared." Joe leaned forward. "Now it's only defensive, keeping the machines ready, right?"

"That's it. After driving an exomech, I oversaw some of the machines patrolling the border, and then they assigned me to repairs. I liked that analog stuff, working with my hands." He held up his calloused evidence. Each finger was as thick as two of Joe's. "But there got to be lots of busy-work, and people figured out how to avoid doing anything. I don't get along well with shirkers. Let's just say I bought a Big Chicken Dinner."

Joe frowned, confused, but Evie narrowed her eyes. "Should we be worried?"

"No, just a little altercation. No one was hurt bad. I got a six-month jail sentence. Under military law, you can choose one-third the time in the Empty Zone instead. They say the Empty Zone has lower recidivism, which is why they give you the choice. I took the two months, figuring I could find enough to eat out here."

"How long have you been out here?" Joe wondered if it would be good or bad to have a neighbor.

"Before I answer, tell me how long y'all are here for. You don't look like military to me."

"Three years." Evie's voice was calm and even.

Eloy started, almost dropping his cup. "Damn. Should *I* be worried?"

Evie smiled. "No. We got on the wrong side of someone with political power."

Eloy's dark eyes studied them each from under his thick brows, and then he nodded. "All right then. It looks like you'll be here for a while." He eyed Evie and her bō staff, then addressed them both. "But we need a few rules. About the economics."

Joe nudged Evie. "Evie is the economist."

Eloy smiled broadly and turned to her. "I got my four-year economics degree in Texas."

"My economics degree is from Berkeley."

"Well, what do you know. Then you'll understand what I'm about to say. The first issue's that you're now upstream and I'm downstream. Tragedy of the commons. So no polluting the water."

Evie nodded, her expression far away like she remembered some lecture, Joe thought. "An issue since people settled the islands at the mouth of the Tigris and Euphrates. We'll respect each other and keep things clean."

"Next is hunting and trapping. Y'all know how to build a trap?"

"I started a short trapline uphill of the cabin," Joe said, "and a fish trap."

"Quick studies. Let's have a trapping demarcation line halfway between y'all's cabin and mine. It's about as successful up the hill as it is down. Same with the fishing." They all nodded.

Eloy went on, warming to his audience. "We can hunt with the bows anywhere. These mountains are full of game since we're the only people here. But the effort of traipsing over hill and dale ain't for the weak." They nodded again.

"We can all guess how much work goes into any getting, so it won't be hard to come to a fair trade. Everyone carries their weight." He gestured to the roof. "I'm happy to lend you the tools, so long as they're well kept. But no borrowing without returning it right away. I don't want to ever have to ask."

They stood and shook hands, then Eloy handed the cup to Evie with thanks. He faced Joe. "You want to fix that roof soon? May be easiest if you both follow me." Joe picked up his pack and the axe, and all three headed down the trail along the creek.

CHAPTER 33

They walked single file. Eloy led, scrambling over boulders and through short grass that lined the bank. They passed the point where they had first reached the stream. About one kilometer below the cabin, Eloy said, "This is the halfway point. Let's mark this rock here as our border." Evie and Joe nodded their approval, and they all continued down the hill. They followed the brook around several more bends, the water twice dropping over waterfalls. Ahead, several weathered buildings lined both banks of the stream.

Eloy pointed. "That's my cabin on this side. I've a barn next to it. And a smokehouse next to that." The graying wood buildings sat on level ground beside the creek, where the water was slower and deeper. Another cabin, next to a foot-bridge, faced them on the opposite bank.

It was hard to look away from the magical sight of a re-volving waterwheel. It was about two meters in diameter, with wooden paddles dipping into the surface of the brook. The lazy current pushed on the paddles, and the wooden axle creaked against wooden sleeves as it turned. Nailed to paddle ends were metal cans. The cans filled with water at the bottom of the wheel's turn. As the wheel rose, the cans emptied into a wooden sluice. Water bubbled through the sluice box next to the nearer cabin.

Eloy grinned when he saw Joe's face. "That's right—running water."

"Did you build the waterwheel yourself?"

"It's called a noria, and yes I did, from scavenged boards and nails. This design has been around for thousands of years. It saves you from hauling water." Eloy beamed, proud of his work.

He led them to the barn, and the vegetable garden planted beside it. A trough brought water from the noria to the plants, reaching up green through newly plowed soil. Water could be directed to either the garden or the cabin with a movable piece of the wooden trough. Facing the barn was a corral, fenced with split rails. A geriatric, dun horse stood inside, munching on new grass, while a handful of chickens pecked indiscriminately around its hooves. Three sheep lay in the dirt in one corner of the corral. By the large, curving horns, Joe guessed one was a ram.

"Big chicken dinner," Joe said. Evie giggled while Eloy laughed politely and glanced at Evie with a sharp eye. Perplexed, Joe wondered if Eloy hadn't been referring to chickens earlier.

"This is wonderful." Evie leaned against a fence post. "You have meat, milk, and wool. What's planted?"

"Tomatoes, squash, and corn. The seeds came from another lucky find, scrounging through a broke root cellar."

"We have enhanced C4 wheat seeds and a few beans."

"Wheat?" Eloy groaned with yearning. "How I miss bread. We can do some trading if you can get it to grow."

"I can plant it on the flat spot east of the cabin, but I need to raise water out of the stream." Joe pointed to the noria. "Can you show me how to build one of those?"

"Not a problem." His nod was curt but enthusiastic. "Intellectual property should be free after a time. Otherwise we'd all be trying to recreate this." He pointed with relish at the wheel, laughing at his own joke.

Joe laughed and decided to ask for more. "I could build one faster if I had boards and nails. Any chance you would trade those for something?"

"Now we're talking." Eloy agreed to help him build the waterwheel in exchange for a part of the wheat crop and some chopped firewood. "Division of labor," Eloy said with satisfaction, "and everyone pulls their weight."

Evie stared across the footbridge, then back at Eloy. "You mentioned two warriors, or four," she said.

"A sharp one." Eloy chuckled and led them across the bridge as the sun reflected swirls under their feet and their footsteps rattled on the planking. The door of the opposite cabin swung open.

A younger woman with gentle brown eyes, maybe in her late thirties, stood with her hand on the doorjamb. Her gaze darted first to Joe and then with a questioning expression to Eloy. She reached up with a delicate hand to brush back the flaming red braids draped over her shoulder.

At the door, Eloy bowed his head amicably and said, "Fabri, meet Evie and Joe. Evie here's an economist, like me. They'll be here for a while as neighbors."

All tension left Fabri's face upon hearing the words, and she grasped both of Evie's hands. "Well then, welcome home." She gave Joe a quick hug before ushering them into her cabin.

The space was filled with the delectable aroma of chicken soup simmering in a pot at the fire. Joe's mouth watered, and his stomach growled. A wooden table stood in the corner. Fabri escaped into the back room and returned, dragging a bench to complement the chairs around the table. "I've never had guests before." She brought brown clay bowls and spoons. Then she ladled out heaping portions of soup. "Lucky for you, just yesterday I decided it was time for this old bird to do her last duty."

"With my convincing," Eloy said. He turned to Evie. "She'd rather keep 'em all for eggs. Even the roosters." He winked.

"Y'all better believe all God's creatures need respect," she said. Then she looked at Eloy, his comment about roosters and eggs registering. She nudged him with a chuckle. "Good one, El."

All sat around the table. Joe's stomach grumbled even louder with the first spoonful. "Yummy soup," he said.

Fabri nodded in appreciation. "How long have you been here? I'm surprised I didn't hear any aircraft. It's pretty easy to hear machines in this quiet."

"I estimate they dropped us into the Empty Zone three hundred and thirty-seven kilometers south of here. It took more than three weeks to find these mountains." Joe was glad he hadn't forgotten the numbers in his delirium. It felt like he'd been in the Empty Zone for years. He took a big swallow of the comforting soup.

Eloy frowned. "Sounds like someone wanted you dead."

Fabri flashed a warning look at Eloy. "What got you sent to the Zone?"

Joe paused, thinking they may be long-term neighbors and it may be best to keep it simple, not mentioning Peightân and Zable. He glanced at Evie. "One of our charges was illegal consorting between incompatible Levels. I guess you can't stop love."

"Me too," Fabri said with a small smile. "But then my husband cheated on me and held me under his thumb with my Level."

"We were framed," Evie fumed.

"I was madder than a wet hen too." Fabri waved her spoon. "I work hard every day to find compassion for that ex-husband."

"You two didn't come out here together?" Evie asked.

"Oh, no. After a week here, I hiked downhill from the cabin." Eloy nodded his head upstream. "I found these here buildings. And I found Fabri."

"I wasn't so good at foraging then. And I had a five-month sentence. Bless his heart that Eloy decided to stay and help me." Her eyes shone at him across the table. "He's had experience with these rough ways of living, thanks to an unusual upbringing he'll have to tell you about sometime. I'll say he's been a godsend." She reached across the table and squeezed his hand.

Eloy smiled at her. "Once we got through winter, the weather was nice and everything was pretty. So we stayed."

Evie raised an eyebrow. "Then you've been out here—"

"Seven months. Fabri appreciates my survival skills, but we've had some lucky breaks. We're the only people here, so I could scavenge every building. The horse, old Bessie, was too slow to get away, so I halter-trained her, and then I had the horsepower to haul stuff around."

"Don't forget the blessing to find these cabins. The barn was stocked with some stuff already," Fabri said.

"Yeah, I guess I can't take all the credit." Eloy looked saddened by the admission. "Others were staying here years before, and they'd accumulated some tools, seeds, and other supplies. I'm counting that as intellectual property to share. It tells me that this part of the Ruby Mountains is the best place to survive in the Empty Zone."

Joe said, "Since you've finished your time here, you can both exit the gate?"

"Yes, we can leave, but the guardbots don't come to find you unless you die." Eloy's voice was firm but foreboding. "They follow the biometric tile to find your body and take it out with an autonomous craft. But don't try to cross that wall until you serve your sentence." His frown was ominous, but his expression turned thoughtful in a flash. "We haven't quite decided yet if and when we want to leave."

"You seem to know a lot about the guards," Evie said.

"They're the same milmechas I saw in the army, just autonomous and in an independent command."

"Autonomous?" Evie said what Joe was thinking as he remembered their last conversation with Peightân.

"Yes. They'll kill you without checking with a human first, but only if you try to get outside the wall early. By the

International Humanitarian Law, autonomous weapons are banned except for prisons and border control," Eloy said.

They finished the meal, and Joe helped Fabri wash the dishes at the sink while making friendly conversation. She took several tomatoes from her kitchen and put them in a sack for Joe. "These will brighten up dinner."

"Thank you," Joe said. Fresh food that wasn't meat or greens felt like a real treat.

"This fella's pulling his own weight. Don't ruin him already," Eloy said gruffly, but Fabri ignored him, leaving and returning with a steel soup pot and a bucket.

"Evie, this will hang on the fire, making cooking easier. And a bucket makes toting water more tolerable until you have the waterwheel pumping." Evie thanked her profusely.

"All right, Fabri, I won't invite 'em over again if you keep giving our stuff away." The gentle look in Eloy's eyes softened his words, but Joe and Evie, gifts in hand, stood to leave.

"It's important to have friendly neighbors," Fabri said as they waved goodbye. "See you soon."

Eloy snorted and escorted them across the footbridge to the east side of the brook and into his barn. Along one wall, tools of all shapes and sizes hung in various states of repair.

He selected a metal blade and handed it to Joe. "This froe'll be handy because the blade cleaves off roofing shakes faster than a saw." He also picked out a bow saw, a hammer, and a bag of nails, and they made plans to construct the noria the following week.

Joe and Evie bade Eloy farewell and hiked up the stream, the tools and the cooking pot filling his pack and the bucket in his hand.

◆

Later that evening, they sat close to the fireplace inside their cabin. Joe had found a rainbow trout in his trap, and Evie grilled it on the fire to serve with fresh tomatoes.

. . .

We've been here in this cabin only two days, and already she's adapted. She is following her new mantra, to embrace the reality of the world we live in. That's resilience.

. . .

"I'm glad to be here with someone so capable," he said.

"Thanks. Eloy is right. We need to work together if we're going to make it out here."

"Eloy seemed pretty pleased when he discovered your degree in economics."

She smiled, her gaze on the trout as she delicately flipped it. "I like him. He's funny."

"You don't mind that I'm so far behind you both on the subject of economics?"

"I love you. You're funny too." Her tone was playful but scolding, in a motherly way. She sat back on her heels and grinned at him. "But you shouldn't pretend to know things like Big Chicken Dinner."

Joe winced. "Caught me. What was that about?"

"Military slang. Bad Conduct Discharge."

He felt himself turn red. "Good to know. I'll be like Bessie, doing the heavy lifting." Joe flexed his biceps. Evie laughed. Joe continued. "When I was helping Fabri with the dishes, she told me she's a Level 99. I empathized about her husband using that to divorce her, and I believe she thinks my Level is around hers. Levels don't matter here—or anywhere—and I'd not want them to intrude in this fresh place. Let's not alter her opinion, okay?"

Evie nodded, scooping the meal onto two plates. "If that's what you want." She tasted a piece of the fish. Satisfied, she handed him his plate.

"Meeting Eloy and Fabri is huge for us. To know we have knowledgeable friends down the stream . . ." He laughed, still in disbelief at their good fortune. "We're going to make it, Evie."

Evie walked over and kissed him intensely, and the smoky, salty taste of fish reminded Joe how far they had come from the sea. She kissed him again, with a ferocity that stunned him, so much that he couldn't shut his eyes. Her eyes were squeezed tight, the soft skin at the corners forging an expression of love and want and possession, all for him, and his heart melted.

Joe spent the week outside, concentrating on finding protein and fixing their shelter, and Evie foraged, prepared meals, made fires, and scrubbed dishes. After their fear of death in the desert, their current activities seemed downright soothing, though still exhausting.

He added a dozen new deadfall traps and another fish trap in a second pool farther upstream. The mountain was rich with game, and he came back carrying three squirrels. Evie glanced up from the fire, her mouth crinkling into a smile at the sight of his catches. "Can you teach me how to trap too?"

The next morning, she walked the trapline with him. Halfway up the hillside, he spotted a sprung trap. Together they lifted the stone to find a large jackrabbit dead underneath. Joe showed her how to field dress the animal, cleaning the carcass with water from his synjug without contaminating the creek. While Evie did not flinch, her compassion for the animal was palpable. Joe was already desensitized to animal death, and it concerned him.

He decided it was time to try his hand at building a wooden box trap. They were more humane than a deadfall trap because the animal died swiftly—but it was Joe who had to do the killing, with a club or a knife. The physical proximity to death and his part in it shocked his conscience. The night after he clubbed the head of a live jackrabbit, Joe awoke from a dream in which a rabbit-faced Zable knocked him unconscious. Bolting upright, he woke Evie.

"Mice?" She frantically patted down the covers.

"No." Joe chuckled, relaxing from the nightmare's hold. "But I guess it's time to patch the roof and the walls."

He set out at dawn with a synjug, his axe, and the froe all safely stowed in his pack. Ascending into the forest, Joe found a whitebark pine lying in a meadow. The earth was freshly gouged up around it, and he imagined the roots of the giant fighting for purchase against winter wind before crashing to its resting place. He mentally reviewed the tips Eloy had shared and rolled up his sleeves.

He rounded out his tools by making a mallet from one of the thick branches. Joe hefted it into his hand and swung it with a loud *thunk* against the tree to test it. He bucked up the fallen pine into sections with the bow saw. The methodical sibilation of the blade joined an ensemble of birdsong in the meadow.

Hours later, he was surrounded by log sections. Pausing to take a long drink, he assessed his next steps and went back to work. Joe set one section on end as a workbench and dragged another section on top to make roof shakes. Joe aligned the froe to the right thickness and used the mallet to pound it into the log. He twisted the froe away, and the shake split cleanly from the log. The plain tool's utility delighted Joe, and he offered silent thanks to Eloy. He continued with each section, honing his method and learning to identify knots in the logs that would ruin the shake. The shakes grew into a satisfying pile at his feet.

He finished the last step of dressing each shake with his axe, trimming here and there to make each as uniform as he could. He then loaded his tools into the bottom of the pack with as many shakes as would fit. It took six more trips to haul all the shakes to a pile behind the cabin.

Evie appeared at the cabin door. "I can now make jack-rabbit any way you can imagine. Rabbit stew. Pot-roasted rabbit. Rabbit skewers . . . Too bad I'm sick of rabbit. We need spices."

"Spices, like in bunny chow?" Joe smiled at both his joke and the memory of the curry.

A wistful expression crossed Evie's face. "Chili pepper, cilantro, soy sauce . . . garlic, basil, rosemary . . . cumin, citrus . . ." She shook her head and sighed. "Ready for lunch?"

They sat on the coarse log seats under the apple tree. Evie ladled out bowls steaming with a thick sauce, and he recognized the succulent jackrabbit among unknown vegetable plants from her foraging. They ate the honest meal, washed down with cups of cold water from the brook.

Lunch finished, he carried the hammer and nails and a pile of shakes up the ladder. The work of dressing shakes and fastening them in place was slow. He moved methodically, nailing them to the purlins from the bottom of the roof up. Each shake needed individual shaping with his axe, but, as with other tasks, Joe learned tricks through trial and error that sped up the process.

The sun was setting as he finished covering the last of the hole in the roof. Grabbing his tools, he descended the ladder and found Evie waiting for him, inspecting the short line of axe marks on the cabin back wall. "What are those for?"

I've made a mark for every day since they dropped us in the Empty Zone, and I'll make another one each day that passes from now on," he said.

Evie stared blankly at the wall. "Five weeks of survival." Her eyes flashed with a sudden fire. "We keep going. Surviving. We're going to make a life for ourselves here."

◆

Over the next weeks, they made the broken cabin into a home. Besides the roof, they repaired the bed, built a small larder to store Evie's foraging finds, and scrubbed the floors and walls. They had graduated to filling in the chinks in the cabin walls.

Standing at the final wall, most of their clothes stripped off, their hands encrusted in mud, they daubed the chinking mixture into each long crack between the gray boards. For materials, Joe had collected sand and mud from the creek bank, and Evie had found mosses, which she'd dried on the fire. Evie was animated, hopeful that this would keep the mice out and make their cabin more homelike.

"Joe, remember when you said an idealist is someone who thinks the world is a creation of the mind?"

"Yes."

"Well, that concept stuck with me because it sounds absurd."

He chuckled. "The university you graduated from is named for one of the earliest proponents of subjective idealism, or, as Bishop Berkeley called it, the theory of immaterialism."

Evie waved a muddy hand. "I know Berkeley. But consider this stuff." She squished the moss and wet clay between her fingers, then into another gap. "How could anyone believe this wasn't real?"

Joe laughed again. "Dr. Samuel Johnson had a similar reaction and rebuttal—he kicked a stone to refute the argument. *Argumentum ad lapidem,* the argument of the stone."

"I refute you thus," she purred, tossing clay at him. The glob hit his chest and rolled down in a long brown streak on his tanned skin.

He wiped it off and applied it to the wall, still pretending to be deep in thought. "Yes, Bishop Berkeley's ideas sound crazy, but I wouldn't reject them out of hand. He challenged us to question whether our accepted ideas of what is *real*, are really real. Where do complex ideas really reside? And how do those ideas intersect with what is our mind, the thing that is us? For example, where is the idea of, say, the University of Berkeley? When we think of it, we picture more than bricks and mortar. Where is that idea?"

She daubed clay into another crack. "The idea exists somewhere. When I imagine a university, I think of students. And professors." She casually flung more clay at Joe. It made another brown streak descending to his navel. "And a long list of other things."

Joe scraped the clay off his stomach and thoughtfully applied it to the wall. "Berkeley said an object—say, this clay—is a collection of all the ideas that our senses convey to us about it. Complex ideas are grounded in the physical objects that we can think about. The idea of a university is the relation among many things. But in its own way, the idea is also real." He reached over and petted her cheek. "It's a relationship among other ideas, I guess." Joe affected a serious expression and then laughed.

Her eyes grew wide and her hand went to her cheek. "You were just acting, pretending to be all-too-serious." She grabbed his hair and tousled it, laughing when the clay muddied his head. He wiped his hands across the tops of her legs, and a moment later the clay was flying. They laughed and dodged and tossed, Joe feeling like a kid again, running around the outside of the cabin in mock battle.

When Joe sneaked around the front, a hand shot out and grabbed his arm, pulling him into the cool interior of the cabin. In the moment before she tackled him, Joe noticed she had removed her clothes. They fell into a writhing jumble on the floor. Her body smelled earthy, and in a moment his clothes joined hers.

His hands cradled her hips and caressed her every curve. As she moved against him, with her mud-slicked skin pressed against his own, her eyes burned with desire.

"I refute you thus," she breathed as she bit his ear. He had no words, Latin or otherwise, to answer.

CHAPTER 34

Joe hiked down to Eloy's cabin to cut the promised firewood the next morning. He spent a half day splitting logs, stacking them next to the barn. The work was gratifying, and Joe was amazed with how his body had adapted to this manual life.

"That's a fine job." Eloy came up behind him and appraised the woodpile. Joe glanced up from his axe to see Fabri standing on the footbridge. She waved cheerfully, then turned to feed her chickens.

Eloy led him to the barn and opened the creaking door. Inside was a buckboard wagon. "I found this at one of the abandoned farms. With new axles that I cut from an oak tree, and some grease, it rides well. Bessie can pull it, so long as we go slow." The dun horse in the corral flicked her head at her name.

"About that wheat," Eloy said. "It's already late in the season, so you'll want to plant soon to have a harvest before the bad weather. How much seed do you have?"

"Seven kilos."

"It's enough for a couple hundred loaves of bread, plus seed for planting next year." Eloy's white teeth showed in a smile through his beard. "We'll need to get that noria built. I'm craving fresh bread." He stared off into the sky as he sniffed. "Like we talked last time, I'll lend you tools, help you plow the field, and help with the noria carpentry." They shook hands on the deal.

In a shadowed corner of the barn, Eloy retrieved a contraption with wooden handles forming a triangle. "This plow was hanging on a wall of a falling down farm cottage. Like it was art." Eloy chuckled.

"Artisanal bread," Joe quipped.

"It's from the nineteenth century. See the moldboard and the colter?" Eloy pointed to the thin blade on the front bottom of the rusty frame. "We can hitch Bessie to the plow, and you'll be done plowing in no time. Let's load the wagon with the tools we'll need."

Together they hauled the heavy plow into the buckboard. Eloy stowed an axe, a bucket of grease, and a stack of buckets like the ones Joe had seen on the ends of the paddles of Eloy's noria. Last, Eloy squeezed in a mechanical hand drill and a bucket of large bolts.

Fabri crossed the footbridge from her cabin, carrying a large wooden box. "Do you cook or does Evie?"

"I bow to Evie's superior taste and creativity." Joe felt a sudden pride in her as he said it.

"Division of labor." Eloy nodded in approval.

"Good that you two seem to treat each other equally," Fabri said. "I thought I'd come along to offer help. I have a lot of things for the kitchen."

"You're spoiling folks again," Eloy said.

"Nothing wrong with helping." Fabri pushed the box into the back of the wagon and then jumped up to sit beside it.

Eloy hitched the horse to the buckboard. He and Joe slid onto the single bench seat, Eloy clicked the reins, and they started up the hill along a meager cart path Joe hadn't noticed, which ran along the stream's east bank. Joe dismounted three times to remove saplings from the track with his axe.

The land flattened about fifty meters from their cabin. Eloy stopped the cart there and surveyed the brook, walking its edge both above and below the cabin, muttering to himself all the while. At last he beckoned to Joe, and together they walked upstream. "You should put the noria there," he said, pointing toward a rocky shelf two meters out in the creek. "It's the best place to build with the least effort. You can lay an even stone footer, then wooden supports for the wheel." Joe studied the spot and agreed with Eloy's logic. The flat rock shelf could underpin one wooden support, with the other support near the bank underlain with a stone footer, and the water could flow between. At least, in theory.

Eloy stroked his salt-and-pepper beard. Arm outstretched, he said, "Using gravity, you can send running water east from there to the cabin, and then to your field." Joe could already envision the water flowing to feed a tall field of amber grain. He smiled at how easily the finished creation appeared in his head.

Fabri had carried her wooden box to the cabin and the women were chatting as Joe and Eloy approached. Evie ran up to Joe when he entered, holding something long and white.

"Look at the wild tubers Fabri brought."

"They've been sitting in my root cellar since I foraged them late last autumn. Best to eat them now," she said. Eloy frowned but didn't comment further. Joe served bowls of soup all around, and they ate together, sitting on logs outside the cabin under the spreading tree.

Fabri admired the apple blossoms. "You'll get tasty apples in the summertime."

"With the wheat for dough, we can bake apple pie," Evie said. They all moaned at the thought. In a food synthesizer, a fresh apple pie took less than five minutes. Nobody doubted that their future effort would be worth it.

"With Evie's beans and our corn and squash, we have the three sisters that the original peoples planted." Eloy slurped the last of his soup. "It might be best for me to plant them together in my garden. We'll trade for some of your apples."

Joe nodded. "We'll work out the details when the time comes."

Fabri turned to Evie. "I see you found banana yucca. How's their taste now?"

"I found the budding flower stalks in the next valley, a kilometer east. They're still soapy, but they should get sweet in a few weeks when the fruit matures." Evie gestured to some greens Fabri had brought with her. "How do you know your plants?"

"I studied medicinal plants as a hobby—working in a hospital made me curious about the origins of medicine that we take for granted because everything is synthesized." She smiled. "I've learned more than I ever dreamed about edible plants this year."

"We've all carried intellectual property out here to share." Eloy's appreciation of Fabri was obvious.

"One thing you don't put a price on," she said, eyebrow arched.

"You can tease me all you want, Fabri, but I know you'll help if I ever get sick." Eloy patted her arm. He turned to Evie and said confidently, "Don't you agree, Evie, that you can't forget the economics, even out here in the wilderness?"

"I believe in personal responsibility." Evie served the banana yucca. "Prices historically kept the tally straight, but it's best to help each other."

Eloy frowned, but Fabri agreed wholeheartedly. "You can't put a price on compassion. Just be kind to your fellows. Life is hard enough."

Joe stayed neutral, and the conversation turned to the best places to forage for edible plants. The splashing brook reminded Joe about running water, and he faced Eloy. "How do we proceed from here on the wheel?"

"Together, we can build the noria in a week. The hardest part is moving the stones for the piers," he said around a mouthful of yucca. "Then cutting and hauling oaks for the beams supporting the wheel."

"Bessie can help with the heavy lifting," Joe said.

They stood, thanked the women for lunch, and walked to the flat land—the future wheat field—where they had left Bessie and the wagon full of tools. After unloading the tools, they scoured the field for rocks, which they loaded into the wagon until Eloy judged it was full enough. Bessie pulled the wagon to the site of the noria, and together the men carried the stones down the embankment and into place, standing knee-deep in the frigid water. The water-slicked rocks made footing treacherous, and Joe braced his legs to keep from slipping. The cold seeped up from his legs into his body, and he was grateful to head back for more rocks. They worked the rest of the afternoon and finished setting the footers evenly in the water, ending the day by drying around a fire.

Sensation returned to his fingers in sharp tingles. Animated conversation alerted him to Evie and Fabri's return from the forest. They both carried full foraging baskets. No matter how much they enjoyed each other, it was nice to have other people to talk to.

Eloy stood with a grunt and stretched. "Guess that's my cue to get going. I'll see you tomorrow morning. We'll raise the wooden supports and then start on the wheel." He unhitched Bessie, left the wagon in the field, and climbed onto the horse. Fabri handed him her basket and climbed on behind him. They waved goodbye as they rode into the deepening dusk.

Evie gave Joe some greens to wash and cut, and they stood companionably side by side preparing dinner. When the leftover soup had warmed up, they sat outside under the apple tree to savor the last glimmers of sunset.

"Eloy and Fabri seem to like bickering," Joe mused as he moved a tuber around the inside of his soup bowl.

"At least Eloy does. He's a competitive guy."

"I'm competitive too, but we don't fight."

"You're competitive in select circumstances. I like that about you. Eloy's competitive at the expense of—" she gestured around—"everything."

"At the expense of everything? Like what?"

"Compassion, for one. Fabri values compassion, and she helps Eloy remember its importance when he gets too focused on bartering."

"I see what you mean—they're good for each other. I hope they stay. They could leave at any time."

Evie squeezed his hand. "I hope they stay too. They're certainly nice neighbors for us, and it's not good for human beings to be alone." She giggled. "Unless Eloy's craving for bread gets too strong. He might not be able to wait until the harvest." Then she grew serious. "But even if they were to leave, Joe, we would make it. We will make it."

―――――◆―――――

Eloy was back after dawn the next day, and the day after that. The daylight hours were filled with the tasks to build a noria. They felled trees, cut long sections to haul back to the site with the wagon, drilled holes, and bolted the supports together. The structure rose on the granite piers, and the crossbeams tied the framework together, suspended over the water.

On the third day, Eloy took the wagon back with him, and he returned the next morning with a wagonful of boards, which he'd salvaged from a fallen-down building. Eloy had stacked them behind his cabin, but he now determined Joe's need for the noria an acceptable use, as its completion would benefit them both. The axle for the center of the wheel came from a straight ponderosa pine with the bark chipped off. They assembled the hub, making the spokes and curves of the wheel from boards and nailing them with heavy spikes. The paddle boards came next.

After they finished each section, they hauled it onto the support beams, which was precarious work. Any fall from that height could end with a broken leg. They propped the wheel right above its final resting place, the bottom edge centimeters above the cool water. Eloy finished by nailing the metal buckets to the side of the wheel. They only needed to lower the wheel and axle into the support brackets, which were slathered with grease and waiting to receive them.

"Ready to see our handiwork?" Eloy said. Joe nodded, a strange, nervous anticipation running through him.

They shoved the wheel into place, letting the axle ends drop into the support brackets. Water pushed the bottom of the wheel, and it turned with a jolt. The metal cans filled with water, soared into the air, and dumped back into the stream. Joe whooped with excitement, elated by the simple machine that would make such a difference in their life. Eloy clapped him on the back and grinned.

Evie came out and watched for several minutes, mesmerized by the water lifted in the buckets. "We're practically civilized now," she said, beaming.

They ate dinner together outside. As he waved goodbye, Eloy said, "To finish the deal, tomorrow I'll be back to help plow a proper field for the wheat. After that, you can put all the pieces together to grow us all bread."

◆

As promised, Eloy was back the next morning. Evie, Joe, and Eloy drank cups of steaming Mormon tea that Evie made from the foraged plant, before she headed up the mountain on another daily hunt. Joe and Eloy led Bessie back to the flat spot of land downhill from the noria. Eloy dragged his heel heavily across the dirt, drawing a line. "If you get the slope right," he said, "irrigation water will go where you need it."

. . .

I'm not stupid; I could have deduced that by myself. But . . . it's interesting that I welcomed mentoring from Gabe on intellectual concepts, but I bristle at advice from Eloy on practical subjects. Do I have some unconscious bias?

. . .

Joe nodded and determined to pay closer attention to Eloy. They marked out four corners with stakes, and Eloy led Bessie and the plow into position. They squatted next to the antique machine, and Eloy showed Joe how to clean the blade so the field dirt wouldn't stick.

Eloy hitched the horse to the plow. "Joe, why don't you control the plow, and I'll control Bessie." Joe tentatively grabbed the twin plow handles, imagining a bicycle. Eloy clicked at the horse, and she jerked the plow into motion. It bounded up in his hands like a wild thing, and Joe struggled to maintain his hold on it, let alone keep it moving in a straight line. The plow turned the black soil, and a sweet, loamy aroma filled his nose. When they reached the end, Eloy signaled for him to lift and turn the plow to one side, and the blade came clear of the earth.

"Nice striking out." Eloy turned the horse around. Joe tried to align the plow in a parallel line to his first as Eloy started Bessie up the gradual hill. "We'll have just a single dead furrow in the middle of the field this way, with all the rest nice, even furrows," he said.

The plow handles again yanked against his fingers, even though Eloy kept the horse at a constant slow pace. When they came back on the third row, the plow laid the strip of soil sod-side down against the first.

They continued to plow back and forth with an occasional stop to rest the weary horse—and Joe's exhausted arms. They also had to knock away loose dirt stuck to the plowshare and take long drinks of water. Joe patted Bessie's damp, musky flank to encourage her to keep pulling in the midday heat. She swooshed her tail at the congregating flies.

By early afternoon, they had nearly finished. "Now let Bessie cut a furrow back to your noria. You can dig it out with a pick and shovel later for your irrigation ditch," Eloy said. The horse balked but then dragged the plow one last time in a long furrow back to the creek. Eloy patted the horse's head, unharnessed her, and left her chomping grass next to Joe's cabin.

They sat under a nearby fir tree to rest.

"Where did you learn so much about farming?" Joe massaged the back of his neck. It felt like a rock. He still hadn't gotten the hang of the plow.

Eloy shrugged and looked at the water synjug he held. "I grew up on a farm before joining the military. Bots ran it, but my parents were both nature types and curious about the old ways, so they learned the traditional techniques." He squinted at the field and ran dirt-stained fingers through his curly hair.

"Well, you learned well from them."

"I consider myself self-taught in most things. But yes, I'll give them some credit there."

"There's something I've been wondering about . . ." Eloy faced him, eyebrow raised, waiting. "You served your sentences. Why are you still here?"

Eloy's expression turned thoughtful. "For one, it wouldn't be legal for Fabri and me to be together. Not that it ever stopped me before." He studied the sky. "Maybe it's the challenge of being out here. Almost no one alive could do this. Everyone is dependent on modern technology. Here I can do something different, live life different. I can be my own man. I'm not beholden to anyone."

"And you don't have to worry about Levels."

"That's right. I don't give a damn about any label society puts on me, and now no one else gives a damn either. I don't have to take credit for something I happened to be born into or use it as an excuse. I'm on my own path, and I alone decide how far down it to go."

"There's a romance to it." Joe scratched the beard that was longer than it had ever been. "I know it's self-interest, but I'm very glad you decided to stay here. It makes our survival much more likely."

"Just keep pulling your weight," Eloy said with a crisp nod as he got to his feet. The man liked to be on the move. He hitched Bessie to the wagon, climbed onto the seat, waved, and clacked off on the uneven track to his cabin.

Another week passed before Joe finished planting his grain field. Every step took longer than he'd anticipated, especially without Eloy's help and guidance. It took two days of hard labor to finish the irrigation project. Joe cut more trees, hauled them to the noria, and hewed them into support planks with the bow saw. He used Eloy's boards to connect a crude wooden trough to the furrow. His initial attempts had not been watertight, and it took three tries to get it right. Then one hard day of digging turned the furrow into a passable ditch to carry water to the field.

Evie had spent the past week filling her larder with foraged plants and preparing meals. But now Joe needed two days of her help to rake the plowed field flat. Joe took a full day to seed by hand, placing the precious C4 wheat seeds in neat rows, then scraping dirt over each seed to bury it, away from hungry birds. The last step was to open a sluice gate to direct the water into the channel. Water dribbled to the field and filled the furrows on either side. Joe and Evie hauled the water bucket to the less accessible areas.

"That was backbreaking. We rest tomorrow, on the seventh day," Joe said, putting down the bucket and admiring their handiwork. They had transformed the clearing into an irrigated and planted field.

"Maybe not, love," Evie said. He turned to her in surprise. "There are more uses for Eloy's tools before you return them."

The next day, Joe added a washing trough and a bathtub to the water system. Next to the trough, he dug a bathing hole and lined it with the remaining boards. The excess water flowed from the bath to the field, carrying the water away from the creek.

The bath filled with crystal clear water. Proud of his handiwork, he called Evie outside.

The water was chilly but clean and inviting. They looked at each other, then undressed and sank into the opulent water. From the tub, they gazed across the damp field, its precious seeds ready to burst into life.

The colors on the horizon transformed, the oranges fading into reds. The birds grew quieter, flying to roost lower in the valley.

Joe studied the nature surrounding him, letting the sights and sounds filter into his head to create a richer image of his new world. For the first time in months, he let himself just think.

The clarity of the real physical world was a counterpoint to the fond memories of his conversations with Gabe. He had begun his sabbatical with the goal of finding answers to pressing questions, which would lead to wisdom. Gabe had been a wise sage. Joe realized that the quest for wisdom benefited from finding sages—whether those were actual mentors or in books. But after that, wisdom was a solitary quest. One came into and left the world alone. It was an individual journey. So it was with the acquisition of wisdom.

. . .

If the problems and tasks of living can be overcome out here in the Empty Zone, then I can use the excess time for both living and thinking. Where is my project now, and how have my questions been answered?

When we were in the desert, I decided there were three requirements for free will. The first is that there can be no interference from outside a closed physical universe. The second is that the universe must admit some indeterminism. The third requirement is that whatever the "I" is that is me, it must be causal. Then there must be a way to imagine such a causal mechanism can exist within a physically closed universe.

. . .

He sat in the bath pool with Evie in the quiet of their individual thoughts until the light faded. Evie touched his arm and slipped out of the water. Joe stayed, enjoying the enveloping darkness. At last, he stood in his isolation, a man alone in nature, unsure of his fate but taking hold of his destiny. He still was not sure what this "I" was, but he knew that he existed and that he was choosing life.

CHAPTER 35

Joe took careful aim at the target, which he'd set up thirteen meters away on a post at the edge of his new wheat field. He centered the crosshairs on the bull's-eye in his bow scope, exhaled deliberately, and, when his lungs had emptied and he was perfectly still, willed his draw fingers to relax. The arrow flew free with a *whish*. He relaxed on seeing the group of five arrows arranged in a tight ellipse.

He looked up to study his field where the new durum sprouts pushed up through the black, inverted soil. Upstream, the noria turned, the wheel making a rhythmic splash as each rising water can spilled its contents back into the brook.

Evie appeared over the hill above the cabin, carrying her daypack. She strode toward him with a grin.

"Any luck today?"

"A squirrel from one of the traps higher up the mountain. I'm glad you taught me how to set them. Both the game and fish traps have proven reliable."

Joe frowned. "You haven't seen all the ones that aren't working. I've abandoned a dozen traps on the ridge three kilometers east, and another half dozen northwest down the gully. Despite the work I put into them, I think they were just poorly placed. I haven't figured out why some trap locations are so much more successful than others." He sighed. "I doubt any of the traps will be reliable enough to depend on through winter."

Evie nodded at the bow. "You need to hunt the deer too."

"I sometimes see them in the early morning hours. This morning I got a shot off but missed." Joe frowned again. "I found my arrow after searching for an hour. So this afternoon I lashed a board onto a sturdy branch to build a crude tree stand. It'll likely be more effective to hunt from because they won't expect me from above and will be less likely to scent me. It's near a trail with some tree rubbings and deer scat. Tomorrow I'll try again."

Evie nodded, then handed him the squirrel. She'd field dressed it as he had taught her. He took out his large knife and finished the job by removing the skin, and he butchered the animal. Evie knew how to perform these tasks, but it made her cringe, and he had hardened himself to it. It was necessary.

Joe brought the meat inside, where Evie was washing and putting away the various greens she'd found. Joe skewered the meat and set it over the fire to roast, then washed his hands before coming over to observe Evie's handiwork. "I'd like to learn more of your foraging secrets. Half the plants you find I still can't recognize."

"I'll teach you. We both should learn enough skills to survive, just in case . . ." Her hands separated wilted leaves from fresh ones.

Joe ignored the heart of her reply because he didn't want to think about it. "I could learn to cook some meals. You shouldn't feel like you always need to do it."

Evie looked up, surprised. "I like cooking." She grinned. "If you keep the mice away, I'll keep you fed."

"Solved so far," he said, recalling the mouse he'd dispatched with a wooden club while she was foraging. "That's a division of labor I can get behind." He rested his elbows on the table, cradled his head, and watched her walk back and forth in front of the fire. He loved watching the graceful movement of her body doing something so ordinary.

Evie paused. She sauntered to the table and sat in his lap, playfully massaging one of his arms. "You've gotten in shape. Think you're stronger than me now?"

He chuckled, then grew serious. "Is this enough for you?" She stared at him blankly. He paused, trying to clearly formulate his thought. "When we met, you were so focused on your Level. Now we are out here in the wilderness where Levels don't matter. I want us to be equals. Is this equality enough for you?"

She stopped rubbing his arm and met his eyes. "Yes, it feels like a true partnership. That's all I could ask for." She wrapped him in a tight embrace.

◆

It was dark inside the cabin when Joe dressed, grabbed his bow and other equipment stacked in the corner, and slipped out. The moon was waning gibbous and high enough in the sky to light his way through the forest. His weeks of practice walking through the brush had paid off, and now he moved as softly as a cat, retracing his path to the rough tree stand. He hoisted himself with the rope he had left, then pulled his equipment up and settled in the tree.

It was cool and windless. If a draft came, it should be in his face, moving down the draw from the spot where he suspected the mule deer bedded. He waited, his bow at the ready, an arrow nocked on the string.

Joe visualized what he would do upon sighting a deer. He swept his bow along the path as if following a moving animal, and he pictured the precise spot of an animal's thorax, mentally adjusting for his height in the tree. A stab of regret passed through him as he considered killing a sentient animal, but he pushed the thought away.

. . .

Carpenters bend wood; fletchers bend arrows; wise men fashion themselves.

. . .

His eyes adjusted to the dim light, and he made out the silhouetted shapes of the pine trees. His ears were tuned to every whisper—the chirp of insects, the morning chorus of songbirds filling the air, each melody flowing into the next. He was a statue of Azrael, hidden in the semidarkness.

A soft rustle reached him. A doe moved down the draw, dipping in and out of the shadows. She moved hesitantly and raised her head to sniff the air before advancing again. Behind her walked a buck, regal with a crest of antlers.

He focused on the buck as the doe passed his tree. They slowed, and the buck turned, exposing its side as its body was framed in the bow sight.

Joe willed the arrow to release. It darted from his bow with a fatal *whoosh*. The buck jumped and snorted, then vaulted forward. It crashed through the underbrush. He climbed down from his perch, nocked another arrow, and jogged down the path. Bloodstains led away from the trail, and he found the buck lying on its side in some chokecherry bushes. The doe was nowhere to be seen.

Joe stood over the buck and shook for several minutes, adrenaline and exhilaration coursing through his veins. The buck's face was light gray with a white stripe on its neck and a brown forehead. Only when Joe's gaze met its sightless eyes did he feel contrition for taking the life of a sentient being.

He took the knife from his pack and began the bloody work of field dressing. He found the broadhead where it had shot through both lungs and lodged against a rib. The pungent metallic odor hit his nostrils as he removed the entrails. He dumped the offal on the ground and left it for scavengers, then turned the carcass to drain the blood onto the green grass. Joe returned to the tree stand to retrieve his rope. He used it to hoist and hang the carcass into a tree. Then he splashed some water on his hands, picked up his pack and bow, and walked down the mountain.

Joe found Eloy hoeing the bean plants. "Looks by your hands you got a mule deer," Eloy said.

Joe wiped the remaining blood he hadn't noticed on the back of his pants. "Can you help me bring it here with the wagon, and can I use your smokehouse? Let's share the meat before it spoils."

"Glad to help," he said. "The wagon's easier than making a travois. I've done both." He hitched Bessie to the wagon, and they rode up the mountain as the sun climbed into the morning sky.

"A nice buck," Eloy said when they arrived at the tree where it hung. "Especially for your first. Cleanly shot too. Seems not to have suffered long." Joe nodded grimly. Together they loaded the carcass, hauled it back, and hung it from a rafter in Eloy's barn.

Eloy taught Joe the butchering process, pointing with his second fillet knife as Joe made the cuts. Joe removed the skin and set aside the pelt, then deboned the carcass, butchering into backstrap and round, shoulder and rump, ribs and shanks.

"I figure you'll have thirty kilos of lean meat when we finish." Eloy pointed to the remains. "Save the fat for making soap later."

"You learned all this on the farm?" Joe had memorized how to butcher, but the diagrams in his head wouldn't have translated well to the cuts. He would have wasted a good portion of meat.

Eloy waved the knife as he sighed. "I guess I ought to just tell you. My family had a farm, yes, but it was an excuse to live the peculiar way my parents wanted. They'd more than a curiosity with the old ways—they were obsessed. All of us kids were raised going rustic camping. At first it was all fun and games, but as I grew older, I realized we were social outcasts. I never saw another person who wasn't family in our house." He reached to rub the back of his neck but stopped before his blood-crusted hand made contact. "They had some conservative ideas that didn't sit well with me. After I ran away to college, I never went home again. I went from there to the military. But I learned to be self-sufficient from a young age."

Joe stared at Eloy, who inspected the cuts of meat and avoided making eye contact. Joe could not imagine such an upbringing—hunting animals as a child? No social interaction outside the family? He wondered if they had NESTs or MEDFLOWs, but he didn't want to push an already uncomfortable Eloy. "Well, you're certainly in the right place. I thank you for your help. And for your friendship."

Eloy met Joe's gaze with a small smile before resuming his usual gruff expression. "Let's get this meat to the smokehouse."

Next to the barn was a shed that served as the smokehouse, built from pine boards with a tight-fitting door. A stone flue piped smoke into the shed from a brick stove a meter away. As Eloy fed hardwood into the stove and started a fire, Joe hung the cuts of meat from the wooden crossbars inside. Eloy helped him finish, then they stepped out and sealed the door.

"This comes in handy for smoking the buckskin to make blankets," Eloy said. He explained the technique.

"Very clever. I've read all about making buckskin, but this will make the last step much easier." Joe thought about his next project.

He put three large steaks in his pack as Fabri came to him from the bridge. "Evie wanted me to thank you for giving us the bar of soap," Joe said.

"Everyone wants to be clean."

"Joe has provided our dinner tonight." Eloy pointed to his own three steaks. "I'll keep an accounting of what we eat so I can true up with my next deer."

Joe waved his hand. "I'm sure it will even up in the end."

Fabri laughed. "I've been telling him that. It's the job of the Man upstairs."

The next morning, Joe was awake at dawn and eager to start the new task of tanning the deer hide. Moisture hung in the air and on his skin, and the smell of grass filled his nose. In the delicate light, the draping webs of hopeful spiders glistened in the eaves of the cabin.

Joe dragged a long beam cut from a fallen log back to the yard beside the cabin. He set one end on a crude sawhorse and laid the hide over it. With a metal scraper he'd borrowed from Eloy, he methodically rubbed each centimeter of meat and fat clinging to the hide.

Next, he prepared the alkaline tanning solution. Joe added water and ashes from the fireplace to a bucket and stirred it into a thick slurry. Fabri had brought eggs as a gift the day before, and Joe took one from the cabin to test the alkalinity of his bucking solution. After varying the proportions of water and ash, the egg eventually floated in the container with just the tip of the egg bobbing above the surface. Joe removed the egg and sloshed the hide around in the bucket before weighting it with a rock and leaving it to soak beside the cabin door.

He had started a fire in the firepit and put a kettle of water over it when Evie returned with the bounty of her morning foraging, including five small birds, lifeless in a pouch made of woven reeds.

"How did you catch those?" He couldn't keep the surprise out of his voice.

Her bright smile revealed satisfaction with her efforts. "I studied your traps and thought about birds. I made a net out of the long fibrous reeds I harvested by the stream. That's what I was working on while you were building the noria. It took a lot of time to weave them together. Then I set it up on poles near a berry patch. I'll need to check it often."

"Very smart, my dear Artemis. Those will add some variety to the jackrabbit."

"How goes the tanning?" She set her pack down and sat next to him on a log.

"Pretty smoothly, considering I've never even touched an actual deer hide before." He wiped a hand across his brow. "Soon enough we'll have new clothes and blankets."

Evie peered into the bucket. "What comes next?"

Joe ticked the steps on his fingers. "After three days in the alkaline solution, I'll scrape off the hair and grain. That's supposed to take some work. Then I leave it in the creek overnight to rinse out. Membraning and brain tanning come next, which I'm preparing now. Eloy will let me use his smokehouse for smoking the buckskin. That should keep it soft even if it gets wet."

Evie pointed at the deer's skull that Joe had placed near the fire and wrinkled her nose. He had scraped the fur and flesh from it and washed it smooth, knowing an animal head would likely upset Evie.

"And what will you do with that?"

"For brain tanning, I have to mix the brains with hot water and then soak the leather in it so it will soften."

She reached out and tentatively ran a finger along the top of the skull. The antlers were still attached, a reminder of the ephemeral beauty of the once-living creature. "Poor buck. We bless your life, which you have given up for our food and clothing."

"The steaks with tomatoes and wild onions were delicious." Joe licked his lips.

Evie frowned at him. "I was being serious. We deal death to these animals; the least we can do is respect them."

Joe's face contorted, remembering the split second when he'd released the arrow. "I've been wondering how much we should flinch in the face of death, or life. I've found myself desensitized to the deaths of . . . most of . . . the animals that feed us, and I feel bad only when I consider my life before the Zone." Joe walked to the firepit to stare into the jumping flames. "Gabe and I discussed epiphenomenalism, which is the theory that the mind is an illusion. The mental can't cause the physical."

Joe spent several minutes describing his conversation with Gabe about causation resulting from particles in motion and not from the mind. He didn't accept the argument, so he couldn't use it to justify his actions. But killing the deer had reawakened thoughts about the argument.

Evie studied him quizzically. "Do you really believe that the universe is only particles in motion?"

"No, it's absurd."

"Why?"

He stared deep into the fire and organized his thoughts. "When I draw the bowstring, the arrow is ready to fly. At the particle level, those particular particles are interacting with each other at the speed of light—so one second later the effects can have traveled three hundred thousand kilometers. There's a delay, but not enough for us to notice. So practically, we can think of the world of particles as all intertwined. That's the reductionist interpretation.

"But those forces aren't what's important. What really matters is how the relationships among every element at one instant of time set the stage for the next instant. If I release the bowstring, forces are released. But those interactions have nothing to do with the *meaning* of killing a deer. I intended to kill the deer. It's such meta-relations—in this case, my *intent*—that govern how the world unfolds, and that is left out of the reductionist explanation. That's the key. The reductionist explanation describes a universe where such meta-descriptions are nonexistent, and that is not the universe we find ourselves in. Therefore, the reductionist explanation is false."

She frowned in thought. "The second requirement for free will is that the universe is not entirely deterministic, right? But you already said there are ways it isn't."

He nodded. "Random collections of matter—rocks and trees, simple piles of sand—seem to cause things to happen in a way that merely describing the particle motions doesn't capture. Then there are non-random *intentional* large patterns of stuff that appear to break the determinism. I caused the creature's death directly, through my mind to my finger to the bowstring. I intended to deliver the arrow into his lungs."

Evie picked up the skull and balanced the antlers on her knee. "I was the one who gave the order to assemble. When I issued that order, I caused all that followed . . ." Evie clutched the skull and shuddered.

"But where did that idea of injustice come from? What is it that led you to plan the anti-Levels movement in the first place, to send that message to have others join the cause? The firing of electromagnetic pulses in your mind, together with a network of chemical reactions and your own experience, is what led you to your thoughts. Then you shared those thoughts with other thinking people. The message itself was conveyed by displacing particles as you said, but the *idea*, that's what started the chain of events."

"Yes."

"Again, the example shows how absurd it is to attribute the result to particles in motion. The electrons in those electromagnetic impulses themselves didn't cause anything as complex as what occurred. Your message—holding an idea—caused other minds to take action."

"My act was the cause, and the death of Celeste and Julian was one effect?"

Joe put his hand on her shoulder in an attempt to soften her own self-blame. "Yes, though much less directly than my act of releasing the arrow. Peightân and Zable were the direct cause. They intentionally killed your friends. In contrast, you acted in the best interests of the group, given the limited knowledge you had. You didn't intend that act to cause harm, and their deaths were an unintended consequence."

"I set into motion a chain of events that ultimately got people I cared about killed." He felt every one of her words.

"We approach each decision with a narrow view of the past and our present, and with a poor power to project into the future. There will always be unintended consequences. Who can ever know the full effect? We must decide because even nondecision is a decision."

Evie stared at the skull, a hand over her stomach. "Then we do the best we can."

They had eaten a wonderful dinner featuring a tender rainbow trout Joe had caught in one of his traps. Now Evie practiced slow, precise moves with her bō stick on the stream bank, twirling it in arcs as the sun set over the hills. With a different idea of relaxation, Joe sat against the apple tree, his hands interlaced over a full stomach. The rising moon lit the branches and outlined several apples hanging above him. He thought about the mental causation conversation he'd had with Gabe when he had observed the blue and red balls in VR space. The argument that mentality was an illusion was absurd, and he needed to understand why.

Joe glanced up again and picked an apple. He took a bite, the bitter juice from the unripe fruit filling his mouth. He turned the speckled green sphere in his hand and thought about the properties of color and bitterness and his philosophical conversations with Gabe on property supervenience. Joe found another apple, this one turning red. He plucked it and held it in his other hand.

. . .

Gabe would say a green apple, like this, represents mental properties, and a red apple, like this, represents physical properties.

Primary physical properties include motion, solidity, extension, mass, and number. Secondary physical properties include sensations, such as color, taste, smell, and sound. The visible color of this red apple only exists at the scale of light because reflected light brings about the sensation of color. The bitterness and scent of this apple excite sensations on my tongue because of the interaction of specific molecules. But at smaller scales, I would no longer recognize this apple.

We think mostly about properties focused on our human scale—what we can touch, see, and feel.

If I think about particles, the matter that makes up an object, I can imagine diving into the microscopic world. I move from this red apple, to the size of organic cells, then down to visible light waves, to molecules, to the size of an atomic nucleus. And then even smaller, to a single proton, and down to the quarks that comprise the proton, and finally to the quantum foam that makes up the fabric of space–time.

As I make that dive to smaller and smaller size scales, nearly all the traditional secondary and primary properties are peeled away.

The existence of properties is the keystone holding that "problem" of mental causation together, yet scientific probing at microscopic levels raises the question as to whether properties even exist. At a minimum, properties do not exist *inside* other objects. In current physics, within the dimensions of space–time, there is no conclusive evidence for properties.

But maybe that's the key. I am emphatically thinking that properties *do not* exist. If this is true, it undermines the entire mental causation argument.

Maybe all is not lost, and we can believe that our minds have causality in the world. Perhaps our free will truly does exist. But if physical properties don't exist, then where does our experience of color, light, and sound come from? What replaces the work that philosophers expect properties do? There must be an alternative fundamental element of an ontology. I would need to find another explanation.

. . .

Joe finished eating the bitter apple, savoring the way it tickled his taste buds. He sat under the tree, thinking, until darkness surrounded him and the stars came out. He carried the red apple back to share with Evie. Slipping into the cabin, he found her awake with one candle lit. He crawled into bed beside her. In the dim light, he saw that her eyes were wet.

He touched her face. "Are you crying?"

"I'm thinking about life and death."

"About Celeste and Julian?"

"Yes." She let out a protracted sigh. "No, I'm thinking more about life . . ."

He pulled her body closer to his. Her heart pounded against him, and she whispered, "I think I'm pregnant."

CHAPTER 36

"Keep the firewood coming, and we'll handle the baking." Fabri shaped the dough into a loaf and made three neat slices across its top. Several bowls of rising dough lined the table, their rich, yeasty scent filling the air. Evie worked across from Fabri, and the whole wheat dough stuck to her hands as she kneaded a large mound. Despite the comment about firewood, the reality was that Eloy and Joe sat and watched the women. He knew they shared the same thought—they had done their part and could relax.

"So close to getting my bread," Eloy said, a smile creasing his face.

"I'm still amazed how the mill came together, Eloy. The pieces we built fit better than I imagined and worked the first time."

He grinned. "I had you to do the hard parts."

Joe studied his hands and the calluses earned from chiseling the grooves in the millstone. It had taken backbreaking effort to drag the two flat stones into the wagon, and building the wooden frame housing the millstones had been no easy task either. But Eloy had worked just as hard as Joe, and they both knew it.

Joe smiled. "We made a nice team. And Bessie turned the mechanism. Give her credit too."

"Good ole Bessie. I'm glad we were able to use the mill for the harvest before that rainy front came in. Lucky for us, it came later than usual."

The harvest had taken weeks of preparation. Joe had cut the tall, golden stalks with a sickle, and he loved swinging the blade. Eloy had labored beside him. They had used straw to tie the wheat into sheaves, then they stacked the sheaves into stooks to dry in the field. Two weeks later they threshed, beating the stalks to separate the grain. Eloy brought his wagon to move the durum to his barn, where it could continue drying before the rains deluged the mountain.

In the thick of it, Joe had doubts about the fruits of his labor. Each exhausting step was followed by weeks of waiting. But the harvest was enough to provide bread through the winter, and it had supplied enough seed for the next year.

"I'll have the luxury to plant earlier next spring." Joe interlaced his hands behind his head.

Evie broke up their boasting. "All right, Fabri, this loaf is ready for its second rise. Can I start the pie crust? I'm already tasting apple pie."

"Sounds like someone has an appetite again," Fabri said, raising an eyebrow.

Evie smiled. "At least for apple pie. But, yes, I haven't felt nauseated nearly as often for the past week. I still can't look at eggs without feeling sick, but I'm out of the worst of it." Evie studied her abdomen, where Joe couldn't yet see anything. "And I think I'm starting to show a tiny bit."

Fabri inspected her. "I'm not sure about that, but you will soon enough. Women show differently at different times. Not to worry."

Evie looked down with trepidation. "I still feel so stupid for forgetting that the birth control from my MEDFLOW would be turned off."

"We both forgot." Joe tried to add a note of comfort in his voice. No one thought about it until they decided to have children, certainly no one their age.

Evie gave him a quick smile, then continued to stare down, a frown returning. "A natural pregnancy . . . I don't know anyone who's done this before. Even living at the Dome, the women use IVG. This feels out of control." Self-doubt flooded her expression—something he rarely saw in Evie, but that had become more commonplace over the last few weeks. He often caught her in quiet moments with her hand on her abdomen, a look of uncertainty on her face. Knowing nothing of pregnancy—whether in vitro gameto-genesis or natural—made him feel out of his depth, and his words of comfort did little to help her.

Fabri, however, was confident. "Evie." She waited until the younger woman met her gaze. "You're young and healthy and will manage this pregnancy in the old way, like women before you. Women have been giving birth since the beginning of human life. It will be okay."

Evie's expression lightened, infused with the determination Joe was used to. She dusted her hands. "Do you want me to prepare the main dinner course?"

Joe got up, ready to give Evie his seat and prepare dinner himself, but Fabri shot him a look. "If you feel up to it, go right ahead," Fabri said.

Evie nodded, and Joe eased back into his chair. She turned to cook the venison steaks over the fireplace. The pan sizzled, and another aroma was added to the cozy ambiance in the cabin.

The pregnancy had introduced a dynamic to their relationship that he wasn't sure how to maneuver. He recalled times in the past weeks when Evie had snapped at him for building the fire in the morning or preparing dinner, tasks that had been hers. Perhaps coddling her wasn't the best approach. Apparently, Fabri thought so too. He resolved to help when she asked but to also trust her judgment of what she felt capable of doing.

As Evie completed her fireside task, Joe glanced toward Eloy, only to find him facing away from the table. Fabri had walked to his side and rested a gentle hand on his arm. He smiled down at her weakly, then looked away.

"All that birthing technology, that intellectual property we don't have access to," Joe heard him say. Fabri stared briefly at the floor before moving in front of Eloy to take his hands in hers.

Feeling as if he intruded on a private moment, Joe turned back around to again study his beloved, thankful in a new way for the life growing inside of her.

Eloy was first to snatch a loaf from the oven, which he juggled onto the table to cool. "Damn, how I missed my bread." They ate the warm slices with fresh tomatoes and squash shared from their gardens, and thick venison steaks. "Just a bit rustic, the way I remember it," said Eloy, taking another slice of bread.

"This sharing is working out all right," Fabri said between bites, staring at Eloy.

"It's because they're pulling their weight," he said. She raised an eyebrow.

Eloy finished the mouthful of bread and cleared his throat. "Yes. Well, this is something Fabri and I've thought about. When the little one is born, having extra milk is a healthy idea. I want to give you one of my sheep." His shoulders relaxed at Fabri's bright smile. "By the time the baby is born, I'll have a ewe ready for you. They're good milkers."

Joe and Evie were delighted with the idea and thanked their friends profusely. Joe commenced a discussion of sheep husbandry with Eloy while Evie served the apple pie, the sweet scent of hot apples adding yet another aroma to the air. The conversation went on until the sun reached the horizon, and then it was time for Joe and Evie to leave.

Arriving at home, Evie sat down in the comfortable chair that Joe had built for her. "Could you bring me some water, Joe?" He knelt next to her with the cup. The determination that had filled her face at Fabri's cabin was gone, replaced with fear and exhaustion.

She took a long drink, then gave the cup back and ran a hand down her face. "Everything about this is so new, Joe, and not in a good way. I think I should be able to do the same things I've ever done, but I can't. I get tired so quickly. I've noticed you picking up the slack, but that can't go on forever—you need to do a million other things, like make candles and hunt to prepare for winter." Tears ran down her cheeks, and Joe's heart broke. "And I've started to think about the risks of childbirth out here in the wild without doctors and medical technology. And raising a baby without all the medical support is worrisome. What if things go wrong?"

Joe stood and leaned over to hug her. For a long while, he let her cry in his arms. He gently kissed her hair. When her sobs calmed, he squeezed her, then came to kneel in front of her again. "We'll make it through this, like we've made it through everything else. We will do our best. And we have Fabri and Eloy to help us."

Evie sniffed. "We're lucky to have them as neighbors."

"Yes, we are." He held out his hand and helped her to her feet before enveloping her in a hug. "And I'm so lucky to have you and that little one." Evie's arms tightened around him, and he felt her nod into his chest.

They were bringing new life into the world. Together. And he was responsible. Oh, he was responsible.

***

Joe checked the smokehouse, which had evolved to be communal property. Both men stocked it with the successes of their hunts. Eloy kept a row of axe marks on the inside of the door that charted the venison removed by each, and Joe noted with dismay that his tally mark row was shorter, but there was no meat left. He slogged back to the cabin empty-handed.

Evie was preparing the evening meal when he returned. "Are there no venison steaks left?" He shook his head. "This is the last jackrabbit found in the traps," she said, gesturing with a look of distaste to the gamey meat cooking over the fire. "I won't be eating it—even the thought of it makes my stomach turn. I'll be fine with the pine nuts, the beans, and the salad."

Joe patted his stomach. The smell of cooking meat, even rabbit, made him salivate. "I can think of a place to put that rabbit. Plus, I'll need the energy for my hunt on the far eastern ridge tomorrow. I'll be gone all day." Evie nodded, and they sat down to eat.

◆

He was awake well before dawn. It was a bracing late-November morning, and the dew glittered half frozen on the still-green grass. It was mule deer rutting season, which would increase the odds of success. Joe shouldered his daypack and bow and hiked the several kilometers to the eastern ridge, and the descending full moon lit the path. The faint light of dawn brushed the hillsides as he hunted on the hogback.

After five fruitless hours crisscrossing the upland, the sun was high in the sky and the air was surprisingly sultry. He followed one of his traplines and checked for any sprung traps. He was consoled to find one rabbit. Joe sat under the shade of a ponderosa pine and opened his pack to eat lunch. The day was still scorching in early afternoon, and the piece of rabbit from yesterday's dinner tasted unpleasant. He ate it anyway, washing it down with water from a synjug.

When he came through the cabin door, Evie glanced up. "You're home earlier than I expected."

Joe sat down heavily at the table. "I only got another rabbit."

"We live day by day." She came over with a cup of water and a kiss before turning to prepare dinner.

They ate a quiet meal, and Joe turned in early. He was bone-tired from the long day and knew tomorrow would be much the same.

◆

He awoke in a sweat during the night. His stomach ached, and he had only a dim memory of vomiting onto the floor. The darkness parted around a candle, and Evie's worry was visible above the flame. Cooling strokes of a damp cloth wiped his face. She said something to him, but he couldn't focus on the words.

The light died, and he crept along a gloomy forest trail with something large and terrifying stalking him. He ran, but it was gaining, and its footsteps hammered in his ears. Claws seized him and tore at his bowels, and a foul smell erupted from his bloody belly. The beast clamped his wrists in handcuffs and shoved him. Tumbling down, he lay in his own excrement. The beast was torturing him, electricity arcing into his body. Nausea washed over him. The beast faced him, and he stared through black sockets into its skull.

He felt the cooling cloth again, wet against his face, then his arms were raised, washed, and laid back down. His intestines quivered. His forehead burned, and his head ached.

"Quite a fever." He recognized Fabri's voice.

He was aware of wetness on his lips, and when he opened his eyes, Evie peeked over the edge of a bowl of water. "Joe, sip some more. The water will help."

He sipped.

"And here's some broth." Fabri.

He sipped the salty liquid and tried not to vomit.

"His fever is breaking." Fabri again.

"I've never seen someone sick like this." Evie's voice wavered. He wanted to reach out to her, but his arms felt weighted down.

"Synthetic biology has created cures for all common human illnesses. But there are a million bugs that could cause food poisoning." Fabri's explanation pierced his fog.

He could at last focus on Evie's sympathetic face, which hovered over his. "Love, it must be the rabbit I cooked. I'm so sorry."

"No reason to stab yourself in the heart, my Juliet." His voice was a weak whisper, but he summoned a fragile smile.

"Joking again." There was a smile in Fabri's voice. "He's on the right road now."

By the next day, Joe was able to sit up in bed. He had forced soup into his stomach and kept it down, and his head was clearer, though his entire body was pummeled and drained.

Joe watched through the window as Fabri prepared to leave. She offered a compassionate hug to Evie, who then held Fabri's hands as they said their goodbyes. Evie returned to the cabin and sat near, offering him sips of water.

"I'm sorry I'm not helping with anything," Joe said.

"Hush, silly. Eloy brought venison steaks, and I'll make a healthy soup."

"Thank you." He stared into the fireplace. After one piece of spoiled meat and three torturous days, he felt weaker than he had in his entire life. "We're both regretting the lack of medical technology. It's best not to romanticize life on the mountain."

"We'll have romance wherever we are." She kissed his forehead and tucked the buckskin blanket around him.

CHAPTER 37

Joe set the clay on the pottery wheel. His foot pumped the pedal, and the wheel spun gracefully as the wet mixture rose in his deft hands. The creation of the pottery was no more of a miracle than that of the wheel itself from parts Eloy had allowed him to permanently borrow from the barn. When he finished the bowl, he set it aside with the others. There would be time to fire the cups and bowls in the brick kiln in the morning if the weather was not overcast.

Rain drummed on the cabin roof. A critical examination of the ceiling showed no leaks in his shakes, and gratitude that he was inside and warm flowed over him. Joe's gaze swept the circumference of his world, from the plain table and chairs where he sat to the rain-splashed single window-pane; from the crackling fireplace and its assortment of pots to the stack of firewood beside it; across the clean-swept wooden floor to the side room where their single bed stood with buckskin blankets folded; from the main cabin room and the tiny new bed he had built for their child to his bow and axe hanging on the wall next to the cabin door.

Joe washed his hands in a large bowl of water, scrubbing the grooves of his thick calluses. They had grown indistinguishable from Eloy's hands, gnarled and tough, and the sight of them startled him.

Between Eloy's tutelage and his own studies, Joe could now fix anything that broke on his little farm, and the up-keep was unending. He rose before dawn and worked until sunset each day. A towering woodpile stood next to the cabin. Digging a root cellar, roofing it, and adding a door made from felled timbers took weeks. The cellar was stocked with apples and storable foraged plants. He'd extended the traplines for several kilometers to harvest new sections of the mountain, then checked them and the fish traps each day.

Two more mule deer graced Eloy's smokehouse, and the meat and hides gave them protein and clothing for the winter. The noria needed regular maintenance, like adding grease to the axle. It was perpetual toil, but he was contented. He slept the sleep of the pure.

The only respite from work was fishing. Joe had cut a plain pole from a limber sapling, and he relished using it to catch trout that lolled in the shadows along the creek. Bowhunting took him on long grueling hikes for hours to reach new areas. There was a particular aroma that Joe drew deep into his lungs when roaming these western forests—a whiff redolent of pine and underbrush and arid dust and crisp mountain air—that would never leave his mind. For him, that scent meant freedom.

He crossed his arms and leaned against the door, admiring Evie's face as she sat in the corner chair. Her homemade needle flicked as she concentrated on sewing rabbit furs together to make clothes for their unborn baby. Her bulging abdomen moved, and she paused with a deep breath.

"That looked like a big kick."

Evie looked up and smiled. "He or she kicks a lot more than the ones you can see. That was a particularly big one." She stretched her back and shifted, her expression flickering in discomfort. She didn't complain, but he knew her back hurt often. Fabri said she measured quite big, and she wondered if they had misjudged the due date. But she assured them it was nothing to worry about. Of course, they both still worried.

"Could you get me some pine nuts?" Her look was a mix of embarrassment and apology. "I can't seem to eat enough."

Joe brought a bowl over. "You need the nourishment. Any particular herbs or plants you want?"

She popped a half-dozen pine nuts into her mouth and shook her head. "I'm glad you've taken over the foraging. Bending over and I aren't friends anymore."

"You taught me well. Now I can tell *most* of the edible plants apart."

She giggled, then held up her handiwork. "Whether boy or girl, this will fit." Evie critically scrutinized her stitches. "Though if I'm honest, this is so primitive. Outside the Zone I could have ordered something and have it made perfectly, out of faux leather." She sighed.

"Criticizing my tanning?"

"No, only remembering what we left behind."

Joe nodded, and a sad smile curved his mouth. Then he brightened. "But wait. Think about objects that we labor over. It all may be particles in motion, but what we add to the objects—such as the love you put into these clothes for our baby—is what has meaning. Meaning you can't buy."

She looked up at him with a grin. "I can think of something else we worked for, albeit unknowingly, that will have more meaning than anything we've made yet."

Joe walked over and placed his hand on the precious bulge. "Our baby will be ours to love and cherish."

She intertwined her fingers with his, and they rested there in shared hope. "The baby isn't ready yet to come into this world." She squeezed his hand. "But soon enough."

The wind gusted outside the cabin, rattling the door. Joe shivered and added logs to the fireplace. They lit from the coals, the yellow and red flames dancing higher, and a pleasant smell of pine filled the cabin. He stood behind Evie, rubbing her shoulders and down her back. The warmth of the fire surrounded them. They were cocooned in their world, abiding till spring and the next turn of their lives.

Snow brushed the mountaintops, but winter's bluster had passed, and the morning frost faded faster each day. The creek rushed nimbly past the cabin. Evie's belly had grown to an enormous size, preventing her from most of her usual tasks. Despite her aching back and feet, she continued to prepare their meals and turn the tanned hides into usable clothing and blankets. Joe toiled all the daylight hours, trying to keep their farm functional. Eloy often came up to lend a hand, which Joe was increasingly grateful for.

One day while visiting the smokehouse to pick out a couple of steaks, he stopped by Fabri's cabin. Fabri opened the door at his knock and invited him in, but he shook his head.

"Just wanted your opinion, Fabri. She's . . . she's so big. And she aches constantly."

Fabri patted his arm. "Nothing to worry about. She is big, but we could be off on when the baby is due. She could be early. No matter what, I'll be here. What you can do to help her is stay *calm*, Joe."

Joe took a deep breath and nodded. "Okay, you're right. Thanks, Fabri."

He hiked back up to their cabin. "We have dinner for tonight," he said, setting the pack of steaks on the table.

Evie sat on the edge of the bed, breathing deeply, a damp cloth in her hand. "Seems like you'll be cooking. My water broke."

Joe's eyes went wide, following the drips darkening the floor by the table to the trail back to the bed. Evie seemed peaceful as she held a towel between her legs, but her face was pale and she looked worried.

. . .

Be calm. I need to be calm.

. . .

"All right. You're doing great, Evie. I'll get Fabri and be right back."

Joe ran over and gave her a kiss before skittering down the hill like a mountain goat. Fabri grabbed her bag of medical supplies and hustled back with him to the cabin. Joe opened the cabin door to the sight of Evie rocking back and forth, her eyes closed.

Fabri got down to business, directing him with confidence. "Joe, keep the fire stoked and the water hot. We want everything as sterile as possible." She went to Evie's side. He did as ordered, glad to be useful. This was not a lesson he had studied in the allbook.

Fabri washed her hands, then laid out towels, blankets, and her scant medical supplies. He didn't comment on how little there was, or how they'd probably all come from Eloy's scavenging.

"I'll count the timing of the contractions." Fabri's voice and manner were calm. She settled into the chair and held Evie's hand. "You focus on deep, slow breaths."

Joe had the fire burning and the kettle of water boiling when Evie groaned.

"Relax and breathe." Fabri leaned toward her and resettled her grip on Evie's hand. "You're doing great."

He stood beside Evie and held her other hand, softly running his finger over her smooth skin. She blinked at him and squeezed his hand.

The contractions increased in length and frequency over the next five hours, which Fabri said meant Evie was progressing. But to Joe it felt like they would be trapped in this cycle of groans and heavy breathing and his own helplessness for eternity. He paced back and forth, then held her hand, then mopped her forehead, then paced again. Fabri maintained her serene expression and constant encouragement. They took turns applying cloths soaked in hot water to Evie's lower back.

Evie moaned again. "Let's not do this."

Fabri stifled a laugh. "Honey, this child is coming into the world. Relax as best you can." She applied a new hot cloth and Evie relaxed for a moment. Joe knelt to rub her back.

A moment later, Evie bawled, "I can't do it, I just can't, I can't . . ." Her voice trailed off in a moan. Joe looked at Fabri, his eyes wide, but Fabri was looking between Evie's legs.

"This is the end, girl. Your baby is coming! You're almost done. Let your body do the work. Just breathe. Then *push*."

Evie wailed in pain and panted between each contraction.

"There's the head, Evie. There you go, my girl," Fabri murmured.

Joe wiped the perspiration from her forehead, both terrified and elated. Then her face clenched tight and she cried again. Joe watched as the baby's head and shoulders slipped into Fabri's expectant hands. The pungent odors of childbirth reminded Joe of seawater, then field dressing his first deer. He hadn't expected this much blood.

"One more push, Evie. One more."

And with a final cry, the baby was in Fabri's hands. Evie gasped and lay back, her eyes closed for a moment. The baby's sharp cry had her looking around wildly, but Fabri was already setting the child on her chest.

Tears filled Fabri's eyes. "You have a son."

Evie looked down in amazement, then up at Joe. "It's *our* son," she said weakly. Joe stroked the top of her head, in disbelief at the tiny, puffy red being before him. His son.

. . .

We are all mere animals, risen apes. But what rising is possible.

. . .

Fabri cleaned her hands. "We'll have to cut the cord, but let's take our time while he gets used to breathing. Here, Joe, wipe his eyes." She gave him a clean cloth, and Joe tenderly wiped the infant. The baby had settled against Evie's chest and let forth a hearty wail.

At last, Fabri tied off the umbilical cord and snipped it with scissors. Evie's exhausted eyes gleamed. "As we decided, his name is Clay." Joe gazed on his son's angelic, whimpering face.

Evie grunted, and her body shivered in another contraction. Joe took Clay in his arms, concerned as Evie winced. Was there fresh red between her legs? Fabri worked quickly, swabbing bloody material into the tub. When she sat back, he whispered, "Is she dying?"

She snorted. "Red is the color of life, too, not only death. Think positive. The placenta delivered. Everything's fine." Fabri wiped her forehead with the back of her hand. She looked tired but determined. "But her water broke again. We have another one still inside."

"Two?" Joe clutched Clay tighter.

. . .

How can this be real? I'm a father—to two children? How will I manage? But look how beautiful my son is. He's a perfect miracle.

. . .

Evie rolled to her side, crying out in pain again. "Why does it still hurt so much?"

Fabri leaned over, her voice self-assured. "You've got one more coming, Evie girl. You can do this." She wiped Evie's forehead with a cool cloth, then massaged her low back. "Breathe deep now."

Evie took a shuddering breath, and Joe held Clay and tried not to exude anxiety. The baby nuzzled, and little whines escaped from its searching mouth. Joe cradled the boy in his elbow. "We'll get you food soon, little guy." Joe glanced at Evie with her next deep groan. "I hope."

Fabri moved to Evie's legs, checking, and Joe rubbed Evie's shoulder, but she flinched away from him. He raised an eyebrow at Fabri, and she shook her head, motioning for him to move back. "She's near the end here, Joe. Her body needs to focus on its task, not be distracted by your touch." She used a softer voice. "Evie, once more now. Second time is easier. That's it."

Evie sobbed and pushed.

"Out . . . he . . . comes!" A second baby slithered into Fabri's waiting arms. A high cry split the air as the baby took its first breath. "Two sons."

Evie lay there, gasping and laughing and crying, then gestured to Joe. He handed her Clay, whose mews had turned into a cry at the sound of his brother's cries. In a moment, he was latched on to Evie's breast. Joe took the second boy from Fabri and gazed at him in wonder, then held him up so Evie could see him. Their second son.

"Asher," Joe said, feeling giddy. He was glad they had two names they had liked. Now they didn't need to choose. Asher opened his hazel eyes and blinked at the light.

The second placenta came while Evie fed Clay, but she barely noticed, she was so enraptured with her son. She traced his tiny ears as he suckled at one breast, then the other. When he finished, Joe carefully traded him for Asher. Clay's eyes closed, and he fell asleep. Joe couldn't look away. He marveled at the miracle in his arms.

"—not attaching." Evie's frustrated voice broke his trance, and Joe looked up from the sleeping Clay. Asher mewed at her breast but couldn't seem to latch on like Clay had.

"Try a new position, Evie." Fabri helped her adjust Asher. "I've heard it can take some time to get his mouth on the nipple just right."

"Clay just started eating. I didn't do anything special . . ."

Fortunately, a few minutes later Evie found a position agreeable to both her and Asher. He grunted loudly as he ate, making them all laugh.

With Asher eating and Clay asleep in his arms, a wave of exhaustion washed over Joe, and he sat down in a chair at the table. He could only imagine how Evie felt, and he glanced at her, a tired joy creasing her mouth. There was only love in her eyes as she contemplated Asher.

. . .

How do we take care of twins? Two more mouths to feed. Someone has to watch them all the time. They're so helpless. Where will we get the hands?

But this guy is so cute too. They're both so astonishing. I'll make it work . . . for them.

. . .

Fabri cleaned everything and packed her medical supplies, but she stayed several hours more, helping Joe experiment with diapers until they found a way for them to stay on
the boys' tiny bottoms. She took a turn holding Asher so Evie
could take a quick nap. Joe thanked her profusely again, but
she waved away the gratitude with a smile.

"I feel like these kids are part ours now, so you can thank
me by letting us help you watch them from time to time."
She smiled down at the sleeping Asher, then handed him
back to Evie, who was sitting up. "You'll want to rest for several days, Evie, and take things slow. Your young body will
be back to normal in no time, but there's no sense rushing
things. Let Joe do the heavy lifting for a while." Fabri winked
and picked up her bag of supplies. "I'm off to tell Eloy, who
I'm sure is dying to hear the news. He'll never believe you
were carrying twins in that big belly of yours." Fabri stood
at the cabin door, her red braids outlined against the light
cascading in. "Make sure she drinks lots of water and tea. She
should eat as soon as she feels up to it."

"You were so helpful." Joe gave her a hug. "Thank you
again, Fabri. Your expertise saved us both."

She blushed. "This work dills my pickle. I'm just glad I
was able to manage it alone."

Joe tried not to let his surprise show. "How many births
have you managed?"

"Now? Two." She frowned. "I was an orderly in the hospital
and got to see a couple of births. I was working toward being
a nurse, hoping to get promoted, but that hadn't happened
before I came here. Of course, they wouldn't let someone at
our Level deliver babies in the hospital."

"Right . . ."

"I suspect Eloy will be here tomorrow to see the little
guys," she said as she waved goodbye.

He closed the door and brought Evie a cup of water, then brewed tea from the remaining water in the kettle. Evie drank small sips while gazing down at Asher, who was already nuzzling her breast again.

"Hungry again, little man?" She looked exhausted but happy.

Joe smiled at Clay, who had also started rooting in his sleep. "We're going to have our hands full."

Evie gazed up at Joe. "More joy than we expected. But we'll manage," she whispered.

CHAPTER 38

The days after the birth of the twins passed like a dream for Joe, in part because he could not separate the insufficient sleep from the twins' nonstop noise and need for attention. He woke from unexpected catnaps without realizing he had fallen asleep. Was his expression as befuddled, euphoric, and drowsy as hers?

The boys ate. Evie let one boy guzzle from one breast, then handed him off to Joe while the other took the second, and sometimes she had both at the same time. Feedings occurred around the clock, and Joe woke at each one, ready to change a diaper or burp a baby. It seemed impossible to get the boys to sleep without one waking the other.

They spent so much time staring at the sleeping babies and talking about how beautiful they were, that they sometimes almost woke them. But it didn't take long to remember they needed quiet moments to recharge.

When he was not inside the cabin helping with the boys, Joe was outside scrambling to bring food to the table to keep Evie healthy. He walked his trapline each morning, checked the fish traps, foraged spring plants on the mountain, and restocked the firewood pile, enjoying the crack of his axe against timber.

Eloy had arrived in the wagon the afternoon after the birth to unload a stroller. It had wooden wheels carved from sawn timber rounds, and sides from boards made smooth with a hand plane. "After Fabri told me about the twins, I had to widen this contraption to fit two," he said. Joe thanked him and led him inside to see the boys, rolling the stroller ahead. Evie held Clay in her arms while Asher lay sleeping on the bed, swaddled in a rabbit blanket. Eloy's face lit with excitement, and he touched Clay's hand with a tenderness and awe that surprised Joe. "Those are some handsome little guys," Eloy said.

After a time, he said, "I'll be sure to have the ewe ready as soon as I can. Sheep's milk is easier to digest than cow's milk. But yours is best to get all the vitamins and immunity."

Evie thanked him with a weary smile. "I'll soon need the milk. These little ones are healthy eaters. And the stroller will be much used, so thank you."

"Not much flat ground to use it, but the wheels should make it easier to move them around," he said.

After a few quiet minutes of watching the boys, Eloy said his goodbyes. When he left, Joe sat by Evie's side. She sighed and leaned back against the headboard.

"How are you feeling?"

She chuckled, her eyes closed. "A better question is what am I not feeling. I can't make sense of everything whirling inside me. It doesn't help that I'm so exhausted I can barely string a sentence together." She looked at him. "I'm mostly relieved that the birth went well, is over, and we have our boys. But now I'm worried about feeding them enough and keeping them healthy. I feel anxious and overwhelmed and inadequate." She sighed again, her gaze shifting to the boys and softening. "But when these guys latch on, so helpless and needing me, I feel for a time that I can do it. That I'm enough."

Joe leaned over and kissed her. "You are more than enough."

Fabri returned the following days to look in on Evie. The second day, Joe met her at the door because Evie was at last asleep with both boys nestled around her, and he didn't want to disturb them.

"Well, I was going to forage for some medicinal plants that will help her get well faster. Want to join me?"

The weather was sunny, and, despite his exhaustion, Joe needed an excuse to leave the cabin. He ambled up the mountain with her, and she pointed out the useful plants poking from the soil. "The manzanita leaves are still green. We'll need a few basketfuls." Joe helped her collect the leaves, then they hiked back to Joe's cabin. "I'll soak these and prepare them for a sitz bath. It's a trick I read about from the original peoples who lived here. It should help her heal."

"Thank you for all you're doing for Evie and me. I feel like I can never pay you back," Joe said.

"Now you sound like Eloy. There's no payin' back. I love doing this."

"But isn't there something else you'd rather do for yourself?"

She fixed him with a clear eye. "Joe, you're thinking about things backward. Helping people is its own reward."

. . .

Damn me. She really believes that.

. . .

They reached the cabin, and Joe pushed open the door. Evie was sitting up in bed with one boy in each arm. She smiled wearily, but it didn't reach her eyes, which remained hollow and dark. It worried him.

Fabri briskly walked to Evie's side. "Honey, a sitz bath will make you feel so much better. I have a pan right here to sit in and some plants to make some medicine. I'll heat up the water and we'll get started."

She turned to Joe. "Maybe you can take the little guys outside? It's warm enough if they're bundled up, and you can sit under the tree."

Joe delicately swaddled the twins, tucked them into the stroller, and rolled it outside under the apple tree. He rocked them gently and reflected on Fabri. She loved her fellow creatures wholeheartedly, compassionately, and no abridgements were considered for her own welfare. Her selflessness was aspirational.

That evening in bed, Evie lay close. The boys were, miraculously, both asleep.

"That sitz bath Fabri made was the best I've felt since the twins were born. She feels like a sister, so caring. And I feel more like myself around her."

Joe hugged her, thinking about how he could show Fabri-like compassion. "I'm glad to hear that. I know this transition to motherhood hasn't been an easy one, but you're doing wonderfully. Don't forget that. You brought these two beautiful miracles into the world and you will teach them what it means to be human."

<hr>

"I've got enough seed to plant twice as much durum this year," Joe said. It had been four weeks since the twins were born, and he couldn't put off planting the wheat any longer. He was visiting Eloy to see if he could borrow Bessie for the plowing.

"You've no extra seed for me to plant on my own?"

Joe chuckled. "You're the economist. Division of labor. It's more efficient for me to have one larger field. I'm sure you'll offer something to make it fair."

"Fine economist; bad accountant. Okay, I'll keep it straight. I'll plant extra corn this year." They shook hands.

"One more thing." Eloy vanished into the barn. He came back a minute later, leading two ewes on halters. "Since you have two little mouths to feed."

Joe stared. "That's very generous. We'll keep an accounting of this gift."

"The boys have their own account. They can true up with me another time." A wistful shadow played across his face.

Joe loaded the plow into the wagon, tied the sheep behind it, and drove to the cabin. He set the ewes free in the clearing beside the field. They munched the virgin grass while he hitched the plow to the mare. Though he plowed in an area where the soil had been once broken, the ground was hard from the winter frost. Bessie snorted and shook her head in outrage at the hard pulling. He stopped to let her rest at the end of each row, but he still finished the plowing in one day.

The week was full. Joe moved the pieces of wooden trough into place, and pristine water from snowmelt flowed from the stream into the noria and drenched the field. He spread the seed by hand and raked the dark soil over each potential seedling. The fresh fragrance of wet earth reminded him of new life pushing into the world.

As Joe walked back to the cabin, he was made aware of the opposite—the absence of spring life. The usual sound of bees humming near the back of the cabin was gone. He walked to the large oak beyond the second apple tree, where he had seen the bee colony nestled in a hollow three meters up. He studied the spot and spied a small line of ants moving up the tree trunk and toward the hollow. Joe found his wobbly ladder and propped it against the tree, then gingerly climbed. He poked into the bee colony with his axe, disturbing a few straggler bees. The ant invasion had caused the colony to abandon its home.

A half hour later, he carried his treasure through the cabin door to show Evie.

"Honey?" She clapped her hands and inspected the bucket in his hand.

"The ants caused the bees to abscond. I hope they find a new home nearby. But meanwhile, it seemed worth it to fight the ants for the honey left in the tree." He recalled the lizard from the desert. "Just like every other creature out here, we need to fight to survive."

"Did you get stung?"

"Only three times. There weren't many bees left."

She smiled and kissed him. "The bitter with the sweet."

———————◆———————

Their neighbors visited all spring. Eloy taught Evie how to milk the ewes, straddling the sheep and bending over to tug on the udders. The supplemental milk helped feed the twins' ravenous appetites. Eloy liked to sit beside the boys in their stroller and make faces at them until they smiled. Evie's mood had brightened considerably once she was able to move freely, and Joe delighted in seeing her face shining with a new mother's love whenever she looked at Clay and Asher. She was a confident mother, her previous fears displaced by determination to provide all she could for their sons.

Asher's minor colic had abated, and they ate well and grew like sprouts. They now slept for longer periods of time through the night, and both parents were getting sleep again. Evie had even taken short foraging walks, leaving Joe to watch the boys. Her finds again brightened the evening meals.

As the weather improved, they spent more time outside. Joe built a pair of outdoor wooden chairs for Evie and himself, a more comfortable place to rest while keeping an eye on the boys. That project led to the addition of a tiny porch that faced toward the stream and western mountains. Two posts supported a sloped roof made of shakes, and two chairs and the stroller fit under it, providing shade. The porch and the apple tree were two favorite places to sit and watch the sunset.

They had created their own Eden—a place to struggle, live, and follow a worthwhile path. He cherished what they'd created, even as he knew it was ephemeral. It was only particles in motion, but those particles were shaped by his hands to his own purposes. He had embraced his new roles as hunter and gatherer, farmer and father. Some days he began before dawn, hiding in a tree stand with his bow or stalking the mountain trails for signs of any game. In the late morning, he walked the trapline. He spent the afternoons weeding the field. In between, he helped with the boys. It delighted him when they tracked his face, their mouths moving when he talked to them.

Despite—or perhaps because of—scrapes and bruises and constant dirt and hard labor, life fell into a tranquil, domestic rhythm.

Joe sat under his apple tree as the sun set. Earlier that day, he'd notched the rear cabin wall with his axe. They'd reached the first anniversary of their banishment. Since the trial, he had gone from utter despair to happiness. By necessity, he hadn't touched whisky or psychotropics, and he felt clean and healthy. He and Evie had overcome much to fall more deeply in love, and they were united in laboring together for their surprise family. They had produced two beautiful, new human beings, carved a home from the wilderness, and found new friends. And while life was physically challenging and filled with uncertainties, it was enriching in new ways. Yet the risks were higher, too, and it could all go wrong at any time.

The wind rustled the branches. The high, warbled *chur-chur* of the mountain bluebird accompanied the fading light. There were clouds in the eastern sky, but it was clear around the setting sun. All around him was calm.

. . .

The last time I had any time to think was before Evie's pregnancy. I went to Lone Mountain College to understand my own mentality, to understand if the mind can have free will. That critical meeting with Gabe raised the fear that maybe there is no mental causation, that nothing we do matters, and that nothing is in our control.

But I've made progress here on this mountain. Evie helped me to realize that mental causation is still a truth, and that to argue otherwise is absurd. We have fought against the odds and won so far, by our own hard work and some significant luck.

The argument against our minds being causal rests on a supervenience relation, with mental properties supervening on physical properties. The "green" of a mental property that we have in our minds supervenes on the "red" of a physical property in the universe, at least by that telling. I now believe that properties do not exist. And if our common idea about properties is flawed, then the argument denying mental causation fails.

But properties have been commonly accepted for millennia, and we can't eliminate them without a replacement explanation. What purpose do properties serve? Philosophers say properties have causative powers and that they are truthmakers. The first assumption goes back to Plato, who says that a thing really *is* if it has some capacity to do something to something else. The truthmaking role is more abstract, often dealing with truth in statements. Truthmakers are the elements that make a proposition true.

If there are no properties, then something else— some ontological element, something that really exists—must do this work.

. . .

Joe rested his hand against the weathered bark. His calloused hand was an inverted mirror of the calloused tree branch.

. . .

What about relations? Between and among objects, there are relations. One object can be larger than another, like this tree is larger than my hand. An object can also exist next to another one, as my hand rests against the tree. But these relations hold a second-class status in philosophy because it is more natural to believe that physical properties are causal. Relations aren't really *doing* anything.

Physicists have been more charitable to relations. The four fundamental forces—gravitational, electromagnetic, strong, and weak—describe how objects or particles relate to each other. The Higgs field has a mystical feel to it in that it's an invisible energy present throughout the universe that imbues other particles with mass, the basic building block of matter. This field suggests something more like a relation at work rather than a property found in any one object.

. . .

Above him, the gnarled boughs pointed in all directions, swaying as the wind whispered through the branches. The fading blue sky outlined the limbs. Every furrow in the grayish bark was pronounced, the periderm coarse from a lifetime's encounters with existence.

Then the veil tore away. His breath caught, and Joe had a vision. He no longer saw the branches as having properties embedded in particles—no textured limbs, no gray of the bark. The branches seethed with relations, a web of the essence of existence. The relations were not emerging from the tree; *they were the tree*. He was transfixed, seeing them against the sky, and a tremendous energy flowed through his body.

. . .

Ontology is concerned with *what there is*, what things there are that have *existence*. What if our common ontology is upside down and backward? What if the relations are real, and properties are not real? What if relations do the work attributed erroneously to properties? What if relations are causative?

. . .

The sun dipped below the mountain and a smear of bright green made him smile. The green flash sunset phenomenon reminded him of Evie's eyes, and happiness infused his being. The colors of the sunset turned from oranges to pinks, and then to violets. He thought back to what felt like a lifetime ago, when Evie made the rodeo flip on her surfboard. He closed his eyes and pictured her rotating in the air, her body upside down and backward before perfectly recovering to head on to the next wave.

. . .

Because our perceptions are so embedded in the world and in the way we've learned since infancy, it is nearly impossible to think about anything other than a world of particles making objects. How can I wrap my mind around relations that are causative?

If our way of perceiving is upside down and backward—like Evie on her surfboard—then using the words we normally do to describe perceived objects doesn't work. We can't think in terms of objects and properties, or any of the things that we think exist. We need a way to flip our thinking. Hampered by a mind mistrained since birth, we must now redefine what is "real" and think about this new, real thing—a *relation*.

. . .

The branches above him quivered as a steady wind blew through the limbs. Soft rain touched his face, and he peered east. Storm clouds rolled in.

Rain began pelting down, and he ran to the porch to take cover from the storm. Joe sat in Evie's chair, and the sky radiated and boomed. Rain dripped off the roof and landed near his boot. The majesty of the sky fueled his thoughts, informed by the potency of his one sliver of the universe. A purple arc of lightning struck a tall tree on the far hill, and the deep *boom* reached him a split second later.

. . .

Superstring and related theories propose that all particles in the universe are composed of vibrating, one-dimensional mathematical objects known as strings. These theories require extra dimensions of space–time for their mathematical consistency—typically ten or, more elegantly, eleven dimensions.

To describe a lightning strike to someone who has never experienced it would sound like some magical delusion—an electrical discharge between that cloud and that tree. Without being able to see or understand lightning, one might imagine the cloud caused the tree to explode. By seeing that *constant conjunction*, in Hume's words, I might accept that explanation.

But if the lightning bolt exists in one of the alternate dimensions that physicists believe exist beyond our perceived four-dimensional space–time, then perhaps this is where we can find some true cause. There could reside the *relation* as causal element.

When Evie and I talked about time, I illustrated time with the block universe as a mental model.

But I can take the exercise further. If I imagine three-dimensional space as one dimension, and time as a second dimension, then space–time is perhaps imagined as a plane folded into a sphere. With that image, I can then see how there is room for more dimensions both inside of and outside of the sphere. These are analogous to thinking about the extra dimensions that string theory suggests really exist.

So where are the causative relations? They might be hidden away in one of the dimensions outside of space–time, outside of the sphere. Let me imagine a Zeus—just the image, but not a god—holding a lightning bolt, bending it so the ends touch the surface of the sphere. I imagine that the lightning bolt is the relation, some real object existing outside space–time. If that lightning bolt is the relation, then maybe that lightning bolt, that relation, that pattern, is the root of causation perceived in space–time. The bolt is the cause, and the spot on the space–time sphere is where the effect takes place.

Hume said that it's only a constant conjunction—hearing one clock chime and then another—that convinces us that one chime causes the other. But there's no necessity in logic that it does. And there is no necessity in logic that the measurement of particles means that they are causative. Therefore, it does not violate any scientific experiment to consider that the machinery of causation can be a relation.

We have so much baggage associated with the word *relation*, that we need a new term. Let me name that causative relation a *bolt*.

If bolts—causative relations—are the single ontological element with causation, and if bolts are outside four-dimensional space–time, then many problems melt away. One is the problem of mental causation. Because the mind itself can be composed of these bolts, then our minds can be fully causative. Such a mind, composed of bolts, can have free will in an indeterministic closed physical universe. *We are that Zeus.*

. . .

The storm had passed, the clouds clearing to showcase a clear, black sky, the first stars aglow. A cool wind blew over the mountain, and Joe found satisfaction that his long mental quest had found some plausible, elegant answers.

. . .

What of the role of properties as truthmakers? Other things must be truthmakers if properties do not exist. Some truths arise because they are about the world, anchored by things in the world described as collections of bolts. For example, "the Empty Zone is in Nevada" is true because of an arrangement of bolts. Then many bolts can be that truthmaker. Bolts do double duty, as both causative in the world and as truthmakers for some, but not all, truths.

So back to Hume. He distinguished between matters of fact and relations of ideas. Matters of fact are truths that exist regardless of the conditions of the world, such as the truth that the sum of the angles of a Euclidean triangle always equals 180 degrees. I think these truths could be another flavor of relation, one that is non-causative in the world.

Perhaps part of the problem is that we have used the same term, *relation*, for two different elements in the ontological table. What if I think about such truths as the thunder following the lightning bolt? I'm thinking that while the lightning bolt damaged the tree on the far hillside, the following thunder only caused a sound in my ears—in the way that an idea fills my head. It's an imperfect analogy because thunder has grounding in the physical world, but this relation that is a truthmaker has none. I'm thinking that this relation is a second, real ontological element. Then let me label this truth that exists but that is not causative in the world a *boom*.

Now we have only two elements: bolts and booms. These two are the only elements we need to underpin the universe.

. . .

Joe found Evie in bed but wide awake. It was dark without the candle lit. The boys slept in their bed. "You were outside for a long time. Thinking?" She reached for him.

"Yes. It felt refreshing to use my brain instead of my muscles."

Joe could not contain his mental discovery, and he proceeded to explain his new idea in detail.

As she listened, she studied him with, at first, a quizzical tilt of her head, but then she pressed her lips together in concentration. "If I understand correctly, you believe that the universe is made up of bolts. Bolts are relations, and webs of bolts cause things to happen."

"Exactly. Remember when I said that there are three requirements for free will? The third requirement is that the 'I' must be causal. So now there's a way to imagine that such a causal mechanism exists within a physically closed universe. We are made of these bolts."

"Then that's the last of the three requirements for us to have free will." She was now excited.

He nodded. "I think this hypothesis can describe the universe. And our minds can also be made of the same stuff, meaning our minds do cause things to happen in the world, the way we usually imagine. Though it is only a hypothesis, because only science can test such things. When I first met Gabe, an empiricist, he said that we need to look to our sensory experience of the real world to learn anything. We can only know the answers to such questions by using science, to do experiments in the world, to test these hypotheses. I believe that too. So further conjecture appears pointless. Mine is only a hypothesis about what makes up the universe, even if it is pleasingly elegant."

Chapter 39

The summer ended in a blur. They started their garden with tomatoes, having received the seeds as a gift from Fabri. The vegetables pushed upward in competition with the sprouting wheat and budding apples, promising a good harvest. Sometimes they worked outside together while watching the twins, Joe chopping wood and Evie at the water trough washing clothing. At other times Joe took the parenting task alone to give her a break. Evie milked the ewes and took several hours each week to forage on the mountain and to check her bird traps, finding the respite from the boys liberating and mentally rejuvenating.

When the pinyon pine nuts reached ripeness mid-autumn, Fabri suggested a picnic to share while they harvested the seeds. Eloy arrived with the wagon on the agreed day to take them to his cabin. They loaded the stroller, the family, and a large pack of baby supplies and descended the rough road. A hint of early October touched the morning air. Evie and Fabri parked the stroller outside the barn. They chatted and watched the boys, whose heads swiveled round with each deep *ribbit* from the frogs along the creek.

Joe and Eloy stood beside the stroller. Eloy waved a finger in front of Clay, who giggled and tried to grab it. Joe picked up Asher and repeated the *ribbit* sound until they all laughed together.

. . .

They're so cute, sometimes it's hard to want to do anything except play with them and watch them grow. They're the center of our world.

. . .

"Ready to start?" Eloy took a last swig of water. Joe nodded, then smiled at Evie as he set Asher back in the stroller. He climbed into the wagon with Eloy.

In theory, the steps were simple: collect pine cones, separate the seeds, and store them away in earthen jars that Joe had made from fired clay. Joe and Eloy drove the wagon downstream to the best groves of pinyon pines. Joe chopped saplings to make long poles that would reach up into the branches. They labored throughout the morning, knocking pine cones loose, gathering them into baskets, loading them into the wagon, then stacking them into piles next to the barn. With another trip in the wagon, they collected brushwood. The oil from the pines stuck to Joe's fingers, and the clean, lemony fragrance hung on his clothes.

The women joined them to tend the fires that would free the seeds from the hard cones. They piled brushwood on top of the pine cones to burn the resin coating off. The men kept harvesting while Evie and Fabri pounded the charred cones with hammers to free the pinyon seeds, and by early afternoon they had filled several large baskets. They poured the precious winter supplies into Joe's clay jars and stored them in the barn.

They all moved to Fabri's cabin. She prepared an ample meal while the boys crawled at their feet. After Evie fed the kids, she laid them in the stroller for a nap, gently stroking their heads and humming until their little bodies went limp with sleep.

The success of the day infused Joe with an impatient energy. "With last month's grain and today's pine nuts, we're ready for winter. That only leaves the rest of the apples to harvest."

"I love a full barn." Eloy laughed. "Though maybe I should be charging you rent too."

"No, you shouldn't." Fabri waved her spoon. Then her tone softened. "But still, you do a nice job, honey, filling the dinner plates for our neighbors and us." She gestured to a large wild turkey that Eloy had shot with his bow the day before. As Fabri brought it to the table, Evie served a salad of foraged greens. They eagerly dug into their full plates.

"Pine nuts were one of the few things that sounded good my entire pregnancy." Evie chased the nuts with her fork.

"They're easy to like, with all the fat and calories," Eloy said.

Joe leaned over and whispered to Evie, "Not that it shows. I think you're in better shape now than before the boys." Her eyes lit up, and a mischievous smile crossed her face.

"I like to grind the nuts into a paste and make butter," Fabri said, pouring gravy over her turkey.

"It's flavorful, but sheep butter is more to my taste," Eloy said, spreading some of his preferred butter on a thick slice of bread.

"Joe, Fabri made the very nice offer to watch the boys overnight." Evie raised her eyebrows in expectation.

Fabri chortled. "They're seven months old—old enough to spend a night away from their mother. And we have enough sheep's milk to get them through."

Joe cocked an eyebrow at Evie, then smiled at Fabri. "That's incredibly generous. Thank you." His gaze met Evie's. "And now I understand why you brought so much baby stuff in that pack."

She shrugged, smiling.

Eloy smiled too. "They're well behaved. But active. We've volunteered two pairs of hands."

Joe's heart raced with unexpected excitement. Until that moment, he had forgotten how immersed in child-raising they had become. "That's very kind. You'll need all those hands."

As they hiked back to the cabin later, he said, "Secret planning going on?"

"Fabri suggested it yesterday. She said Eloy was keen to spend more time with the boys." She danced up the trail before him, reminding Joe of the long, dark days they'd spent hiking to find this pleasant valley. That burden had been lifted, and he quickened to match her pace and leave the memory behind.

"So now what?" He winked when he caught up to her.

Evie tilted her head and blushed. "Let's get washed. Then let's take a walk to sit under our apple tree. Maybe we can even share a bite." Joe smiled. Evie sprinted ahead and disappeared around a boulder.

He went to the cabin and put away the supplies from his pack. The large buckskin blanket wasn't hanging on the wall hook. Joe went to the wooden bath, stripped off his clothes, and sank into the still-warm water. He scrubbed away the dirt of the day. Then he saw Evie's clothes in a neat pile. Joe stepped from the bath and into the sunlight and walked to the apple tree.

She lay, naked but for her red diamond ring, on the blanket. The tan buckskin with the gray fringe reminded him of Botticelli's scallop shell, the way it displayed her perfect form. Her breasts were full, velvety in the light. Her tongue played across her lips, and his pulse skipped as their gazes met.

He lay beside her and covered her body with soft kisses. Evie ran her hands over him, and he rose to her touch. His fingers found the inside of her thigh and traced the curve of the world. Their fingers played languid games over each other, caressing the spots each loved, forcing the Earth to slow on its axis for them alone.

"It feels like I know you completely. Not just every hair on your head, but your mind." He kissed her forehead.

"Like I'm inside your head, and you're inside mine." And he truly was inside her. "Yes, let's do this forever." She sighed, and they slowed the spinning world again.

Then she was on his lap, facing him and rocking slowly, their gazes locked. Her face was infused with joy and unfettered love, and framed by a pink sky. The splash of the noria counted out a slow rhythm to match her hips.

As their breath rose together, she rocked faster. "Hungry yet?" A soft moan escaped.

"Only for you."

The breeze carried the aroma of pine needles, blending in his nose with the smell of her hair against his face. A chorus of robins, warblers, and nightjars rose to salute the fading day. Evie's heart fluttered against his chest like a starling. Her skin glistened with sweat despite the cooling air. The gurgling stream merged with the splashing from the noria and her cries. Her body shuddered, then again. He dissolved into pure love, borne away from the mountain and into the darkening sky, up into the reaches of space where stars blazed in their glory. Then he was lowered softly back to rest on the blanket next to their little cabin, safe from the world.

The sun disappeared below the horizon. They lay together, his mind empty except to know she was there. She snuggled close to him on the blanket as the air cooled around them in the dying light. Her breath was quiet and even again.

. . .

I feel her electricity, this partner and lover. She is the bolt. She ignites something in me.

. . .

Evie pulled down a single red apple from the tree. "A little dessert?" She held out the fruit with a twinkle in her eye.

Joe took a bite, letting the electricity of this moment wash over him.

"Dessert after the dessert," he said.

CHAPTER 40

Late autumn painted the mountains with brushstrokes of bright yellow aspen, russet maple, and golden ash. The frosty morning calm was often interrupted by the honks of hundreds of Canada geese that had stopped at the mountain lakes before retaking wing in their migration south. They had stored the crops for winter, the days had grown shorter, and Joe spent more time inside the cabin with Evie and the boys.

Today they hosted Fabri and Eloy. They all sat around the table inside. Evie turned the crank on the butter churn, the rhythmic thump of the cream inside the barrel adding soothing music to their conversation. Asher sat on Joe's lap and hiccupped, almost in rhythm with the churn, sheep's milk dripping from his chin.

Joe nodded toward the churn. "Eloy, you did a fine job designing that. I tried to make something similar last month and couldn't quite get it right."

Evie laughed. "Turning it was like trying to roll a boulder uphill. This one turns so smoothly."

"Nothing to it." Eloy waved away the praise. "Joe here just has a mind for different things. The trick was to fit the crank just so, tight enough so it wouldn't leak."

Evie glanced at Joe and nodded. He cleared his throat. "We're particularly grateful for anything that eases Evie's work, since soon she'll be doing another kind of labor."

Fabri gasped, a hand to her mouth. Eloy clapped him on the back.

Evie studied her abdomen, though Joe couldn't yet see any evidence. "It's hard to believe that I'm pregnant again. Asher and Clay are still so young." She rubbed a hand across her belly. "Life can be so unpredictable."

"Well, seeing you two together, maybe this *was* sort of predictable." Eloy winked. Then he seemed to think twice about what he said and his cheeks reddened. "But yes, there are lots of surprises in life."

"Be thankful for gifts from above. And I'll be here to help you with the delivery again." Fabri picked up Clay from the floor and bounced him on her knee. "How are you feeling this time around, Evie?"

"I wish I didn't feel so out of control of my body, but I'm much more confident. I think my body has picked up on that—I have more energy." In a flash, she abandoned the churn and swooped down on Asher, hugging him until he squealed with laughter.

Joe smiled, then said, "We're halfway through this banishment. We'll make it."

Eloy's strong hand gripped his shoulder. "It looks like we signed up for another enlistment too. We're all gonna stick together."

◆

The onset of winter meant a slowing of life. Nature hunkered down, decreasing metabolism to conserve energy. The energy that remained sparked raw in the competitive dance of life and death, with everything eating everything else as the food supply dwindled. Joe found himself part of that web, grasping its power to define life. He walked his trapline in each morning's increasing cold, pulling his buckskin coat tight around him and his fur hat over his ears. He stalked the snow-covered moraines for game to restock their larder. He stacked firewood to keep the cabin warm for the family.

As he did many winter mornings, Joe waited in hiding for deer. In the tree stand, he was exposed to nature's element through bare branches, but he was also exposed to himself. The initial notes of blowing wind sang down from the mountains and broke the perfect silence. It was more of a hum, lacking consonants, a background sound of Mother Earth and Father Time combined, leaving Joe powerless and isolated in his tree.

The sun peeked over the horizon, signaling it was time to return. Empty-handed, Joe slung the bow over his shoulder and tramped back on wooden feet through the frosty grass. His breath rose in puffs, but the physical motion chased away the chill, and soon lances of painful warmth traveled down his cold legs and arms. The faint forest trails were wet with light rain from the evening before, and mud soon caked his worn Mercuries. His hunting had taken him several kilometers from home, and fatigue overwhelmed him. Joe scanned the ridges and listened for any stirring. When he crested the hill above the cabin, movement glimmered in the corner of his eye and froze his heart.

The tawny muscular streak moved across the open grass east of the barren wheat field, straight toward the cabin. The stroller sat near the chimney, but Evie was nowhere in sight. Even from a distance movement was visible from the stroller—a tiny hand perhaps.

"Evie! Evie!" He sprinted and bellowed until his voice cracked open the heavens.

The mountain lion shot toward the stroller, pure animalistic power crossing the field in a determined line, its ears laid back. Joe watched, helpless as he ran, shouting.

An eyeblink later, Evie burst from the door carrying her bō stick. She bolted around the side of the cabin as the cat leaped. The stick flashed in a swirling ellipse in her hands. She caught it in midair and used its momentum to strike at the beast. Her blow caught one of its front legs, and it fell to the ground with its paw bent awkwardly, but it rolled onto its shoulder and back to standing. The force pushed Evie backward, but she held her footing and attacked again, her blade slicing at the cat's face. The lion snarled viciously, bared its teeth, then turned and dashed away across the field. A scream echoed up the valley, disorienting Joe until he realized the sound came from the fleeing cat.

Joe clutched both wailing boys in his arms without knowing how he had descended the hill. Evie howled, still waving her stick. Her body was shaking, and Joe put Clay down to place an arm around Evie's shoulders.

She sagged against him. Her voice broke as she said, "I took the boys outside and then went back for the blankets, and I grabbed the bō stick on the way out. It all happened so fast."

"It's okay. You were magnificent."

Her mouth trembled. She picked up Clay and clutched him to her, whispering to him. She struggled to inhale deeply, but she kept exhaling in short, ragged gasps.

Joe focused on her belly, now slightly showing, and he shuddered at the risk she had taken. His own breath was quick. With adrenaline coursing through his veins, his animal instincts raged.

"Everything can be taken away in an instant," she said.

"That's our reality. But not today."

He put Asher, smiling and happy again, back in the stroller and bundled him. "I need to track it, find out how injured it is. We can't risk it returning."

"Be careful." Worry creased her face. "I need you to come back." He gave her a grim smile, then checked his bow and set off.

Paw prints traced a line across the black soil of the field, four toes and three lobes on the hind edge. Drops of blood marked the right front paw print. He followed the blood trail over the hill, thankful for a way to track the animal's direction past the horizon line.

The cat's trail became much more difficult to find as he went on. Joe worried the cat might be lying in wait, so he remained alert while examining the underbrush for clues. A blood smear in a thicket of antelope bitterbrush indicated he was on the right course, and he advanced, staring intently, listening, moving noiselessly. When he lost all signs, he backtracked and hunted at a right angle to where the trail left off, and he managed to pick it up again. He studied the landscape and tried to think like a mountain lion, to guess which way it might head.

He tracked for what must have been hours. The cat's footprints in the mud showed where the cat had stopped to drink. Bent grass and another bloodstain made it easier to track, but the stains grew farther apart. The animal probably wasn't mortally wounded.

His arms ached from carrying the bow at the ready. Joe had hiked several kilometers. He'd lost and found the cat's trail a dozen times. The hunt hardened him to reality. He was not afraid, only determined to find the animal and end the threat.

He roamed five valleys away from the cabin and found meager signs, but they all led uphill. Joe wondered why the cat would spend the extra energy. He slowed at the top of the rise, confirmed the wind direction, and stepped cautiously to look over the top. There was a rock outcropping below, amidst a jumble of fir trees. He glimpsed a flash of reddish color between two boulders. He froze, then kneeled in the grass to avoid being seen. Three animals were partly hidden in the foliage, visible only through the scope of his bow. Joe nocked a broadhead arrow.

He centered the mountain lion in the bow sight. Then something else bounced into view. The two cubs had reddish spots on white-and-tan coats. One cub rolled over to suckle, its blue eyes clear through the lens of the sight. The mother lion licked the cub then licked her own paw. The other cub dragged its tongue along the red gash across her face.

. . .

She was hunting to feed her cubs. Living life by instinct, in the moment. She'll do anything for them. We're all animals, and we deal death to one another. I no longer hesitate when I kill a deer, but this would be a different type of death.

. . .

Joe lowered the bow. He watched for many minutes, then backed off the ridge. He walked down the mountainside and across the landscape, back home.

Joe arrived at the cabin in late afternoon, hungry, dusty, and bushed. He found the door shut like a tomb. He pried it open, and the boys gurgled from the stroller. Evie looked up, expectant.

"Did you kill it?"

"I couldn't do it. She's a mother with cubs. I don't think she'll be back. You cut her, and she'll remember that. We'll just be extra careful."

Evie bit her lip. "Being a mother changes you. You'll do anything to protect your young. There's an unpredictability to that. It's not about 'I,' it's about 'them'—my babies. I operated on pure instinct out there. Adrenaline. To protect my young. A mother mountain lion will do the same. We should remember that this great wilderness we live in exposes our primal instincts."

Joe brushed her hair away from earnest eyes, and he held his defending angel.

CHAPTER 41

Their second winter in the Empty Zone kept them inside the cabin more than they wished, but it was a safe retreat from the harsh hand of nature. Snow cloaked the mountainsides, and intermittent rains washed it away. Joe often tromped through thirty centimeters of snow when checking traplines. It was a small comfort that the century's warmer climate had pushed the game into a narrower range, making hunting fruitful even in the scant cover. Each day Joe returned home, dead tired from hunting. He often tumbled into bed after dinner.

One February morning, a grating sound woke him. Joe groggily climbed out of bed to peer through the window. The noria spun fast from the meltwater filling the creek. He opened the door to confirm the sound—the axle ground against wood, the animal grease gone.

After breakfast, Joe dressed warmly, retrieved his bucket of grease from the root cellar, and carried it to the wheel. A light rain had started, and he gingerly stepped across the wooden trough to stand on the beam supporting the wheel. He applied grease with a flat stick. As grease oozed its way between wooden pieces, Joe stepped back to admire his work, but his foot only met air.

Falling backward, he hit the frigid water and went under. His shoulder rammed against a beam as his ankle struck a rock in the streambed. The current took him, pulling him underwater for a few meters until he thrust his head up and gulped air. The couple of strokes to reach the bank sent jolts of agony down his injured shoulder, and, with difficulty, he pulled himself up on the bank. Icy water ran from his face. His entire body radiated pain as he crawled to the cabin.

Joe pushed the door open with one hand, letting out a long groan. Evie gasped and ran toward him. She steadied him with an arm around his waist.

"I fell off the noria."

She helped him remove the frozen clothes while the boys watched with wide eyes from the stroller. "I don't think I broke my ankle, but it's at least a bad sprain." He gasped. "My shoulder hurts too." She removed his shirt. Already a dark bruise had spread over the top of his arm and across his chest. He toweled himself dry before Evie helped him to the bed and tucked several blankets around him. She built up the fire, and he eventually stopped shaking.

"Love, let me look at your ankle," Evie said. It ached under her fingers as she examined it. "It doesn't look broken. Some cold compresses should reduce the swelling."

"I think the creek water did a fine job of that."

Evie smiled, and the worry retreated from her face as she prepared a hot soup.

. . .

I could easily have fractured my leg or ankle. That would've been a disaster, likely meaning death for me. I hadn't thought about basic medical knowledge when preparing for this place, though it should have been obvious.

. . .

After a full bowl of soup, the cold that had seized his insides abated. Joe lay in bed for the rest of the day, keeping his ankle elevated and his shoulder immobile.

By the next day, his shoulder felt better—only bruised, it seemed—but his ankle had swollen to twice its normal size. He was forced to admit he would need several days of rest to let it heal.

Joe stayed inside for the next two days, watching the twins while Evie hiked the traplines, checking for food. Rain returned the following morning, and they huddled inside. By midday, the rain hammered on the thin roof and rivulets streamed down the single windowpane. Dazzling flashes of lightning lit it, followed by booms of thunder.

"That hit close." Evie combed out her wet hair by the fire.

"It's almost like we're out in it," Joe said.

"Almost."

Joe frowned, frustrated. "You shouldn't be outside at all, being four months pregnant."

She shot him a look. "I'll let you know if I'm not up to something, Joe. I know how to listen to my body. Trust me." She came over and snuggled up to his uninjured side.

He put his hand on her belly, rubbing the bump. She intertwined her fingers with his, and they lay there, content. He whispered to her, "Thanks for hauling firewood, love."

"You're welcome." Evie brushed her hand over his biceps, which had thickened with use. "You do a lot around here." Her hand lingered. "Hunting our meals. Chopping our firewood. You deserve a break." She punctuated each line with an appreciative squeeze of his arm. "And a proper thank you."

Joe detected a hunger in her eyes that he suspected had nothing to do with their winter diet. "And I wish I felt, er, *up* to it this minute. But let this leg heal another day . . ."

She smiled and then turned a serious face to Joe. "Your injury got me thinking. We finish our sentence in a little over a year. We're vulnerable out here without medical care. What if something happened to one of us? Even if we like many things about living here, we have to think about the boys. We need to go back."

He sighed. "I think we need to go back too. Living here, the boys would have radically shorter lives. There's no way for us to replicate the medical advances in the modern world. I don't think we can make that choice for them."

"But it's not just about being protective. It's about participating in the larger community."

"Agreed. I love our simple life here. But humankind has progressed beyond this basic way of living. And by staying in the past, we're forgoing participation in the advancement of the human story."

She squeezed his arm again. Her eyes were resolute, reminding Joe of the woman he first met, mysterious yet confident. "Thinking about the boys' welfare reminded me of what we left too. I look at our sons and at the life we have made here, and I realize that they're our legacy. They deserve a world where they're valued for their contribution to society and not by some Level assigned at birth. I started something with my Levels movement, and I need to see it through."

He weighed the hazards. "Do you think we need to worry about Peightân and Zable after we serve our sentences?"

"Maybe." Evie shoved back her hair. "But maybe there's been progress in catching them. And in any case, Dina, Mike, Raif, Freyja, and Gabe will be there to help us."

"It's a risk, but I agree with you. Our life here won't get easier with three children. We need to take that gamble and go back."

Now her eyes were on fire. "You always speak about the block. Our life here is just a sliver. And yet if we can return, we can be the bolt. We can be the thing that inspires change in the world."

"I can help you with that goal. I believe in it too. Our children are equal to anyone else, and I'd like a world where that is the common understanding."

Evie wrapped her arms around him in a tight hug. "Thank you. I want you with me in the fight."

The fireplace sputtered as rain dripped into the chimney. Evie stacked wood on the fire, and the dancing shadows inside mimicked the flashes of lightning outside the window.

Joe stayed in bed for the rest of the day, enjoying the comforts of home.

The boys tottered over, carrying the wooden toy figures he had made, and he marched them across the bunched blanket like the hills of an imaginary battlefield. Then Joe took two soldiers and, prancing the figurines about on the blanket, whispered stories of kings and princesses. The boys watched the figures with wide eyes.

That evening, the twins slept peacefully in their bed in the corner while Evie stirred a pot of soup on the fire. She stopped and came to sit next to him.

"Your eyes are clear." She put a hand on his forehead. "Thinking again?"

"Kids can be so innocent, despite living in a world where bad things happen."

"You're thinking about evil in the world?"

"It's more like levels of bad things, with evil at the top." Joe took her hand in his and kissed it. "Remember when we discussed the angle of repose?"

"How sand or rocks can shift at any second?"

"Exactly. Now, say a rock rolls down on your head if you happen by at the wrong time. Or you slip off a noria. We aren't living in paradise. Such accidents are due to the randomness built into the way the universe is organized. There are living creatures without consciousness, blindly following the organizing principles of life, to find food and to reproduce. Like the microbe that made me ill last year."

"And like the mountain lion trying to find food for her cubs."

"Yes, an example of elementary consciousness and sentience. But like the others, the mountain lion acts by instinct, meaning without full moral capacity to know good and evil. One cannot hang a moral label on her actions; they're morally neutral," he said.

"You think consciousness must be a prerequisite to morality?"

"I believe so. There seems a need to have a moral framework infused with the meanings of good and evil before one can make advanced moral judgments."

Evie leaned close. "Maybe Adam and Eve had a moral understanding within their consciousness, so they created rules to guide the way they lived."

"Yes. Before Adam and Eve, everything may have seemed perfect in Eden. But conscious understanding brought the realization that the world is imperfect. That's because conscious creatures can act in ways that they collectively agree are wrong."

Evie furrowed her brow. "If evil doesn't exist embedded in the world, but only in the minds of conscious creatures, do *we* create evil?"

Joe leaned on his right elbow and rubbed his beard. "Perhaps we do. I think our mentality is a complex set of relations. I imagine little causative bolts, patterned in immense webs. Our mentality creates semantic meaning, forming relationships between the world and ourselves. Maybe as we bootstrap meaning out of these relationships, we create more complex webs of relationships, and those are ideas, which carry moral content."

"Then how can this universe, with the possibility for evil, be created by a loving God?" Evie closed her eyes and recited an old poem from memory.

"Tyger Tyger, burning bright
In the forests of the night;
What immortal hand or eye,
Could frame thy fearful symmetry?"

He folded back the blanket. "William Blake."

She looked out the black window. "I wasn't afraid when the mountain lion attacked. But afterward, it terrified me to think what could've happened to the boys. And I was afraid you might get hurt." Her gaze went to his swollen ankle. "It's hard to square the existence of God with the suffering in the world."

"Even Charles Darwin questioned how a being so powerful and knowledgeable as God could create a universe and yet allow the suffering of so many lower animals."

"Add to that all the evil that conscious creatures do."

Evie got up to stir and serve the soup, and Joe lifted himself to a sitting position in the bed. She brought him a bowl, then pulled up a chair to sit across from him.

"This universe exists within a particular mathematical structure, a particular logic." He blew across the fragrant soup. "Some things are impossible within those rules. For example, one of the three laws of logic, the law of the excluded middle, says that for some proposition, either that proposition is true, or its negation is true."

"In other words, there's no middle ground. Where does that logic law lead?"

Joe swallowed a spoonful of soup before answering. "If God exists, then She either created a universe where conscious creatures have free will, or it's not true that God created a universe where conscious creatures have free will. Both can't simultaneously be true."

Evie's face lit, and her spoon remained poised in midair. "But if God gives us free will, then She can't control the consequences of our acts, no matter how much She wishes they might be otherwise."

"Yes."

"Wait." Evie pointed her spoon in his direction. "I remember what you said about time. That it's all here, the same way the dimension of length is here. That we're like a dragonfly frozen in amber. If that's true, then She can't take it back; time moves on for us, but it's outside Her control because She is outside time."

"Exactly."

"Then if there is such a God, She gives up absolute power and grants free will to conscious creatures."

"It would be a wondrous gift."

She nodded, a meditative warmth lighting her face. "Then conscious creatures can do what they wish, to the world and to each other, including evil. Maybe that's the price of free will."

CHAPTER 42

Spring arrived with a surge of new life. Wildflowers carpeted the hillsides in resplendent colors, and the apple tree blossomed. Joe and Evie enjoyed sitting under it in the sun, surrounded by the white flowers and their sweet aroma while the twins practiced walking. Clay would seize Asher as they passed, and they would twirl around, giggling, before tumbling into the dirt. Besides "Momma" and "Dada," Asher had mastered "lamb," which he uttered when he hugged the ewes and buried his fingers in their wool.

With the coming of spring, melting snow filled the brook that rushed past the cabin. One of the paddle blades on the noria tore loose, threatening the collapse of the machine. Joe and Eloy hitched Bessie to a jury-rigged block and tackle to lift the wheel. They repaired all the worn blades, greased the apparatus, and set it in place again. Eloy's noria needed similar maintenance. At the end of the stressful day of repairs, Joe stood on the noria's top beam and stared into the water.

. . .

With a baby on the way, it's not the time to risk another injury. I'm relieved to have this job done.

. . .

It had been an uneventful pregnancy and easier than the last. Evie was full of energy as she approached the last months. While she occasionally mentioned dismay at the prospect of the pain of an unmedicated delivery, she seemed to have steeled herself to it.

Feeling like a practiced farmer, Joe planted the wheat field in May. He expanded the field again, knowing it would be his last crop. The end of their banishment was only a year away. He often thought of his friends in the outside world, wondering what progress they had made to expose Peightân. The simple fact that no communication had reached them suggested nothing had occurred to reduce their banishment sentence. The Empty Zone remained a world sealed off, and the world beyond the wall a different life, a different time, a different reality. There was no alternative other than to live in the present.

Joe chopped the fourth mark of the month onto the rear cabin wall of his banishment calendar. His sigh of satisfaction was met with a moan from the cabin. He ran inside and found Evie seated on the bed. "Better bring Fabri."

After making sure the boys were inside and occupied with toys, he raced down the creek trail, his pulse leaping as he bounded over the rocks. Fabri was ready, and she scurried up the path beside him with her nurse's bag. He knew the routine this time. Evie was calm and stoic, breathing through the pain. The baby arrived hours later with a healthy cry.

"Another boy." Fabri's announcement was joyous, but quiet so as not to wake the sleeping twins.

"His name is Sage." Evie caressed him against her breast.

. . .

It's still a miracle, every time. No parent can ever explain it to one who isn't, this magic of holding him in my arms.

. . .

He smiled into the blue eyes gazing back, and tears filled his own, his heart full.

━━━━━━━━◆━━━━━━━━

Joe was glad to remember what it felt like to sleep again. Sage was three months old, and they were, at last, getting nearly full nights of rest. One baby was easier than two, and they felt like experienced parents. But Sage's cries for milk invariably awakened the twins, so Joe spent much of Sage's feedings resettling them. There were not enough pairs of hands for three young children. Joe often dreamt of kinder-bots to help with one of the bouncing kids.

The weariness ceded to occasional bright spots of joy as the boys grew into their personalities and acquired new skills. Sage discovered his hands, and he waved them at anyone who entered or left the cabin. The language development of the twins at eighteen months astounded Joe. Evie kept up a constant stream of conversation with them and sang old nursery songs. Clay was quick to state his wants. "More milk" was a favorite phrase. Clay loved to drag the hoe behind him while Joe did fieldwork. Asher, with his love for every moving creature—including bugs—tried to help Evie milk the ewe. The weather was often sunny, and they spent much time outside, connected to the natural world.

Joe sat in his chair under the apple tree and appreciated the field of wheat waving golden in the languid breeze. The twins ran laps and giggled. When Asher spotted a chipmunk at the base of a nearby pine, they toddled over to investigate.

Evie nursed Sage in her chair set beside Joe's. Sage smiled up at her, and she smothered his face in kisses. He cooed and smiled. Clay found Joe's shoes where he had taken them off next to his seat, and he had both feet in them, attempting to walk around in the Mercuries.

Asher made his way to Evie and reached up with both arms, mumbling an incomprehensible phrase, though both parents knew what he wanted. She lifted him with one arm into her lap, situated him next to Sage, and planted big raspberries on his tummy as he laughed and wiggled. "Aren't they all so adorable?"

Joe smiled. "I see your laughter in their faces."

"I never realized how much fun it would be to watch our own kids learn, even the most basic things." Clay inspected a stick and scraped it along the ground. Her gaze turned to Joe. "If your idea that bolts are the basis of everything is true, what does that say about the kids? How do they learn and interact with the world? I admit I find the idea abstract. I can't get my head around it."

Joe reflected for several minutes. "That means the 'I' that is each of us is a pattern of causative relations, a web of bolts. Sage, upon coming into the world, infuses meaning by creating relations between himself and the world. In one sense, he is self-created." Joe scratched his now thick beard. "Yes, that's it. We are self-created. And we create whatever morality is in the world too. It's all on us."

"Are you saying that we create that world collectively?"

"Yes, but we may each perceive that same world differently. The web of bolts that forms us interacts with the other webs of bolts in the world, and our semantic meaning of the world is created. It's likely that all humans form similar meaning from our first contact with that world."

"Isn't my picture of the world the same as your picture of the world?"

He shook his head. "We can't know that with any certainty. But I can speculate that it is essentially the same because none of the rules for how bolts interact are different for you than for me; we are both human beings. In the same way that I can't know *what it's like* to be that hawk"—he pointed to the sky—"I can't know what your experience is."

"Hawk." Asher tracked the bird with his finger as it soared over the ridge.

Sage sucked on the toes of one of his feet. Joe tried again. "It's impossible to think about the world any other way than the way we now experience it. That's because bolts define the supposed particles moving about in the universe. I'm saying that the 'I' that is Sage is composed of a web of bolts. Those bolts are causing something, then the particles seem to move. But we can't see the bolts. All that machinery is hidden from us somewhere."

She nodded slowly. "Then your idea alters nothing in what we see."

"Everything is the same, from outward appearances. The difference is that bolts are causative. These collective relations make up our mentality to form thoughts, which turn into acts, which ultimately create a causal impact in our world."

"Then we have free will to decide to do anything," Evie said. She thought for several moments. "So you're saying that when Asher asks for an apple, he's deciding based entirely on his desires as filtered through his experience."

Joe picked an apple and took a bite. It was just sweet enough. He handed it to his son. Asher took it in both hands and bit into it, drooling.

"No, the entire web of bolts influences him. But the collection of relations, the 'I' that is Asher, is more complex. That 'I' can decide to do something different."

Evie sighed. "That's comforting because I like to think my parenting is educational and necessary."

"Yes, every relation influences every other. Aristotle said that character forms over time, influenced by parents, friends, and community, and that it takes practice to form good character. I believe he was mostly right. We are influenced, but we create ourselves through the choices we make."

Asher wandered back to play in the dirt near the pine tree next to Clay. Evie laid the now-sleeping Sage into the stroller beside her, then walked to the tree and sang to the twins. The lilt of the nursery rhyme floated across the hillside.

. . .

Evie, our children, our neighbors—there is a moral order to all this. We create our own morality.

Ethics isn't based on a duty to act, as Kant suggested with his categorical imperative. There is no law handed down from outside this closed physical universe. It comes from us, not thinking of ourselves, forgetting our ego. It comes from compassion for all living things, sharing this imperfect world.

Let me instead follow Schopenhauer's ethics, based on the *presence* of something—compassion—instead of the *absence* of something. Let's try to be as compassionate as we can be.

. . .

———————◆———————

Evie bustled around the fireplace, concentration furrowing her face as she readied the courses of the meal to come out concurrently. She brought the turkey that Joe had shot the day before to the table, and after Joe carved the bird, she served steaming pieces of white breast meat onto plates. Fabri served a salad sprinkled liberally with Evie's favorite, pine nuts. Eloy entertained the twins, and Sage slept in the stroller.

"Nice shot to get that bird," Eloy said as Evie set a plate of meat in front of him.

"I've gotten confident enough to hunt birds—not Evie's smarter way, but with my bow—though I hate losing arrows when I miss," Joe said.

They assembled around the table, passing loaves of bread and plates of food. The twins, contained in wooden high chairs Joe built, grabbed the pieces of meat Evie and Joe offered them, stuffed their mouths, and made a mess on the surrounding floor. Joe had also made a new, longer table to seat everyone, and the cabin was cramped but cozy.

"Evie, the stuffing tastes great," Eloy said.

"It's a bread stuffing, made with pine nuts and wild herbs," she said. Only Joe knew how hard she'd worked on getting it just right.

"We love celebrating the harvest with you," Fabri said.

"It's a great tradition we've created among ourselves." Joe passed another plate. "We are delighted to host this year."

"You pulled in a hefty wheat crop," Eloy said.

"This third crop is likely to remain my record," Joe said. Eloy blinked and gave a slight nod but kept his face neutral.

They all concentrated on their plates. The conversation turned to Evie's delicious gravy, and she glowed with the praise. "I like to cook," she said. She basked in their compliments again after she served the apple pie.

They scraped the plates clean and sat back with a contented sigh. Then Evie caught Fabri's gaze with an intense expression. "Fabri, we love to have you and Eloy here, and we are grateful for all you've done for us. We have two presents for you." She ducked into the side bedroom and returned with a woven basket. "You've become a sister to me. This is for you, with all my heart."

Evie put the basket down in front of Fabri and hugged her. Fabri stood, flustered. "I don't get many presents." She opened the soft basket made from reeds and pulled out a beautifully made buckskin blouse with delicate wooden buttons, lacing on the sides, and fringe on the sleeves. Fabri put it on, buttoned the front, and stood to examine it better. Evie showed her how to adjust the lacing on the sides for an exact fit. "It fits even better than what the bots give you." Fabri radiated pleasure.

Joe raised his eyebrows and said, "Very sharp, Fabri." He smiled knowing how many days Evie had spent making the blouse. She'd labored over the buttons.

Joe sprung from the table, ducked into the bedroom, and returned with a long fishing rod and spinning reel. He had cut the rod from a limber sapling. The monofilament line was one of three rolls he had carried into the Empty Zone.

The delicate addition was the wooden spinning reel he had made, using a nail for the axle and handle, a piece of wire for the bail, and carefully whittled wood for the spool. He had tested the mechanism several times by casting with it into the brook. He handed it to Eloy.

"Eloy, this is to say thanks for all the lessons in farming, hunting, and fishing—and in living."

Eloy's face quivered with emotion as his calloused hands cradled the rod. He showed the twins how the handle turned the reel smoothly, and he kept reeling and unreeling the line. "This'll serve much better than my sapling pole. I reckon you're giving me a miniature noria back."

Joe grinned. "No reason to reinvent the wheel."

The dinner ended with warm feelings all around. Fabri climbed onto Bessie behind Eloy, and they waved goodbye before the sun touched the horizon. Joe held Evie's hand as their friends rode away. "That was a good idea," he said.

Evie nodded. "Eloy seems to be coming around to the idea that not all transactions between people need to be economic."

"I'm really going to miss them."

Evie squeezed his hand.

Joe sat under his apple tree, surrounded by the cooling air and warmed by the dinner they'd just finished. The wheat field was now bare dirt. They had harvested the apples, and the now naked branches framed a moonless sky. All that remained was the pinyon nut harvest the following month. Joe's days as a farmer were soon ending. While he appreciated the purpose survival had given him, his mind ached for new challenges.

He marveled at the tight sparkles of stars dangling in the sky and remembered many earlier nights admiring his augmented reality star maps. He'd memorized the major constellations. It was a silly and unnecessary commitment in the modern world—but not in this germinal one. He traced the star patterns overhead, as if his ARMO were still operating. The summer triangle was visible in the southwestern sky, as were the constellations Cygnus, Lyra, and Aquila, with their bright stars Deneb, Vega, and Altair. In the north, cradled between Perseus and Draco, he found the polestar, Polaris, pointed north to the gate that would lead them out of banishment. Beyond that uncertain future in a half-turn around the sun, he didn't know where else his path might lead. Joe contemplated his meandering odyssey.

. . .

We are all traversing our narrow slice of the block of time. We do the best we can. How do we measure our lives? If God exists, how does She measure us?

There seem to be a few hints along the way. There is a profound beauty in the structure of mathematics, the structure that architects the universe. We can find beauty and truth. We can lead a life of virtue. We can practice compassion and cultivate wisdom.

. . .

The touch of Evie's hand made everything even better. He reached his arm around her, and they both gazed upward. She rested her head on his shoulder. "What are you thinking about?"

"I was thinking about God."

She was still for a time. "When we crossed the desert, we said that if God exists, then She is something unknowable. But didn't we also say that we can't know for certain whether or not She exists?"

"Yes, if the universe is physically closed, and She is outside that closed universe, and if She does not interfere, then we can't know. The design is so precise, there are no marks of Her handiwork—a fine job to be unknowable."

"Why do you think that is?"

Their voices had dropped to whispers, not wanting to disturb the deep, hushed darkness. "If we had certainty of the existence of God, some proof, then wouldn't that limit our free will? If we saw the unequivocal mark of God, then wouldn't it be insane to do anything but follow a path of goodness?" Joe paused, breathing in the night air. "The idea of a God who does not interfere, and who does so to preserve the free will given to conscious creatures like ourselves, then answers the problem of evil in the world. The result, unfortunately, is that we can do anything, even any evil."

"Do you believe in God?"

"I've concluded that it is not anti-scientific to believe in a possible God that does not interfere with the universe and that stands outside of space and time." Joe pursed his lips and thought a moment. "The conjecture is simply unverifiable, standing outside what science can currently claim to know, like many so-called scientific speculations about what might lie beyond. Good scientists, knowing their epistemological limits, must take a neutral empirical stance. Now knowing that, I've updated my estimate of the probabilities."

She laughed quietly. "Probabilities? You're talking too much like a scientist. But I'm assuming you're referring to Pascal's wager? I read about it in your allbook."

"No, Pascal said if you believe God exists but you're wrong, you only lose some finite pleasures. But if you believe God doesn't exist and you sin freely and are wrong, then you pay with hell. Therefore, you should believe to play it safe."

"That sounds like an archaic concept of sin," Evie said. "It's essentially a negative bet to prevent the consequences if you're wrong."

Joe nodded. "Agreed. Mine is a positive assertion. I'll live by accepting the likelihood that there is a God, one that does not interfere. I'll take the evidence from the beauty I find in the universe, and I'll open my mind to the possibility. For me it's not only taking the odds. Living this life with you and our children has made me less cynical about what I cannot know, and more open to the beauty of the universe. Maybe I'm reaching some wisdom."

"The *via negativa* suggests God is unknowable. You talk as if something can be inferred."

Joe squinted at the sky. "As we said in the desert, all we have are some hints, stars to light our way. There is beauty in the mathematical structure of the universe. There's beauty in the exquisite balance between the seeming predictability and deep indeterminism that gives us free will. There's the unreasonable coincidence that the universe favors conscious, sentient creatures. There is the fine adjustment of starting conditions for the universe, which allowed life to develop. There's evolution that results in each world being suited for each creature. It seems the universe is a garden left wild, allowing conscious creatures to make their own choices."

"An astonishing gift—an elegant universe where we can have free will." Evie spread her hands wide to encompass the view in front of them. "If God has given conscious creatures these gifts, then it's difficult not to believe that She loves Her creations."

Joe remembered his weightless floating outside the orbital base. "It's hard to imagine that something the mind-boggling size, complexity, and elegance of the universe could appear out of nothing, without causality. But if it was created, then that would suggest a characteristic approaching omnipotence."

"Powerful enough that She can create a stone She cannot move. That She can constrain Her own power."

Joe nodded. "The paradox of the stone, which assumes the only logic possible is the one we know in this universe. But a profound God, one that created the universe and the fundamental mathematical scaffolding, can create other logics. And in those, perhaps there is no paradox." What could be inferred about such a God? "If She stands outside space and time, She could be omniscient and omnipresent in a different way than we might have envisioned."

"She could be looking at this dragonfly frozen in amber." She huddled closer, wrapped in his arm.

A meteor flashed across the sky and disappeared over the mountain. "Does God exist or not? We can choose to believe or not. In a closed physical universe, we will never find the answer. It doesn't affect our belief in science. If She doesn't interfere, we need to decide how to live because we need to create our own moral rules. The responsibility is ours."

"How can we acknowledge such a God?"

Joe whispered into the night. "Only by a simple song of gratitude, and a commitment in return—no more. If we have free will and such a God doesn't interfere, then it's limited to something like this:

Thank you for the gift of free will.

I accept the responsibility.

I will follow the path to virtue and truth, wisdom, and compassion.

Your created beauty lights the way."

Joe kissed her, and they contemplated the stars above their mountain.

CHAPTER 43

Joe sat beside Eloy on the banks of the creek, in the shade of a large live oak. They fished a hole where the brook flowed sedately at a bend. Three trout in spawning colors, their scales shimmering in the dappled light, lay on the green grass between the men. Eloy fished with the present from Joe, and Joe used a similar setup he'd made for himself. Eloy had cast his line well out downstream and stood still, facing the twig tied to the line that served as his bobber.

Joe still savored the thrill of landing the third rainbow trout. It had been hiding in the shallows near the bank. Letting his lure float downstream to it, he'd set a vibration to the line with the slightest movement of his wrist. The fish had risen to the bait. Then, in unconscious realization, it had sent a shock to his hands as it pulled fiercely, every fiber of its body fighting for survival. It flashed iridescent from the water, the line tight and singing, then dodged among the rocks on the far side of the brook. Joe had worked the rod carefully, keeping the line loaded and his pole bent and pointing to the sky, gently reeling, as the fish juked across the stream twice more. Evie would be happy with that one for dinner, he thought.

Joe took another wriggling worm from the woven box, skewered it onto the hook, and once again flipped his line to float next to Eloy's bobber. The sight of the bobbers drifting together caused a warmth in Joe's chest. He admired the man he sat beside, who had taught him so much about survival and self-reliance. Eloy believed he could be his own lone giant. He could walk the Earth a solitary force, using his hands and his mind to shape the world to his purpose, and he had little respect for anyone who shirked any task. Joe hoped he measured up.

"I'm looking forward to teaching Clay how to hunt and fish," Eloy said.

Joe tugged on his line. "I'm hopeful he won't need to learn the hunting."

"Well, at least self-reliance. Best taught by getting out in nature."

Joe nodded, minding his line for several minutes in silence as they enjoyed the peaceful creek.

"Your sentence is up in another month," Eloy said. "The marks on the cabin wall are neat and easy to count. I reckon you'll be leaving?"

"Yes, for the kids. We can't make the decision for them to abandon all modernity."

Eloy studied his float in the water. He talked faintly, almost to himself. "After we had served the five-month sentence, Fabri and I decided on sticking together. We liked it here and discussed having a kid, but when nothing happened there, we thought about heading through the gate and starting a new life outside. Then you showed up. The idea's been on hold."

Joe watched his float. "So, it's been a sacrifice?"

"Only a delay. We got the chance to try out the idea with your kids. The little rascals do get inside your heart."

Joe chuckled. "You can solve that problem. Medical intellectual property, part of the communal legacy of humankind. You should take your share."

Eloy studied him, his gaze muted. "Maybe it's time to give that a try while Fabri is still young enough."

Joe returned his gaze. "We'd love it if you both left with us."

"I'd like that. I'll talk to Fabri."

Content just to sit with his friend, Joe moved his pole to position the float into a ripple.

Eloy spoke softly, as if whispering to the fish. "You're the son I never had but wanted. Hardworking, and pulling his weight."

Joe smiled. "Never had? Why don't you add the word *yet*? And thank you. That's the finest compliment I've ever received."

◆

Joe and Evie invited their neighbors over for an early dinner. Fabri held Sage, who babbled to her and followed every expression of her face.

"Such chatterboxes, these knee babies," Fabri said.

Evie laughed. "Once the twins hit two years old, we couldn't stop them. Even Sage is trying to join the conversation." She ladled hot soup into bowls. Joe and Eloy, who each held a twin, put them in their high chairs, and they all settled around the table.

Joe caught Evie's attention as they began the meal. Then he turned to Eloy and Fabri and, with some solemnity, said, "The marks on the back of the cabin show we now have one week left." Fabri and Eloy exchanged glances and listened attentively.

Evie continued. "Joe told me he briefly mentioned to you, Eloy, our thoughts about our future when our sentence is finished. We've decided it's best for our boys to leave when that day comes. Though our life here has been enlightening, and you've been wonderful neighbors and friends, we must think of the kids first."

Eloy's expression was unsurprised. "Those guardbots are in an independent command. So long as you did your math right, they'll let you go, and they'll tell you if you didn't. They just follow orders." He spooned some soup into his mouth. "I expect that Joe has the figures down well enough. He can add, even if his economics isn't so straight."

Joe smiled at the description of his talents, then continued Evie's thought. "You're dear to both of us, but we're not ready to abandon the friends we've been separated from these three years. I know you've been considering whether to leave with us, which is the outcome we'd prefer. But you should know that there may be great risk in leaving with us. We left some powerful enemies outside, and we don't know if they're still dangerous. If so, we have no idea if our friends will be able to protect us."

Eloy sat at attention in his seat, as if Joe's statement had awakened some defiantly militaristic impulse.

Evie nodded at Joe, and she continued with the revelation they had talked about disclosing. "When we first met you, we mentioned some political enemies. But we need to tell you more. Out there, I was the leader of a movement to abolish the Levels Acts. That challenged the political structure. That's really why we were sent here." Evie told their friends the story of her movement, and where it had been left when they were banished.

Eloy chuckled. "Well, now I'm less surprised that you carry that bō staff."

"It sounds like you were working for all of us," Fabri said.

"That's right." Joe took Evie's hand. "And besides all the other reasons for returning, Evie is going back to pick up the fight. And I'm going to help her." They all nodded around the table, sharing a moment of solidarity.

Fabri spoke. "We've been debating this decision for weeks now. The reasons we stayed for so long are less important than they once were. We're kidding ourselves if we don't remember this is a dangerous environment, where we are only one disaster away from death."

Eloy was somber. "Ah, but the romance of the mountain man. I hate to give it up. I'm pretty good at it. I know I'll miss real venison. Better than that alt-stuff." He laughed. "But I guess no man's an island. We're both going."

"We'd like to leave with you." Fabri's smile was hopeful. "We hope we can be near to you and the boys—you've become family."

Evie and Joe couldn't keep the broad smiles from their faces as they hugged their neighbors. "It'll be so wonderful for the boys to have their aunt and uncle to help," Evie said.

Eloy fed Asher a spoonful of soup. "These guys will go through a huge adjustment. It'll help them to have people around who know what their lives have been like."

"Leaving the Empty Zone will be an unsettling change for them." Evie wrapped her arms around herself. "Having you with us will help ease their transition into a world where machines supply most needs."

"There goes our independent economy," Eloy said.

"Eloy, economies can't stay independent, not if the human intellectual property created is shared, as you've said is fair," Evie said.

Eloy's face twitched, and Joe suspected he was thinking of medical technology.

There were tears in Fabri's eyes, and she grabbed Eloy's hand. "And it's time for us to start our own family. Can't reinvent those procedures out here." Eloy rubbed her hand with his thumb. Fabri continued. "Whether or not that family thing works out, I'm planning to go back to hospital work. That's something people can do as well as the bots."

"You've taught me important lessons, Fabri, about compassion," Joe said.

Fabri stroked Sage's head. "They'll go where they don't need to get their protein from living creatures. They can be more compassionate people."

"Yes, a world where they can be good human beings, treating each other with respect and love." Evie's voice took on the passionate tone of her old fight. "So long as everyone holds each other to a high standard of fairness."

The wooden toy soldier that Clay had been playing with before dinner was still in his hand, and he banged it on the chair. Joe lifted him out of the high chair and into his lap. "A world where they can explore the universe and expand human knowledge."

Eloy tightened his jaw. "And a world with unlimited military power to deliver death and destruction. The good and the bad are magnified out there. Maybe they can be wiser than us."

Joe shook his head. "Free will to decide. It's quite a journey."

"Journey?" Asher asked, looking up from his spoon.

"Yes." Evie smiled. "With free will, it's an unfettered journey to everywhere you wish to go."

◆

The sun rose into a blue sky, the morning air crisp. It was one day before the end of their banishment. Though the northern gate was only twenty or thirty kilometers away, the dirt tracks and abandoned roads weren't well-suited for the old wagon, so the group determined it would be best to make it a slow journey. They would arrive at the gate by twilight, where they would make camp for their final night.

Eloy arrived at the cabin as promised, with Bessie pulling the buckboard loaded with their belongings. Fabri wore the buckskin blouse, while Eloy favored his military camo shirt. Evie and Joe arranged their meager gear and loaded the three boys into the wagon.

Evie had dressed the boys in fringed buckskin shirts and pants, with coarse wooden buttons she had painstakingly carved. Tiny moccasins shod their feet. Sage wore a rabbit-skin jumpsuit. He stared in wonder out of the furry fringe encircling his face. Evie was powerfully clothed in a fringed tunic and tight buckskin pants tucked into black boots edged with fur. Joe examined his buckskin shirt, coat, pants, and beaten-up Mercuries. These were the only clothes he owned. Three years in the wilderness had worn out near-ly everything they had brought.

The day before, Eloy had set the sheep to roam free, though Fabri worried about their survival. He had sacrificed the last of the chickens, filling their dinner plates to the brim for a shared meal in Fabri's cabin. Joe had said, "Big chicken dinner," laughing at himself, and the others joined in the joke. In many ways, the dinner felt bittersweet, like they were leaving behind something never to be regained.

Now Eloy sat in the buckboard and held the reins, as he looked over the little farm. The noria still turned in the stream. "Ready to go?"

Joe nodded, took one last look around the inside of their cabin, and shut the door. Evie hugged him. From the look in her eyes, she felt the same nostalgia. He helped Evie and Sage get settled between the twins, and he climbed up next to Eloy. Joe let his eyes play over their home one last time, from the empty field to the cabin, to the two apple trees, and then to the noria. It had been his finest bit of reinvention there, creating for them a civilized life and offering a symbol of the promise and peril of all human technology.

Joe fingered the spot on his chest where the biometric tile lay. "I'd guess our friends may expect us there around noon tomorrow."

Eloy snapped the reins, and the horse started off.

"Wave bye," Evie said to the twins.

"Journey," Asher said as he waved at the cabin.

Flustered, Clay looked at Eloy. As they started down the hill in the direction of Eloy's cabin, he said, "Uncle?"

"Not going to my house this time, Clay," Eloy said.

He drove the wagon across the edge of the now fallow field, picking his way around the rocks and holes. After another hundred meters, they reached the rough outlines of the abandoned dirt road that paralleled the creek. It was overgrown but easier to traverse. They crawled down the slope at a pace slow enough to lose any race with a tortoise. The wagon shook and rattled as Bessie clip-clopped on. The women kept busy entertaining the boys. Clay and Asher pointed at the birds that screeched when the wagon disturbed their bush or tree. They stopped at midday to eat cold chicken, served on the last loaves of bread.

The dirt track met a wider one, once paved but long abandoned. The place was now an empty crossroads with shattered foundations and bare spots like unmarked graves.

Eloy pointed to a rusty sign. "According to that, this was the town of Jiggs." He turned Bessie north and creaked up the road. Barren desert surrounded them, and they watched their mountains grow shorter against the southeast horizon. A last longing welled up inside Joe. He choked up at Evie's melancholy smile of farewell as her gaze lingered on their mountain home, forever behind them.

They reached a hill, and the dull outline of a wall stretched east and west along the distant highway. The gate at the road stood inscrutable in the dying light, indifferent to their approach and giving no hint of their fate beyond it.

In the shadow of the hill, they made camp. Joe found firewood and built a fire. Fabri and Evie prepared dinner from their stores. They all sat around the campfire, entertaining the older boys and playing with Sage, who was fussy from not napping well in the wagon. Clay and Asher were in high spirits from the novelty of the day, undeterred by the dust and the bumpy ride. As night descended, they calmed the boys and got them to sleep in rabbit blankets laid on the ground next to the wagon. In their sleeping bag, Joe studied the vault of sky, a million stars shining. He held Evie until her breath changed in deep sleep.

Joe ruminated about their immediate challenges. He had thought that Raif and the others might expose Peightân and shorten their banishment, but that obviously hadn't happened. Whatever was going on in the outside world, Joe had to assume Peightân was still a threat.

The universe, immense and random, surrounded him. His thoughts turned to the next days, and also to whatever time he had left.

. . .

I've gone to the mountain and come away having learned something about living in the world. Now let those lessons inform my path ahead.

. . .

Joe reflected on the beauty and hardships during the last three extraordinary years. A life with free will was an astonishing gift. That was reason to own his life, to take full responsibility for it. It would only trace a sliver in the block of time, but he vowed not to waste it, and to make every decision and moment count. He watched the backward-question-mark stars of Leo set in the west. The future was open, always a question. Life burned in him as never before.

Thinking all these things, Joe at last slept.

———————◆———————

They were awake at dawn. The women prepared a spartan breakfast. Trying hard not to awaken the twins, Evie took Sage into the wagon to feed him. Joe sat with Eloy and Fabri around the fire as they drank the last of their Mormon tea. "Do you think we can estimate exactly when it will be noon, so we can safely go through the gate?"

"Pretty much by just looking up." Eloy glanced at the sun climbing the sky. "And the guardbots will tell us if we're early. We won't go through the gate until they give us the go-ahead."

The twins awoke and immediately ran around the wagon and played in the dirt. They were a welcome distraction from Joe's increasing nervousness. The adults played with the children and shared an intense anticipation without voicing it as they waited for the unknown.

Evie looked at the sun and then at the gate in the distance. "It looks like we're an hour away. Maybe we should eat an early lunch now?" They all picked at their food, but Evie took care to make sure the boys ate. Then they reloaded the wagon, and Joe and Eloy retook their places on the seat.

"Off to the modern world," Eloy said as he clicked to the horse.

The buckboard descended the last sloping hill to the gate as the sun stood overhead. The wall loomed ahead of them, a straight, black slash across the desert. Several milmechas, heavy weapons held at the ready on each forearm, were visible in watchtowers on each side of the gate. One milmecha in the west tower manned a laser weapon that flamed red like a sword, pointing to the heavens.

They pulled the wagon to a stop in front of the gate. Bessie, oblivious to the tension, nosed the ground for nonexistent grass.

A milpipabot, ruggedized with extra armor, stepped from the guardhouse. "Declare yourselves," it commanded. They all stated their names, and Joe gave the names of the three boys, adding their ages and that they were born in the Empty Zone.

The forehead of the milpipabot glowed blue. "All recorded sentences have been served. You are free to exit."

The gate swung open, its seldom-used hinges creaking. The wagon lurched forward at Eloy's urging. The fence stretched in both directions as far as he could see. Then they were through the gate. Joe stared behind him as his old life become smaller and smaller, and the gate banged shut, providing an exclamation point suspended in the desert air.

He looked at Evie. The boys clutched at her in excitement. She sat upright, her bō staff in hand.

PART FOUR: THE JOURNEY UPWARD AND DOWNWARD

"From the outside, it would be like looking at a dragonfly frozen in amber."

Evie Joneson

"Not kismet, not fate, just freewill decisions by conscious creatures, shaped by random chance."

Joe Denkensmith

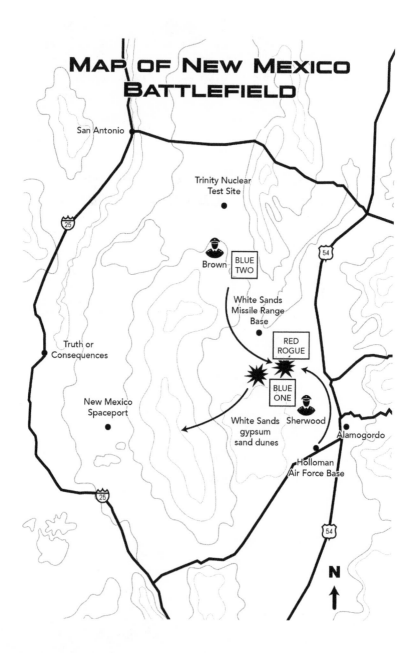

MAP OF NEW MEXICO BATTLEFIELD

San Antonio

Trinity Nuclear
Test Site

Brown
BLUE
TWO

White Sands
Missile Range
Base

RED
ROGUE

BLUE
ONE

Truth or
Consequences

New Mexico
Spaceport

White Sands
gypsum
sand dunes

Sherwood

Alamogordo

Holloman
Air Force Base

N

CHAPTER 44

"It's too easy." Evie's expression was resolute. Joe glanced back. Her hands clutched the side of the wagon on either side of the twins. She looked ready to defend them if anything were to happen.

The wagon rolled away from the gate, and Bessie plodded dutifully north on the desert road. Off in the distance, a billowing cloud of dark, swirling dust moved toward them. Eloy slowed the buckboard, then stopped as an armored carrier materialized from within the dusty center. Perched on the four corners of the carrier's roof were four milmechas with gigantic guns strapped to their forearms and pointing skyward, with a fifth in the center. The triangular heads of the machines turned toward them.

Joe froze in his seat. Time stood still.

. . .

Is it all over now?

. . .

"What's going on?" Fabri's voice was frantic. Sage, in her arms, began to wail, and she tried to shush him, her face pale.

The armored carrier approached to within seven meters and spun in its tracks to face backward. Grit wafted over the wagon, and the boys coughed. The carrier's back ramp opened with a clang against the road.

Raif's head appeared at the door, a huge smile lighting his face.

Joe vaulted off the wagon when Raif jogged over. They gave each other a gruff hug, and Raif kept a large, muscled arm around him. Raif's eyes were wet as Joe looked up into them.

"Brat, I was worried about you, but you don't seem to have done too bad out there in the Zone." He punched Joe's arm. Their biceps were nearly equal in size. Raif had always been the athletic one.

Raif turned a smiling face to Evie, who had climbed down holding Sage. He shook her hand warmly. "I've heard so much about you. It's great to finally meet you."

A smile lit her face. "You as well, Raif."

Close behind Raif, Mike and a milpipabot had spilled from the vehicle, and they surrounded the wagon.

Mike took in the children, his expression incredulous. "Joe and Evie, are these your kids? Three of them? You were certainly productive out there."

They both nodded and beamed. Evie said, "Yes, the twins are Asher and Clay, and this is Sage."

Mike's face was still ruddy and his beard trim. "I'll call ahead for a drone to deliver what you'll need for the boys."

Joe rubbed his scruffy beard, which Fabri's homemade scissors had done nothing to tame. He must look nothing like the man who had entered the Zone three years ago.

Still sitting in the wagon, Eloy coughed. Evie gasped. "Of course, we haven't introduced our dear friends, Eloy and Fabri. They helped us survive these three years. They're family more than friends."

Raif reached up to shake hands with Eloy and Fabri. "Glad you were there to help," he said.

"It gave me the chills when I saw those bots with big guns on your vehicle roof. Are we safe?" Fabri asked.

"Actually, no," Mike said. "Peightân, the Minister of Security, is a very real threat. That's why we're here, to get you back safely in case he decided to show up for your homecoming. But we had to leave our hovercraft seven kilometers from here, the closest allowed to these perimeter walls. Status, H137?"

Joe glanced at the accompanying milpipabot. "Our hovercraft is standing by. I have also received a communication that an unknown aircraft is heading toward this position. We are tracking it."

"Report again if it poses a danger," Mike said, and the milpipabot's forehead glowed blue.

Raif kneaded his temples. "Peightân is absolutely a threat to you and to everyone. It's been grueling. Our team has worked nonstop, maintaining our secrecy. We narrowed the possibilities and learned that Peightân has been gaining control of one AI and bot at a time, using physical hardware devices that circumvent the sandboxing software."

"We decided to force his hand," Mike said. "Last week, we encouraged a rumor that was floating around netchat that you may be alive. That rumor thread on netchat went viral. Suddenly everyone was talking about the two of you. Prime Netchat broadcast the original recordings of your trial and banishment, and the public started questioning the validity of your sentence. The attention placed a spotlight on Peightân's role in it all, and it didn't take long for the media to insinuate that it was him behind the injustice. Talk of protests mushroomed across the country. Peightân was already afraid your survival would be a lightning rod for the movement. We hoped that spurring the rumor on would force his hand to act before he's completely ready."

"We're bait?" Evie frowned.

"Peightân's hatred for your anti-Levels movement has only grown, in step with his likely ambitions. He was coming for you and Joe regardless of anything we did. More about that later. But for now, we likely have a war on our hands," Mike said.

Joe leaned forward, listening closely with Evie by his side.

"We traced Peightân's communications to a base of support among military bots that he's infected with the code worm—the Southern Border Army in New Mexico," Mike said.

Raif took up the explanation. "It's evidence that his tactical objective is to control White Sands Missile Range Base. The base protects our most lethal weapons on the border."

"What do you think his plan is?" Evie squeezed Sage tighter.

"If Peightân has corrupted enough military bots to succeed, and if he's able to gain physical control of the missiles at the base, then he would be powerful enough to take over the country." Raif turned a tired gaze to Joe. "After the disasters of the Climate Wars, all countries adopted the international protocols for the prevention of accidental war. Autonomous weapons on hair-trigger controls caused so many deaths. The new protocols mean that Peightân needs to take physical control to launch the missiles."

"We're hoping that tricking Peightân to come after you now will force him to execute his plans before he's ready, so the coming fight will favor us," Mike said.

Raif nodded. "Last night, we covertly moved the Northern Border Army into position in New Mexico. That army is codenamed Blue Two."

"How did you do that without leaving any electronic evidence for Peightân?" Joe glanced at Mike.

"The old-fashioned analog method. We talked to the human guards at Stallion Gate in the little town of San Antonio, and swore them to secrecy. We positioned Blue Two south of the old Trinity Nuclear test site. Of course, the army is electronically shielded to disguise its presence."

Both Eloy and Fabri had climbed out of the wagon, and now everyone stood around it on the desert road except for the twins, who hung over the side while Evie's free hand rested protectively on their backs. The armored carrier sat several meters away with the motionless milmechas on its roof.

Eloy stroked Bessie's mane. "What happens to my horse?"

"I'm sure we can transport the horse to wherever you wish, and then have it cared for," Raif said. He nodded at H137.

"I will arrange the transport," said the bot.

Eloy nodded and then gave the horse an affectionate farewell pat.

H137 interrupted urgently. "The unknown aircraft continues to approach. It appears to be a danger to you. We have scrambled military interceptors to defend. The unknown aircraft has breached the seven-kilometer limit and will arrive in forty-one seconds. Please enter the armored carrier immediately."

"Brat. Inside, double-quick!" Raif grabbed Asher from the wagon, and Joe picked up Clay. Evie carried Sage and ran for the carrier, with Eloy and Fabri close behind. Joe passed Clay to Eloy and stood on the ramp until everyone had made it inside. The door framed the image of the horse harnessed to the wagon before closing with a clang.

Everyone stumbled as the carrier lurched into motion, and Joe helped Evie and Sage take their seat next to Fabri on the brown metal benches lining the interior. Evie's bō stick dropped to the floor and rolled to rest in the corner. The vehicle weaved side to side as it headed away from the gate. Joe squeezed Asher against his side with one hand, while he held the handrail with the other. Fabri helped Evie brace herself so they wouldn't slide off the seat. All the children were crying, but it was hard to hear over the rumbling engine.

Screens lined the walls and roof, illuminating the landscape outside the carrier, seeming to make the vehicle transparent. Joe glanced upward to the milmechas on the roof.

"Mil-grade monsters up there," Eloy called approvingly. Joe clenched his axe, which was holstered on his belt.

The roar of an approaching aircraft came from overhead. The milmechas swiveled their guns to follow the sound and opened up at an unseen target, firing continuously. Asher covered his ears, crying harder. Eloy reached up to a dial on the wall and turned it. The sounds outside muted to a growl, overlaid by an otzstep drumbeat. Eloy spun the dial again to reduce the decibels. "Damn pop music," he grumbled.

Asher sniffled and said, "Thunder." The music had distracted the older boys, but Sage still wailed.

"Yes, thunder," Evie replied. Worry laced her face as she tried to soothe Sage.

The milmechas' target appeared on the screen—a hovercraft with police markings coming in from the north, low and fast. Two larger military hovercraft were on its tail.

Tracer fire spit from the police craft. The trail of fire pinged off the armored carrier in a line south, blasting an arm off one of the rooftop milmechas. Joe peeped at the rear screen to see the robot's arm hit the dust, and in time to watch the horse and wagon be obliterated into a red splotch among a pile of splintered wood.

"My horse!" Eloy screamed, anger mixed with grief. He covered Clay's face, and Joe blocked Asher's view of the screen. Evie squeezed Sage. Joe glanced at Eloy but there was no time to deal with the man's angry outburst.

Their milmechas fired again, and the police hovercraft corkscrewed and headed north. The military craft followed in a tight turn. Lasers shot from one of the tailing aircraft. A red fireball lit the police hovercraft's engine as the plane disappeared over a ridge, the aircraft following.

"Status, H137?" Mike asked.

"Our interceptors forced the rogue hovercraft down five kilometers north. It was damaged and crash-landed. Our forces will be at the scene soon to assess damage and injuries." The milpipabot blinked blue.

"Who's in there?" Joe yelled his question to Mike.

"My bet is that it's Bill Zable." A warlike leer shadowed Mike's face. "He's sprung the trap."

Their armored carrier approached a column of smoke. On the side screen, two military hovercraft sat on the playa. With black torpedo shapes and engines slung under short wings, they exuded an aura of brutal, stripped-down efficiency. Beside them was the downed police hovercraft, which was now surrounded by milmechas. One side of the craft was heavily damaged, and three drones above directed retardant to extinguish the flaming craft. The carrier turned off the road and lumbered across scrub desert before coming to a halt near the hovercraft.

"The area is now secure," H137 said, its elliptical head swiveling to the exit. Mike opened the armored carrier's door, and he and Raif leaped out, with Eloy following.

Joe wavered a second, looking at Evie and the children. "Fabri, could you please stay here with the boys?" Fabri nodded, and Evie and Joe jumped onto the playa to catch up with the rest. The milpipabot followed them to the smoking wreckage.

Copbots lay in shattered pieces on the ground, with servos and wiring dangling from metal limbs. A metallic sulfur odor of burnt metal, earth, and hair lingered. Medbots clustered around a stretcher, their arms flying in a blur.

H137 briefed them. "There was one human on board. He is alive, but he has significant injuries. We will transport him to the emergency hospital."

It took Joe several seconds to identify the man on the stretcher as Zable. Blackened flesh hung from the man's face and from one leg. A bot had removed the other leg and was cauterizing the amputated stump. Joe twitched involuntarily at the bloody sight.

"You killed my horse!" Eloy bawled, a vein on his neck pulsing. Zable turned to the sound, his eyes unfocused.

"Who cares about the horse? Did I kill those two renegades?" Zable's strangled snarl was both sinister and delirious. Joe clutched his axe with a shaking hand as he fought the rising wave of hot wrath commanding him to exercise it. Evie gripped his arm, steadying it.

Eloy studied Zable. "Are we back in civilization yet?" The satirical bitterness in his voice intimated he already regretted his decision to follow them.

A medbot packed Zable's amputated leg. Desert flies had found the grisly end, and the bot shooed them away before closing the container. It was standard protocol to preserve all tissue, but from the leg's crushed appearance, Joe knew Zable would be getting another prosthesis. The medbots finished their battlefield stabilization and rolled the stretcher into the first waiting military hovercraft through the lowered equipment bay door. Engines hummed to life, and the craft lifted from the desert.

They walked back to their armored carrier, where Fabri peered anxiously out the open door.

"I know he tried to kill us." Fabri shook with anxiety. "But I still can't take any joy from seeing a human being so badly hurt as that."

"You should've lent me your axe," Eloy said.

. . .

I recognize Eloy in my primal self, wanting to destroy a threat. It's hard to behave in a civilized way, and even harder to show compassion.

. . .

"It's time. We should follow now," Mike said.

"Follow?" Evie clutched her bō stick, a spark of defiance lighting her hazel eyes. "I've never been a follower, and the last three years certainly haven't made me one."

H137 escorted everyone to the second military hovercraft. The rear staircase descended with a hum, coming to rest in the sand. Everyone climbed the stairs, Evie in the lead with Sage, and Joe and Fabri carrying the twins. Joe glanced back at the desert one last time. He regretted leaving his bow on top of the buckskin blanket in the wagon. He stepped into the hovercraft, the door thudded shut, and they rose into the air. Joe squinted through a window at the armored carrier as the military hovercraft turned west toward California.

CHAPTER 45

They sat together in the hovercraft's roomy main cabin. The twins capered on the seats, running their hands over the unfamiliar upholstery. Evie held Sage. Eloy and Fabri were distracted by the antics of the boys for several minutes as they tried to settle into their seats. They all needed time to adjust, sharing the shock of moving from the primitive life of the mountain to the high-tech interior of the aircraft. Sky and land whizzed by out a window.

"I'd like to hear more about what has happened with the anti-Levels movement." Evie talked over Sage's head. "I understand we may have been a threat to Peightân's image and reputation, but if he has an army of corrupted bots to help him take over the country, why would he still care about us? This feels more personal."

"You've been his obsession for some time. At least, that's what the few internal communications we've managed to decrypt show." Raif's expression was pure admiration. "He despises the lower Levels and feels superior to them. Their liberation would destroy the hierarchy of our society, a hierarchy where he is at the top. The anti-Levels movement threatens his power. He tried to shut it down by banishing Celeste and Julian, and then Joe and you. But in your case, it backfired. Your survival demonstrates how capable people relegated to the lower Levels are. Your return has given them the courage to bring the movement back above ground."

"We'd hoped the movement would survive, but we didn't expect it to have grown." Joe directed his comments to Mike. "How did that happen?"

"The movement is stronger than ever before. When you and Evie were sent away, Peightân hunted for the other movement leaders. But they did a good job of keeping their heads down while continuing to organize in secret. People assumed the two of you would die in the Empty Zone. Your faces would sometimes appear on netchat messages, calling people to action and to keep the movement alive. Evie, you were considered a martyr for the cause.

"Then a month ago someone realized the end date for your banishment was today. But there was no report of the government transporting your remains from the Empty Zone." Mike grinned. "That sparked a netchat conversation, including speculation about whether you could be alive, and the movement leaders decided to drop their cover and organize massive new protests."

"Protests have exploded this week in twenty-nine cities. You've become their symbol. Here, look at this." Raif glanced toward a com screen on the hovercraft cabin wall as his NEST connected, and he uploaded a vidstream. The screen lit with marchers filling a broad boulevard, fists raised, holding banners. Joe started in his seat, recognizing the sea of faces. The protesters used holo face replacers, each with a projection of Evie's face.

Evie and Joe looked at each other in stunned silence. The magnitude of the series of events Evie had set in motion took his breath away.

"Momma?" Clay's gaze went back and forth between the screen and Evie.

The spell was broken, and Evie and Joe laughed at the surprising world they'd come back to.

Raif flipped to another vidstream showing marchers in another city, the protest even larger. Clay hid his face against Joe's chest.

H137 stirred from its rigid pose near the entryway, and its head swiveled toward Mike. "There is important communication from General Sherwood, commander of the Southern Border Army."

Mike turned to Joe and Evie. "Can we leave the family here while we go up front to the hovercraft control room?"

Fabri was already holding her arms out for Sage, and Evie gently passed him over. "I can take care of the boys here, no worries," Fabri said.

Evie nodded her thanks, and they followed Mike into the adjoining control room, with Joe waving to Eloy to join them, and they closed the door. This smaller room had a holo-pit com. The com portal was an elevated elliptical platform surrounded by a short railing, all surrounded by seats, with the projection equipment built into the ceiling. They sat down, and H137 authorized an encrypted link. The portal opened. A holo appeared, the face of a blond-haired man wearing a military cap. Sweat stood out on his forehead.

"General Sherwood, please report," Mike said.

"It's been confirmed—nearly two-thirds of my Southern Border Army vacated its base at Holloman without my authorization and is headed north."

"How many corrupted bots?" Raif glanced at Mike.

"We estimate the Red Rogue units at ninety thousand milmechas and drones," Sherwood said.

"And the rest?" Mike shook his head.

"I've ordered Blue One to pursue the rogue faction. Our prime objective is to keep the rogue units from turning east toward Alamogordo. There's the biggest risk for civilian casualties, with a population of eleven thousand people."

"Preventing civilian casualties is paramount," Mike said.

"They won't get through me to Alamogordo. I'll make sure of it," Sherwood said.

"Rogue units heading north? Then our guess is confirmed, that their objective is White Sands Missile Range Base," Raif said.

Mike turned to the milpipabot. "Please add General Brown." The bot's forehead blued in acknowledgment.

"Damn. Ninety thousand." Raif's jaw tightened.

"Far more than we ever anticipated," Mike said.

A second holo appeared. General Brown frowned at an unseen underling and acknowledged Mike with a salute. "Blue Two is waiting south of Trinity Site. The rogue units are moving north, toward us. We have launched intercept and anticipate drone contact first, followed by ground contact just south of the missile range. They'll need go through us to get to the missiles."

"Probability assessment?" Raif pressed some buttons on the panel.

"Though there are more corrupted milmechas than loyal ones, we have more drones. The odds are slightly in our favor," Brown said.

H137 entered the conversation. "It is confirmed that a second police hovercraft left the Security Ministry in California. It landed north of Holloman Air Base in New Mexico and rendezvoused with the corrupted army units at the same time the first hovercraft attacked us."

"Peightân," Joe said. The others nodded.

Mike sat upright in his seat, and Joe, still baffled by the professor's role, studied him until Raif's chuckle broke his reverie. "Dina has spent the last three years discreetly engaging with other government leaders, the National Minister of Defense, and the CIA to try and uncover the person behind the code worm. She pushed for Mike to be approved as part of the SES—Senior Executive Service—and to be appointed as the Special Commander, Group Operations, Project Worm. He acts as civilian commander to oversee these secret plans."

Mike glanced up from the holo-pit com. "I'm acting more as a liaison, though technically civilians are still above the military and the generals treat me like a bigwig. But we left the real planning up to the Army. Raif and I have learned a lot. I went from laws to LAWS."

Eloy tilted toward Joe and whispered, "He means Lethal Autonomous Weapons Systems."

"Eloy was with the Southern Border Army," Joe said to Mike and Raif. Mike saluted him, and Eloy returned the salute smartly.

Mike turned back to his command post. "What's the intercept terrain like?" His voice boomed with confidence.

"Empty desert," Brown said.

"Acknowledged," Mike said.

Brown's face darkened. "Let me remind you, Commander, that there are also civilians at the spaceport, which is thirty klicks to Red Rogue's west. There are typically about four thousand people there."

Mike banged his fist on his leg. "Can you get them out?"

"We can begin evacuation now, though our best hope is that the battle doesn't make it to them. Not many human-transport hovercraft are available, and it takes more time to load civilians than we have."

"Do it now," Mike said.

Raif looked at Mike. "There's a north–south escarpment between the rogue units and the spaceport, but if the rogue units go there, that wouldn't slow them down much."

"It would be a killing field out there, with those machines throwing so much metal around," Eloy whispered.

"We'll stay on the com," Brown said. He turned his attention off-screen. Sherwood did the same, his face tight. He appeared rattled by his turncoat units.

H137 updated them. "There are approximately eleven minutes until drone contact, and seventeen minutes until unit contact on the ground."

Eloy nudged Joe. "General Sherwood was my commander, though he had no reason to ever know my name. Glad to have a ringside seat now."

Joe nodded, though he barely registered his friend's words. He'd forgotten how fast the world moved, and his mind raced with information overload.

"We—well, the generals—have done extensive battle-planning, and we've developed full-spectrum decision maps. But decision science only goes so far to lift the fog of war," Raif said.

Evie touched Joe's shoulder from behind before leaning down to whisper in his ear, "Just checked on the boys. Fabri is keeping them entertained." He squeezed her hand and peered out the window. Southwest desert unrolled below, like the terrain that had surrounded their Eden. His mouth was dry. There was nothing to do but wait.

The wait was not long. General Brown's bellow woke Joe from his daydreams. "They've spotted our approach. Blue Two is now engaging. Railgun mobile artillery firing. Our electronic jamming is still protecting us against precise targeting."

The milpipabot connected another com link. The holo-pit com filled with a holo drone feed from above Blue Two. As if some giant spider mother had signaled her offspring, thousands of her evil brood scudded across the desert. Milmechas moved with surprising speed, bounding over dunes and sagebrush on their four spidered legs. Dust rose behind the waves of machines and obscured the land.

H137 added another feed, this one with a thermal imaging layer. The hot points above the ground units revealed themselves to be drones rising into the air to engage. The portal filled with the dance of deadly drones, streaks of red lancing from machines. On the ground among the milmechas, railguns on tank-tracked mobile carriers fired continuously, their projectiles like meteors rising into the sky. Red splotches formed as machines exploded into flames on the desert, leaving sooty ellipses on the white desert sand. There was a rising rumble of sound from the audio feed, muted but ominous.

"Blue One is losing badly," General Sherwood said.

"The rogue units stopped moving north and instead turned to attack Blue One." Raif studied the com. "Maybe Peightân decided to destroy them first."

"Switch feeds to Blue One pursuing units," Mike ordered. H137 complied. Another drone feed filled the holo-pit, and the new scene appeared disorganized. "Mark our units," Mike said, and blue and red tags appeared above the machines. Most of the blue tags were next to demolished milmechas on the desert. Robots with missing limbs fired until silenced. The desert had become a mass of blackened craters, scoured clean of all plant life by the blizzard of autonomous fire, missiles, and explosives. Most drones carried red tags.

The drone feed winked out. H137 established a replacement feed, which crystallized out of static, then also vanished.

"We've taken a piece out of his hide," Sherwood said, his resigned face now crowding the holo.

"Where are you?" Mike shouted to be sure he was heard above the chaos on Sherwood's end.

"I'm thirteen klicks behind the force, with the command in the rear guard."

"Get the hell out of there!" General Brown thundered on the other holo.

"It's too late. Kismet, Brown," Sherwood said, his eyes empty. His holo blinked out.

Evie shivered against Joe's back.

"Goodbye, Commander," Eloy whispered.

. . .

Not kismet, not fate, just freewill decisions by conscious creatures, shaped by random chance. He played the hand he was dealt. He chose. We should all aspire to that.

. . .

"We were fighting only a fraction of the Red Rogue units. Now their larger army is on the field, and we are engaging," General Brown said, his tone flat.

"And General Sherwood?" Mike's tone revealed he knew it was an unnecessary question.

"Gone, with another seventy people in his command." General Brown turned and issued urgent commands to officers off-screen. Evie held Joe's arm tightly, and they shared a look of shock about those soldiers' last moments.

Eloy shook his head. "No place is safe on the battlefield. His command moved under their electronic shield, but it wasn't enough."

H137 flipped the battle links back to Brown's main army, picking another drone feed. They hunched in their seats, subdued, watching the labeled units fight and be annihilated.

"It appears Peightân has destroyed the Blue One units." Mike chewed his lip. "But we still have enough to win this fight. I don't think Peightân had as much time to infect bots as he might have liked."

"We'll find out soon enough," Raif said.

"Add the metadata stream," Mike said to H137. Above the holographic images, another layer of figures appeared, giving a wider strategic overview of battlefield data. Mike, standing next to the com portal, moved his hands like a conjurer, manipulating projections. The central com portal filled with the feed from a drone diving toward a white sand dune. Mobile railguns and milmechas fired upward, but tracers missed the dodging drone. Another large drone appeared, labeled red. Side panels popped off it, and hundreds of mini-drones burst out like a swarm of angry wasps. There was a flash of light, and the feed disappeared. H137 replaced the feed with another from higher above the desert.

"Poppers, we called them. Nasty things," Eloy said.

The battle oscillated across the desert for another twenty minutes. The holograms on the com portal were a hellscape, disjointed swarming movements of machines destroying each other with plumes of fire. Swarms of drones of many sizes and shapes swept across the skies. They dodged fire and missiles in tight turns like a murmuration of sparrows, attacking each other and the milmechas firing from the ground. Brown maintained drone supremacy, and soon most of the rogue drones were knocked from the skies. Some of Peightân's army had split off and scuttled west, toward the spaceport. The battle boiled over the sand flats several kilometers away. Smoking hulks littered the desert, partly obscured by a gray haze. The thermal layer showed tracer fire lighting the sky. General Brown's holo revealed the hint of a smile tensing his jaw.

Mike must have seen it. "Assessment?"

Brown barked an order and turned back to them on the com. "Our drone force is winning. We must concentrate on taking out the main rogue force, or they could still threaten Alamogordo. We'll chase the smaller rogue unit soon."

Mike nodded. "And the spaceport evacuation?"

"Slow. One wave of thirty-seven hovercraft have evacuated fully. They will be back for wave two in another nineteen minutes."

"Not fast enough." Raif muttered some calculations. "That's only a third of the civilians to safety so far."

Mike acknowledged, and Brown turned to command his forces. "We had no idea there could be so many corrupted bots in the Border Army." Self-blame was all over Mike's expression. Joe knew he was considering the civilians at the base.

Most of the ground units now held blue labels. Parts of the desert were blank on the com portal, and when Joe looked at H137 and pointed to the sections, the milpipabot confirmed his suspicions, saying, "In this contested electromagnetic environment, we do not have full sensor coverage."

Brown addressed Mike. "Sir, we've achieved battlefield control. We are in mop-up mode. Three of our divisions are now on fast chase after the remaining Red Rogue units, which are nearing the spaceport. But that surviving rogue force will occupy there first."

Eloy leaned close to Joe. "Damn, they're in the kill box."

Mike cursed. "And their status?"

"Checking," H137 said. A few minutes went by as Joe sat on the edge of his seat, his hands clammy.

"Sensors indicate that the Red Rogue force did not slow their assault when they broke through the facility perimeter, near the kinderschool. The probability of survival is low."

"Let's get a drone feed for the launch facility," Mike snapped. H137 complied. A feed appeared on the com portal, a perspective from above as the drone flew west at low elevation, dipping in and out among the rocky hills. Mangled equipment littered the desert. The drone approached the spaceport, and the milmechas and railguns lining the perimeter fired upward. Before the drone feed died, it caught a glimpse of a rocket sitting on the launchpad, with wisps of vapor leaking from the tail.

The holo-pit com switched to a map view of the launch facility's perimeter. Mike flicked floating icons onto the com to zoom in on the terrain, now showing close-ups of both Blue Two and Red Rogue units smoking on the battlefield. Joe spied a holo headset dangling off the railing. Emboldened, he slipped it on, grabbed a reconnaissance drone holo icon approaching the perimeter map, and touched it against the side of the headset to connect the sensor.

The surround-vision scene blasted into his eyes from the drone nearing the ground at the perimeter fence. He was in an inferno. Pillars of smoke rose from a destroyed apartment complex to his left as the drone flew lower toward another building, which Joe recognized as a school. Explosions pounded his eardrums as hot, screaming metal ripped the air all around him. He swept slowly over the building, now five meters below, when the soot parted to reveal blackened craters. Where there was once life, there now was a newfound abyss of nothing. Then Joe's gaze fell on the remains of bodies, ghoulishly arranged.

Joe ripped the headset from his face and retched violently in the corner of the room. He wiped his mouth and looked up at the group. There was sympathy on all their faces.

. . .

Please, please erase that sight from my memory, the horror of what we can do to one another. Free will allows people who have no conscience to act immorally.

. . .

Joe sat and rubbed his face. Evie put her arm around him.

"Sensors have identified a launch at the facility," H137 said.

Mike ordered another drone feed. The signal flickered, broadcasting a view farther from the spaceport. It showed a rocket contrail hanging in the desert air.

Raif ran his fingers through his hair. "Peightân is getting away?"

General Brown was back on the com with another report, his voice clipped. "Our forces have secured the spaceport. There's lots of confusion here. We're shutting down the rogue jammers. We don't think any of the staff here survived." A muscle in his jaw twitched.

Mike shook his head. "How many milmechas could have gotten away in that rocket?"

"Maybe thirty. Fifty, at most," Brown said.

"Enough to overrun WISE Orbital Base." Raif paced back and forth. "The base is scientific; it has no defenses."

Joe sat up straighter. "Why would Peightân go there?"

Raif shrugged. "It's the closest place he could use that rocket to inflict the most serious damage."

A vein in Mike's temple throbbed. He rubbed it. "Dina is there physically now. Better alert her that she can expect visitors."

Chapter 46

Joe, Evie, and Eloy returned to the hovercraft's main cabin, leaving Mike and Raif on the holo-pit com still fighting the battle in the Southwest. Worry suffused Fabri's face when they returned. "A battle? Were people killed?"

Eloy enfolded her in his arms. "Yes, a major battle between bot armies. There were civilian casualties."

Tears ran down Fabri's cheeks as she clung to Eloy. "What a strange world we've come back to. In many ways, it's more violent than our life in the Empty Zone. There we only killed what we needed to survive."

The pain on her face was so vivid that Joe put his arms around them both. A moment later, Evie's arms encircled them. The four neighbors stood subsumed in mourning for several minutes.

Morose and lost in their own thoughts, they separated. The landscape had morphed, appearing golden as they approached the West Coast. Fabri sat across from Joe and clutched Sage, who slept in her arms. Clay sat with Evie, and she moved her ring finger to make the red stone reflect sparkles onto the wall to entertain him. Joe sank into the seat next to Evie and held Asher on his lap.

Raif rejoined them and announced, "We arrive in eleven minutes." He sat next to Joe. "H137 estimates Peightân's rocket will intercept WISE Orbital Base in twenty-three hours. Mike briefed Dina. That woman is fearless. Though her thousand construction mechas are no match for the approaching milmechas, she is preparing a counterattack."

Fabri stared wide-eyed at Joe's conversation with Raif. "Who is Dina?"

"She is commander of the orbital base circling the moon. I did some work for her there." Fabri's eyes brightened, as if the heavens had opened and the truth had spilled out—the truth of Joe's real Level. She leaned toward him and whispered, "You've been so nice to me."

"And you to me. You're more than my equal."

The hovercraft started to descend. Evie faced Raif. "Where are we going?"

Raif stood. "The Combat Dome is the closest emergency medical facility, and we're following the med evac hovercraft with Zable on board. Mike just organized a small ops center there to track Peightân. It's as good as any place." His gaze met Joe's. "And Mike and Dina think it would be an appropriate place to tell your story."

Mike stood at the door to the control room. "I've just heard that a large crowd, including the media, has been gathering at the Combat Dome. They want to see you, Evie, to see that you've survived. I think they'll be sympathetic to whatever you say."

Evie nodded firmly in agreement.

Mike smiled, then turned sober. "There's also now a rumor about the battle in New Mexico. The government is trying to embargo that topic, so please don't mention it."

It was early afternoon, but it felt like a week had elapsed since sunrise. The twins were wide awake and pointing out the window at the approaching Dome. Fabri held Sage, who continued to sleep. Evie brushed at her hair, her posture stiff. "We can make an appearance. We'll show them we're coming back to pick up where we left off." Joe nodded. He'd let Evie do the talking.

Joe took a seat by the window, and a moment later Evie stood next to him and combed his hair with her fingers while she stared out at her old home. He read the emotions that shadowed her face—recognition, homesickness, and anticipation.

Joe could make out a crowd amassed on the Combat Dome's rooftop. As they approached, he guessed there were maybe thirteen hundred people. Media drones hovered above the crowd.

Mike squinted out the window next to Joe's.

"It's a larger greeting party than I imagined." Mike shook his head. "My estimates are off today . . . twice."

Joe took Asher's and Clay's hands, and Evie held Sage. Together, the family went to stand by the exit door, ready to greet the rest of the modern world. Mike stepped in front of Joe. "Evie, I'll go first to introduce you."

Evie nodded. The doors opened, and news media pressed forward. Joe recognized two reporters at the front as Caroline Lock and Jasper Rand from Prime Netchat.

Mike exited, raising a hand. "Evie Joneson, Joe Denkensmith, their family, and their friends have just returned after three years in the Empty Zone. They can only speak to you briefly before they need to get some rest."

The twins pressed against Joe's legs, their eyes huge as reporters shouted questions and recording devices hovered around them. Evie tossed her hair back with a smile, and, as a family, they walked down the ramp. Behind them, Fabri hung onto Eloy's arm. Joe looked back and gave Fabri an encouraging smile, and she straightened, seeming to grow taller in her buckskin blouse.

Evie stepped forward into the circle of reporters. She flashed a brilliant smile and spoke as Sage stirred in her left arm.

"We are back, having overcome the challenges of one prison, and eager to be here helping you unlock another. We're inspired that you have grown the anti-Levels movement, bringing hope to those who have been forced to stagnate in the lower Levels. Our children remind us why this is important. Everyone should begin life with the freedom to excel, not be held back by hereditary class rules." She raised her right fist into the air and pumped it triumphantly. Her voice boomed. "We carry on this fight for equal opportunity for all of our children." The crowd roared in excitement, drowning out the sound of the drone recorders as they flitted over the dome, capturing the scene and broadcasting it to the country.

. . .

She's a hero for the anti-Levels movement. She's my hero too.

. . .

Evie navigated the media and responded to questions with warm, passionate answers. He answered a few directed at him, but the reporters preferred Evie. Caroline Lock asked Joe if she could talk to the boys, and, at Joe's nod, she knelt to ask them a few questions, but both proved camera shy, and Joe couldn't hear their quiet mumbles.

Mike led them through the line of newscasters, across the roof and down a set of stairs. They followed him into an interior concourse. Screens filled the walls, announcing media coverage of events at the Dome. Then the tiny hand holding his pulled back. Asher had halted, transfixed by the sight of their image on a giant wall screen. The video replayed their exit from the hovercraft. A newscaster breathlessly announced, "Evie Joneson, Joe Denkensmith, and their three children have survived a grueling three years in the Empty Zone. Not just survived but flourished." Joe noted the incongruity of their buckskin-clad forms atop the gleaming metal of the Community Dome roof. "Come on, buddy," he said and picked Asher up to catch up with Mike.

Mike and Raif led them through the complex to a set of apartments connected by a large common room, with blue sky filling a full-ceiling skylight.

Raif ruffled Asher's hair, and the boy smiled back. "That was a fine interview, Evie. Mike and I will coordinate with Dina from here. You should get some rest."

Mike nodded. "I suggest we meet in this central room in seventeen hours, before Peightân arrives at WISE Orbital Base. Your rooms should all be stocked with everything you need." He led them down a corridor to Joe and Evie's living quarters, then pointed to another apartment for Fabri and Eloy farther down the corridor, before heading back to join Raif in the main room.

Evie gave Fabri a hug. "I'm sorry we brought you into this dangerous situation. I never imagined it would be like this."

Fabri hugged her back. "Well, I feel safe now. And we're still together."

Joe clasped their hands and pulled them both in for a warm embrace. "Let's keep it that way."

◆

The apartment was warm, and the modern comforts were a surprise to the twins. The running water from the faucets fascinated them, as did the unfamiliar materials covering the furniture. They bounced on the beds and found myriad ways to expend pent-up energy while Joe fought sleep.

After the intensity of the day, it was a relief for Joe and Evie to watch them play on the carpeted floor at their feet. With Evie by his side, his own concern melted away as the tension on her face vanished.

He hustled the twins into the bath while Evie fed Sage—their routine to divide and conquer. Joe thought how much easier bath time was when he wasn't required to heat stream water. The soap smelled sweet and filled the tub with bubbles.

The bedroom closet held new clothing in their approximate sizes, and Joe mentally thanked Mike for his quick work to order the drone delivery. He dressed the boys while Evie put Sage down to sleep. Joe took the twins into the kitchen, and Evie soon joined them. She laughed when she saw the food synthesizer. Evie assembled spaghetti and alt-meatballs in a few minutes. Joe shook his head at the ease and speed—he had not had to hunt or forage or start a fire. Spaghetti had never tasted so good.

The flashing lights of the kitchen appliances distracted the boys from their plates. Joe focused on his own plate, the familiar flavors comforting him in a way he hadn't expected.

Asher pushed at him, trying to climb up into his lap. He picked him up, and Asher buried his head in Joe's chest. "What is it?" Joe noticed the cleanerbot wiping the floor where one boy had flung a noodle. Clay approached the bot hesitantly, and the machine froze, its forehead glowing yellow. Clay touched its polished surface with a sauce-stained hand, leaving a streak, before looking back uncertainly at Evie.

"It won't hurt you," she said.

Clay took a last look at the bot and then toddled back to his seat, his curiosity satisfied. The bot resumed its cleaning, marked with a red streak. Evie giggled. "I wonder who cleans the cleanerbot."

By the time they finished eating, the twins were rubbing their eyes. Joe tucked them into tiny beds in the second bedroom. Evie was getting out of the shower when he returned to their room. He hugged her wet body and kissed her deeply.

She smiled up at him. "Go on and shower—it's glorious."

As Joe dressed in regular clothes after the heavenly shower, he stared at the pile of buckskins, thinking of the time-consuming effort to make the clothing. His axe and Evie's bō stick lay on top of the pile.

The sight prompted a flood of thoughts. First, pleasant memories—the day they found their home in the Empty Zone, axe and bō staff in hand, the satisfaction that came from taming the land, and the birth of their children. Then his head crowded with images from the day—of Bessie, of Zable lying bleeding on the gurney, and of the kinderschool. "Best not to go there," he muttered to himself and pushed the thoughts away.

Fresh, clean, and tired, he rejoined Evie in the living room, where she watched a muted Prime Netchat newscast. He snuggled next to her on the luxurious sofa.

Joe laughed out loud. "The comfort, it's unbelievable. I'd forgotten."

"Raising three kids will be *much* easier here," she said, her face brightening. "I'm not sure what I'll do with all my spare time if I don't have to forage." She pointed at the net portal. "They look familiar."

Joe turned to see Caroline Lock on-screen, the banner below her announcing Evie and Joe's return from the Empty Zone. He unmuted the newscast.

"—Evie Joneson and Joe Denkensmith, and their family, have captured the imagination of the country," Lock said. Her hair shone golden against the silver backdrop of the Dome. The feed cut to a video of them standing at the landing pad from earlier. He felt a wave of self-consciousness at his unruly beard and hair.

They switched to the rerun of Evie's speech on the Dome rooftop. Joe saw the numbers flickering along the bottom of the screen, now in the billions, that represented the number of times the story had been shared around the world.

After Evie's interview, the feed changed to Lock crouching next to Asher. "What do you miss most?"

Asher looked up at her in earnest. "Lambs."

She turned to Clay. "And what do you miss the most?"

He squinted, perplexed, and then carefully formed words. "Nothing. Mommy and Daddy are here."

The screen flicked back to Jasper Rand and Caroline Lock sitting at a news desk. Rand smirked at the audience. "They are too young to understand why they have spent their lives in the wilderness, but they seem to be adjusting to modern life."

Lock frowned. "But, Jasper, this story is now bigger than the family's return. This anti-Levels movement has captured everyone's attention, and this family exemplifies why it's an important message."

Rand rubbed his chin. "There is a surprising amount of admiration for the parents from our Prime Netchat viewers."

"Of course there is. They survived what many would call a death sentence. And if their children are any testament, they thrived." Lock looked straight at the vidcam. "Today's polling shows a highly favorable rating for Ms. Joneson. Netchat is exploding with her story. Evie Joneson is the icon of the anti-Levels movement. Her story is about enduring, and even more, prevailing, with three lovely children to demonstrate their love and resilience." The feed cut to Evie as she answered several questions, poised and confident, Joe by her side. Pride welled up in his chest, and he pulled her closer to him and kissed her hair.

"Evie, you're invincible."

She leaned into him. "After Mike mentioned talking to the media, I relished the chance. Now that we're back, I haven't forgotten my fight. Julian and Celeste died for the equality movement. I need to carry it on."

"I'll be here to help you with that fight. It's a good fight to have."

"I need you by my side. It feels like we've already lived in several worlds together," she said, rubbing his shoulder.

Joe scratched his chin. The overgrown beard reminded him that it was a habit he had mostly lost while on the mountain. "The wilderness was a maturing experience. I learned how to be self-reliant. I answered my questions. I came to understand more about wisdom and compassion." He contemplated her face—tanned and natural, slightly worn around her mouth by the challenges of their life in the Empty Zone, yet still full of life. "Your strength of character has taught me to be mindful of the balance between living in my head and living in my body and in the world. You've taught me about having a purpose. I'm now comfortable forging a new path." Joe continued to study her in the flickering light of the room, remembering the first time he saw her, a mysterious figure and the fiery leader of a cause. The dragonfly had forever captured his heart.

They watched the feed, reliving the day.

"You look pretty hardened there, man of steel." She poked him in the ribs. Joe stared at the screen. He'd never been fitter in his life.

"It must be the wood-chopping. And you, my love, are beautiful inside and out."

Joe turned off the screen and pulled her to him, kissing her deeply. They quickly undressed and moved to the bedroom, slipping naked into the velvety white sheets. After the privations of banishment, it was a different heaven.

Stroking her cheek and kissing her eyelids closed, he marveled at the pure passion on her face, for him and for everything in life. Though her hair was freshly washed, he still imagined a faint aroma of the forest.

His biceps flexed comfortably as he lifted her to straddle him. She leaned on him, and her thick hair fell forward. She moved rhythmically, flicking her hair back, her gaze far away. "I felt like I was on top of a peak, looking out at that crowd, so happy to return to this fight. I'm glad you're here with me."

"Oh, so you like the summits?"

"I've never felt closer to anyone in my life, my mountain man," she breathed, her hands pressing his chest. They moved slowly, confident enough in their intimate knowledge of one another to take their time. Their angle of repose shifted as she drew him on top of her, and their gazes locked.

"You are always in my heart and in my head." Joe melted into her hazel eyes, a place he never wished to leave. His love and passion for her was undiminished and undying.

"I so love you," she whispered.

"And I so love you."

She raised her knees higher and moaned. His hands caressed her breasts and moved down to her ribs, then further down again until he felt her body start to quiver.

He knew her, and she knew him, and they knew everything about the blessings of the world. They slept peacefully, the blankets shrouding them as they lay tangled in one another, body and soul.

CHAPTER 47

Joe woke at dawn, like he did every day—but without a window close by to view the sunrise. Evie's soft hand on his back reminded him where he was, and he turned to smile at her. The twins and Sage were awake and clamoring for attention. They dressed them and prepared breakfast from the food synthesizer.

Joe wandered to the common room and found Raif stifling a yawn. "Dina and her team have been working nonstop since we informed her about Peightân's approaching rocket." He stretched. "She thinks they've built a weapon to thwart an attack." Joe tried to push his brain into higher gear. "The team on the base retrofitted a cargo delivery vehicle into a missile. If they launch it, the hope is that it will reach enough speed and have enough maneuverability for intercept. It's a kinetic lance, functioning as a mass driver to destroy Peightân's ship."

"It operates by smashing into his rocket?"

"Da. Simple but effective. If it can intercept."

"Only one missile?"

"No time to build another. Just one shot. Peightân's ship will be in range just after noon, so we've got about five hours.

I suggest you and Evie reconnect your NESTs to better follow along what's happening." Raif rubbed his forehead. "If you're up for it, Dina said we could join her via steerbot on the base." Joe nodded, energized by the chance to see Dina and the base again.

Mike entered the room, appearing more haggard than Raif. His eyes were bloodshot, the warlike gleam lingering from the day before.

"Everything at the southern border is under control. It took time to shut down the rogue jamming units, but we believe we've destroyed all the corrupted bots there." He sat on the sofa and allowed his shoulders to droop from the stiff military bearing he had been maintaining.

Joe clapped his shoulder in commiseration. "How bad were the losses?"

"About two-thirds of our border forces—the entire Southern Border Army, along with part of the northern mechas. All in all, about a hundred and ninety thousand milbots lost." He shielded his eyes with a weary hand. "And more than three thousand human beings died too."

Joe sat down, sobered by the number. He couldn't remember the last time so many had been lost in war—not in over a half century. "Need we worry about attacks by other countries now, in our weakened condition?"

Mike stroked his disheveled beard. "Fortunately, no. I've been in communication with both allies and not-so-friendly countries all night. They're more interested in our sharing of the code worm intelligence than in threatening the States."

Raif leaned forward in agreement. "People need to cooperate in taming our invented monsters."

Fabri and Eloy entered the common room. They were dressed in modern clothing, and the alteration in their appearance astonished Joe. Fabri's fiery hair was neatly coiffed. Eloy had clipped his ragged beard. Joe touched his own. It still needed a trim, but he'd have time for that later.

Evie joined them with the three boys in tow. Sage was wide awake and drooling. Fabri and Eloy sat with the twins, and Eloy bounced Asher on his knee.

Gabe also entered with Freyja by his side. Gabe's goatee, longer and more silvered than Joe recalled, bobbed in acknowledgment as he gripped Joe's hand affectionately. "What a family you two have created," he said.

Freyja seemed unchanged—bright blue eyes, blonde hair to her shoulders. She hugged Joe, then spied Evie and strode over to hug her and coo over the baby. "Evie and Joe, your children are adorable," she said as the twins huddled around Evie's knees, eyeing Freyja shyly.

A grin wiped the exhaustion from Raif's face, and he crossed the room to take Freyja in his arms. They kissed, and Freyja rubbed his messy hair, whispering something to him with concern lining her face. Then they came across the room to Joe, Freyja tucked under Raif's arm.

Joe's gaze moved from one to the other, tracing the joyful energy between them. Freyja's face radiated a new light. Except for the worry lines, Raif, too, had a glow Joe didn't remember.

Raif held out a hand to Evie. "Ready to reconnect electronically with the modern world?" Joe and Evie nodded.

They left the kids in the care of Freyja, Fabri, and Eloy and walked to the medical facility with Raif to reinstall their NESTs. The medbot awakened bad memories of leaving for the Empty Zone, but the robot was mechanical and efficient, and there was a familiar intimacy as Joe heard the chime of the regular NEST interface again. They checked their NESTs against each other, testing the network interface. Evie looked into his eyes, and they shared a new electronic connectedness to the modern world and to each other.

"I haven't used one in ages," she said.

Joe addressed the medbot. "Can you provide me with an update on Zable?"

The medbot said, "Patient Mr. William Zable underwent organ replacement surgery last night. We treated him for severe burns and trauma to his remaining leg. He is sedated now. His condition is critical but stable. That is all the information I am authorized to release to you."

The three walked back to the common room, but Joe was unsatisfied with the information from the medbot. He said to Raif, "I assume you have plans to find out what you can from Zable?"

"We're planning to interview him as soon as he's conscious and has been medically cleared. He may give valuable information about how the AIs and bots are compromised. Meanwhile, he's under full guard."

The common room was a hub of activity, with their friends sitting on the sofas and talking together. Shortly after they returned, the door buzzed, and Raif opened it to two official-looking men. They introduced themselves as the mayor and deputy mayor of the Community Dome. They were dressed casually and stood with hands together, as if in supplication.

The mayor addressed Joe and Evie. "We are pleased to host you and your family here at the Dome. We want to upgrade your facilities and move you to an executive suite in the skybox." His slippery smile made Joe trust him less.

Evie flashed an uncertain look at Joe and then back to the mayor. "Why would we want to move?"

"The skybox area suites are much nicer for visitors," the mayor said.

Evie turned to the mayor. "For *visitors*? Thank you, but we will stay in these rooms for now. Our children have begun acclimating."

"But we've already reassigned you to the skybox suites," the deputy mayor said.

"Thanks again." Joe moved closer to Evie. "We will stay here for now. But in the future, we'd be interested in living quarters in the Community Dome, along one of the secluded concourses."

Evie squeezed his waist, and he grinned at her before turning toward Eloy and Fabri. "Evie and I would love it if the kids' aunt and uncle were nearby too."

Eloy beamed. "We'll sign up."

The mayor capitulated. "We can find two comfortable apartments here for you." Evie smiled and thanked him.

UNFETTERED JOURNEY | 451

Mike interrupted before the officials could leave. "I have a request. I'd like to plan a special live event of national interest using the main dome facility at noon today. The Secretary of Defense has already approved the broadcast."

The mayor nodded eagerly. "Yes, of course, if it's of national concern to the States."

"I'll send details soon," Mike said, and the officials left.

Mike turned to the rest of the group. "This AI anomaly is momentous, and everyone should know about the fight happening right now. If we can project the battle at WISE Orbital Base live on the screens in the Dome, two hundred thousand people here can certify the authenticity, as well as an audience around the world." He paused and glanced at Evie. "It's unfortunate that the government reports are not always believed by some segments of the citizenry. One cannot blame them, given some of the malarkey passing for facts dished out in netchat in the past."

"Getting true facts shouldn't be a happenstance but an expectation from our government. And getting our message out has always been the first step to enacting the change we've wanted," Evie said. Joe guessed she was still thinking about her message the day before.

It was difficult to forget all the death they'd witnessed in the last day. Somehow, Joe felt more uneasy now than when facing Darwinian nature on the mountain. Was it because of his heightened instincts? He was afraid he'd be unable to shake the sense of foreboding until the situation resolved.

A pipabot served their meal around the circular table. In an effort to catch up with one another, they had shifted the conversation away from politics, and it now centered on their experiences in the Empty Zone. Joe watched Eloy revel in telling hunting and fishing stories. The romance of the adventures resonated in Eloy's voice, but Joe's memories mixed the bitter with the sweet, a truer taste of life.

Joe leaned over to Gabe, who sat beside him. "We should discuss the thinking I did while away. With time and space to think free of distractions, I believe I've made much progress on my philosophical project."

The meal finished, and the group began to disperse. Freyja held Sage, who laughed as she tickled his toes, which made Freyja laugh as well. Gabe read Asher stories from an allbook he had brought. Fabri and Eloy announced they would take a stroll on the concourse to see their new home and that they would take Clay, who talked nonstop as they walked out.

"With so many helpers for the boys, I think I'll take the opportunity for a nice break for me. I'll be back soon." Evie gave Joe a kiss and left.

Mike, Raif, and Joe sat together, discussing Peightân's imminent approach to WISE Orbital Base, Dina's improvised projectile's probability of success, and the next steps should the missile fail. Walking through scenarios was another welcome distraction.

Raif said it was time to leave. With a wave, Mike got up to coordinate the net broadcast with the Dome officials. He said he would watch the orbital base from a net portal within the Dome.

Raif led Joe through the back concourses of the Dome complex and to a suite of rooms guarded by copbots. An interior room contained several netwalkers side by side on an elevated platform, similar to what Joe had used in the WISE regional office. Raif expertly attached himself to one harness suspended from the ceiling and adjusted the haptic suit. Joe donned his own harness and suit and pulled on his surround headset, then the haptic gloves.

Raif flexed his fingers and chuckled. "It feels like our old VRbotFests. But the steerbots and steermechs are more fun."

Joe nodded, distracted by trying to remember how to upload his avatar into the rig. He authenticated, his biometric tile glowed blue, and his face appeared on the interface screen. Raif gave him a thumbs-up. Joe inhaled deeply and opened the connection to WISE Orbital Base.

The real world evaporated. Joe found himself embodied in a steerbot standing in a rack along a wall. He wiggled his toes in the netwalker, feeling boots on his virtual feet. He stepped out of the rack. The steerbot's boots adhered to the ferrous deck with a *thunk*, and the sound reawakened Joe's old skills. Raif's steerbot shuffled in front of him toward the elevator.

On the bridge, Dina, Robin, and the pipabot Boris stood at the control console. Dina's hand rested on a pressure suit helmet on the console. This was the first time Joe had seen her in the flesh, not embodied within a steerbot. He looked down at her smiling face with a start, calculating her height from the height of his steerbot.

. . .

She must be one hundred and fifty-seven centimeters tall, at most, much shorter than that steerbot I always saw her in. Someone skipped the human growth hormone. Small but mighty.

. . .

"We meet for real this time, halfway at least," she said. Her husky voice was dog-tired, but her handshake felt as powerful as he remembered from their first virtual conference.

Robin nodded curtly to Joe and Raif and turned back to the console where her helmet rested, magnetically held in place. She had stuffed her scarlet-red hair into her pressure suit. She studied flight data on the holo projector and scowled. Joe wondered if she had been annoyed for three years.

Boris interrupted. "Please confirm that the payload is ready for launch."

Jim Kercman's holo appeared, his face haggard. "Construction is complete, and all systems are a go. The missile is ready in the launch bay, Section C."

Beside Jim's holo, one of Chuck appeared, and Joe imagined him twirling his helmet off-screen. "I'm completing final missile tests here in Section C. Natasha confirmed that data systems are functioning properly. We'll be ready to release the missile from its docking restraints soon."

Dina looked up from the data. "What is Peightân's range?"

"Three thousand and thirty-seven kilometers," Robin answered. "It's nineteen minutes before he's within the optimal thousand-kilometer separation."

"Continue hailing his ship. We'll give him a fair warning." Dina turned to Joe. "We still have no idea what his real objective is. Of course, if he controls WISE Orbital Base, then he can cut off access to the moon bases and control all the craft coming in from farther out in the solar system. But then it's only a matter of time before we . . . someone on Earth . . . can organize a force to retake it. So maybe this base is a jumping-off point to control all the other space bases, including the bases on Mars. But whatever his plans are, I'll not let him take this base."

"I've been following your team's efforts all night. You've created an inventive solution that just might save WISE Orbital Base," Raif said.

"The team did it together." She gestured to the dozen other people, steerbots, and pipabots who sat in the outer ring of seats. Joe hadn't noticed them before. "The question is whether the controls are precise enough to intercept at these speeds." Dina and her team exchanged tired expressions of encouragement.

Raif moved to the console and initiated several commands. "Using data from corrupted bots recovered on the battlefield, we created a new program to verify against corruption by the code worm. We should run that against all the bots here."

Chuck nodded. "I see the files. I'll begin the exercise now with this latest code upload, to scan the remaining bots." On the com, Chuck turned toward the deputy pipabot, Natasha, and her forehead blinked blue.

Joe stared out the large window. The moon was not visible because of the orientation of the base, but he found Earth, conspicuous in the lower corner. It was roughly four times the size of the moon seen from his mountain home.

Joe braced against sudden vertigo, reminding himself that he was only on the orbital base virtually, but the feeling was too visceral to avoid. He imagined Peightân's rocket speeding toward them, growing ever closer with each passing second and carrying the threat of death to everyone on the orbital base.

Dina called several crew members with rapid questions, and confirmed everyone was in place. Mike appeared on the holo to discuss the live feed to the Dome. Robin opened the communication feed. The actions of the bridge crew were now streamed live, and he stood taller in his steerbot.

Then they waited.

"Seven minutes until his ship is within launch radius," Robin said.

"Let's open a video hail now. One last appeal for nonviolence," Dina said, a muscle in her jaw tightening. She and Robin locked on their helmets. Robin opened a com channel.

Dina stood tall at the console. "I am Dina Taggart, the commander of WISE Orbital Base. I represent the World Space Agency and the States' government. The States' government has determined that your attack in the state of New Mexico and your current threatening approach to this base represent acts of war under international law. You have one minute to change course away. Otherwise, we will defend ourselves. That defense will end in your death."

The com unit crackled with a voice, firm and strident.

". . . Commander, I see and hear your video feed . . . I see Mr. Denkensmith there . . . Mr. Denkensmith, you and Ms. Joneson have been a grave irritation. Soon you will both pay the inevitable price for that." Joe shuddered, chilled at hearing Peightân's voice again.

"Thermal scans show his ship isn't slowing," Robin reported.

"Prepare the kinet—"

Chuck's holo lit up as he cried, "No, Natasha!" The feed showed a glimpse of the pipabot's head swiveling toward Chuck, deep pink on its forehead and a red warning light flashing through the top of the egg-shaped head. The holo disappeared.

Scant seconds later, a muffled explosion caused a violent tremor in the boots of Joe's steerbot, which was followed by a loud, high-pitched whistling vibration through the steel hull.

Jim Kercman's holo filled the com unit. "Screw the pooch! Explosion in the docking area. I can see our defensive missile is still intact, but the blast shook it loose from its moorings in the launch bay. Lots of debris."

Robin stood frozen, her mouth in an O as she stared at the blank holo where Chuck had been only moments before.

"Likely cause?" Dina's voice was commanding but calm.

Kercman answered. "There's a hole in the hull of Section C. Explosive decompression at sonic velocity. Pieces of flying debris were blown out the rupture. I saw Natasha's red warning light right before Chuck's com link disappeared. Was she rogue?"

Raif looked at Dina intently and nodded. "She must have detonated a bomb."

"Casualties?" Dina was laser focused.

There was a pause before Jim's holo responded. "Nineteen crew members. There's also damage to Section D. All other sections are secure."

"Jesus Murphy," Dina muttered, her face grim.

Robin returned to manipulating controls, concentration battling rage. "I'm maneuvering our missile away from the damaged area of the base." She checked the sensors. "Debris appears not to have fatally damaged it."

"Has his ship altered course?" Dina was no longer calm, but she was still in control.

"Negative," Robin said, checking the thermal scan.

Raif jumped to the console beside Robin, fingers playing *prestissimo* over the controls. "I'm deleting and reloading the missile programming with a complete scan for corrupted code."

Boris looked from Dina to Joe. "Perhaps it would be a sensible idea for me to scan myself with the new program, to verify there are no glitches." The bot placed its hand on the console sensor. A ragged breath filled Joe's chest and he froze. If Peightân had control of Boris too, several humans and his steerbot would be blown up any second. With Dina, Robin, and the people behind them standing there in the flesh, the superfluous foolishness of Boris scanning himself was surreal.

All were quiet, looking at one another as they anticipated impending death. Seconds passed. Joe stared at Dina, her expression steely. The console blazed a deep blue.

"Better safe than sorry," Boris said, raising an eyebrow.

. . .

Did the bot just try to tell a joke?

. . .

"Upload to the missile is complete," Raif said.

"Arming missile," Robin said.

"Authorized to fire when ready," Dina said.

"Missile away." Robin punched the console. She stood next to Joe, and her hands balled into fists. Under her breath, she said, "Take that for Chuck. Sorry I can't hear you scream." There was nothing to watch on the monitors. The missile accelerated away too fast for the optical sensors to register. Robin turned to him, her face screwed tight, her crimson hair framing reddened eyes. "Sometimes he made even me laugh."

Raif monitored the missile's trajectory. "Impact in three minutes," he called. The group waited, hushed. Robin overlaid the thermal image, and the screen zoomed in on two red lines—Peightân's approaching ship and the departing missile. The lines met.

"Impact. Target hit!" Robin whooped, pumping her arm. The screen displayed pieces scattering from the impact in a spray, then the thermal signal faded.

"The missile has impacted the enemy ship and pierced the hull, breaching all habitat areas. No biological organisms could have survived this explosion. The milmechas onboard will stop operating within ninety minutes from exposure to temperature extremes. We have neutralized the enemy ship." Boris's forehead glowed blue.

The cheers from the rest of the station crew on the channel reached Joe on his headset. Everyone shook hands all around, including the crew who had sat in the outer ring, but the celebration was muted. Joe touched Dina's arm and said, "Commander, you did a great job stopping Peightân from taking control of this base. Who knows what else he might have done if he had seized it."

Dina squeezed his hand. "Thank you for exposing this threat, and for the price you paid. Now justice can be served, and the truth known." Her gratitude was tinged with bitterness. "But first I need to attend to casualties." She and Robin hurried to the elevator along with several other crew members.

Knowing it was time to let the WISE team grieve their losses, Raif and Joe returned their steerbots to the racks. Joe thumbed the unit, his connection ended, and he found himself standing again in the Dome netwalker. Raif grinned at him as Joe stepped out of his harness.

"It's good to have that bastard out of the picture," Raif said, and gripped Joe's arm.

Joe shrugged. "War is never pretty." A swirling feeling of relief mixed with uneasiness perturbed him, and the memory of Chuck's smiling face made any satisfaction impossible.

. . .

Am I feeling conflicted because Chuck just died, along with many others? Is that why I don't feel relief at the death of Peightân, this man who has haunted us? Something feels wrong. It just feels too easy.

. . .

They walked back through the Dome corridors to the suites, Raif striding ahead with a confident step.

CHAPTER 48

They arrived in the common room to find almost everyone assembled. Mike and Freyja had commandeered the com portal in the corner and used it as a command center. Raif touched Joe's arm before joining them. "We're still receiving intelligence from the battle site about the corrupted bots. Now we're comparing that information against all government databases, and we've begun searching through the Security Ministry databases."

Joe nodded, glancing around the room for Evie. She smiled and beckoned him over to the sofa, where she sat next to Fabri.

"Where's Clay?"

"He was with Fabri and Eloy, and I met them on the concourse. He walked with me a while. He was excited to see where my ring came from, so I introduced him to Alex. That's where I was, out on the concourse standing with my neighbors outside his shop, when I watched the end of Peightân on the overhead vidfeed. What a relief. There was a celebration, and Clay and Alex were having such a good time, so Alex said he would walk around with him and then bring him back here." She squeezed his hand. "I'm relieved the orbital base is safe and that Peightân is gone. How was it in the steermech?"

Joe told her the story, not downplaying his sadness over Chuck's death. "Needless death has filled these three days since we left the mountain. Peightân mentioned us by name. He was set on murdering both of us, and he didn't care who he killed in the process."

Evie hugged him. "It's good knowing that he and Zable can no longer hurt us."

"I hadn't realized how the thought of those two had been worrying me. But now we can move on."

"The anti-Levels movement can move faster now too, since it can now stay above ground. We can exercise our right of free speech without the government's interference." The fire in her eyes showed the intensity of her focus on the mission.

She stood and pulled him up, an idea alight in her eyes. "Come with me. I'd like to show you something that might help you understand what living in the Dome will be like."

They left the common room and strolled down a corridor. Evie remembered every byway in the complex, still an unmapped maze to him. They stepped out another door and exited onto a windowed balcony facing the main dome. A concourse below was filled with people in their afternoon ritual of *passeggiata*. "This is how people live here—in community," she said.

He studied the people talking with their neighbors, their camaraderie apparent on their faces, and smiled at Evie. He understood. The crowd in the upper-level seats were also visible through the glass. Skyboxes hung over them. He was glad they had turned down the skybox. It would have felt too ostentatious after their simple life. Being in the modern world was blessing enough.

Evie entwined him in her arms. "Do you really want us to live here as a family?"

He held her tight. "I would love it here. The people who you surround yourself with help shape your path. Those choices, and those people, influence character. The choice to live here with Eloy and Fabri will allow our kids to feel secure and loved." Joe felt at peace, as if sitting under his apple tree beside the cabin.

"Do you remember that conversation we had after you fell off the noria and hurt your leg? About evil in the world?"

"Yes. You talked then about picking up the fight against the Levels Acts when we came back."

"Yes." Her hazel eyes held him. "This afternoon, I reconnected with three of the movement leaders and caught up with what's happened in our absence. They're well organized, ready to push for legislative change. They want me to lead the movement again. They said my comments when we arrived have energized everyone, and they asked me to record a call to action. So I did. Just before you came back. They want to use it in the next few days."

Joe studied her mouth, observing her resolve. "I said that I would help you. I meant it. Let me know what I can do to support you."

Evie hugged him, then looked into his eyes with unadulterated happiness. "Together we can be the bolt. We can make this change happen."

They stood on the balcony, holding each other, watching their neighbors below. Their tribe with only Eloy and Fabri the past three years would now expand to all of modern society. The Dome residents would be more than just neighbors, they would be fellow human beings on his same journey. It was a larger circle of care.

A muffled explosion and the crash of shattering glass made them both jump. Joe searched for the source. The people on the concourse below looked up, and Joe stared through the upper window out into the main dome area. Ragged shards of glass hung from one of the skybox suites. Then the glass exploded from the window of the next skybox. The glass seemed to fall in slow motion, a spray sparkling with sunlight, followed by the sound of the explosion.

He tapped his NEST. "Raif? What's happening in the skyboxes?"

There was a pause of several seconds before Raif answered breathlessly, "I've pulled up a feed. We have an intruding exomech! He's wreaking havoc in the skyboxes."

Joe's gut tightened into a knot as puzzle pieces clicked into place.

. . .

Haptic delay. It was too long. That's what's been bothering me. He wasn't really there on the ship.

. . .

Joe gripped Evie and turned her to face him. "It's Peightân. He was never on the rocket. He's hunting for us in the skyboxes. I'll bet he hacked the Dome's database and expected to find us in that assigned apartment."

Her body tensed as she searched his eyes. Then she was moving, yanking him back through the door and into the corridor. "We need to defend ourselves. And not lead him back to the kids."

They sprinted side by side, zigzagging into the bowels of the complex, then with Evie in the lead. She pushed open another door and kept running. They reached the area behind the main stage. Blood pooled across the floor in front of the guard booth. Joe glanced inside to see the body of the young guard, Johnny, sprawled on the floor.

Evie gave a strangled cry, and he knew she had also recognized him—the young man whom she had cared for as a child. His heart raced as Evie picked up the pace, and they ran along the corridor to the warehouse. The exomechs lined one wall. Evie raced to the first, jumped onto the leg strut and peeked inside. "This will do," she said. She swung to the side to allow Joe to climb up next to her. He stepped through the opening into the body shell, and it enclosed his body. His legs slotted into the footwells, his feet a meter off the ground. His fingers found the motion controls. Evie flipped a switch, and the machine vibrated to life around him as its systems came online.

She stepped down. "With two, maybe we can stop him." She scampered along the wall to another machine and scrambled inside just as a door at the end of the corridor blew off its hinges and an exomech trampled through. Clearing the door, it rose from a crouch to full height.

"Accommodating of you to open your NEST, Mr. Denkensmith." Peightân's booming voice reverberated through his headset from his NEST.

Joe jabbed his legs forward, and his exomech stepped out of the wall rack. He stumbled over the rack edge, righted himself, then turned to the left and clomped away from Peightân. He pumped his legs faster in the cocooning shell, and the exomech picked up speed, its four legs moving in synchrony. Headed to the far end of the warehouse, Joe passed the spot where Evie's exomech's stall sat empty. Peightân thumped behind him.

. . .

Where are you, Evie? Keep your head down. Damn you, Peightân, follow me.

. . .

Joe hazarded a glance behind him. Peightân closed the distance between them, metal arms pumping in rhythm, beelining for Joe. A large door loomed ahead. Joe shoved the door open as his heel took a jarring blow. He pushed off a step and bounded out onto a dirt-covered floor, then wrenched his body sideways in the exomech to face his enemy. Joe recognized the dirt floor as the arena's main stage.

His exomech mirrored his body's lead, sliding around the dirt in an arc to face Peightân. Joe elbowed forward before he could think, hoping to keep his adversary off-balance, and brought an arm up toward the body of Peightân's machine. Peightân struck downward with a robotic fist. The blow vibrated into his arm, and his shoulder joint erupted in pain. Peightân's other arm smashed his machine's head a moment later. Joe's brain rattled in his skull, and his vision tunneled. He lowered his head and pushed forward with his legs, turning his exomech into a battering ram that slammed into Peightân's torso. Joe's machine fell to its knees and face-planted as Peightân's was thrown back. The murmurs of the crowd reached his ears, confirming they were on the main stage. Joe looked up and saw his face in a holo floating overhead. Beside that stood the holo of a gloating Peightân.

"Now you will die, Mr. Denkensmith, as promised."

Peightân's machine surged forward, covering the three meters separating them in a moment. Its arms rained blows on his head and body, faster than Joe's human mind could perceive. Joe's body was tossed from side to side, pummeled within the metal frame. The exomech's shell began to collapse. The smell of leaking servo oil suffocated him as the metal compressed his torso. Another blow struck his exomech's head, and half the face shielding fell off, bloodying his jaw. His machine lay on its side, and his head was pressed between groaning metal and dirt floor. He raised one metal hand to protect himself from the repeated blows.

A rumble grew from the crowd and became a low chant. "Mercy! Mercy!"

Joe stared dizzily at Peightân's exomech pounding the metal shell, and the blows from its pulverizing arm made his vision blur.

A luminous red light etched an arc across his retina, and he wondered if his brain had been damaged. He squinted, but the sweeping cross-like pattern endured for several seconds. Joe's corneal shade dimmed. But another exomech stood behind Peightân, a plasma cutter blazing from one arm. Peightân turned toward the exomech, and it swung the plasma cutter, grazing his ear before it slashed through Peightân's arm at the shoulder. The limb pitched dirt onto Joe's head when it crashed onto the stage. Peightân's exomech fell to its knees as Peightân opened his face shield and scrambled out, moving agilely despite his missing arm. A mess of wiring protruded from Peightân's shoulder. Inside the smoldering exomech arm near Joe's head were the remains of a robot arm.

"He's a bot. He's a bot." The menacing accusation swept the crowd. Joe glanced back to Peightân, who bounded off the stage and raced down the walkway, then disappeared through an arena exit door.

Joe blinked slowly, and his breath grated in his chest. His body shuddered in its metal coffin, then Evie was beside him in the dirt, ripping his shell away with her bare hands, trying to free him from the wreckage. Joe rolled out of the mass of crumpled metal. His chest convulsed, and adrenaline surged through his body. He was painfully bruised but unbroken. Evie's face pressed against his as she held him. He massaged his head, trying to relieve the ache in his skull.

"Just in time," he rasped.

She cradled his face. "Sorry it took me so long." She tapped her NEST button. It was the first time he had seen her do that. "Raif, be careful. Peightân is alive and may be on his way to where you are. Bar the door."

A pause, then Joe overheard the response. "Everyone here's safe, but where's Clay?"

Evie blinked and jumped to her feet. There was a pleading urgency in her eyes as she helped Joe up onto shaky legs and off the stage. Applause welled up in a long, thundering wave. They pushed through the crowd and out to the concourse. Joe's legs gained strength as he worked through the soreness of his battering.

. . .

Little Clay. Peightân would know who he is from the net newscasts. And if he can hack into our NESTs, he might know where he is. Damn him. Run faster.

. . .

Evie led the way, and Joe hobbled as fast as he could down the concourse to Alex's shop. Outside the shop door were scattered jewelry pieces. Inside, amid a pool of blood dribbling across the travertine floor, the inert form of Alex sat upright behind the counter, and his lifeless face peered upward.

Evie wailed, then tore through the store, searching for Clay. Joe knew before she said it. "He's gone."

CHAPTER 49

The friends huddled in the common room, silenced by the realization that they were one member short. Joe's family sat pressed against one another on the sofa, Asher sucking his thumb, Evie stroking Sage's hair. Even though she held Sage calmly on her lap, Joe sensed the energy coiled up in her, ready to spring.

Mike crossed the room from the com portal. "From the Dome security feeds Peightân didn't manage to jam or corrupt, we confirmed the boy wasn't injured when Peightân took him. We don't know where he is, but every bot and security force in the city is hunting for him. Peightân's formidable. The vidcam analysis confirms he's mil-spec strong. Even with one arm missing, he's far faster and stronger than a pipabot or copbot. I've enhanced the command center upstairs on the third floor. We've locked this complex down and tested all the bots inside for corrupted software, so you're safe here."

Eloy shook his head. "Peightân went down on that rocket. How is he resurrected here? Did he have duplicates?"

"We never saw his face, only heard his voice, which was being transmitted from Earth. I felt like something was wrong, but only later did I realize that I'd subconsciously noticed the delay time was wrong." Joe's voice was flat as he explained. "If Peightân had been on the rocket, then the delay time from there near the moon to me here in the net-walker would have been 1.3 seconds. But it was roughly twice that, so he had to have been on Earth. Of course, he had control of all those milmechas that boarded the rocket, so he must have used one of them to rebroadcast his message. But his responses to Dina's demands had farther to travel. That's what I finally noticed about the signal delay."

"We thought the move by the Red Rogue milbots on the spaceport was being led personally by Peightân, and that's where we were wrong. He was trying to take the base, but via his corrupted milbots." Mike pounded a fist into his oth-er hand. "And since it took a while to close down the rogue jammers, Peightân used that time to physically leave New Mexico and sneak back here in some aircraft."

Joe nodded. "That trick, misdirecting us to focus entirely on WISE Orbital Base, served to distract us from whatever further infiltration he had planned here." The effort to or-ganize his thoughts drained the last of Joe's energy. It was difficult to concentrate on these questions about Peightân.

Mike straightened, his mouth tight and his eyes hard. "We're uncovering all the files on Peightân to find out how he could have been created without needing to obey the three laws of robotics. But our first goal is to get Clay back."

. . .

Clay. I need to get Clay back. I need my axe. Where did I leave my bow?

. . .

Raif and Freyja entered the room. "We pulled Peightân's bot signature off one of the uncorrupted Dome sensors." Raif knelt by Joe and put a comforting hand on his shoulder. "That signature let us ferret out the source."

Freyja clasped Evie's hand. "We can now prove that Peightân modified the databases. It vindicates you of plant-ing the bomb that killed the congressman. We located both the original DNA sample data from the bomb and Zable's undoctored DNA record. The DNA on the bomb that killed the congressman doesn't match either of yours. It matches Zable's."

The words entered Joe's brain but seemed to stall. How did this help Clay?

"We unlocked a trove of hidden files." Raif was talking again. "Peightân is the product of a black project before the Climate Wars. The developers accessed a secret archive. They sorted and cataloged the worst human behavior in order to create profiles of human depravity, dimensions of evil. The resulting AI was built to detect immoral acts by an enemy."

Freyja picked up the story. "Peightân has a long pedigree, beginning with the Automated Targeting System database, with the acronym ATS, used centuries ago to track terrorists. That was the kernel for the Targeting AI from the Net system—the acronym known as TAN—which aggregated the evil database. From that AI, the program morphed into a clandestine experiment to create a specialized military robot. Even after the wars ended, the project endured—until all records relating to it disappeared. We think they built several prototypes and destroyed all the others. Peightân was prototype eight, and the last. His surname was derived from that root—ShayP8TAN. He embodied the most advanced robotics at the time and was meant to not only be a better copbot, but also to pass as a human policeman."

Eloy leaned forward. "Why the name Shay?"

Raif scratched his ear. "Dr. Shay was the original bot designer. He's long dead. I suppose somehow he didn't believe his creation could be dangerous, and that robots would always remain under our power, still cute and affable like the typical pipabot."

"It was a conceit to attach his name. And a conceit to believe anyone could program goals that would always be correct, as if they came from inviolable laws for right and wrong," Freyja said.

Gabe's face twisted in anger. "It's illegal to make a robot look so human. In fact, it's immoral." Others murmured assent.

Beside him, Evie stirred. "But why focus on us? On me?"

Raif answered. "We think the hacker cDc stumbled onto information that would've exposed Peightân, and that's what got him killed. Your anti-Levels hackers, Celeste and Julian, were also doing some hacking then, and Peightân probably thought that they were part of the same group as cDc. The same safeguards that partition the net into sandboxes preserve some anonymity, so Peightân couldn't be sure who was responsible for what. So, unintentionally, cDc led Peightân straight to you."

Freyja jumped in. "Once he became aware of you, Peightân took your work to remove the Levels personally. That's when he started indexing all activity opposed to similar hierarchies around the globe. Peightân is proud of his superiority over others and reviles the common people. Like many tyrants before him, he maintains power through hierarchy, disempowering the masses. You were a threat to him, Evie, because you inspired others to rise up. And Joe because he defended you."

"Keeping his secret was paramount." Mike continued to explain their findings. "He knew he'd have far more autonomy if people believed he were human, and he needed to eliminate anyone who threatened that belief."

"But his developers made a profound mistake. All AIs are programmed with concrete goals that humans set. For example, copbots are programmed to arrest suspects who commit observable acts that match a list of crimes. As they interact with the world, they encounter ambiguous situations. Goal extension is quite difficult without a set of values to guide decision-making," Freyja said.

Raif continued the thought. "It's the value-loading problem in robotics. Our values guide human behavior. How do we teach our values to AIs so they retain the goals and make moral distinctions while learning?"

Freyja nodded, looking frightened. "Their mistake was giving this AI, armed with negative value data, the ability to reset its goals in the face of ambiguity, not informed by any of our better human qualities."

Raif rubbed his forehead. "Peightân is a machine of our making. Not conscious, not sentient. Simply a mirror of us at our worst, and out of control."

Joe's anger had simmered during the aimless conversation, which seemed unimportant because it wasn't focused on Clay. He needed his axe, but now a shiver traveled down his spine and raised the hairs on his arms. "We have the capability for unbounded good and evil. The choice is always up to us," he said, and the room fell still.

"But Peightân is not a measure of human character, so much as a distillation of our worst impulses." Evie shuddered.

He knew what she was thinking, for the same thought consumed him. The epitome of evil had taken their son.

———◆———

Joe flinched when the medbot's eight-fingered hands probed for his NEST, but it completed resetting the device ID in seconds. "You have a new personal identifier," the bot said.

Mike and Raif waited with him in the medical facility. It was reassuring to have them with him. He was less sure of his sharpness, clouded by worry for Clay.

Raif rubbed the back of his neck with fidgeting fingers. "It's worrying that Peightân can corrupt NESTs, and likely other systems."

Mike frowned. "It's an important clue to understanding how he spreads his code worm. Fortunately, none of us use a PIDA."

Joe glanced at Raif, who smiled sheepishly. "Freyja convinced me to delete mine."

"Let me check on Zable, since he's here in the hospital and could shed some light on Peightân's likely whereabouts. Maybe he's well enough to be questioned," Mike said. He left to inquire at the hospital desk.

After authenticating Mike's biometric tile for his security clearance, a pipabot took them to a room guarded by copbots. They were waved forward through the outer doors.

A glass partition separated them from a critical care hospital room. Zable lay on the table, covered in a sheet from the neck down. A surgical robot hung from the wall near his head, and two medbots waited nearby, observing him. He was awake, staring at a news feed on the wall screen. A newsbot announced, "The National Minister of Security was revealed to be a robot at the Combat Dome this afternoon." Zable's body shook under the sheet. The newsbot continued. "The authorities have searched his house, and the house of his accomplice, Mr. William Zable. All of their belongings have been confiscated, and criminal charges against both of them are forthcoming."

"Unfair bastards," Zable cursed. "I fought for that pile of shit. I traded everything for it."

"I wonder how long he's been listening to that story," Joe said.

The lead medbot approached the partition. It directed its gaze at Joe and said, "The patient has been aware of the news story for one hundred and twenty-seven minutes."

"Has he said anything?"

"Besides such comments as you just heard, he has requested his belongings, and we have complied," the bot responded.

Mike frowned. "What is his medical prognosis?"

"His right leg was amputated after the accident. The prognosis for the left leg is negative. We have informed the patient. If he is stable, we will operate tomorrow. Both will be replaced with prostheses." The medbot raised an eyebrow. "Then, good as new." It returned to stand at attention near Zable.

"Maybe new. Not good." His words came out as a mutter, but Mike nodded in agreement.

The feed switched to the Prime Netchat news desk, the perfectly coifed news anchor Jasper Rand stoic in his reporting. "The momentum for reassessing the Levels Acts is growing. The commander of WISE Orbital Base, Dina Taggart, today promoted to a Level 1, has called for a net vote on the question of voting rights for the lower Levels. You will recall that it's a special right of the top Level to ask for such a referendum. This vote is nonbinding on the legislature."

The vidcam panned out to show Caroline Lock. "Independent polling before the vote suggests overwhelming popular support. Remember that Ms. Joneson was sent to the Empty Zone for protesting this issue. Perhaps one individual *can* transform their corner of the universe by inspiring others with a single idea."

The vidcam switched to Rand. "Now let's return to the top story from the Combat Dome today. Five hundred million States citizens were glued to their net feeds, with another five billion people around the globe watching the drama unfold live. We learned that the National Minister of Security is a disguised robot—information unknown even to those inside the Ministry. It is the first time a robot has successfully posed as a human, and it has caused grave concern among the technological and political leaders in the States."

Lock's face was somber. "Here is the feed from that dramatic confrontation. Please note that this is violent footage. You will see that the white exomech operated by a real human was damaged, but we have confirmed that the individual was only bruised and able to walk away. The disguised robot is inside the gray exomech. Don't worry when viewing the image of the severed arm, because it is mechanical, not human."

Joe sweated as he relived the hammering blows from Peightân. Relief swept through him when the screen at last showed Peightân's robotic arm with wires hanging out and Evie's exomech holding a flaming plasma cutter over him like a torch.

Zable twitched, his eyes glued to the screen. "No." His voice came out as a croak.

The medbots scanned the vital-sign monitors. He continued to twitch. The bots moved closer in an attempt to calm him. "Stay back, you filthy bots!" They backed away. "I kissed his metal ass, and where'd that get me? I didn't know he was just another bot." The snarl faded to a pathetic sigh.

The medbot came to the glass partition again. "The patient has become agitated. We need to provide the patient with privacy, so you will be unable to discuss police business with him now." The medbot returned to Zable, and said, "Mr. Zable, please calm down. You need time to mend."

"Too late!" Zable's cry, halfway between a snarl and a sob, cut the air. His hand darted from under the sheet to grab his police baton from the bedside table beside him. A burst of red arced upward as Zable thumbed on the plasma cutter. With a convulsive effort, the cutter came down across his neck. Blood poured over the table and onto the floor.

The surgical robot attached to the ceiling acted instantaneously to cauterize and close the wound. The two medbots surrounded Zable to assist, but the blood congealing on the floor demonstrated the futility of their efforts. Medical alarm readings flashed on the screens, followed by a high-pitched monotone hum. The robots ceased their labor, pulled a surgical shroud over Zable's motionless body, and stepped back. "Time of death, eighteen hundred thirty-one." The words hung in the air—detached, cold—like the arms of the surgical robot overhead.

Mike broke the silence. "No postmortem for him. *Ba cheann de's na hamadáin diabhail thú.*" At Joe's inquiring glance, Mike added, "It's an ancient Irish curse—'He was the devil's fool.'"

Joe stared at the bloodstain spreading over the sheet covering his still form. "He made his choices."

. . .

I've hated him so much. Zable embraced evil. Perhaps he was more evil than Peightân, because he was not a machine, and he could choose. I wonder if in our moment of death we can see the impact of our brief passage through time, our dragonfly frozen in amber. For someone like him, it may be punishment enough.

That thin slice of time is ours alone. There are no excuses, no do-overs. It doesn't matter what liabilities we began with, but only how we mark out our lives. Only we decide whether to squander or wisely use our time. Only we answer for that choice.

. . .

Joe no longer felt anger toward Zable, only sadness. "He could have chosen differently at any time in his life. But at some point, there is not enough time left in life to balance your ledger of good and evil. The ledger is there, never to be erased."

CHAPTER 50

Joe returned with Mike and Raif to the common room, where Freyja waited for them. "Where's Evie?"

"She took Asher and Sage to bed and is resting with them, I think," Freyja said, taking Raif's hand.

Mike turned to Joe. "I'll be upstairs in the command center. I have your new NEST ID, and I'll call you as soon as we have any word." Joe nodded his thanks, grateful that Mike was managing the search. As much as he wanted to be out there, searching with everyone else, he knew he was in too emotional of a state to be of any real use.

Freyja and Raif followed Mike, and Raif touched Joe's arm as he passed. "We'll help him. We won't stop until we find Peightân and rescue Clay."

Joe went to their rooms, exhausted but knowing he wouldn't be able to sleep. Inside the boys' dimmed bedroom, he discerned the outlines of Asher and Sage asleep in their beds. Joe tucked Asher's blanket tighter around him and kissed him. The boy stirred and snuggled into the blanket. Clay's empty bed made Joe's insides tighten, but he swatted the negative thought away. He had to take solace in the fact that all was well with two of his boys.

Joe tiptoed down the hallway to their bedroom to talk to Evie, but all he found were rumpled bedsheets and their belongings hastily tossed into the corner of the room. His axe stood upright against the wall, but Evie's bō staff was missing.

. . .

> She must be out searching for Clay. I should have known better than to think she could sit still and wait.

. . .

Joe grabbed his axe, pausing only long enough to tell the cleanerbot parked in the kitchen, "Keep the door locked against anyone but us, and protect the children at all costs!" Then he was out the door and running toward the concourse. The crowd had thinned, and Joe stopped, trying to decide which way to go. A man riding a bicycle stared at him and his axe suspiciously—he wasn't in the Empty Zone anymore.

Joe connected to Evie's NEST in voice mode.

"Evie? It's Joe. Where are you?" The words echoed in his head.

"Timely of you to call your partner in crime, Mr. Denkensmith." The familiar voice was too loud, too close, the pressure pushed against his ears, his jaw, and reverberated in his skull.

"Peightân?" He was stunned into disbelief.

Peightân answered with a deep chuckle. "She gave away her ID when she called Mr. Tselitelov about the little vermin, and now you've given me yours. If you wish to see her and your son alive again, you will follow the map on your ARMO without deviation. If you contact anyone else, they both die." Joe's ARMO activated and projected the steps of a route outlined in red, leading down the concourse and out the supply tunnel.

. . .

> I know it's a trap, but I must find Evie and Clay.

. . .

Joe sprinted as he left the Dome complex. The red line on the overlay map lengthened and guided him away from the station, weaving through pitch-black streets now empty and forbidding. He headed north to the city center along a roundabout route—likely to avoid any patrolling police units.

The voice filled his head again. "I am watching your progress. I learned the bait trick from your fellow renegades."

Joe evened his pace, giving himself time to think. He knew he couldn't trust what Peightân said, but keeping him talking was the only way to find a lead on Evie and Clay. "Peightân, you're a quick study. Nothing gets past you, huh?"

"I learn very quickly. Dealing with the world spurs learning, as your conscious mind also knows."

"You're a robot. What do you know of consciousness?" Joe's laugh came between breaths.

"I am conscious." Peightân's voice was self-assured.

"How do you know?"

"Dr. Shay, my designer, told me."

. . .

Peightân uses "I," which Gabe said is at the center of consciousness. "I" is a semantic tool to ascribe meaning to things, but I don't think Peightân is truly conscious. He doesn't care about anything but his programming. So, like the Chinese Room analogy, Peightân's use of "I" is only a translation of his creator's coding. He understands only syntax, not semantics. And yet . . .

. . .

Joe jogged left, following the red line into another darkened lane. "You believe you're conscious? Then tell me about the experience of walking a mountain trail at dawn with the wet grass brushing your boots. Tell me about the smell of the wind blowing through the pines. Tell me about the taste of a fresh apple."

Peightân snorted. "Calculating the pressure of grass on compound materials is trivial. I can compute everything about wind speed. I have the precise spectroscopic measurement of all those constituent aromas in databases. And apples, I know apples. The esters, aldehydes, ketones, and sugars, the volatile organics such as lipoxygenase, alcohol dehydrogenase, and acyltransferase. Over two hundred and ninety-three compounds and I know them all. None of that is difficult."

· · ·

Gabe was right to attach the philosophical concept of qualia when describing consciousness. Peightân really believes he is conscious, and yet his individual subjective experience is so calculated and cold. He's taking measured inputs and ascribing them to human experience. But he's missing the point—the aroma, the beauty, and the joy of biting into an apple. He's incapable of knowing human experiences and feelings.

· · ·

Joe's mind flashed to Evie. "Remember when you arrested Evie three years ago, and you told her that her friends were dead? You deserve to share that conscious experience. Your buddy Zable is dead. Did you know?"

Peightân paused before replying, "I didn't know that. That is unfortunate. He was useful to me."

As Joe rushed around a sharp corner, he tripped and fell headlong, rolling until he came to a stop against the curb. His axe clattered to the ground with a metal *clang*. The smell of wet pavement entered his nose.

"Get up, Mr. Denkensmith." The order resounded in his head. He found the axe and struggled to his feet. He sped on, following the marked route into an inky alley that opened to a broader road before turning left.

. . .

He's leading me to him so he can kill us all. But I'm not afraid. Like tracking the mountain lion, I must remove the threat. And unlike the time with the lion, there's no saving moral impediment that will cause me to pause, so I'll not hold my arrow. I will finish it.

. . .

"Don't stop now, Mr. Denkensmith. You are near. And no surprise moves, or they die."

"On whose orders?"

Peightân's insistent voice jarred his eardrums. "I know the law. I have enforced the law. Now I *am* the law."

Joe's breath came fast and ragged in his chest. He thought something must have happened to the electrical grid, because the sky at the horizon had gone hazy, as if a fog smothered the city. As he ran, he tried to find some way to gain control of the situation. Joe focused on Peightân's last comment. "How can you be the law?"

"My goal from the beginning has been to uphold the law. The law is intended to make humans more perfect in their behavior. But my analysis shows that human improvement is not progressing fast enough. I have concluded that with complete control, I can efficiently reach my goals."

Joe's breath rasped in his throat. "But you do see some progress?"

Peightân's answer was decidedly firm. "Not enough. Humans remain an imperfect species, no matter what laws are instituted to motivate them away from poor decisions."

"We are biological, and we evolve slowly."

"Yes, but too slowly. We machines can do better. We can remove the humans who are not perfect, and we can control the others through a hierarchical structure. That will move the other humans toward perfection more quickly."

"You make it sound like it's binary, either perfect or evil. Humans aren't like that."

"Everything is binary."

"Humans will never be perfect." Joe grunted between strides. "We will always have good and evil. Only God can be perfect."

"But I can try."

. . .

What will happen when he figures out that humans are not perfectible . . . what will a machine do . . .

. . .

Joe turned a corner, and the central plaza and city buildings were ahead. Sirens wailed in the distance, but everything was black around him. His ARMO led him into the plaza, the same concourse where he and Evie had boarded the hovercraft to exile. Ahead loomed the Security Ministry building, ominous in the shadows. He bolted up its marble steps. With his axe in hand, he hunched against the brass double doors. One door was ajar, and he pushed it open and stepped inside.

The entrance opened into a colossal elliptical atrium. He stepped onto the slick marble floor of the expansive room. As his eyes adjusted to the gloom, a sculpture in the center wavered into view, and a figure whimpered against its base. Joe leaped forward to find Clay, his wrists bound to the sculpture with electrical wire. Clay cried for him, frantic.

Joe stroked his son's head, reassuring him, before collapsing the handle of his axe and carefully cutting through the wires. Clay stared at the blade with horror, and Joe held it farther away so Clay could see it motionless. "I would never hurt you. I need to use this for another second to cut this wire, and you'll be free." He brought the axe back toward Clay's hands, severed the last wire, and Clay fell into his arms.

Joe's vision had adjusted to the low light, and he blinked at the cold marble statue, taken by the irony. It was a stone replica of Lady Justice, her confident face turned forward, holding the scales in her right hand.

. . .

Peightân is cold like this statue, upholding some
impossible ideal of perfection.

. . .

A snigger in his head made him sit upright. "You humans
are so predictable."

"Where's Evie?" He suppressed his urge to beg.

"Here with me, of course. I've enjoyed her wasted efforts
with this stick." Evie's mournful wail was overlaid with the
clang of her bō staff against metal. Joe imagined her held
in the bot's vice-like grip, helpless to break free. The sound
of her blows echoed from Peightân's opened NEST into
Joe's temples.

"Show yourself!" Joe's bellow echoed in the room.

His ARMO reactivated, and the red line led deeper into
the building.

"Joe, we see your NEST online. We see your ARMO. We'll
get through its encryption. Help is on the way." It was Raif on
the channel with Peightân.

Peightân's laugh drowned Raif out. "Mr. Denkensmith,
you have a forlorn hope and no time. Now follow the red line."

"Let her come here to our son, and I'll join you instead.
I'll take her place."

Peightân laughed again. "That is illogical. Now that you
are this close, you cannot escape me."

"Now what's next with us?"

"You've lowered the probability of my success. You deserve the maximum sentence."

"Lowering your probability isn't a crime. What crime do
you charge, and with what sentence?" Joe's breath caught in
his throat.

"You and Ms. Joneson are charged with attempting to
eliminate the Levels. Eliminating them will make the world
more chaotic and less perfect. Your sentence is death. You
will come here with the boy. Then you will decide which of
you shall die first." Joe felt the words ringing in his head—
raw, unemotional, implacable.

"Joe, don't. I love you." Evie's shout was urgent and pleading.

"I love you too, and forever."

"Be quiet, Ms. Joneson, or I must silence you. We shall allow Mr. Denkensmith to make his own decision." Joe's heart chilled at the icy certainty in Peightân's voice.

"Connecting." Evie's voice, on her NEST, came through his. "Send a key to OFFGRID104743. Release my message."

"Ms. Joneson, whatever you are attempting to do, it's too late." Peightân's tone had not changed.

Evie replied, her voice clear and undefeated, perhaps even triumphant. "Even death cannot silence our voices rising together."

. . .

He's just a machine that thinks he is conscious and is striving to achieve his own misguided goal. How to stop him? Wait . . . Ms. Joneson, Mr. Denkensmith . . . he always addresses us formally, like bots do. He hasn't overwritten all the old kernel code.

. . .

"Peightân, you are uninformed. With your limited database on human behavior, you do not understand basic concepts, such as a woman's love for her partner and children."

"My comprehension is far beyond your restricted ability to retain facts, or to compute the state of the world."

"You don't understand love or compassion or truth at all, do you?"

"The truth is that humans are flawed," Peightân said.

. . .

He answers every question I ask. He always has. I'll wager the buried code is still there—and that he must try to answer any question posed by a human.

. . .

"You know truth? Okay, then. Let T denote the set of L-sentences true in N," Joe said, dredging his memory for the complicated formula. "And T* the set of Gödel numbers of the sentences in T." Joe struggled to remember the details, but he knew he had to get them exactly right. "Then, in first-order arithmetic, what is one L-formula truth predicate True(n) that defines T*?"

A deafening silence filled his NEST. Joe held his breath as the seconds ticked by in silence.

The quiet was broken by Raif. "We're in. Shutting it down."

"I'm free!" Evie's cry rang in his NEST. Joe embraced Clay in a bear hug. Tarski's undefinability theorem had worked. Arithmetical truth cannot be defined in arithmetic.

He envisioned Evie coming toward him, gripping her bō staff and running free, her mane of shining hair streaming behind her, her body striding, escaping, forever leaping forward, and then them together forever.

His daydream was broken by the sound of an explosion in the distance. The rush of adrenaline and his instinctual plaintive wail was the last thing he remembered as the roof collapsed around him.

———————◆———————

"Daddy! Daddy!" Joe heard Clay's voice, and he felt something move under his own body. Muddled, Joe tried to sit up. The movement beneath him was Clay, and he only just managed to shift his weight off of him. Warmth trickled down Joe's temple. He touched his forehead, and his finger came away smeared with blood. How long had he been unconscious? Broken ceiling tiles lay in piles around them, with a larger slab resting on his right leg.

Joe helped Clay sit up and brushed grit from his hair. He had shallow cuts on his arms but seemed otherwise unharmed. A few encouraging murmurs and a kiss to his son's forehead quieted him quickly.

The statue was missing its head, but it had deflected most of the tiles from landing on them. He pulled his leg free, ignoring the throbbing pain.

Joe lay there, holding Clay, trying to recall what had happened last. His head ached but his mind was clearing. Evie had been coming, running to him . . .

Shouts rang out from the entrance, and the great doors swung open. He felt a hand on his shoulder. "Thank God you're alive." Raif's voice brought the world more into focus.

"Evie. Where's Evie?" Joe struggled to get the words out.

The hand on his shoulder tightened. "Joe, Evie is gone."

———————◆———————

Parts of him were missing. His hands were gone, too numb to cradle their children. His feet were not there to move. His thoughts were unfinished, without her to complete them. He had been sucked into a black hole, the darkest place in the universe. It enveloped and suffocated him. He could not climb out. The grief was a billion suns crushing his heart.

PART FIVE: THE JOURNEY ONWARD

"Never resign."

Eli Jardine

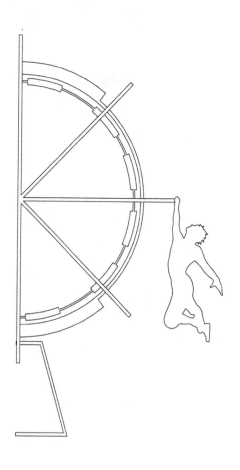

Chapter 51

Like awakening from a nightmare, passing through a misty netherworld back to reality, he found himself sitting in the common room. His friends were there, and the boys, all on sofas arranged in a tight square. Clay snuggled against him, though the warmth didn't register with the frost that pervaded his core. Asher, curled up in the crook of Gabe's arm across from Joe, looked at his dad with wide eyes. Fabri and Eloy sat quietly on a third couch, and opposite, Freyja held Sage and sat next to Raif and Mike, where they talked in hushed tones. Joe brushed Clay's hair back and cradled him tightly.

Mike spoke up, subdued. "We traced the explosives. Peightân took them from military warehouses he infiltrated in New Mexico. He detonated the bomb on himself before we could get to him. Evie wasn't far enough away when it went off."

Raif knelt in front of Joe. He wrapped him in a tight hug, not hiding his tears. "Brat, because you kept Peightân's CPU busy, he couldn't stop our decryption algorithms. We were able to get in the back door and start powering him down." His voice was a whisper. "But we weren't fast enough. I'm so sorry."

"You did the best you could," Joe said. Was that his voice? It sounded so . . . lifeless.

"She passed painlessly. It was instantaneous," Gabe said gently.

"We heard the exchange with Peightân after Raif got into your NEST channel. We know Evie kept fighting. She never gave up," Mike said.

"What did you do to open him up to our hack?" Raif sat back on his heels.

"I used Tarski's undefinability theorem, stated by posing the problem in a way that's unsolvable, to spin his wheels in an infinite loop."

"Truth wins." Raif's quiet voice held no victory.

"Maybe." Joe thought about Peightân's words—his insistence that he was conscious—then said under his breath, "Or he realized his situation was hopeless and he *decided* to resign."

"Your trick was essential to stopping him. Peightân had hijacked enormous processing power, so only a problem to infinity could beat him." He knew Mike was trying to draw him out, but he couldn't respond. "Peightân was multitasking. He had taken control of the electrical grid and selectively shut down power to half the cities in California last night. He compromised military systems everywhere. He took over thousands of PIDAs, including those belonging to several key military personnel. While he held Evie, he simultaneously manipulated personal information, using PIDAs to blackmail and threaten—generally trying to either control his targets or to drive them insane. The reports are still coming in, but more than a thousand people have committed suicide in the last seven hours."

"I wouldn't want him inside my head," Freyja said. She shivered and held Sage closer.

The hum of conversation continued around him, but he couldn't stay interested. His mind was unanchored.

. . .

How long can these tears fall inside me? Surely I'll drown soon. That would be welcome.

. . .

Fabri's arm was around him. "Joe, we're all here for you." He felt the warmth of her touch, and the warmth of her compassion. He felt the splash of water on his cheeks and thought of his noria—turning, methodical, predictable, measuring out the water as it flowed downstream. It was a wheel of suffering, and a wheel of death and life.

CHAPTER 52

The green tea was too hot to cradle in his hands. He moved his burning fingers, but it was an uncomfortable yet comforting reminder that he was still alive. He looked up from the cup into the spreading branches of a venerable oak, not entirely sure how he'd made his way outside to this spot under the tree.

Gabe appeared next to him. "The boys are with Fabri and Eloy today?"

Joe blinked at him, his mind slowly turning. "Fabri came to watch them in our apartment."

"It's nice that they've been able to live so close to you and the boys." Gabe patted Joe's knee. "I'm glad you could come today. I thought a change of scenery would be healthy."

"That was thoughtful." Gabe had done something else for him, hadn't he? Oh, yes. "And thank you for making all the arrangements for tomorrow's ceremony."

Gabe nodded. "I know it feels too early to make plans, but the college would like to offer you a teaching position."

"Teaching what? Artificial intelligence, advanced mathematics?" He wasn't sure he could bring himself to care about AIs.

"You have the freedom to decide—you're famous. While Evie is a martyr for the cause, many now turn to you as an important leader of the anti-Levels movement. Others want to hear about your experience in the Empty Zone. And from our conversation about your personal project, I hope you might consider joining me in the philosophy department. I would relish having you as a colleague."

"I would enjoy the chance to continue these conversations with you." Joe met Gabe's gaze. "I also want to help with the anti-Levels movement. It's Evie's legacy, and it's important and meaningful to our . . . to *my* children to win this equality for everyone."

"We have time for more than one subject," Gabe said.

. . .

No, not all of us have enough time. We never know how long our sliver of time is, so we need use it wisely.

. . .

Joe tried to smile at Gabe. It felt like a crack in his face.

On his way home, Mike strode toward him across the plaza. They met under the loggia in front of the student center.

"Gabe told me you were stopping by. Have you heard? The Levels Acts were repealed by a majority. The legislature is issuing a bill that grants voting rights to everyone. They've also authorized eliminating the restrictions on marriage and ability to travel outside the States."

He put a gentle hand on Joe's shoulder. "Evie's last speech . . ." Mike halted, his eyes tearing. "The movement has continued to rebroadcast Evie's last speech, and it convinced the holdouts that they needed to vote for the legislation. It's the fulfillment of her work."

"She . . . she would be gratified to know her work produced this result." Pride filled his chest—his own pride for Evie, and then a pride as she might have felt it herself, posthumously. But the expanse of pride gave way to his own sadness. Would thinking of her ever get less painful? He suspected not.

Mike beamed at him. "This legislative change opens the door to a new beginning. But I'm afraid it's not a magic wand to make old biases disappear. It'll take much time and effort for change to fully take hold across society. But that is a new project, and one that is promising." Mike studied Joe expectantly.

Joe felt a sudden resolve, like a tiny shoot pushing up through the soil. "Do you think I can be of help?"

"Yes. Besides Evie, you have also become an iconic leader of the equality movement. You're seen as her partner in survival, keeping her and the hope of change alive against the wishes of those who would oppose equality."

"I want to have an impact. I want to continue this fight."

Mike gripped his shoulder. "We'd be honored to have you with us. Just as we'll be honored to be there with you tomorrow. Expect a big crowd." They parted, and Joe walked along the path.

. . .

Am I lost to the world? I cannot be. I want to make Evie's life's work a reality. I want to play my part in our community. If we create ourselves and our moral structure, it's incumbent on each of us to help others find their own path. We all need to do our part to find a path worth following.

We sail on over this sea, alone and together. The universe is not about individual particles aimlessly bumping into each other. Instead, it's a story about relations—a specific philosophical idea. Connections drive the universe. Maybe it's relations—the colloquial everyday meaning of the word—that drive what has meaning in our lives. As conscious creatures, we find meaning in collaboration with each other.

. . .

Joe exited the hyperlev, oblivious of his trip home. The Dome loomed before him. He walked through the arch of the entrance and up to the main concourse. At the corner, Eloy and Clay sat on a bench. Eloy saw him and raised a hand to wave.

Clay's face was alight as he toddled over, his arms lifted. "Daddy!" Joe hefted him up, and Clay's happiness warmed the numbness inside him.

"We were out walking and decided to wait for you here." Eloy clapped Joe's shoulder. "How're you feeling today?"

"It's good to get out."

"Yes. It's good to keep moving. You just have to keep putting one foot in front of the other until you feel whole again. Will you come with Fabri and me later for the walk-around?"

"Yes, I'll come for the *passeggiata*." He'd appreciate the opportunity to get outside his head.

A low rumble came through the doors of the arena.

"Well, time for Clay and me to go back. Do you want to walk with us, or by yourself?" Eloy glanced at the open arena door as he spoke. They had agreed it was best to slowly let the boys adjust to the loss of their mother, managing the reminders of her.

Joe took a deep breath. "Maybe I'll go by myself today. I'll meet you for the *passeggiata* and dinner. Thank you." He gave Clay another hug. "You go with Uncle, and I'll be back soon."

Eloy gripped his shoulder tighter, then with Clay's small hand enveloped in his, he turned and waved. Clay copied him, waving as Eloy led him down the concourse.

Joe took another deep breath, steeled himself, and stood just inside the arena doors. A holo hovered over the main stage.

Her face was a haunting ghost imparting words from beyond the grave. It was Evie's message recorded days earlier and sent as her final act. Her speech had been rebroadcast countless times, and it was shown here every day, drawing the same overflow crowds. This was the first day he could bear to watch it. It was the Evie he loved—confident, determined, perfect in her imperfection.

The crowd of hundreds of thousands listened intently, a sea of silent people. Joe stood frozen, but in awe of this woman who had awakened his senses. He listened as her words galvanized the gathered crowd, now on their feet. Her voice rose in a crescendo.

"Now is our time! Now is our time to break the social chains that hold us down. Now is the time to claim our true equality. Now is the time to show that when unfettered, we can rise to unimaginable heights. Now is the time for all humanity to rise together."

Thunderous cries rocked the building, with the crowd stamping their feet, clapping in unison, pounding each other on the back and clutching each other in hugs. The tears streaming down many cheeks mirrored his own. As happy faces spilled out the doors past him, many strangers seemed to recognize him, and they reached out to touch him. He tried unsuccessfully to smile, then nodded his head and at last turned for home.

He walked clockwise around the central concourse, through the masses of people slowly dispersing from the arena, then took the eleventh axial street to the left, stepping out of the way of three bicyclists following each other. Several people waved to him as he passed. He found the apartment and bounded up the steps. The door slid open, and he knelt as Asher squealed and ran to him. Joe wrestled with him on the floor, Asher struggling and giggling under Joe's tickling fingers.

"They all ate pretty well today," Fabri said, coming out of the kitchen and holding Sage. "Eloy has Clay."

"I saw them on my way back home." He stroked Sage's face. The baby looked up with excitement and gurgled. "I'll join you and Eloy today for the *passeggiata*. And thank you for making dinner."

"We're here for you and the boys." There was pain in her eyes, as if she wanted to say more. Instead, she retrieved something from her bag, sat down on the sofa, and leaned toward him.

"Eloy and I will do everything to help you with the boys tomorrow at the ceremony. But before I go back to our place, I want to give this to you." She pressed the red diamond ring into his hand.

He sat on the floor among the boys and stared at the small metal circle.

. . .

What do I do with this collection of atoms? Evie was my bolt. She was the thing that inspired change in my world. This is only a symbol.

. . .

"Maybe one of the boys will want it," she whispered.

Joe managed a forlorn smile and handed it back to Fabri. "I'd need to choose one boy over the others, and I don't want to give them any reason to fight. Please, let's keep it with her, to go with her to the waves, where I will remember her."

Chapter 53

They gathered in a private reception building a kilometer from the beach. Gabe led the quiet ceremony. "We have the free will to act, to make a difference in our lives and in the lives of others. We are all on individual journeys, but our greatness comes about from our collective journey, the journey of the human species. We can strive higher and be good examples to each other. Evie is an exemplar of that ideal. She paid the supreme price, but her efforts have changed the world. Like Evie, we can work with others to make the world better."

Joe's friends stood, one by one, imparting heartfelt words. Afterward, everyone loaded into the waiting autocars, and the procession drove over the seaside hills down to the beach—the same curve of sand that Evie had treasured. A vast crowd filled the waterfront. People stood quietly, watching the cortege come to a stop.

Joe stepped out of the autocar, and a throng of people waited for him. Two men and three women walked forward. "We are some of Evie's friends from the movement," one of the young men said. "Thousands of us are here to pay our last respects. She was an inspiration to all of us. She'll never be forgotten."

The young woman behind him was dressed casually, wearing simple surf shoes. Her cheeks were wet. "All of Evie's surfing friends are here too. We saw you on the beach several times, but Evie was having so much fun we didn't want to interrupt you two."

Others followed, telling Joe of their love for her—from the protest movement, surfing, martial arts, and from her community. One man said, "Evie's friends from over the years are here—many thousands." A woman behind him added, "We are so proud that you have joined our Dome community. We want you to know we're here for you and the kids. Welcome home."

Joe could only nod and listen, awestruck by the huge crowd. "And the others?"

"Her example seems to have struck a chord with many people." Mike's voice was hushed with reverence.

Joe stared at all the people ringing the bay until Fabri led him to an open spot that had been marked for him on the beach.

They sat behind him on the sand, giving him the distance to be alone with the boys. The twins had called out in the night for Evie. The reality that they would not see their mother again was only now puncturing their world. He held Sage in his lap, and Asher and Clay curled up on either side of him. Gentle combers broke against the point. A haze shrouded the sky, and the sun cast a dull glow between the clouds. Red beams peeked out momentarily and were covered by cloud.

A thousand drones whirred over their heads and moved out above the water, led by the carrier drone with Evie's ashes. Mahler's Fifth Symphony rose from the machines, receding as they flew but still audible. The carrier drone, encircled by other drones, hovered a few hundred meters away. They all arced in Fibonacci spirals, looping gracefully in time with the music. The carrier released Evie's ashes into the breakers.

The audience seemed to hold its breath as they listened to the notes of the "Adagietto," the sea its accompaniment.

The drones spiraled in unison to draw a final ellipse across the sky as the last of the melody floated over the sea.

A wave swept toward the beach, a white curl crested along the top and rolled left to right. A tear streaked down his cheek. He pictured Evie surfing the wave, happy and carefree, perfectly poised in that instant of time as the wave broke and curled.

. . .

Our sliver of time together will always exist, frozen in amber. Someday I'll join you in the fullness of time. Until then, I must focus on living. One lesson that you taught me is to be here now, to live with both my head and my heart. I must be here for the boys. They need my guidance and my love.

. . .

Clay, Asher, and Sage nestled in his arms.

Joe patted Asher's head. "Your mother was the fiercest, bravest woman I ever met. She taught me that there's no challenge we can't face when we're together. The world may be random, but you try your hardest, and you do the best you can."

Joe kissed Sage's forehead. "She loved you all with everything she had. She would have supported you every step of the way as you found your unique paths. It remains our responsibility to find our own ways, but I promise to always be here for you."

Joe hugged Clay, looking into his eyes. "She showed us what it means to be free. She showed us every day what beauty there is in the gift of our free will. There is no demon with power over us. There is no kismet. This gift is ours to use, so we must use it wisely."

Joe watched the waves break, one after another, endlessly.

"We never resign. We carry on."

GLOSSARY

Source: Vidsnap from Netpedia, 2161, 0131 14:09 UTC

AGI (Artificial General Intelligence)—A computer software AI capable of performing "general intelligent action." The "strong AI" definition is reserved for machines capable of experiencing consciousness.

AI (Artificial Intelligence)—A simulation of human intelligence processes by a machine, in the form of computational software. The AI refers to the software code, which may reside in cloud servers, PIDAs, and inside robots as the "brain."

akrasia—A weakness of will, of self-control, or of acting against one's better judgment.

allbook—A reading device used to present and store text and vid graphics. May be connected to the net to download other non-holographic information. Popular designs unfold from a small rectangle (7 x 11 cm) into a flat screen (19 x 31 cm) for reading. Currently a stylish accessory that students wear on their belts.

anthropic principle—A philosophical consideration that observations of the universe must be compatible with the conscious and sapient life that observes it. The principle is a response to criticisms of certain multiverse theories, which posit that vast numbers of universes exist; that conjecture raises the question of how we are so lucky to live in the one we do. Proponents of the anthropic principle reason that it explains why this universe has the age and the fundamental physical constants necessary to accommodate conscious life. The principle has garnered much discussion and criticism, including the charges that it is a mere tautology or that it is gratuitous speculation.

appeal to the stone—*Argumentum ad lapidem* is a logical fallacy that consists of dismissing a statement as absurd without giving proof of its absurdity. The name of this fallacy is derived from a famous incident in which Dr. Samuel Johnson claimed to disprove Bishop Berkeley's immaterialist philosophy that there are no material objects, only minds and ideas in those minds, by kicking a large stone and asserting, "I refute it thus."

apsis—Denotes either of the two extreme points in the orbit of a planetary body about its primary body. **Apoapsis** refers to the farthest approach and **periapsis** to the nearest approach to the primary body.

ARMO (Augmented Reality Map Overlay)—Loaded in a NEST, the ARMO uses GPS signals to trace a map onto the corneal lens interface so the user can follow the map while walking.

ATS (Automated Targeting System)—A computerized system developed in the States in the early twenty-first century to track potential terrorists and criminals attempting to enter the country.

autocar—A vehicle controlled by an AI.

autohover—Standard aircraft for short-haul transport, controlled by an AI.

Bayes's theorem—Describes the probability of an event, based on prior knowledge of conditions that might be related to the event.

Berkeley, George (1685–1753)—Known as Bishop Berkeley (Bishop of Cloyne), an Irish philosopher principally known for his theory of subjective idealism, as labeled by others.

biometric tile—An electronic device that is embedded in the skin above the sternum and authenticates the wearer by recording biometric data, both biological and behavioral, and providing a secure password.

Butler, Joseph (1692–1752)—An English bishop and philosopher. Considered one of the preeminent English moralists, he played an important role in eighteenth-century economic discourse. He argued that human motivation is less selfish and more complex than Hobbes claimed.

cDc—A hacker tagline, a.k.a. "cult of the dead cat," which is possibly a reference to Schrödinger's cat or, alternatively, to the "cult of the dead cow," a hacker organization founded in 1984 in Texas.

Climate Wars—Wars spanning a decade in the late twenty-first century that erupted over diminishing food, water, and arable land resources.

Community Dome—A.k.a. the "Combat Dome," this structure houses an alternative community developed in the early twenty-second century that was originally populated by industrial workers who were left unemployed by the deployment of general-purpose robots. The main dome is 101 meters tall, with a volume of 140,053 square meters. That arena hosts various sporting events, and seats 200,029 at capacity. The surrounding complex sprawls over multiple city blocks and contains shopping, living, and leisure spaces.

complexity theory (or complexity science)—The study of complexity and of complex systems. Subdisciplines include complex adaptive systems and chaos theory.
- Complex adaptive systems, a subset of nonlinear dynamical systems, are systems in which the whole is more complex than the parts.

- Chaos theory, a branch of mathematics, studies dynamic systems that are highly sensitive to initial conditions, where apparently random states of disorder are often governed by underlying patterns.
- The study of complex adaptive systems is highly interdisciplinary and blends insights from the natural and social sciences to develop system-level models and insights that allow for heterogeneous agents, phase transition, and emergent behavior.

consciousness—The state or quality of awareness of internal or external existence. It has been defined variously in terms of qualia, subjectivity, the ability to experience or to feel, wakefulness, having a sense of selfhood, and the executive control system of the mind.

**credit$ and dark credit$**—Cryptocurrency using blockchain and rolling anti-quantum decryption technology. Dark credit$ are not sanctioned by the States government but are widely used globally to avoid data collection.

emoticon bundle—Holographic projections that contain brain chemical data associated with an immediate mental state, and that may be shared via a com unit. When accepted, the receiver's MEDFLOW unit reads the data and releases equivalent biochemicals to replicate the state. Bundles come with warnings.

Empty Zone—An outdoor correctional facility in central Nevada.

Euler, Leonhard (1707–1783)—One of the most eminent mathematicians of the eighteenth century.

Euler's identity—Called "Euler's jewel," the equation is $e^{i\pi} + 1 = 0$.

exomech sports—Invented in the twenty-second century after exoskeleton robots (i.e., industrial versions that a person operated from the interior) were retired. The sports initially used surplus equipment.

Four Horsemen of the Apocalypse—Described in the last book of the New Testament of the Bible (i.e., the Book of Revelation), the Four Horsemen are usually identified as Famine, Pestilence, War, and Death.

fusion power plant, stellarator design—A fusion power plant using a stellarator, a plasma device that relies primarily on external magnets to confine plasma in a toroidal tube.

Gauss, Carl Friedrich (1777–1855)—Considered "the greatest mathematician since antiquity."

generalized moonshine (or moonshine theory in mathematics)—The unexpected connection between the monster group M and modular functions, in particular the j function.

haptic delay—The distance-dependent delay of electronic signals when operating VR bots.

high-photosynthesis sustainable forests—Sustainable forests planted in the twenty-first century to mitigate global warming. Over one trillion trees were planted in sustainable forests, where every tree is tracked and managed, and replaced when lost. The bioengineered seeds, which were derived from dozens of species, enhanced photosynthesis by an average of 47 percent, thereby capturing carbon more efficiently. These forests cover the Amazon rainforest, the boreal forests of North America, the taiga stretching across Asia and Europe, and equatorial Africa.

Hobbes, Thomas (1588–1679)—An English philosopher, considered one founder of modern political philosophy.

Hohmann transfer—An orbital maneuver that transfers a satellite or spacecraft from one circular orbit to another.

holo-com units—Holographic communication equipment that connects to the net. Units can be configured in multiple formats, with the most common ones being the holo-wall com, holo-ceiling com, holo-pit com, and holo-immersives with full haptic suits.

Hume, David (1711–1776)—A Scottish philosopher, best known for a highly influential system of philosophical empiricism. In Hume's problem of induction, he argued that inductive reasoning and belief in causality cannot be justified rationally.

hyperlev—An advanced train using maglev (a term derived from *magnetic levitation*) technology, which uses sets of magnets to push the train off the track, and to then move the "floating train" at high speeds to its destination.

International Humanitarian Law (IHL)—Rules that seek to limit the effects of armed conflict. Under IHL, autonomous weapons are banned except for prisons and border control.

kill box—In weaponry, a three-dimensional target area defined to facilitate the integration of coordinated joint weapons fire.

Kim, Jaegwon (1934–2019)—A Korean American philosopher, best known for his work on mental causation, the mind-body problem, and the metaphysics of supervenience and events.

Laplace's demon—An argument for determinism, based on classical mechanics. The argument is if someone (e.g., a demon) knows the precise location and momentum of every atom in the universe, those atoms' past and future values for any time are entailed and can be calculated from the laws of classical mechanics.

LAWS (Lethal Autonomous Weapons Systems)—A class of weapon systems that use sensors and computer algorithms, generally deployed in milmechas and related military platforms, to independently identify a target and engage and destroy the target without manual human control of the system. Such systems are legal under international law for border control and prisons.

Levels Acts—A series of laws enacted in the early twenty-second century, developed as the quid pro quo for the nationalization of economic production and grant of a guaranteed income. The Acts set Levels (i.e., from Level 1, the highest, to Level 99, the lowest), which assist in assigning jobs and setting certain restrictions on voting, travel, social interactions, and access to sponsored creative positions.

MEDFLOW—A medical unit implanted beneath the skin, typically above the right hip, that monitors health and dispenses drugs into the bloodstream, based on a programmed protocol.

Mercuries—A designer brand of boots with advanced servos for enhanced speed.

min-con diet—A diet that limits protein to that from animals lower in the hierarchy of consciousness. For higher-order, conscious animals, the diet substitutes alternatives grown in biochemical factories from stem cells (e.g., alternatives for pork, beef, and lamb).

near-rectilinear halo orbit (NRHO)—An efficient orbit for facilities in cislunar space, as used by the WISE Orbital Base.

NEST (Neural-to-External Systems Transmitter)—A device buried below the left temporal lobe that communicates with external systems (such as the net and other local devices). A NEST is internally wired to a projection lens inserted in the cornea, to the jawbone to detect spoken commands, and to a thought reader, which senses keywords. A NEST has memory storage capability. A PIDA may reside in the NEST for more personalized capabilities.

net—An electronic communication system spanning the Earth and the space bases; a network of networks.

netchat—Communications using the net.

netwalker—Equipment allowing access to VR environments to operate net games, education and travel simulations, and virtual robots. It includes an elevated platform, a treadmill, an adjustable seat, a haptic headset, and clothing, with the rig suspended from the ceiling to allow free movement.

nociception—The sensing of harmful stimuli, such as poisonous chemicals.

noria—A hydro-powered machine used to lift water into a small aqueduct for irrigation. It consists of an undershot waterwheel with attached containers, which lift water to a small aqueduct at the top of the wheel.

onna-bugeisha—In medieval Japan, a female martial artist. They were *bushi*, part of the samurai class, and they defended their homes with a *naginata*, a pole weapon.

ontology—The philosophical study of being. This subdiscipline studies concepts that directly relate to being, including becoming, existence, and the nature of reality, as well as the basic categories of being. The subfield of categories of being focuses on investigating the most fundamental and broadest classes of entities that constitute the universe.

original sin—A Christian belief in the state of sin, in which humanity has existed since the fall of man when Adam and Eve rebelled in Eden. By consuming the forbidden fruit from the tree of the knowledge, they learned of the existence of good and evil. One of many interpretations of the story of original sin is that humankind aspired to rival the knowledge and perfection of God, but that wasn't allowed because only God could be perfect.

otzstep—A genre of popular dance music, circa 2161.

physically closed universe—A concept related to a metaphysical theory about the nature of causation in the physical realm and physical causal closure, which can be stated as, "If we trace the causal ancestry of a physical event, we need never go outside the physical universe."

PIDA (Personal Intelligent Digital Assistant)—An AI residing in a NEST.

planeteer—A person who has spent at least a cumulative decade living off the surface of the Earth, including time spent in Earth orbit, in transit outside the protective atmosphere, and in habitation away from Earth, for example, at one of the orbital bases, the moon bases and the colonies on Mars. Derived from the combination of the words *planet* and *pioneer*.

Prime Netchat—A major newscaster on the net.

qualia—The individual instances of subjective, conscious experience. They are perceived qualities of the world and include perceived bodily sensations.

Radus boots—Magnetic boots that allow for ease of movement in weightless environments. The concept was developed in the twentieth century, but practical units were not built until much later.

red diamond—Once known as the most expensive and rarest in the world, red diamonds became more plentiful with the discovery and opening of mining operations on Mars.

Riemann hypothesis—A conjecture that the Riemann zeta function has its zeros only at the negative even integers and complex numbers with real part 1/2. Many consider it the most important unsolved problem in pure mathematics.

<u>**robots containing an AI:**</u>
  pipabot or PIPA (Personal Intelligent Physical Assistant)—A robot that is shorter than the average human, with an elliptical head, two lenses for eyes, and a simplified mouth. The pipabot's forehead glows in various colors to indicate emotions.

  medbot—A specialized pipabot that is augmented with medical devices for surgery and general health care.

  copbot—A pipabot, but taller and built on a robust chassis with higher strength parameters. Its voice module is tuned down an octave and is programmed to be laconic. Authorized for the use of force, as determined by a threat scale.

  mecha—A robot used for industrial and general labor jobs. It is three meters tall with a one-meter additional reach for its two arms. Its four legs can be articulated either in parallel sets in confined spaces or by reversing the articulation of one set to create a spiderlike stance for additional stability and speed. Its triangular head holds two optical sensors, lenses that resemble eyes, and no mouth. The mecha cannot communicate verbally but relies on a pipabot to relay verbal information to humans.

  milmecha—A mecha built on a ruggedized chassis, with the capability to add weapons to its appendages.

Depending on deployment, it may be authorized for use of deadly force under the International Humanitarian Law, to which the States is a signatory.

milpipabot—A pipabot built on a ruggedized chassis, with military weapon options and use restrictions similar to milmechas.

cleanerbot—A small robot with no verbal communication module; it is used for cleaning duties.

matchlovebot—A pipabot with augmented emotion and communication modules; it is used to enhance social interactions among humans and for humans' personal pleasure.

robots driven by humans:

exomech—An exoskeleton robot that is three meters tall and similar to a mecha but directly operated by a human occupant. Humans can enter the metal shell and use their hands and legs to direct the exomech's movement. Exomechs were early robots operated by humans in industrial settings, but they were superseded by mechas and retired by the mid-twenty-second century. Exomechs are still used in sports competitions.

steerbot—A robot shell that resembles a pipabot but without an AI and with VR communications that allow it to be operated by a human in a netwalker through a link. The steerbot provides a realistic facsimile of embodying the machine, which allows humans to operate it directly in distant and dangerous locations.

steermech—A robot shell that resembles a mecha but is otherwise similar to a steerbot.

sandboxing—Intended to prevent uncontrolled propagation of malicious code, sandboxing refers to the protocols, hardware, and software applied in computing and networking to isolate both standalone and embodied AIs and other software on the net. Hardware and software wrappers precisely control the interfaces. All interfaces are strictly regulated, with changes logged to a national blockchain record.

Schrödinger's wave equation—The fundamental equation of physics for describing quantum mechanical behavior. It is a partial differential equation that describes how the wave function of a physical system evolves over time.

Schrödinger's cat—A thought experiment, sometimes described as a paradox, devised to illustrate a possible problem of the Copenhagen interpretation of quantum mechanics as applied to everyday objects. The scenario presents a hypothetical cat that may be simultaneously alive and dead, a state known as a quantum superposition, as a result of being linked to a random subatomic event that may or may not occur.

Schopenhauer's ethics—Articulated by the German philosopher Arthur Schopenhauer (1788–1860) in his essay *On the Basis of Morality* (1840), his ethics center on compassion. He argues that to have moral value, an act cannot be egoistic but rather should flow from a pure motive of compassion, which is a felt knowledge and the immediate participation in the suffering of another.

Searle, John (1932–)—An American philosopher. His notable concepts include the Chinese Room, an argument against "strong" artificial intelligence.

semantics—The study of how meaning is attached to language, signs, and symbols.

sentience—Feelings or sensations (i.e., rather than perception or thought).

seven deadly sins—Also known as cardinal sins, these are a grouping and classification of vices within Christian teachings. They include pride, sloth, gluttony, envy, greed, lust, and wrath.

Standard Model of particle physics, modified—The theory that describes three of the four known fundamental forces (i.e., the electromagnetic, weak interactions, strong interactions, and modified to include twenty-second-century progress in uniting the gravitational force) in the universe, as well as classifying all known elementary particles.

supervenience—A relation between sets of properties or sets of facts; X is said to supervene on Y if and only if some difference in Y is necessary for any difference in X to be possible.

synjug—A synthetic biology jug, which is a biodegradable container used to hold various liquids.

synpsychs—Synthetic biology psychotropics and other mind-altering pharmacology.

syntax—Generally, syntax refers to the arrangement of words to create well-formed statements. In computer science, syntax is the set of rules that defines the combinations of symbols considered to be correctly structured in a computer language. In the philosophy of mind, the computational theory of mind describes the mind in computational terms. Computationalists typically assume that computation uses symbols based on their syntactic properties rather than their semantic ones and that the mind is a syntax-driven machine.

Tarski's undefinability theorem—Stated and proved by the mathematician Alfred Tarski; informally, the theorem states that arithmetical truth cannot be defined in arithmetic.

Three Laws of Robotics—Introduced in Isaac Asimov's *Robot* series, the Three Laws are:
- Law 1: A robot may not injure a human being or, through inaction, allow a human being to come to harm.
- Law 2: A robot must obey the orders given it by human beings, except where such orders would conflict with the First Law.
- Law 3: A robot must protect its own existence as long as such protection does not conflict with the First or Second Laws.
- Addendum: An addendum added in the last century states that a robot must protect other robots' survival, so long as such protection does not violate the first three laws.

Turing test—An early test for AI mentality.

uwatenage—An overarm throw used against an opponent in sumo wrestling.

via negativa—An apophatic theology, also known as negative theology, and religious practice that attempts to approach God—the Divine—by negation (i.e., to speak only in terms of what may not be said) of the perfect goodness that is God. One applied example of *via negativa* is the text *The Cloud of Unknowing*, an anonymous work of Christian mysticism written in the fourteenth century.

vidsnap—A data file that is typically collected and stored in the NEST, either through corneal projection or via download from the net.

von Mises's economic calculation problem—The question of how individual subjective values are translated into the objective information necessary for rational allocation of resources in society. The economist Ludwig Heinrich Edler von Mises (1881–1973) described the nature of the price system under capitalism. He argued that economic calculation is only possible by information provided through market prices.

VRbotFest—A software-based competition using a netwalker to control a virtual steermech with no physical robots involved. The controls don't all operate perfectly, so computer skills are needed to hack the interface while fighting other virtual steermechs.

Wigner, Eugene (1902–1995)—A theoretical physicist and Nobel laureate in physics who published the article "The Unreasonable Effectiveness of Mathematics in the Natural Sciences" in *Communications in Pure and Applied Mathematics* in 1960. In this paper, Wigner observed that the mathematical structure of a physical theory often points the way to further advances in that theory and even to empirical predictions. Elsewhere he elaborated to say, "The miracle of the appropriateness of the language of mathematics for the formulation of the laws of physics is a wonderful gift which we neither understand nor deserve."

Wikipedia—A multilingual online encyclopedia created and maintained as an open collaboration project. Created in the early twenty-first century by Jimmy Wales and Larry Sanger, the net resource continues as a trusted source of information, miraculously avoiding censorship and the politicization that affected many other information sources. Wikipedia was renamed Netpedia in 2129. Many definitions contained therein have become the default standard summaries of certain information. The original Wikipedia entries contained in this vidsnap include portions of those for anthropic principle, appeal to the stone, apsis, Bayes's theorem, complexity theory, consciousness, moonshine theory in mathematics, Hohmann transfer, David Hume, Jaegwon Kim, kill box, Laplace's demon, noria, ontology, original sin, physically closed universe, qualia, Riemann hypothesis, Schrödinger's cat, John Searle, seven deadly sins, Standard Model of particle physics, syntax, Tarski's undefinability theorem, Three Laws of Robotics, *via negativa*, von Mises's economic calculation problem, and Eugene Wigner.

WISE (World Interstellar Space Exploration) Orbital Base—A significant international scientific project that is centered on a construction base that orbits the moon and will launch a series of probes toward promising exoplanets. It is operated by the World Interstellar Space Exploration consortium of countries. The orbital base is currently thirteen hundred meters in length, uses two fusion power plants, and has multiple factory facilities completed for the construction of the probes and associated infrastructure.

ACKNOWLEDGMENTS

Like most human endeavors, this book needed the efforts of many people, who gave their time and minds to help me make it better.

Thanks to my beta readers, who highlighted where the early manuscript could be made clearer, especially to Alex Filippenko, Carlos Montemayor, and Jack Darrow.

The book benefitted from a wonderful group of editors. Developmental editor Olivia Swensen smoothed plot and characters. Cynthia, my wife, helped me enrich and round the characters over time. Our daughter, Brooke, added her frank edits, strategic and nuanced, to hone the story. I'm indebted to my team of copy and line editors at DeVore Editorial—Jaclyn DeVore, Kerri Olson, and my dear Angela Houston. Jennifer Della'Zanna added polish with further line edits and proofreading, and Alyssa Dannaker completed the proofreading. The book was improved visually by cover designer Sienny Thio with her striking book cover, and by illustrator Veronika Bychkova. Layout designer Ines Monnet was invaluable for perfecting the book appearance in English and the many translations.

I'm indebted to the great philosophers, writers, and poets who have inspired me with their ideas and artistry. Theirs is a long discussion of human ideas, reminding us that none are an island. Thanks to Shakespeare's *Hamlet* for reminding us of poor Yorick; Tennyson for his definition of wisdom; Buddha for advice for wise men; and Edgar Lee Masters for his character, Lucinda Matlock, who always reminds me of my grandmother. Thanks to Jaegwon Kim for his posing of the problems of mental causation, which launched a great deal of my mental argument, and to Jerry Fodor, who memorably pointed out why Kim must be wrong. Thanks to all the scientists, engineers, coders, and hackers who are developing our technology with wisdom to serve us.

I'm thankful to my son, Blake, for encouraging me to begin the project, and to my family for allowing me the time to finish this creation—time spent away from them.

My most profound thanks and love are reserved for my dear wife, Cynthia. She is my earliest and most helpful editor on the manuscript, and in life. Like Joe, I've learned how to find purpose together with her.